MOMENT OF CONCEPTION

MOMENT OF CONCEPTION

Charles O'Donnell

MOON LIT. PUBLISHING

Moon Lit. Publishing
Westerville, Ohio
www.moonlitpub.com

MOMENT OF CONCEPTION
Copyright © 2019 by Charles O'Donnell
All rights reserved.

Lyrics from "Let The Day Begin" by the Call reprinted
with permission
Copyright © 1989 by Michael Been

This book is a work of fiction. Any references to real events, people, or places are used fictitiously. Other names, characters, places, and incidents are products of the author's imagination. Any resemblance to actual events, places, or people, living or dead, is entirely coincidental.

5-16-2019

Author's website: www.charlesodonnellauthor.com

ISBN: 1-970041-07-2
ISBN-13: 978-1-970041-07-1

To my wife Helen
For every time that you asked me "Are you writing?"
I owe this book to you.

Also by Charles O'Donnell

The Girlfriend Experience (Matt Bugatti #1)
Shredded: A Dystopian Novel (Shredded #1)
Shade (Shredded #2)

Contents

1

LIDDIE

"LIDDIE IS DYING."

Ann Novotny heard the words but they made no sense. *Liddie is dying? What does that mean?* Her little girl, not yet sixteen, was sick—that she knew—but Liddie had been sick before. Children get sick—they don't die. She stared blankly at her husband, Lew, as he repeated, "Liddie is dying." She shook her head. He might as well have been speaking Swahili.

‡ ‡ ‡

Liddie Novotny turned the page.

"Ever kissed a boy before?" Evan asked with a devilish, devastating grin.

"Of course I have!" Ashlynn lied, melting as Evan's smile grew wider, his brown eyes crinkling adorably. "Lots of 'em. As many as you've kissed girls, I'll bet."

"That's not very many. I only kiss really special girls, and only ones I really like. And not many of them want to kiss me, so that narrows it down. Nah, not many at all."

Ashlynn got a shiver when Evan touched her hand, a shiver that spread through her whole body. She felt Evan's hand slide up her arm as she leaned back on the sofa. "How do you know I want to kiss you?" she asked.

"I don't. I'm just hoping."

She gasped as his lips touched hers in a soft kiss, tentative at first, becoming more insistent as she kissed back, a kiss she'd imagined a hundred times, a thousand times better than she'd dreamed.

Liddie closed her eyes, sighing as she laid the book on her chest, imagining a lingering, loving kiss.

Her eyes popped open when her phone chimed at the arrival of a text message. She smiled when she saw the sender.

MINDY   *sup?*

She tapped out a reply:

LIDDIE   *nada*
MINDY   *star$?*
LIDDIE   *def*
MINDY   *20 min*
LIDDIE   *ciao*

Liddie spent the next twenty minutes choosing her outfit —jeans and heels, and a purple tank top tight enough and low enough to show off her developing breasts and barely discernible cleavage. She put on makeup, removing it and applying it again, stopping after the third try to look at herself in the mirror, turning from side to side. *Just right.*

From her bedroom window she saw a car pull up to the curb. Her friend Mindy waved from the passenger side window. Liddie pulled on a khaki jacket and ran downstairs.

"Mom, I'm going out," Liddie shouted as she left through the front door.

"Call if you're going to be late," her mother Ann called after her.

"Hi, Mindy! Hi, Mork!" Liddie said brightly as she hopped into the back seat.

Liddie could see Mindy's brother Danny looking at her in the rear-view mirror. "Ha, ha," he said with a mocking sneer.

"Oh, so sorry," Liddie said. "I meant to say, 'Hi, *Dork!*'"

"Ha, ha, *ha!*"

"How did you talk Danny Boy into driving?" Liddie said with a smirk.

"All she had to do was ask," Danny interrupted. "What better way to spend a Saturday than chauffeuring my little sister and her little friends around town?"

Mindy turned in her seat to face Liddie. "He's going to meet James at the skate shop."

Liddie's eyes grew wide and her mouth formed a tight *o*. "*Ooh! James!*"

"Stop it," Mindy said.

"Danny, you do know that your sister has a fatal crush on James, don't you?"

"Stop *it!*"

"It's not exactly a fucking state secret," Danny said. The girls giggled as Danny pulled away from the curb.

Liddie continued her conversation with Mindy on the way to Starbucks, distracted by Danny's frequent glances in the mirror. She wasn't sure what he was looking at—his chin was raised and his head was tilted—but she was sure that the rear window was not in his line of sight.

Liddy had known Danny since she was eight, a loud, gangly girl, all knees and elbows, inseparable from his sister Mindy. Liddie and Mindy—hardly anyone ever said one name without the other. At fifteen, Liddie looked almost nothing like that ungainly child. Her dark blond hair was sun-streaked, her formerly chubby cheeks showing high cheekbones, setting off her large, blue eyes. Liddie liked the changes. They'd happened so fast—Liddie wished they had come faster.

At a stoplight, Danny stopped glancing and started looking in the mirror continuously. Liddie puckered her lips in a mock kiss. Danny raised his eyes to get a better look at the neckline of Liddie's tank top.

Starbucks was nearly deserted. Liddie and Mindy sat at a high table by the window with two Mocha Frappuccinos. Liddie hung her jacket on the back of her chair, exposing her bare shoulders, warmed by the sun streaming through the window. From where she sat she could see Danny sipping a black coffee, chatting up the girl at the counter. He stole glances in Liddie's direction whenever the counter girl looked away, and sometimes when she didn't. After his fourth glance, Liddie looked down at herself, to see what Danny found so fascinating.

It was not only Liddie's face that had changed. She had curves. Her breasts were small, but promising. Her hips were no longer skinny and androgynous but had widened noticeably. She looked up just in time to see Danny turning away from her and back to the counter girl.

Danny, Mindy and Liddie arrived at the *Noise Forest Skate Shop* just before closing. Danny's friend James was applying grip tape to a new board, expertly trimming the edges and smoothing the seam with a file. He cut openings for screws and attached the trucks with machine-like speed as Mindy watched with doe eyes. James finished assembling the board and handed it to its new owner.

"Hey, Danny," James said. "Hey, ladies." He leaned against the workbench with both hands. He had the sleepy eyes of a stoner and the beginnings of a beard, his brown hair tied back into a pony tail, spraying out into a generous, curly bush.

Danny gripped James's hand. "Ready to knock off?"

"*So* ready. What's the plan?"

"Our options are limited. I got my little sister and her friend with me."

Mindy scowled.

"Mindy, right?" James said with a wave. Mindy's scowl turned into a broad smile as she waved back.

James put one hand on his forehead and wagged a finger at Liddie. "And you are…?"

"Liddie."

"Sure. Hiya, Liddie."

"We're up for anything," Mindy said. "Right, Liddie?"

Mindy gave Liddie an imploring look. Liddie turned to Danny, who shrugged slightly. She thought she saw him smile.

"Sure," Liddie said. "So what are we doing?"

The four of them ate at an Applebee's. James was laconic but Mindy paid him rapt attention, laughing at his jokes—even the lame ones—touching his arm as she did so. Danny's glances at Liddie became more frequent and less discreet. Halfway through the meal, Liddie tugged her tank top higher and pulled her jacket closed.

Mindy tapped Liddie's hand. "I need to check my lipstick," she whispered.

Liddie followed Mindy into the ladies' room. Mindy checked the stalls to confirm that she and Liddie were the only two in the room.

"James wants us to go back to his place," Mindy said.

"He does? Did he say that?"

"Yes! Didn't you hear him?" Mindy leaned closer. "He has beer," she whispered. "And *weed.*"

Liddie shook her head. "Mom's expecting me home."

"Call her. Tell her you're at my house."

"What if she calls?"

Mindy rolled her eyes. "How many times have you told your mom you're at my house? About a hundred. And how many times has she called? Zero."

Liddie hesitated before fishing her cell phone out of her bag. Mindy grinned as Liddie tapped the screen and put the phone to her ear.

"Hi, Mom?"

‡ ‡ ‡

James's apartment was shabby, in a cheap part of town. It was furnished with a mismatched collection of salvaged chairs and tables, and a couch that retained the smell of all its previous owners' unhealthy habits. Liddie and Mindy sat together on the couch while Danny and James pulled chairs around a small table. A bag of marijuana and assorted smoking paraphernalia lay in the center next to six cans of beer. Liddie watched the others as they passed the pipe. She imitated their technique, inhaling deeply and holding it in. Her lungs burned and her eyes watered until she gave up and hacked out a cloud of smoke, falling sideways on the couch. Mindy, Danny and James laughed until Liddie recovered enough to laugh along.

Through two bowls, James's chair inched closer to Mindy's end of the couch. Mindy leaned closer each time James handed her the pipe. As the conversation grew increasingly animated, they touched each other more frequently, until James's hand remained on Mindy's waist and Mindy's on James's thigh. Danny's glances at Liddie turned into stares. Liddie occasionally stared back.

"Want to see my pet turtle?" James said. "He's in the bedroom."

"A *turtle?*" Mindy giggled. "In your *bedroom?* Yeah. Show me your turtle. I want to see him. Is it a boy turtle?"

"Let's go find out." James held Mindy's arm as she stood. The two of them went into the bedroom and shut the door.

Danny moved to the couch beside Liddie, opening another can of beer and offering it to her. She took a sip and handed it back.

"How are you feeling?" he asked, his words booming in her ears, as if they were in an echo chamber.

Liddie's eyes closed and opened slowly. "A little tired," she said. Danny filled another bowl and lit it, puffing it to life. He sidled closer to Liddie and offered her the pipe.

"I've had enough, I think."

Danny set the beer and the pipe on the table. "You're really pretty," he said.

"Thanks."

He put his hand on Liddie's knee and slid it up her thigh.

"Danny, don't."

His hand slid up to her waist as he leaned closer, putting his other hand on Liddie's breast. She tried to pull away but he pinned her against the arm of the sofa.

"Danny, please don't."

Liddie stiffened her body, keeping her mouth closed as Danny pressed his lips against hers, probing with his tongue.

Danny pulled her closer, grabbing her breasts harder, wedging a hand between her thighs. Liddie struggled as a blizzard of thoughts blew through her mind.

She thought of the short, awkward, one-sided sex talk her mother had given her on her thirteenth birthday—the stories Mindy had told her about her sexual experiences, and how Liddie had pretended to know what she was talking about— the times she'd touched herself to orgasm, wondering if sex felt that way, or if it was better—the way Danny had looked at her all day, in a way that he had never looked at her before, and how she had looked back.

She thought of Mindy and James in the bedroom.

Then she stopped thinking and put her tongue in Danny's mouth.

‡ ‡ ‡

Mindy surveyed the scene through bleary eyes. Danny was sprawled on the floor, face down, wedged between the couch and the table. Liddie was asleep on the couch in her tank top and panties, her jeans, jacket and bra draped over the back of the couch. Mindy kicked her brother's leg.

"Hey. Take us home."

Danny was unresponsive. A second and then a third kick roused him. He rolled over, pushing against the table. Liddie didn't move as beer cans clattered to the floor.

"What time is it?" Danny rasped.

"Six-thirty. Can you drive?"

Danny sat up. He shook his head and looked around, turning toward the young girl on the couch. He stared for more than a minute, at her pale thighs, at the mound under her flower-patterned panties, at the budding breasts under her tank top. He turned back to his sister.

"Yeah. I can drive."

"Go in the bathroom for a while. I'll take care of Liddie."

Danny obeyed. Mindy sat on the edge of the couch and shook Liddie gently until she came to.

"Hey, girlfriend. Let's go home."

‡ ‡ ‡

In the car, Liddie tried to remember what had happened, and, more importantly, how it felt. Danny had kissed and nibbled her nipples. That felt good, until he got carried away. He'd stroked her under her panties—she liked that. She remembered that Danny wasn't very big, comparatively speaking, if Mindy's stories were to be believed. Even so, it hurt when he entered her, a lot at first, and then not as much, but it never stopped hurting. She didn't come, and she didn't feel it when Danny came inside her.

Liddie turned to the window and bit her lip.

It didn't feel like much of anything.

‡ ‡ ‡

Danny dropped Liddie off at her house. She left the car without a word and walked to the door while Mindy and Danny watched.

"I see you got *your* rocks off, asshole," Mindy said. Danny didn't respond right away. Halfway to their house he spoke up.

"Just remember, this was all your idea. Did you get what *you* were after?"

Mindy rubbed the inside of her thigh. "Mission accomplished," she said.

‡ ‡ ‡

Liddie's mother woke her in time for Liturgy. She struggled to stay awake through the service, imagining, in her sleepy state, that every person they greeted stared at her with condemnation. She was certain that the priest scowled at her from the dais; even the icons seemed more disapproving than usual.

After Sunday dinner, Liddie went to her room and laid down. Feeling cold, she hugged herself to keep from shivering. She closed her eyes but she didn't fall asleep; instead, she slid her hand down between her legs and pressed. The pain made her groan.

"Sweetie, are you all right?" her mother asked from the other side of the door.

"Fine, Mom, I'm fine." She lay still for another minute before getting up. She found her cell phone and tapped out a message.

LIDDIE   *hey*

The response came in seconds.

MINDY   *hey u ok?*
LIDDIE   *not really*
MINDY   *shit u need me to come over?*

Liddie thought for a minute before replying.

LIDDIE   *no. talk tomorrow, ok?*

Liddie went to her computer and opened a search screen. She typed in *morning-after pill.*

✝ ✝ ✝

Liddie found what she was looking for in the pharmacy section of the supermarket. She made sure that the aisle was deserted before picking up the box.

MOMENT OF CONCEPTION

Backup
Emergency Contraceptive
Reduces the Chance of Pregnancy if Used Within 72 Hours of
Unprotected Sex or Primary Contraceptive Failure
Increases Resistance to HIV Infection

Liddie held the box close to her chest as she looked over the checkout lines. She went to the one tended by a young girl, not much older than she was, timidly placing the box on the end of the belt, as close to the checker as possible. The checker scanned and bagged it without raising an eyebrow. Liddie ran home, went straight to her room, and swallowed the pill. She looked at herself in the mirror and sighed. Then she burst into tears.

Over the next few days, Liddie remained uncharacteristically reserved. Her schoolmates noticed and asked if she was okay, but Liddie assured them that everything was fine. Some went to Mindy for an explanation but she told them nothing.

By Wednesday, Liddie experienced cramps and spotting, which she took as a good sign. She felt better by Thursday, but on Friday the cramps returned.

Liddie left her ten a.m. algebra class. She'd paid no attention to the lesson—she was unable to focus on anything other than the growing pain in her abdomen. She went to her locker but she was unable to dial the combination. Finally giving up, she leaned against the row of lockers as she fumbled in her backpack for her phone. A few students noticed her distress; one whispered that someone should get the nurse. Liddie tried to operate her phone but her vision was too blurry. She kept trying until a pain tore through her like a jagged saw.

Every head in the hallway turned toward the unearthly groan. Students gathered around Liddie's unconscious form, lying on the floor, the crowd silent at first, until one boy shouted "Oh Jesus! Call an ambulance!" when he noticed the dark red stain spreading in the crotch of Liddie's jeans.

‡ ‡ ‡

Lew and Ann Novotny sat together in the waiting area outside the recovery room. *Type five cardiorenal syndrome* the doctor had told them. Liddie's heart was failing, and her kidneys had shut down. Lew insisted on knowing more but the doctors had nothing more to tell him, other than that Liddie was bleeding internally and that surgery was necessary. She had been wheeled into the operating room an hour before.

Lew was the first to see the surgeon as he came through the door. He wore blood-stained scrubs, his surgical mask still hanging from his neck. Lew and Ann stood facing the doctor. The doctor stopped. He shook his head very slightly from side to side.

Ann's grip on Lew's arm failed as she slid to the floor.

2
ROBIN

THE CAR PULLED to the curb in sight of the protesters lining the sidewalk. The woman in the passenger seat, dressed in a long, brown coat, buttoned to the neck, looked at the driver with wide eyes and a trembling lip. The driver touched her passenger's arm. "Robin, don't be afraid. I'll be right beside you," she reassured her.

They left the car and walked toward the crowd. The trembling woman kept her eyes down as her escort walked beside her, holding a protective arm around the woman's shoulders. From a distance they could see signs held overhead, with graphic photos of aborted fetuses and hand lettered captions.

ABORTION KILLS CHILDREN AND HURTS WOMEN
JESUS WANTS YOUR BABY TO LIVE
PITTSBURGH FAMILY PLAN MURDERS THE
UNBORN

A man raised his hands and prayed with his eyes closed and his face to the sky. "Lord Jesus, we pray that this woman will open her heart to you, and that you will reveal to her the awful truth of what she is about to do." Those next to him prayed more quietly, but no less fervently. As the two women walked past the line, the demonstrators talked to them directly.

"Sister, don't do this. You have options."

"You are carrying a person inside you. Your baby deserves a life."

The escort kept her eyes forward, while the woman in the brown coat looked at the people pleading with her. As one protester held out his hand, she reached out to touch him. Her escort pulled her away.

"No contact!" she shouted. "You can talk but you can't touch. You don't even know this woman is going for an abortion."

"Yes, we do," said the praying man. "We know. You don't provide escorts for mammograms."

The escort hurried the woman forward. The woman turned back to the man and smiled.

‡ ‡ ‡

"Ms. Kline?"

The nurse stood in the doorway of the waiting room of the Family Plan Clinic. The woman in the brown coat stood and followed the nurse into the examination room.

"Please get completely undressed and put this on." The nurse handed her a well-used gown, with fraying edges, faded from too many washings. "I'll be just outside. I'll check on you in a few minutes." The nurse left and closed the door behind her.

The woman removed her coat and laid it carefully on a chair. She removed her clothing and donned the gown, then sat on the edge of the examination table to wait.

The nurse opened the door for the doctor, a middle-aged man with graying hair and tired eyes. He carried a file folder labeled KLINE, ROBIN.

"Ms. Kline," he said, in a soft, caring voice, "I'm Dr. Coble. Nurse Yoder and I will be performing the procedure today. First, I'll need to ask you a few questions. Then I'll do a brief examination."

Dr. Coble put on a pair of reading glasses that dangled from a tether around his neck and looked over the forms in the file. "I see it's been twelve weeks since your last period. Have you experienced anything unusual? Any discomfort? Nausea?"

The woman didn't answer, but instead slid off of the exam table and walked to the chair. She picked up her coat and reached into the pocket.

"Ms. Kline?" the doctor asked.

Robin Kline pulled a cell phone from the coat pocket. She flipped it open and put her thumb on the '#' key.

"Forgive me, Jesus. I am heaven sent."

"Ms. Kline, what…"

Before Dr. Coble could finish his sentence, Robin pressed the key.

3

RONNI

RONNI BARRAKET SAT at the table in her office studying the file: a police report, an FBI investigation brief, profiles of the perpetrator and victims, and a news item:

TWO DEAD, ONE CRITICALLY INJURED IN ABORTION CLINIC SUICIDE BOMBING

Dr. Eugene Coble, 59, of Braddock Hills, died Tuesday in a bomb explosion at the Pittsburgh Family Plan Foundation, a provider of abortions and reproductive health services. The bomb was exploded by a patient, Robin Kline, 32, of Pittsburgh, who was also killed. Kirsten Yoder, 29, a nurse at the clinic, was injured in the blast. Mrs. Yoder remains in critical condition at UPMC Presbyterian Hospital.

Family Plan Foundation officials reported that Ms. Kline had made an appointment for an abortion that morning. She was provided with an escort, a standard practice since crowds of anti-abortion demonstrators became a regular presence at the clinic. The escort, Shelly Nadler, 45, of Pittsburgh, reported that Kline had appeared nervous, but that it was common for women to be anxious before having an abortion.

MOMENT OF CONCEPTION

The FBI has taken over the investigation. The clinic remains closed for the foreseeable future.

The article quoted clinic workers who remembered Dr. Coble as a dedicated professional, but one who was unsettled by the controversy surrounding the clinic, and who looked forward to retirement. Protesters denounced the bombing, but they often added a postscript—*at least this doctor won't be killing any more babies.*

Robin Kline's social media pages revealed little—no suicide note, no manifesto—just a few links to religious and right-to-life sites that might have suggested the woman's leanings. She lived alone and had never been married; her neighbors described her as "pleasant enough."

The FBI profile of Robin Kline was only slightly more revealing. She was born in Pittsburgh and had lived there her entire life. She had no passport; it was likely that she had never been out of the country. She enrolled in a community college after high school but dropped out after a year. She lived in a one-bedroom apartment and worked stocking shelves in a supermarket.

The report detailed the history of the Pittsburgh Family Plan Clinic, the focus of anti-abortion protests for more than a year. The courts had imposed a two hundred foot limit around the clinic; demonstrations were prohibited inside the buffer zone. On one occasion, federal marshals were called in to remove protesters who had harassed patients and clinic workers, but for the most part demonstrators followed the rules.

Ronni moved on to the forensic analysis of the physical evidence. The bomb was a sophisticated device, consisting of plastic explosives and an electronic detonator, triggered by a modified cell phone. When the bomb went off, both Robin Kline and Eugene Coble died instantly.

Kirsten Yoder, the nurse, would have died as well if she hadn't been shielded by Dr. Coble. She was rushed to the hospital and admitted to the intensive care unit. Doctors allowed the authorities to question her briefly before putting her under sedation.

Ronni was reading the transcript of the FBI's interview of Kirsten when she stopped suddenly.

Q: Did the perpetrator say anything before she detonated the device?
A: Yes. She said, "Forgive me Jesus. I am heaven sent."

Ronni gasped as she dropped the file.
Heaven Sent.

‡ ‡ ‡

The lobbying firm of Stivers and Cartwright had hired Ronni Barraket two years before, she having attracted the attention of Jay Stivers while working as a staffer for a Republican congressman from New York. It was her third congressional staff position in five years—her reputation as a brilliant legal mind and a savvy political strategist made her a prime target for recruitment. Jay Stivers recognized her talent while working with Ronni on a bill to limit EPA authority. She was perfect for Stivers and Cartwright: brilliant, personable—and conservative. And he knew that her stunning good looks— tall and slim, with long, black hair, blue eyes, dark complexion, and a model's face—would open doors.

Stivers quadrupled her salary and gave her one of Stivers and Cartwright's premier accounts: the American Life Defense League—the ALDL. It was to prepare for a meeting with Tony Marino, executive vice president of the ALDL, that Ronni was studying the file on the Pittsburgh Family Plan clinic bombing.

"Ronni, Tony's here."

Jay Stivers stood in Ronni's doorway with Tony Marino. The contrast between the two men could not have been more stark: Marino was an affable, portly man, barely five- six, while Stivers was tall, lean and muscular. Marino had a chubby face with narrow eyes and an ever-present grin; Stivers's stern face, with intense blue eyes, rarely smiled when he wasn't drinking and dining with a legislator. Marino had a head of thick, curly, salt-and-pepper hair; Stivers was completely bald.

"Hello, Tony," Ronni said as she greeted Marino with a hug.

"I'll leave you to it," Jay said. "I've got to get to a meeting with the speaker."

Ronni had learned to interpret the subtle emotional cues in Tony's face. He was smiling—he was *always* smiling—but she knew that he wasn't happy.

"We'd like you to prepare a press release about the Pittsburgh bombing," Tony began as the two of them sat down. "We're greatly saddened by this terrible thing. But the public, and even some on the Hill, are liable to associate this, whatever we call it—this *crime*—with legitimate right-to-life groups and with the ALDL in particular. We can't allow that. A suicide attack is not persuasion. It's terrorism."

"I know, Tony," Ronni said softly. "I'll have a draft for you by this afternoon. And don't worry about the Hill." She handed Tony a single sheet of paper. "Here are the talking points. We've already scheduled meetings with our key allies in Congress."

Tony scanned the list. "Yes, these are perfect, as usual." He laid the paper down as he shook his head. "That poor, misguided woman. What do we know about her?"

"What they've reported in the paper, of course," Ronni said, "but we were able to get our hands on this report through one of our contacts in the judiciary committee."

Ronni opened the file. "Thirty-two, unmarried, lived alone. She worked at a grocery store." Ronni paused. She turned the file around so Tony could read it. She put her finger on one line of the transcript of Kirsten Yoder's interview.

"Tony, I think you should see this."

Tony peered at the paper. His narrow eyes widened, and his mouth dropped open.

"Heaven Sent?"

"Yes."

"You don't think *they're* behind this, do you?" Tony asked.

"I doubt it. They've vandalized clinics, they've blocked entrances, they've publicly shamed doctors and patients—but they've never taken a life. This would be a new low, even for them. Besides, Heaven Sent has already denied involvement."

Tony looked down again at the file. "Then she really was just a disturbed individual."

"And that's what we'll say in the press release."

"Send me the draft as soon as you have it." Tony patted Ronni's hand before leaving her office.

Ronni went to her computer and clicked on a folder, filled with news items, press releases, and reports on the radical anti-abortion activists who called themselves *Heaven Sent*. There seemed to be no action too extreme in their holy war —but they had always stopped short of murder.

Ronni picked up the Family Plan bombing file and re-read the profile of Robin Kline.

Single woman, barely graduated high school, dropped out of community college. Probably never set foot outside of Pennsylvania.

She picked up the forensic report.

C4 military-grade explosive. Remotely-controlled electronic detonator.

Ronni laid the report on the table as she gazed at the wall, looking at nothing in particular.

This woman did not make this bomb.

4

CAMERON

THE SHOOTER STOOD ready as he waited for the puller to load the trap with targets. He was tall and slim, with sandy hair, and dark brown, almost black eyes. He was young, and he *looked* young, with round, pink cheeks and smooth skin. Though he was in his early thirties, he could easily pass for a twenty-year-old.

The day was cool, hazy clouds diffusing the sunlight and softening the shadows. The wind sock fluttered, half-extended, in a cross-range direction. The shooter pulled back the bolt of his shotgun, a Browning Twelvette double automatic that he'd owned since he was a child. He loaded two shells into the receiver, then lifted the weapon and sighted downrange.

"Puller ready?" he shouted.

"Ready!"

"All right, let's see one."

The target rose from the traphouse as the shooter pointed and fired. The target sailed downrange, intact.

The shooter closed his eyes as he lowered his gun, inhaling deeply, followed by a slow exhale. He paused to clear his mind before opening his eyes again and sighting the gun.

"Pull!"

The target rose. The shooter fired. The target evaporated.

As he lowered his gun, the cell phone in his range bag chimed. He reloaded as he waited for the chime to stop. He was about to raise his gun when the phone chimed again.

He retrieved his phone from the range bag and checked the display: *Francis Compton*. The shooter pressed *Ignore*, shut off the phone and returned it to his bag. He readied himself for the next shot.

"Pull!"

‡ ‡ ‡

"Was it a good day, Dr. Stroud?"

The shooter laid his bag on the counter at the Delaware Valley Skeet Club. He opened his wallet and handed a credit card to the man who had addressed him.

"Thirty-eight out of fifty, Eddie, not counting the free shot."

"And *with* the freebie?"

Dr. Cameron Stroud smiled. "Thirty-eight out of fifty-*one*."

Eddie chuckled. "That's why we don't count 'em."

Eddie rang up the bill while Cameron took his phone from his bag and powered it on. The phone buzzed in his hand as the display filled with a list of missed calls, six in all, every one of them from Francis Compton. He was about to clear the list when the phone chimed with an incoming call. Cameron put the phone to his ear.

"Yes, Francis," he said. "To what do I owe this distinct pleasure?"

"Cameron, I've been trying to reach you for an hour."

"We're talking now. How may I be of service?"

"The report, Cameron. It was supposed to be on my desk this morning."

"Now, Francis, we discussed this. The report is still under review. You will have it when it's complete."

"You told me it *was* complete."

Cameron signed the receipt on the counter and handed it to Eddie with a smile.

"Francis," he said, as if addressing an impatient child, "the *trial* is complete. The *report* from the trial is not suitable for the non-technical reader. The conclusions must be restated in appropriate terms."

"Cameron," Francis said slowly, "I have meetings in two days with the FDA. They know how to read a clinical trial report. You can take as long as you want to write your summary, but I need the report *now*."

"The details of the clinical trial will be appended to the report, of course, but do you want to risk an incorrect conclusion because it was not properly explained?"

"Cameron, I'm not having this conversation with you again. Be in my office tomorrow at nine a.m. *With* the report."

The phone went dead. Cameron smiled as he tapped the screen a few times and held the phone to his ear.

"Charlie? Stroud here. I just got a call from Mr. Compton. Y'all better finish up that report."

‡ ‡ ‡

At five minutes past nine Cameron Stroud walked into the office of Francis Compton, Chief Executive Officer of Compton-Genencraft Pharmaceutical. Francis was seated at his table with Robert Hendrickson, vice president of business development. Cameron smiled; neither Francis nor Robert smiled back.

"Good *morning*, gentlemen," Cameron said brightly. "I trust you're having a *wonderful* day."

"I don't see the report," Francis said.

Cameron took a chair at the table. "Francis. As I have explained more than once, the summary of the trial report is *crucial* to its proper interpretation. It's like that annual report y'all fuss over every year. Why don't you just send the shareholders the financial statement and the auditor's report? You know why—because it's not just a report. It's a *sales job*."

"*I* can sell it," said Robert. "You're the head of research. *I'm* the head of sales."

"Oh, *Rob*," Cameron snorted. "You couldn't sell fertilizer to a farmer if you weren't at a retreat in Barbados. This is the federal Food and Drug Administration, not liquored up doctors and insurance execs. If *anyone* needs someone to explain a trial report to him, it's *you*."

"Fuck you, Stroud." Robert's round face was dark red. "Fuck *you*." He turned to Francis. "I'm god-damned sick of this little shit treating me like I'm an idiot." He turned back to Cameron. "I have a PhD in biochemistry from Penn and an MBA from Wharton" he said, tapping his chest. "I don't need *you* to tell me how to read a report."

"Biochemistry?" Cameron said with a smile. "I had no idea. That *is* impressive. I have an opening for a technician in my laboratory. Why don't you send me your résumé?"

Robert stood up, almost knocking over his chair.

"Why the hell am I even here?" He turned to Francis as he pointed at Cameron. "From now on, you can deal with this asshole. I don't want to be in the same room with him."

Francis held up his hand to quiet Robert. "When will I have the report?" he said to Cameron.

"Francis, I'll go check on its progress right now. But I can't make any promises about when it'll be done. This is too important to risk sloppy work."

"Then *check on it*."

"Right away," Cameron said as he left the office.

"Fire that son-of-a-bitch," Robert said, "or smack him around. He doesn't treat you with any more respect than he does me. And he *works* for you. Why do you put up with it?"

Francis sighed. "That man makes this company millions. Hell, have you checked your portfolio lately? He's probably made a million just for you, personally."

Francis walked behind his desk and sat down. "He almost single-handedly saved CG Pharma when he invented the *Backup* formulation. And it was his expert testimony that helped push *Backup* through the FDA as a non-prescription drug. I know he's hard to take. But he makes us rich. If this new Alzheimer's treatment pans out, we'll be richer still."

"And you'll put yourself in line to succeed the old man," Robert said.

Francis stared at Robert. He was right—another success like *Backup* would solidify his position as the successor to the chairman of Compton Industries, Elliott Compton—his father.

"If I do take over, you'll be my successor. Think about *that* the next time you tell me to fire Cameron Stroud."

‡ ‡ ‡

"Charlie, show me what you've got."

Chief lab technician Charlie Beaver laid a fifteen-page report on Cameron's desk. Cameron scanned it, taking less than ten seconds to read each page as Charlie and two other technicians looked on. After a few minutes Cameron frowned as he dropped the report on the desk.

"Charlie, where did you learn English? I never did see such a mess of misused and misplaced words and punctuation. Hell, even an old Alabama boy, such as I, knows where to put a comma. And didn't we talk about structure? *State* your conclusions, boy, don't toss them around carelessly in hopes that your reader will stumble over them. *State* them, *build* your case, and state them *again*."

Charlie and his colleagues looked down with rounded shoulders as Cameron pushed the report toward them.

"I suppose I could do this myself, but I'll give you one more chance. I want another draft by four. Maybe, *finally*, you'll learn how to do it properly."

Charlie picked up the report and wordlessly followed the other technicians out the door.

"And, Charlie, I saw at least three irrelevant citations. Check them all. And close the door."

Charlie complied before trudging back to his cubicle to rewrite the report.

Cameron lifted the lid of his laptop and opened a browser window. He clicked on a bookmarked link, displaying a list of folders. He clicked on one labeled *B Alerts*.

The folder contained a list of links to newspaper articles.

SERVICES ON THURSDAY FOR ABIGAIL SANFORD, 14, OF MODESTO
CARRIE ROYBAL, 16, LOSES HER BATTLE WITH CANCER
DONNA GUTHRIE, 13, BELOVED DAUGHTER, PASSES AWAY

Cameron scanned the list of death notices. Cancer. Accidents. One suicide. Mostly teenagers, with a few in their early twenties. He stopped scanning when he reached a link near the bottom of the list.

LYUDMYLA NOVOTNY, 15, DIES AFTER SUDDEN ILLNESS

He clicked the link.

Lyudmyla Novotny, aged 15 of Kenosha, known to her friends as "Liddie," passed away suddenly on Friday after a brief illness. Ms. Novotny collapsed Friday afternoon at Orson Welles High School after complaining of abdominal pain. She was rushed immediately to Aurora Medical Center. Doctors reported that Ms. Novotny died of heart and kidney failure during surgery.

Services for Ms. Novotny will be held Wednesday at Sts. Constantine and Sava Orthodox Church at 2 p.m. Mourners may pay their respects at Nowacki Brothers Funeral Home on Saturday from four to eight p.m.

Ms. Novotny is survived by her parents, Lew and Ann Novotny of Kenosha, and her maternal grandparents, Miroslav and Natasza Burczyk of Gdansk, Poland.

Cameron read the notice twice before closing the folder and turning off his computer. He closed his eyes, leaning back in his chair, his hands together, pressed against his lips.

After a few silent moments he whispered, *"One."*

5

CLARA

Święty Boże, Święty Mocny, Święty Nieśmiertelny, zmiłuj się nad nami.

The mourners chanted the words of the *Trisagion* in unison: *Holy God, Holy and Mighty, Holy and Immortal, have mercy on us.* Ann and Lew Novotny stood in front, just a few feet from the casket where Liddie lay, dressed in blue, her hands folded over the cross of the Orthodox Christian Church. Ann kept her eyes down as the priest led the Liturgy, unable to bring herself to look on the young face. Lew kept his eyes on his dead daughter throughout the service.

The church was nearly full, with almost all of the students of Orson Welles High School in attendance, as were many of their parents. The week had begun with the announcement of Liddie's death, and notice that grief counselors would be available throughout the week, beginning immediately. More than a dozen students took advantage that same morning, ranging from close friends of Liddie's to passing acquaintances. The depth of their sadness varied, but they all asked the same question: How could a teenage girl be healthy one day and dead the next?

"In a blessed falling asleep, grant, O Lord, eternal rest unto Thy departed servant Lyudmyla and make her memory to be eternal!" the priest intoned at the conclusion of the service. The congregation responded in Polish, *Wieczna pamięć: Memory eternal! Memory eternal! Memory eternal!*

Clara Kildee stood in the rear of the church as mourners filed past the casket. She watched Ann as she looked on her daughter's face for the first time since the opening procession. Ann sobbed and turned away. Lew held Ann as her body convulsed, before gently turning her back to the coffin. Ann stroked her daughter's hair and kissed her on the forehead. Lew did the same, and then he kissed the cross in Liddie's hands. *How does someone survive a blow like that?* Clara wondered.

Clara stopped to buy a deli tray on her way to the Novotny home, where she cleared a spot for it on a corner of the kitchen counter, amid casseroles and cakes. She found Ann in the living room, seated on a wooden chair, daubing her eyes with a tissue as she accepted condolences.

"Ann, I'm Clara," she said. "Clara Kildee. We've met before."

Ann shook her head as she looked at Clara through red, swollen eyes. "I…I'm sorry."

"That's all right. We only talked briefly at a school function. Liddie was a friend of my granddaughter's."

Ann nodded and pressed a tissue to her eye, saying nothing.

"It was such a shock to hear about Liddie. So young. Do they know anything more about what happened?"

"No, nothing."

"But they must know *something*. Do you think they're hiding something?"

"They could…I mean…" Ann stammered.

"Did they do an autopsy?"

Ann's breath caught as she shut her eyes, holding a wad of tissues to her face and sobbing into it.

"Excuse me."

Clara looked up to see Lew Novotny standing behind Ann's chair.

"You're Lew, right?" Clara said.

Lew put a hand on Clara's arm and led her away.

"Yes, I'm Lew. And who are you?"

"Clara Kildee."

"Oh," Lew said. "Kildee. I've heard of you. You're a reporter for the *Advocate*, aren't you?"

"I was," Clara confirmed. "I'm retired now. But I still write the obituaries. I wrote the notice for Liddie."

"Clara, I know old habits are hard to break, but I'll have to ask you not to interrogate my wife. You can see how it upsets her."

"I'm not *interrogating*," Clara blurted. She looked up at Lew, who was a good foot taller than she, to see a stony face looking back. He had broad shoulders and a thick neck. The hand he laid on her arm was huge, with short, thick fingers, resembling the paw of a bear.

"I didn't mean anything by it, Mr. Novotny. When I called the hospital they were very vague. It just doesn't make sense that a young girl should..." Clara stopped and looked down. "You're right. Old habits *are* hard to break. Looking for answers just comes natural to me."

Lew's expression softened. "They didn't tell us anything either, other than that they did everything they could. It all happened so fast. I don't think they have a clue."

Lew removed his hand from Clara's arm. "I'm sorry," he said. "I didn't mean to be harsh. It's been a hard couple of days."

Clara touched Lew's sleeve. "I understand. My sympathies to you and your wife."

Lew nodded. "If you *do* find answers, please, tell us."

"I will."

Clara went back to Ann. "Mrs. Novotny, I'm sorry if I was too forward. Please forgive me."

"It's all right," she said as she dabbed her nose. "You said Liddie knew your granddaughter. Who is she?"

"Mindy Schatz."

"Oh yes, of course. Mindy."

‡ ‡ ‡

Clara parked her car in the lot of the Aurora Medical Center at just past four p.m. She watched the door for the next half-hour. Thirty-two years of reporting Kenosha city news had taught her a few things, the schedule of doctors and staff at major hospitals being one of them. At four-thirty she spotted her man: Dr. Michael Fincher, head of internal medicine. She left her car and ran to intercept him.

"Mike! Mike!"

Dr. Fincher looked in Clara's direction and forced a weak smile. "Clara Kildee. It's been a long time. What are you after today?"

Clara leaned against his car as she caught her breath. "I want to ask you about the Novotny girl."

"Clara, please. You know I can't say anything about the case. That would be against hospital policy and a breach of my professional ethics."

"C'mon, Mike, we've known each other for thirty years. You've confided in me before."

"Only to find my words in print the next day."

"One time. Just *one time* in thirty years. And I never mentioned you by name. Besides, I'm retired from the newspaper."

"You still write the obits."

"Only part time."

"That still counts."

Clara stomped her foot. "Mike, why are you being so difficult?"

"Why are *you* so curious?"

"Because a *lot* of people want to know how a bright, healthy, normal girl can suddenly drop dead. Because they have sons and daughters who are wondering the same thing." Clara bit her lip. "And because I have a granddaughter the same age as Liddie Novotny."

"All right," Mike sighed, "off the record." He scanned the parking lot, looking back at the hospital entrance. They were alone.

"Clara, this is a head-scratcher. I handled the case myself. That girl came in comatose and bleeding internally. I opened her up hoping I could find the source. I've never seen anything like it. The lining of her uterus had sloughed off with necrosis of the surrounding tissue. I removed the uterus and tried to stop the bleeding but she kept hemorrhaging. She sprang two more leaks for every one I stopped. In the end her whole system just shut down."

Mike opened his car door and tossed his jacket onto the passenger seat. "The autopsy revealed nothing—no cancer, no pathogens." He lowered his voice. "It's as if her body were attacking itself."

"Thanks, Mike."

"Clara, don't breathe a word of this. The hospital board met this morning over this case. They're totally paranoid."

"Why? A lawsuit? No one can blame you. She was gone when you got her."

"No, not a lawsuit. We always get like this when we don't have all the answers. In this case, we don't have *any* of the answers."

Clara walked away but turned back just as Mike was about to close his car door.

"Say, Mike…did you do a tox screen?"

"Yeah. It was clean, except for a little cannabis."

✞ ✞ ✞

Clara edited obituaries that were submitted to the paper, and she wrote obituaries on request. These showed up each morning in her email account. She started her day at eight, sitting at her kitchen table with a mug of coffee next to her computer and her cat at her feet. Most of the edits went quickly—she did those first—but the requests took time, each requiring at least one phone call to a relative, hospital, or nursing home. Some involved a search of various databases to which the newspaper subscribed to verify birth dates, marriages—all the milestones that punctuate a life. In the six years since her semi-retirement, she had become highly efficient. The latest the paper would accept final versions was three p.m., a deadline that Clara never missed.

The Kenosha obituaries for the remainder of the week were of people who'd lived long, full lives, or had succumbed to prolonged illness—sad, but nothing compared with the shock of losing a daughter in her teens without warning. Most of the departed had made arrangements in advance, including the obituary. It was light work, done by eleven each day.

Yet Clara remained seated at her kitchen table. She spent each afternoon searching medical websites for terms like *necrosis* and *cardiorenal syndrome*. She searched for the symptoms that Mike Fincher had described and came up empty.

One afternoon, Clara called her granddaughter.

"Hi, Mindy, it's Grandma."

"Hi, Grandma. How are you?"

"I'm fine, honey. How are *you?* I'm sure it's hard getting over Liddie."

"Yeah."

"Have you talked to a counselor?"

"No."

"You should. They're there to help you."

"Okay, Grandma. Maybe I will."

"Mindy, I have to ask you something."

"Okay."

"Do you know if Liddie ever smoked marijuana?"

"What? No! Who told you that?"

"I'm just trying to make sense of what happened. I'm looking into any possibility."

"Weed's not poison, Grandma. Besides, Liddie never smoked any marijuana."

"How do you know?"

"I just know, Grandma. She's not like that."

"All right. I just had to ask."

"Well, she doesn't."

"You know you can call me any time, Mindy. I love you."

"I know. I love you too. Goodbye, Grandma."

Late Sunday evening, Clara logged on to InMemoriam.com, a national database of obituaries. She ran several searches for death notices of young girls, each of which yielded hundreds of results. Clara scanned the list but found nothing unusual. She was ready to call it a night when she tried one more time, adding *orthodox* to the keywords. The search returned fifteen results. The third one caught her eye.

KATARINA MATZEK

Services for Katarina Matzek, 16, beloved daughter of Nicholas and Janet Matzek of Secaucus, will be held at All Saints Ukrainian Orthodox Church on Wednesday at one p.m. Katarina passed away suddenly after a brief illness...

Clara printed out the notice. She tried more searches, varying the keywords. By two a.m. she had printouts of five obituaries, all of young girls, all sudden deaths—and all Orthodox Christian funerals.

The next morning, Clara disposed of her workload in record time. She spent the rest of the day working the phone, calling her counterparts at five other newspapers for details. Some were helpful, others were dead ends. She called hospitals, funeral homes, schools—any lead she could follow. By sundown she was paging through a stack of notes as she absent-mindedly consumed a chicken pot pie.

Holy shit. Same symptoms. Similar age. Similar ancestry—Polish, Slavic, Ukrainian. She set down her fork and put her hands to her face.

What is killing these girls?

6

YOLANDA

The floor manager adjusted the microphone on the senator's lapel as the senator studied the list, printed on the letterhead of the lobbying firm of Stivers and Cartwright, titled:

PITTSBURGH FAMILY PLAN—TALKING POINTS

"Can we get a mic check, Senator?"

"Testing, one, two, three. Security, prosperity, liberty."

The floor manager formed an *O* with his finger and thumb.

The earpiece in the senator's ear clicked. The audio volume increased slightly.

"We're joined now by Senator Yolanda Herrera Peña from our affiliate in Columbus, Ohio. Senator Herrera, thank you for joining us this morning on *Politics Weekly Forum*."

"It's my pleasure, Steve."

"Senator, you're a rarity: a pro-life Democrat from a northern state. What's your perspective on the recent bombing in Pittsburgh?"

34

"Steve, my Catholic faith teaches respect for all human life, not only the lives of the unborn." Yolanda's eyes darted down to the list of talking points. "This act of terrorism—there's no other word for it—is an affront to my beliefs and the beliefs of everyone I know in the pro-life community. I cannot condemn it strongly enough."

"So, Senator, do you think it's a bad thing that this clinic is no longer performing abortions?"

"It's a bad thing that fanatics resort to violence to achieve their ends."

"You say that these *fanatics*, as you call them, use violence to achieve their ends. But aren't these *your* ends, too?"

"Steve, advocacy for the rights of the unborn and terrorism are not equivalent, and I resent your implication that they are."

"And yet, Senator, you have voted to withdraw federal funding for Family Plan Foundation clinics providing abortions, whether or not those funds are used for that purpose. You've publicly stated your opposition to the free availability of contraceptives, and you advocate an abstinence-only approach to sex education. If you're being honest, wouldn't you admit that, if these extreme tactics succeeded in shutting down abortion clinics, you would not be displeased?"

Yolanda clenched her jaw. "Choice is one thing; using taxpayer money to end a human life is another. And you are mischaracterizing my position on contraceptives. This administration…"

"But, Senator…"

"Steve, *excuse* me, *I'm speaking*." The talking points paper crinkled softly in Yolanda's grip. "As I was saying, this administration, members of my own party, have made it their mission to circumvent parental authority by making this so-called morning-after pill, *Backup*, available without a prescription. At the direction of the secretary, under pressure from the pro-abortion lobby, the FDA waived their standard approval process to rush this product to market. Now any girl, regardless of age, whether or not she is mature enough to make such a decision on her own, can find this product on the supermarket shelf, like a box of cereal. I'm sure many of them also believe this false claim that the drug prevents HIV. They believe they can do whatever their urges dictate without consequences—have a wonderful time and take a pill the next day. Is that the morality we want to foster in America? Steve, if you think we're not in a war for the future of our children, consider that the drug company Compton-Genencraft, which stands to make millions from this product, has spent huge sums of money on their lobbying efforts to influence the FDA. As for my position on abstinence…"

Yolanda paused. There was a barely audible hiss in her earpiece.

"You were saying, Senator?"

Yolanda drew a breath. "The courts have ruled that the use of contraceptives in an adult relationship is a matter of privacy. That's good enough for me. My personal values certainly influence my voting decisions, but they are not, nor should they be, the law of the land."

"Very well, Senator, we'll leave it to our viewers to judge whether that statement and your previous statements are consistent. On another topic, you are a Hispanic woman with a national profile from a swing state. You were elected to your second term last year by an overwhelming majority. Many in your party, and a few in the Republican Party, are calling for you to run for the presidency. Senator, what are your plans?"

"Steve, the people of Ohio have honored me with a second term as their senator. I intend to respect that choice by serving them as their representative in the United States Senate."

"So you're ruling out a run?"

"Serving Ohio in the Senate is a full-time job."

"So you're not running?"

"I believe that I've answered that question, Steve."

"I believe that you've avoided answering that question, but we're out of time. Thank you, Senator Herrera."

"You're welcome, Steve. I enjoyed it."

The monitor went dark. The earpiece went dead. Yolanda jerked it from her ear.

Shit.

‡ ‡ ‡

Senator Herrera's staff meeting began promptly at nine every Monday morning and was over by nine-thirty. She met with her appointment secretary from nine-thirty to nine-forty-five. That left fifteen minutes travel time to the meeting of her political advisers at the offices of Stivers and Cartwright. Item one on the agenda this Monday was the senator's performance on *Politics Weekly Forum*.

"I thought it went well, Senator," said a young man to Yolanda's right, a research associate at a progressive think tank.

"You thought it went well? Is that based on your PhD in economics, or is it a gut reaction?"

The young man didn't answer.

Yolanda looked at the next man at the table, a professor of international affairs at Georgetown University. "How about you, Anthony? How do *you* think it went?"

Anthony cleared his throat. "The discussion was limited to domestic policy, Senator."

"Oh, yes, that's right. You don't form opinions on matters that don't involve world conflict or global trade. And the rest of you? Do you share our young economic adviser's opinion?"

Everyone in the group looked nervously at one another— all except one.

"May I speak frankly, Senator?" said Ronni Barraket.

"I insist on it."

"Your Latin temper will ruin you. Steve Melson knew exactly what buttons to push and you fell for it. We've talked about this a dozen times. I know you're passionate on this issue but there's a fine line and you crossed it yesterday. Our polling tells us that the public is sympathetic to pro-life sentiments but they support abortion rights by a wide margin. You ended where you should have started—your personal beliefs are not a basis for public policy."

Yolanda stared grimly at Ronni before looking around the table. "Why is it that the only one of my advisers with the balls to tell me the truth is a woman?" She turned back to Ronni. "The talking points were excellent. If I'd stuck to them, perhaps the morning talk shows wouldn't be referring to me in the past tense." She picked up a newspaper from the top of a stack. "At least the *Columbus Dispatch* liked my performance, but what do they know?"

Yolanda took the group through the rest of the agenda before adjourning the meeting. They filed out, leaving Yolanda and Ronni alone.

"Ronni, how bad is it?"

Ronni pulled a sheet from a file folder, holding it out for Yolanda. "We ran a quick poll yesterday and another one this morning. The impact is minimal. There'll be a few reverberations in the echo chamber, but that'll die down. Senator, we need to focus on the long game. Your position on the *Backup* controversy is a winner. The American people may favor choice for women, but they're protective of their daughters. The fast-track approval of *Backup* by the FDA doesn't sit well with the public. Stick with emphasizing the need for consistency and oversight, and keep talking about CG Pharma as an uncaring, profit-driven mega-corporation with a massive lobbying budget."

Yolanda smiled. "What does Jay Stivers think about that tactic? Such disparaging comments about a great American company! I wouldn't be surprised if CG Pharma was a client of Stivers and Cartwright."

"They're not." Ronni smiled. "Yet."

‡ ‡ ‡

Yolanda paged through her copy of the *Dispatch* during the ride back to her office. She noted articles of particular interest to her constituency, scanning each and reading some in detail: *OSU Recruiting Practices Called Questionable By NCAA, Dayton Plant Closes After 47 Years.*

An article on page four caught her eye:

MYSTERIOUS MALADY STRIKES DOWN TEEN GIRLS
Clara Kildee, Kenosha Advocate

As she read the article, Yolanda pulled her cell phone from her bag and punched in a number.

"Yes, Senator," the other party answered.

"There's an article in the *Columbus Dispatch* you should see."

"I know—the one from that Kenosha paper. It was picked up by the AP. I just read it in the *New York Times.*"

"What do you think?"

"Someone has connected the dots."

7

ANONYMOUS

THE PRODUCER ENTERED the green room in a rush, tapping her tablet computer as seven guests of *The Dr. Rob Show* glanced uncertainly at one another.

"All *right!*" The producer looked up and smiled. "Let's get ready to talk with Dr. Rob. First, who's Clara?"

Clara Kildee raised her hand. The producer flashed a big, showy grin.

"Clara, you're the expert. You're our star. Dr. Rob will start with you and end with you."

"I'm not an expert," Clara said. "I'm a reporter."

"Oh, sure, sure. Just the facts, right? But don't minimize your role. You uncovered this epidemic."

"I'm not sure I'd call it an *epidemic*. The Centers for Disease Control is studying. No one knows what it is."

The producer scrunched up her face. "It's a good thing we're having this talk, Clara. The segment is titled *Debutante Epidemic: What—or Who—is Killing Our Daughters?* We need to sing the same song. So let's just stick with *epidemic*. But the CDC—that's good. Make sure you bring that up."

"What do you mean, *or who?*"

"What?"

"You said 'what, *or who*, is killing our daughters.'"

The producer studied her tablet. "Matzek, Novotny, Blaskovich." She looked at the three couples seated in overstuffed chairs beside tables loaded with sandwich trays and soft drinks that remained untouched. "New Jersey. Wisconsin. Florida. You're from all over the country. Plus, we know of six more couples just like you, with teenage daughters who've died suddenly. And you're all Eastern Orthodox Christians. Isn't it just possible that these are religiously motivated killings?"

"That's insane," Lew Novotny grumbled.

"It certainly is," Clara said. "Why would you even suggest such a thing?" She put a hand on Ann Novotny's arm. "It's sad enough that these sweet girls died the way they did. I can't even imagine that someone could have, well, *murdered* them."

"Hmmph."

The sound came from a short man with a dark tan and graying hair, standing in the doorway, his hands folded under his chin. He entered, bending low to shake the hand of each husband, and pat the hand of each wife, offering condolences in a deep baritone. He stopped in front of Clara and stood straight.

"Hello, Clara. I'm Dr. Rob." He crossed his arms and placed a finger to his chin. "The CDC is studying nine deaths that occurred over a two-week period. We all know the details—they're the same in every case—but the CDC has found no common history. There's no Patient Zero. And they've all but ruled out disease, drugs and poison. Something, or some*one*, struck these girls down at random. Isn't it especially strange that they're all of the same religion?"

"We agreed to be on this program to raise public awareness," Clara said, "not to make up crazy theories."

"We'll let the public decide if it's crazy."

"You just said that drugs and poison have been ruled out," Clara countered. "Even if these deaths *were* intentional, how did they do it?"

Dr. Rob tapped his chin. "Good point. Then perhaps these deaths are *God's* punishment on these girls."

Lew Novotny sprang to his feet, looming over the diminutive Dr. Rob.

"That's just vicious! Are you *trying* to upset these people?"

Dr. Rob flinched involuntarily but stood his ground. He smiled, nodding at the producer before leaving the room.

The producer's stage smile returned. "All right!" she chirped. "We're on in five!"

The segment quickly degenerated into a spectacle. After the parents gave heartbreaking accounts of their children's deaths, Dr. Rob put forth his Hand of God theory and the audience latched onto it. During the question and answer session one audience member after another accused the dead girls of sinful behavior, deserving of divine punishment. Some were certain that God was passing judgment on the false Orthodox religion. Lew and the other fathers stopped shouting at questioners just long enough to comfort their sobbing wives. Clara tried to keep the discussion factual, but her protests were lost in the noise.

The producer watched from the control room, nodding as the director called the camera shots, alternating among close-ups of angry husbands, wide shots of the escalating hostilities, and the occasional full-frame, three-quarter face shot of Dr. Rob nodding gravely. Once the melee began, Dr. Rob remained largely silent, stepping in occasionally to keep the action going when it threatened to peter out.

The assistant producer appeared at the producer's side. "How is it going?" he asked.

"Beautifully. How's the response?"

"That's why I'm here. Take a look at this." He handed her a tablet computer. She read the screen, knitting her brow.

"Is this for real?" she asked.

"Yep. For real."

By the end of the break, the floor manager had restored calm and everyone was in their assigned seats. As planned, Dr. Rob called on Clara for a summation.

"I knew Liddie Novotny, and I feel I've come to know Kat Matzek and Cindi Blaskovich and these other girls who were taken from us. And I can tell you that *God did not kill these girls.*"

The audience murmured as Clara continued. "Even if you believe that God does such things, which I do *not*, these young women didn't deserve to die. And anyone who thinks otherwise is cruel and sadistic."

The murmuring turned to shouting, until the floor director and Dr. Rob motioned for silence.

"We need to know what *really* killed these children," Clara said, "and if appearing on this show somehow speeds up the process, then all this nonsense was worth it. That's our only reason for being here."

"Thank you for that, Clara," Dr. Rob said. "Thanks especially to the parents for sharing their daughters' stories. Our hearts go out to you."

The director called for a full-face close-up.

"And, Clara, it seems your being here *will* make an impact. During our show, fourteen parents called to tell us that their daughters died in this same horrible way."

Clara muttered to herself, "Okay, *now* it's an epidemic."

‡ ‡ ‡

In another city, the credits of *The Dr. Rob Show* scrolled up a TV screen. The viewer turned to a computer keyboard and sent an email to obituaries@kenoshaadvocate.com.

‡ ‡ ‡

Clara had long since turned over her obituary-writing responsibilities to an intern and was back at the *Advocate* full-time with a staff of three. She put them to work the morning after *The Dr. Rob Show*—by that time another twenty-four reports had come in.

Clara and her team worked late into the evenings, contacting every caller to the show. Some of the calls were bogus, but by the time they had checked out all the reports, the count stood at thirty-nine. Most of the new cases agreed to allow the CDC to contact them. Only a few of them were Orthodox Christian, but all of them were of Eastern European descent. Clara kept busy writing daily updates, every one of them making it to the front pages of national newspapers.

Clara looked in on her intern on Monday of the week following the Dr. Rob appearance. She found her in the middle of writing a notice for a great-grandmother who had passed away at the age of eighty-five.

"Clara, do all journalists start out in obits?"

Clara laughed. "Not all, Penny. I didn't. I started in classifieds. But I ended up in obits."

"That's not true." Penny held up a copy of the *Advocate*. The headline read:

TEEN DEATH TOLL AT 48, CDC PRESSED FOR ANSWERS

"You're still in the thick of things." She picked a copy of *USA Today*. "Your byline is in every big paper. This is Pulitzer Prize material."

"If only the topic weren't so gruesome. My years writing obits should have prepared me for this, but they didn't."

"I get *that*," Penny said. "Writing these things is really depressing. But I did get something last week that distracted me for a bit."

"Like what?"

"An email that made it through the spam filter. The title was kind of weird, something like 'where are you looking?' The sender was anonymous and the message had just one word."

Clara cocked her head. She pulled a chair up to Penny's desk. "Do you still have it?"

"Maybe." Penny opened the trash folder and scanned the list. "Here it is."

From: anonymous@nopa8tyy1kzx0rtu.onion
Subject: Are you looking in the right spot?
To: obituaries@kenoshaadvocate.com

Backup

Clara read the message.
"Penny, forward that to me. And don't empty the trash."

‡ ‡ ‡

"Mindy, it's Grandma."
"Hi, Grandma."
"Are you all right? You sound strange."
"It's nothing."
"Are you sure?"
"Yes, Grandma, I'm sure. Why did you call? You must be really, really busy with all your national newspaper writing."
"That's actually what I'm calling about."
"Figures."
"Mindy, honey, I need to know what happened the week Liddie died."
"I *told* you all that already. God, isn't it obvious that I don't want to talk about it anymore?"
"Did Liddie have sex that week? Did she take a morning-after pill before she died?"
There was a pause.
"Oh, Jesus. Oh, Jesus fucking Christ."
"Stay home, Mindy. I'm coming over."
Clara arrived at her daughter's house to find Mindy, Danny and their mother seated in the living room, their eyes red and swollen, wads of tissues littering the coffee table.
Mindy repeated the story she had just told her mother, and which Danny had confirmed. In addition to describing what had happened in James's apartment, Mindy told Clara that Liddie had taken an emergency contraceptive called *Backup,* and that Mindy had promised Liddie that she would never tell a soul.

45

8

ELLIOTT

ON THE MORNING of the CDC announcement, all productive work ceased at the offices of Compton-Genencraft.

Of the forty-eight girls who had died, eight of them were known to have taken *Backup*, and the drug could not be ruled out in any of the remaining cases. None of the autopsies revealed *direct* evidence of the drug; instead, the CDC confirmed the eight cases by interviewing families and friends of the victims, acting on a tip forwarded by Clara Kildee. The fact that one out of six of the girls had used *Backup* made it unlikely—*highly unlikely,* in the words of the CDC director—that there was no connection. The director decided to make the findings known immediately.

Cable news had the CDC press conference on an endless loop. A day later the offices and laboratories of Compton-Genencraft were surrounded by demonstrators, numbering in the hundreds, demanding the recall of *Backup* and an investigation of its manufacturer.

Every Compton-Genencraft employee was either watching the media blitz or talking about it, including a small group of senior executives who were holed up in the board room.

The officers of the company sat at their usual places, each with a copy of the CDC report and a brief on the development, testing, and FDA approval of *Backup*. Wall monitors displayed silent feeds from four cable news channels, all featuring nonstop coverage of the controversy, two of them showing live video of the mob in front of the Compton-Genencraft building.

Francis Compton paged through the CDC document as the other officers looked on. He turned the last page, placing his hand on the report as he scanned the grim faces around the table. "Gentlemen, let's hear our options."

The portly vice president of procurement spoke up. "Issue an immediate recall. Anything else would be considered a halfway measure. The longer we delay the more damage is done to CG Pharma's image." He pointed at the monitors on the wall. "This circus won't go away."

"I have to agree," Robert Hendrickson said. "I can cite a dozen examples of other companies in similar situations. The ones who act quickly survive, and the ones who drag their feet never recover." He held up a sheet of paper. "My team has already crafted a press release—an immediate, voluntary recall and a promise to do an internal investigation. No admission of fault."

The vice president of operations spoke next. "I agree. We need to take control of the situation."

Each of the officers voiced their assent, until only one was left to be heard from.

Cameron Stroud looked around the table at his colleagues. He bent his head forward and pressed a knuckle against his lips, as if he were holding in a laugh.

"I never did see such a bunch of old women in my life. This drug has been judged *safe* and *effective* by the federal government." Cameron held up the *Backup* brief. "These test results show no evidence of serious side effects. And remember, this is *not* a new drug. It's a new formulation of two existing drugs. In fact, both the contraceptive and the anti-viral components have a long history of safety. Are we going to recall those drugs, too? You might as well send everyone home and lock the doors right now."

"All of that is irrelevant," Robert said. "What matters is perception. We've checked retail outlets in twenty states. Sales of *Backup* have fallen by eighty percent. By the end of the week they'll be nonexistent. We've got to get ahead of this."

"Robert, who'd have thought it?" Cameron said. "I actually agree with you. This *is* about perception. And how do you think folks will perceive it when we admit that the CDC is right, when we know they're not?"

Robert pressed his fists to the table and rose a few inches from his chair. "First, we're not admitting *anything*. Second, I *don't* know that the CDC isn't right." He dropped back into his chair. "My god, forty-eight girls dead. At least eight of them used our product. If there's even a *chance* of a connection..."

Robert was interrupted by a knock at the door. A middle-aged woman poked her head in.

"Mr. Compton, there's a call for you. It's the chairman."

Francis closed his eyes and inhaled deeply. "Thank you, Sandy. We'll take it in here." He punched a button on the conference phone.

"Good morning, Elliott," he said in a loud voice. "I'm here with the whole team."

"Francis, I'm watching CNN right now and it's not pretty." The voice from the phone sounded nasal and thin, but not the least bit uncertain. "What are you doing about it?"

Francis looked at Cameron as he replied, "We will issue an immediate recall and announce an internal investigation. It's important that we respond decisively and take control of the situation."

The phone was silent for a few seconds. "You will do no such thing."

"Excuse me?"

"This CDC business is being blown out of proportion. If you issue a recall, you'll be admitting that your product is unsafe, when it's been proven otherwise."

Francis pressed his fingers to his forehead. "Elliott, in the eyes of the public, it's impossible to overreact to the deaths of forty-eight girls, many of whom took our drug."

"Many? I don't see it that way. And neither does your head of product development."

All eyes turned toward Cameron.

"I took the liberty of informing our chairman of *all* the relevant facts," Cameron said. "Of course, I copied you on the email, Francis."

"Dr. Stroud," Elliott said, "please bring Francis up to date."

Cameron leaned toward the phone. "Yes, sir. As I wrote in my email, a recent survey shows that one in five women, age fifteen to twenty-four, have used emergency contraception. Our own sales figures tell us that the overwhelming majority have used *Backup*, and the rate has increased sharply since the drug was approved for non-prescription use. The conclusion is obvious: Pick any forty-eight women at random, and eight to ten of them will have used *Backup*."

The room fell silent. Robert was the first to speak. "How do we know the CDC will agree with those findings?"

Cameron pushed the paper across the table. "They'd have a hard time disputing it. It's *their* report."

"Clear the board room," Francis said. "I need to talk with the chairman in private."

The officers of Compton-Genencraft filed out of the room.

"Dad, we've got to issue the recall."

"Francis, were you not listening? If you issue a recall, not only will you signal that your product is at fault, you'll also stop the search for the real cause. You'll put more young women at risk *with* a recall than *without* it."

Francis leaned closer to the phone and softened his voice. "Dad, when you put me in charge of Genencraft after the acquisition, neither one of us knew a thing about the pharmaceutical business. Well, I've learned a lot in the last year and a half. Success is as much about politics as it is about science. And I've got good people who know their stuff. We all agree: recall."

"Dr. Stroud doesn't agree, and I've got to wonder if your personal feelings toward Dr. Stroud aren't affecting your judgment."

Francis clenched his fists. "Dad, that's not true."

"I hope not. I didn't get where I am by ignoring sound advice just because it came from a son of a bitch. And I didn't make it here by knuckling under to government bureaucrats."

"It's a different time, Dad. Look at your cable feed. Check the Internet. News doesn't just travel fast, it gets *amplified*. Six news channels can't fill twenty-four hours with objective journalism, not when they're competing for eyeballs. If they don't *know* the facts, they'll make them up. The story they're telling, the story that millions believe, is that *Backup* killed these girls."

"Don't lecture me, Son. I'm not the throwback to the Cronkite era that you think I am. Hell, I know what these media types are up to—that hasn't changed in three hundred years. *News* doesn't sell ad spots, *controversy* does. You're letting your enemies control the story line, and you're ignoring your friends."

"Friends?"

"Hell yeah, friends! The pro-life wing nuts and the anti-corporate Luddites have joined forces to take you down, while the pro-choice lobby and corporate interests are left with no grounds to defend you. Why give your enemies ammunition when your friends are ready to stand up for you?"

"What do you suggest?"

"Damn it, Son, do I have to spell it out? You've got a story to tell—tell it! The cable channels will pick it up just to stoke the fire. And get your own people out there. If the talk shows don't call you, then you call them." There was a pause before Elliott added, "If you want to be the chairman, act like the chairman."

Francis heard a beep as Elliott ended the call.

Francis leaned back in his chair, folding his arms, looking at the floor. After two deep breaths he tapped the keys of the conference phone.

"Robert," he said, "meet me in my office. We're going in a different direction."

51

9

THE PRESIDENT

THE PRESIDENT LEANED against the Resolute Desk as he re-read the Compton-Genencraft press release. A group of a half-dozen people had gathered in the Oval Office, among them Communications Director Walt Petri, Health and Human Services Secretary Kay Cardin, and Senator Yolanda Herrera Peña.

"So. Our CDC Director goes off half-cocked and CG Pharma doubles down."

"Mr. President," Kay Cardin said, "the director felt that the situation was urgent enough that it merited an immediate announcement."

"Yes. Well, he's put us in a hell of a spot. After ram-rodding this *Backup* pill through the process to get it on supermarket shelves, a mandatory recall would make us look like political opportunists or incompetent boobs."

"I'm sure you'll recall, Mr. President, that the director was never comfortable with the fast-track approval."

"That's no excuse, Kay. Policy is policy, and procedure is procedure. The communications office clears all public announcements." The president held out the Compton-Genencraft press release. "And then there's this. CG Pharma could have announced a voluntary recall and looked like heroes. Now they're lining up against us. What is Elliott Compton thinking?"

"Sir, they do make a valid point in their press release. The percentage of women who have used *Backup* is about the same as the percentage of confirmed users among the victims. As for Mr. Compton, wouldn't you have some insight? He's your friend."

The president gave Kay a stony look. "He's not a friend, he's a donor." He pointed with the paper at Yolanda. "Senator, what do you think?"

"Mr. President, it was a mistake to approve this drug. Now is your chance to correct that mistake."

"Mandatory recall."

"Yes."

"I'm sure the pro-life caucus would love that. And what if there is no recall?"

"Mr. President, the pro-life caucus, and the pro-life public, would view your lack of action as further proof of a radical agenda to promote abortion."

"This is not an abortion pill," Kay interjected.

"The jury is still out on that question," Yolanda said. "But that's irrelevant. Mr. President, you asked what the pro-life caucus would think and I told you."

The president rubbed his chin. "Kay, what do you recommend?"

Kay looked at Yolanda for a moment before turning to the president. "Mandatory recall. We need to stand by the director."

"Walt?" the president said.

"Mr. President, it's too early. This drug is part of basic reproductive health care. We need more information before we deprive women of this option."

When the president finished polling the group, half recommended a mandatory recall, and half counseled the president to wait. He dismissed them.

When he was alone, he picked up the phone and pressed a button. "Dot, I need to speak to Elliott Compton."

10

DEBBIE

DEBBIE MELNIK SAT in her room, holding an orange tablet in her hand, staring at the computer screen in front of her. It displayed the results of a search for *backup pill:*

COMPTON-GENENCRAFT DENIES BACKUP
HEALTH RISK
FDA DELAYS MORNING-AFTER PILL RECALL;
"MORE RESEARCH NEEDED," SAYS SECRETARY
CARDIN
CRISIS OVER? DEATH TOLL HOLDS AT 48

She looked down at the tablet.

Condoms aren't supposed to break.

She put the pill in her mouth and washed it down with a diet soda.

A week later, Debbie Melnik died of a massive hemorrhage on the way to the emergency room.

11

MATTEO

"IN 1963, THE mathematician Stanislaw Ulam attended a symposium. While listening to the presentation of a long and very boring paper, his mind wandered."

Professor Matt Bugatti stood in the well of a lecture hall at the University of North Carolina as he addressed the first session of *Introduction to Discrete Mathematics*.

"To occupy his wandering mind, he wrote down the natural numbers, starting with one, and spiraling outward."

Matt touched a key on the keyboard at the lectern. A numeral *1* appeared in the center of the projection screen, then to its left a *2*, and below the *2* a *3*, then *4*, continuing in a square pattern. The image zoomed out as the spiral grew, the numbers appearing as dots on a grid.

"Then Ulam circled the primes."

Matt touched another key. Thousands of dots flashed and glowed, each glowing dot corresponding to a prime number, indivisible by any whole number other than itself and one. Among the seemingly random scattering of bright dots, straight lines appeared: horizontal, vertical, and diagonal rows along which prime numbers were concentrated, and other parallel lines along which primes were largely absent.

"These patterns surprised Ulam. And why the primes should appear preferentially along these lines is still a matter of conjecture."

Matt touched a key and another series of images appeared: an ink-black circle from which electric filaments erupted like lightning bolts, a spiral of delicate structures resembling lacework, a parade of psychedelic seahorses.

"Benoit Mandelbrot studied the set of values resulting from the iteration of a simple recursive equation. The equation has only two terms, yet the Mandelbrot set is arguably the most complex structure in mathematics."

Professor Bugatti looked at the faces of his students. After four years of teaching, he'd learned to gauge their level of interest and comprehension. Some, he knew, would succeed brilliantly, some would struggle, and the rest, no matter how hard they—or he—tried, would fail.

"As you pursue your studies of mathematics, you will experience a progression. At first, many of you will struggle with the concepts. This is normal. *Knowing* that this is normal is *not* sufficient to prevent panic."

A wave of laughter spread through the hall.

"I advise you to do two things. First, work with each other. Discuss the concepts. Share your insights with your classmates. You're not in competition. I don't grade on a curve."

There was more laughter, mixed with groans.

"Second, master the techniques. That means practice—*lots* of practice. Technical skill is the first step toward understanding. Once you grasp the concepts, after much work, you'll make rapid progress. New concepts will come to you more easily. Then, your progress will slow down. I call this the *plateau of competence*. If you reach this stage, you should be proud. You'll be skilled mathematicians."

Matt pointed into the lecture hall. "Some of you will transcend that plateau, when you begin to see *concepts* as *structures*, when what was once abstract becomes real, even visceral." He pointed at the exquisitely detailed image on the screen. "The images of Mandelbrot's Set and Ulam's Spiral are compelling, because they are *visual.* However adept you are at doing the math, until you can *visualize* the structures behind the equations, your understanding will be incomplete. And when you *can* visualize them, it will be as if a veil has lifted."

Matt's attention was drawn toward the door, and the person standing there: Nels Coffman, head of the Department of Mathematics.

"Time's up," Matt said. "And my boss is here. Reading and exercise assignments are in the syllabus."

The students filed out, a few pausing to ask questions. When the hall had emptied, Nels stepped in.

"How do they look?"

"It's a mixed bag, Dr. Coffman. But they seemed engaged for the most part."

"*Dr. Coffman?* Matt, you're a tenured professor. When are you going to stop addressing me as Dr. Coffman?"

Matt grinned. "Sorry, Nels. Old habits. What's up?"

Nels sat in a seat in the first row. "Matt, have you been keeping up with this controversy over the morning-after pill?"

Matt shrugged. "It was all over the news a couple of weeks ago. Forty-eight deaths, right?"

"Forty-nine, now—all young girls."

"That's so sad. Do they know what happened?"

"This drug *Backup* is implicated. The FDA just pulled it from the market. That's why I'm here."

"Do you mean, that's why we're talking? I don't get it."

"This is a major embarrassment for the administration. They could have pulled this drug from the market but they didn't. Then another girl died. The pro-life factions are accusing the FDA of caving under pressure from the pharmaceutical industry and the pro-choice lobby. The pharmaceutical industry is closing ranks around the company that makes *Backup*. The pro-choice lobby is trying to change the subject to violence against abortion providers. The president has called for a commission to investigate."

"Okay. I still don't get it."

"They want you on the commission."

"*Me?*"

"Yes, you. This situation is hugely contentious. All sides are doing their damnedest to pack the commission. The president wants at least one neutral party. He asked for you by name."

Matt's jaw dropped. "The *president?* Of the United States?"

"The very same."

"Why would the president even know who I am?"

"Matt, you're a national treasure—the first American to win the Fields Medal in more than two decades. You're proof positive that the United States is not yet a second-rate country. You're a symbol."

"I guess. But why me? I'm a math professor. I don't know anything about medicine. Aren't there any doctors who are national treasures?"

Nels stood and put a hand on Matt's shoulder. "It'll be great exposure for you and for the University."

"What about my students?"

"We can turn over your introductory classes to an associate professor. I can teach your advanced class."

"No disrespect, Dr. Coffman—*Nels*, I mean—but you haven't taught a class in years."

"I taught *you*, Bugatti," Nels said, with a hint of a growl. "Don't forget that."

The two of them walked out the door.

"You didn't answer my question," Matt said. "Why me?"

"I did answer," Nels said. "You're a symbol. But you're more than that—you are the voice of reason."

12

LUCY

Lucy Seidman got the call at just past nine a.m. *We have your test results* was all they said. By nine-fifteen she was on the bus for the forty-minute ride to the clinic. She looked out the window at the pedestrians on the Atlanta sidewalks, wondering where they were going, and whether they wanted to go there, or had to, and if they were afraid of what waited for them when they arrived.

Lucy sat in the only vacant seat in the clinic waiting area, expecting a long delay. She was surprised to hear her name called after a few minutes. The nurse led her to an examination room, where she was surprised again to see the doctor already there, holding a folder in her hand.

"Hello, Lucy," the doctor said. "Are you feeling okay?"

"Yes, Dr. Coleman," Lucy said. "Still some pain in my stomach."

"Well, you go ahead and sit down here, dear." Dr. Coleman motioned to a chair, then sat on the edge of the examination table as she opened the folder.

"Lucy, I'm afraid there's not an easy way to tell you this. It's cancer, cancer of the ovaries."

"Oh, Lord," Lucy said, her voice breaking. The nurse put a hand on her shoulder.

"Normally, we can treat this cancer, but your case is rather advanced." Dr. Coleman looked at the folder. "I see you don't have insurance."

"No, ma'am."

"Lucy, you can wait here. There'll be someone in shortly to discuss your treatment options."

The doctor left the room. Lucy sobbed into her hands as the nurse rubbed Lucy's shoulder.

A minute later a man entered, wearing a short-sleeved shirt with dark stains at the armpits, and a frayed tie hanging loosely from his neck. He had short hair and a pinched face, both shining from perspiration.

"Lucy, I'm Donald Lominger. Nurse, you can leave us."

Donald closed the door after the nurse. "Lucy, I'm so sorry about your condition. I'm here to discuss your options."

"Yes, sir."

"Do you have a family, Lucy? Someone who can provide care?"

"No, sir. My momma and daddy passed, and I live by myself." Her eyes filled again with tears. "Am I going to die, Mr. Lominger?"

"Lucy, the Lord takes all of us eventually. Some of us are prepared and some are not. Do you believe in Jesus, Lucy?"

"Yes, sir, I do. I believe that Jesus can work a miracle."

"Indeed He can," Donald said. "And sometimes, Jesus sends us a sign, a sign that He wants *us* to work a miracle for *Him*." Donald settled on his haunches in front of the chair. "Lucy, there's wrong in this world, terrible wrong. It causes Jesus great pain that such terrible wrong should go on. But Jesus has only us, His people, to right the wrongs. And sometimes He will choose one of us to work His will. And He rewards those who do His work, Lucy. Do you believe that?"

"Yes, sir, I suppose I do believe it."

"I know you do, sister." He pulled a card out of his shirt pocket and placed it in her hand. "Lucy, I want you to call this number. They will help you."

Lucy looked at the card. It read simply:

404-555-4507
Heaven Sent

13

FLORA

Espresso in the sitting room was the customary end to dinner in the home of Flora Bugatti, and the coffee, as usual, was excellent. Over decades as the hostess of her restaurant, *Da Flora*, she had taken pains to ensure that her customers' last impressions were as memorable as their first.

Matt Bugatti savored the taste and aroma as he recovered from a magnificent *braciole*.

"Giovanni would have been so proud," Flora said. "Your father knew you would do great things."

"I think Dad would have been as confused as I am," Matt said, as he set down his cup. "What a math teacher can contribute to this investigation escapes me."

"*Caro*, they need smart people, to understand…" Flora stopped.

"Mom?"

"What is the thing? The committee?"

"It's a commission, Mom, to investigate the deaths of forty-nine girls."

"Oh, that's right," Flora sighed, "the poor girls."

"Mom, are you all right? You seem tired."

"Of course I'm tired. I've been cooking since one o'clock." She peered at Matt's cup. "Would you like another espresso, *caro?*"

"Sure, Mom, why not? I didn't plan on sleeping tonight."

As Flora went to the kitchen, Matt looked around the sitting room of the home where he grew up. From where he sat, he could see the gallery of photos in the hall.

He went to the hall, walking past the row of pictures as if they were paintings in a museum, stopping before a large portrait, taken almost fifteen years earlier, of Matt and his father, Giovanni. Matt smiled when he saw his own image, that of a boy in his mid-teens. Then he looked at the picture of his father.

His smile disappeared. The face looking back was his. The old man's face had a few more lines, and his eyelids drooped, but there was no mistaking—Matt had become his father. It was unsettling.

Then Matt realized it was not only the picture that had troubled him. He turned and looked back at the empty sitting room.

Matt went into the kitchen to find Flora standing motionless at the counter, staring at the espresso maker, holding a bag of coffee beans.

"Mom?"

"What was I doing?"

"Making the coffee, Mom."

Flora looked at Matt with a blank expression as she held up the bag. "Is this the coffee?"

14

TYLER

MATT WAS THE first passenger to disembark from the Raleigh to Washington, D.C. flight. As he entered the terminal, he came face-to-face with a tall, unsmiling man in a black suit, with the coiled cord of an earpiece behind his right ear.

"Dr. Bugatti?"

"I'm Matt Bugatti."

The man flashed his identification card. The words *Secret Service* jumped out at Matt.

"Agent Baldwin, Department of Homeland Security. I'm here to escort you to your first appointment."

"Okay." Matt looked down the length of the terminal as passengers streamed past. "I need to pick up my bag."

"We've already retrieved your luggage, Dr. Bugatti. It's waiting in the car."

Matt followed Agent Baldwin out of the airport to a waiting limousine. The agent held the door for Matt, then got into the back seat with him.

The car left the airport and crossed the Potomac, passing the dome of the Jefferson Memorial, continuing north through the Mall. To Matt's left was the Washington

Monument; to his right, in the distance, was the Capitol dome. The car continued north through the Mall.

"I thought that the meeting was to take place near the Capitol," Matt said.

"No, sir. Your first appointment is at the White House."

"The White House?"

"Yes, sir. With the president."

‡ ‡ ‡

Matt sat among a half-dozen others in the West Wing lobby, glancing occasionally at the others in the room. He wondered what their story was, and what role they would play on the commission. They spanned a range of age and appearance—they seemed to have nothing in common—and none of them looked like a world authority. *But neither do I*, Matt thought.

Over the course of an hour, Matt witnessed one dignitary after another pass through the lobby—two senators that he recognized, several more that he didn't, and a few in the uniforms of high-ranking military officers. The routine was like clockwork, almost precisely at ten-minute intervals: A visitor entered through one door, signed out, and exited another door; the phone on the receptionist's desk beeped, and the receptionist called a name.

"Dr. Bugatti, the president will see you now."

Matt looked around the room. "Just me?"

"Yes, sir. The guard will escort you."

Matt followed the guard down a hallway until they came to a closed door. The guard opened the door and motioned for Matt to enter.

Matt stood at the entrance, moving only his eyes as he looked into the Oval Office, the scene seeming at once both familiar and surreal.

"Sir?" the guard asked.

Matt looked down and watched his feet as he stepped over the threshold.

The president stood behind the Resolute Desk, continuing to read a file without looking up. Matt turned around as the door closed behind him.

"Dr. Bugatti, welcome to the White House."

Matt turned quickly to see the president striding toward him, his right hand extended, his left hand holding the file.

"Hello, Mr. President."

The president looked directly into Matt's eyes without smiling as he shook his hand. "Please, sit down," he said.

The two men sat facing each other. They were barely seated when the president spoke.

"The director of National Intelligence briefed me on your background." The president opened the file. "Doctorate from the University of North Carolina. Winner of the Fields Medal for discoveries in the mathematics of prime numbers." He flipped a page. "And you have some history with the National Security Agency."

Matt swallowed hard. "Yes, Mr. President."

The president closed the file and dropped it on the table.

"When your name came up, I had to admit that I didn't know who you were. When I heard about your role in this NSA program—*Cygnus*, I believe it was called—and this unfortunate business with the Chinese, I was against naming you to the commission."

Matt recalled his work on the highly classified *Cygnus* decryption system, the breakthrough that led to his Fields medal, and his encounter with the Chinese secret agency *Guoanbu*, to which he had turned over classified information, nearly losing his life. "Yes, sir," he said, barely whispering.

"But an old and trusted friend insisted. He said you're brilliant and dedicated to the truth. In other words, perfect for a fact-finding commission."

"Yes, Mr. President. Thank you, sir."

The president walked to his desk and looked out the window for a moment before turning back.

"Dr. Bugatti, I could have prevented this. I could have pressed for further trials, or forced the FDA to release *Backup* as a prescription drug. But it was politically expedient to fast-track the approval for over-the-counter use." The president took a breath. "*Expedient,*" he whispered.

"When the possible connection with *Backup* came to light, I could have issued a mandatory recall. Many of my advisers recommended a recall. But the adviser I listened to was the one I should have trusted the least. Elliott Compton assured me that a recall was unnecessary. And that was what I wanted to hear—a rationalization to relieve me of responsibility, permission to avoid a public-relations predicament. And then another girl died."

The president clenched his jaw, looking at the floor, tapping the edge of the desk with his fist. "Matt—may I call you that?"

"Certainly, Mr. President."

"Matt, you're a mathematician and an academic. In your work, you start with axioms that are accepted without question, and you demonstrate your conclusions with logic. I, on the other hand, am a lawyer and a politician. In my world, there are no universal truths. We persuade by any means necessary—we stoke fear, we appeal to self interest, we pander to prejudice and resentment. Logic plays a minor role at best. Abandonment of reason and adherence to dogma— these are symptoms of a deeper sickness, one that distorts judgment and inverts priorities, one that elevates ideology above outcomes. It's contagious. I've been infected myself. Curing this disease is the greatest challenge of my administration."

"Yes, Mr. President."

"Matt, you'll serve on this commission with six others. They were selected from among dozens of candidates. Like you, they're all highly accomplished individuals, but they are *unlike* you in one important respect."

"In what respect, Mr. President?"

"*They* were chosen by a committee of politicians, less for their expertise than for their affiliation. On the matters before this commission, there are no neutral parties. These six commissioners are not investigators. They're advocates for their respective positions."

"And me?"

"*I* chose you. Whatever biases these commissioners bring to the task, whatever outcomes they desire, the findings of this commission must be faithful to two things: the truth, and the memory of forty-nine young women."

"I understand, Mr. President."

"Very good." The president touched a button on his phone. "Darlene, you can send Tyler in now."

A young man entered the office. He was an inch short of six feet tall and slim, almost gaunt, wearing a short-sleeved shirt and thin tie that did nothing to make him appear more robust. He had a narrow smile, close-cropped red hair and green, unblinking eyes.

"Matt, this is Tyler Ross. Tyler will be your executive director during the term of the commission. He's young, but he's knowledgeable and whip-smart. He'll take care of the protocols and logistics."

Matt and Tyler exchanged greetings as the president continued.

"I believe you're due at the Rayburn Building in half an hour. The other commissioners are waiting for you."

"Then you've already briefed the rest of the commission?" Matt asked.

"No. You're the only one I intend to meet with."

"Mr. President, may I ask why?"

The president looked at Tyler. "Wasn't he told?"

"Apparently not, Mr. President."

The president turned to Matt. "I'm sorry for the oversight. You should already have been notified. This is the Bugatti Commission. You're the chairman."

Tyler put his hand on Matt's shoulder. "I'll brief you on the way, Dr. Bugatti."

"Tyler will answer all your questions," the president said, "unless there's something you'd like to ask me."

"No, sir," Matt said. "Wait, there is one thing. Who is your friend, the one who recommended me?"

"The deputy director of National Intelligence, Josef Hofbauer. I believe you worked with him on the *Cygnus* project. He was highly complimentary."

‡ ‡ ‡

"Don't worry about the first meeting, Dr. Bugatti," Tyler reassured Matt during the short drive to the Rayburn Building. "I'll do the introductions and take you through the agenda. You should concentrate on what you're going to say to the commission. You need to set the tone. I'm sure the president told you to expect a free-for-all."

"Not in so many words, but I get the idea."

"Here's my advice: Show no weakness. Don't bully them, but don't back down. If one of them says something that sounds like a crock, it's probably a crock, and you need to call him on it. You're the chairman, but everyone in that room will know in five minutes or less if you're their leader. And never forget what the commission is about—finding those responsible for this crime and bringing them to justice."

Matt looked at Tyler. Tyler's eyes were wide and his jaw was clenched.

"I don't know that a crime has been committed," Matt said. "This is an investigation, right? Not a trial."

Tyler's eyes widened a bit more. "Right. Investigation."

The limousine drove past the Capitol and turned into the entrance of the Rayburn Building. Matt and Tyler got out of the car just as Matt's cell phone vibrated in his coat pocket. The display read *Da Flora*.

"Hi, Mom?" he answered.

"Matt, it's me, Marie."

Matt was surprised to get a call from the manager of Flora's restaurant.

"Hello, Marie. What's going on?"

"It's Flora. I think she's asking for you."

Matt looked at Tyler. Tyler looked at his watch.

"What do you mean, you *think* she's asking for me?"

"I think she wants you, but she's not asking for you by name. She's asking for Giovanni."

15

Background

"Get me everything you can find on Dr. Matteo Bugatti."

Ronni Barraket hung up her phone, confident that no detail of Dr. Bugatti's life would escape the notice of the research department of Stivers and Cartwright. She idly ran her thumb across the edges of the six file folders stacked on her desk, one for each of the commissioners—two former legislators, a medical ethicist, a retired CEO, a Nobel Prize winner, and a minister. They shared a common trait, which had motivated Ronni to compile a thick dossier on each of them, long before they had been tapped to serve on the Bugatti Commission: Each had publicly and forcefully taken a stand on the issue of abortion.

But Bugatti was an unknown. A quick Internet search retrieved a short biography on the faculty web page of the University of North Carolina, but beyond that, there was nothing—no Facebook page, no Twitter account—no social media presence of any kind. Ronni hoped that the research department would uncover *some* reason that this academic from an esoteric field belonged on a presidential commission, let alone was qualified to lead it.

‡ ‡ ‡

The officers of Compton-Genencraft Pharmaceutical were present in the board room at eight a.m., with two exceptions: CEO Francis Compton, and vice president of research Dr. Cameron Stroud. At a few minutes past eight, the attendees exchanged puzzled looks. Although Stroud was almost always late to meetings, Francis Compton never was.

At five past eight, Cameron strode into the board room. He looked at the empty seat at the head of the table, raising his eyebrows, smiling faintly as he took his seat across the table from Robert Hendrickson. Robert peered at the cell phone he held below table level as he tapped out a message:

HENDRICKSON   *He's here*

A minute later, Francis entered the room and took his seat. He scanned the faces in the room, coming finally to Cameron, for whom he saved his sternest look.

"The topic of this session is the newly appointed presidential commission," Francis said. "You each have a copy of the charter of the commission and a list of its members. I want to hear your thoughts on what our public stance will be."

"There are two former pharmaceutical executives on the commission," Robert said. "That's a good sign."

"It might be," Francis said. "But I wouldn't consider Virginia Van Hollen a friend of ours. When she was running Rohrbacher she made it her mission to destroy Genencraft."

"And she's pro-life," the vice president of operations said. "I doubt she'll be objective."

"What about Cory Christensen?" Robert said. "Pro-choice, former head of research at Labbé, and a Nobel laureate. I'd say that trumps the CEO of Rohrbacher."

The discussion continued for another ten minutes before Cameron interrupted.

"Y'all are missing the main point—*again*."

Francis lowered his eyes to the table. "What point?" he asked.

"Half pro-life, half pro-choice. Two pharma execs, and they're split, too. Three against three. They'll fight to a draw. This thing was set up to fail."

"What about Bugatti?" Robert asked.

"Well done, Rob," Cameron said. "Bugatti is the wild card. When this bunch gets deadlocked, Bugatti is the only one who can kick them off top dead center. He could be our ally or our enemy. And what do we know about him?"

The executives exchanged blank looks.

"Dr. Matteo Bugatti," Cameron continued, ticking off points from memory. "Graduated from the University of North Carolina at seventeen. Got his doctorate in mathematics at nineteen. Author of more than forty papers. Won the highest award for mathematicians under age forty. Damn, those southern boys are smart. Went to work for a little computer company in Wisconsin and cashed out for more than twenty million. Now he teaches school. And he's not even thirty years old."

"How do you know so much?" Robert asked.

"It's called *doing your homework*, Rob. You should try it."

"Don't start on me, Stroud."

Francis held up a hand. "Cameron, what else do you know?"

"One thing I *don't* know is whether Dr. Bugatti has even *thought* about pro-life versus pro-choice, or any other controversy outside of the field of math. I suspect he hasn't. Judging from his record, Bugatti is only interested in one thing."

"Which is?"

"The truth."

"Then we've got nothing to worry about," Robert said.

"Oh, Rob, that is precious," Cameron said. "That is so sweetly naïve. And you were doing so well."

Robert curled his lip as he looked down, mouthing the word *fucker*.

"Gentlemen," Cameron continued, "in the Roman Empire, it was the first general who made it back to Rome after a battle who wrote history. How little has changed in two thousand years. It's not the truth that matters, it's the narrative." Cameron leaned back in his chair. "We're in a race to Rome."

"What do you suggest?"

"Tell the world that CG Pharma will cooperate fully with the Bugatti commission, and that we have complete faith in the integrity of the commission and of its leader." Cameron paused. "Then, *we* have to get to Bugatti first."

‡ ‡ ‡

Ronni was impressed—the Stivers and Cartwright research department had once again lived up to its reputation for thoroughness. The report on Matt Bugatti included his family history going back to his ancestors in Italy, details of his childhood, and of his academic and professional career.

The first page was a summary.

Born, June 30, 1988. Father Giovanni died April 2, 2004, age 48.

Mother Flora living, occupation: restaurateur.
Pastimes: Competition pistol and rifle shooting.

Ronni paused. *Shooting?*

Political affiliation: Unknown—no record of party registration.
Estimated net worth: $26 million.
Source: Sale of shares in Connectrix Corporation, provider of computing systems to the National Security Agency.

Ronni put a finger to her lip. *Who* is *this guy?*

Marital status: single.

She looked at the photograph. Dr. Bugatti was handsome, with thick, dark hair. He looked his age, except for his eyes—steel-gray, and too old for his face.

She read the last paragraph of the summary, then closed the file and smiled as she slipped it into her bag.

Perfect.

‡ ‡ ‡

"The commission was ideally constituted. And now this."

Senator Yolanda Herrera Peña made the comment at her Monday meeting of advisers. "All perspectives represented and evenly matched. High profile, life-and-death stakes. The perfect talk-show topic. I could have counted on two dozen media spots to praise or condemn the direction of the commission, confident that they would never reach a conclusion." She closed the file. "Then the president fucked it up with this math professor. Who is he?"

She asked the question generally, but everyone knew that it was Ronni Barraket who would provide the answers.

Ronni pushed a file across the table. "Senator, we've completed the background on Bugatti. His profile is interesting."

"*Interesting*, Ronni? It's not like you to give me data with no conclusions."

"Senator, the first page is a summary. If I could direct your attention to the final paragraph."

Yolanda read the page. "Well, this is promising. We can build a strategy around this, assuming we can get to Bugatti."

"Senator," said a middle-aged man at the far end of the table, a former congressional aide. "One thing is for sure. The commission is packed with seasoned pros. Bugatti is a political rookie. However serious he is about the investigation, he'll have to contend with the rest of the commissioners. They won't be led easily."

Yolanda nodded. "You might be right. I wonder why the president would toss this young Daniel in among that pack of lions."

"He's not alone," Ronni said. "The president has appointed an executive director."

"A director? Who?"

"Tyler Ross."

"Is he that crew-cut *wunderkind* from the White House political office?"

"That's the man. He's as savvy as they come."

"Damn. *He* won't be an easy one to get past."

Yolanda scanned the faces at the table, then looked down at the folder labeled *Bugatti, Dr. Matteo*.

"*Shit,*" she whispered.

16

DARRYL

DARRYL MEEKS SAT at the Atlanta intersection in his rented car, waiting for what seemed like an eternity for the light to turn green. He picked up his cell phone from the passenger seat and checked the display.

Donald Lominger
Destination 3.5 mi.
22 min.

"Twenty-two minutes to go three and a half miles," he muttered. "I hate city driving."

Darryl pulled into the driveway of a one-bedroom house with no garage, parking behind a nineties-model Ford Fiesta that was leaking oil on the cracked concrete. He got out of his car and looked around. The house was one in a row of tiny houses, all needing paint and repairs to their roofs and gutters, many with rusted bicycles, toys and non-functional appliances scattered in their front yards.

Another white-trash neighborhood.

Darryl closed his eyes.

O Israel, ye approach this day unto battle against your enemies: let not your hearts faint, fear not, and do not tremble, neither be ye terrified because of them; For the Lord your God is he that goeth with you, to fight for you against your enemies.

Darryl knocked at the door. A short, stout man with a pinched face answered.

"Donald Lominger?"

"Yes, you must be Brother Meeks. Come in! It's an honor to meet you."

Darryl followed Donald into a house filled with ragged furniture, smelling of mold.

"Please, sit down, Brother Meeks. Let me get you some tea."

"Don't bother, please."

Donald grinned. "It's no bother, really. It's already made." He disappeared into the kitchen, returning a moment later with a tall glass of iced tea. Darryl took a sip.

"It's very sweet."

"Yes, sir, that's how we like it."

Darryl set the glass on the coffee table and laid a stack of papers next to it.

"Brother Lominger, I understand you have a new recruit."

"Yes, sir. Her name is Lucy. She's a young woman with ovarian cancer. It's untreatable, I'm sorry to say."

"How sad."

"Yes, sir. But she's joyful. She's found a new purpose, praise Jesus."

"Hallelujah."

"And she's prepared. Any time and place you say, Brother Meeks."

Donald leaned forward with his elbows on his knees. His face was eager. Darryl studied it. *Only say the word—thy will be done.*

Darryl picked up a folder from his stack. It was labeled *Bugatti, Dr. Matteo.* He opened it to the summary page. *Religious affiliation: None.*

He closed the folder.

"Not yet, Brother Lominger," he said. "But soon."

17

MARLIN

MARLIN CASTOR RECOGNIZED the voice of Darryl Meeks as he answered his phone.

"We have found another Soldier for Christ."

"Right. When and where is the induction ceremony?"

"Atlanta. In one week."

"Same uniform as before?"

"No, larger."

"The last one was a size three. How big do you want it?"

"Five. She will make a joyful noise unto the Lord, hallelujah!"

"Right. Hallelujah."

Marlin put his phone aside at the end of the conversation. He went to his basement workshop and checked his inventory. *One-half kilogram of C4 grade explosive. Two class B blasting caps. Two trigger assemblies and parts to make one more.*

Marlin looked over the array of armaments. He would need more C4. The last device used three kilos, but apparently Meeks was not satisfied with the result. Marlin had quoted a price for a five kilo device and Meeks went for it without even a counteroffer.

Left money on the table.

Marlin wondered what dumb shit social outcast Meeks had conned into blowing herself up this time. He chuckled.

Soldier for Christ my ass.

18

PRESSURE

ASSOCIATE JUSTICE ALONZO of the United States Supreme Court stood before Matt Bugatti, holding a bible.

"Raise your right hand and repeat after me."

Matt raised his right hand, leaving his left hand at his side.

"I, Matteo Bugatti, do solemnly swear…"

"I, Matteo Bugatti," Matt repeated, "do solemnly affirm…"

Justice Alonzo hesitated. "That I will support and defend the Constitution of the United States against all enemies, foreign and domestic…"

Matt repeated the oath, except the last line.

"So help me God," the justice said.

Matt lowered his hand and held it forward. Justice Alonzo, still holding out the bible, shook Matt's hand. "Congratulations, Dr. Bugatti."

"If I could have the commissioners seated here," Tyler Ross shouted. He stood behind a row of seven chairs arranged in front of a blue backdrop and six American flags. "Dr. Bugatti, we need you in the middle."

The commissioners sat down. A lean man with a mane of sandy brown hair, grayed at the temples, sat to Matt's left and offered his hand.

"Dr. Bugatti, I'm the Reverend Hunter Gibbs."

Matt smiled and took his hand. "It's good to meet you, Reverend Gibbs. I'm looking forward to working with you."

"And I with you. Dr. Bugatti, I couldn't help but notice your reluctance to swear the complete oath. I'm curious—do you have a religious objection to swearing an oath?"

"Hardly, Reverend. I take the oath very seriously. It wouldn't be honest of me to swear an oath to God."

"Not honest? Why is that?"

"Because I believe there is no God."

"Can I have your eyes this way, please?" the photographer said.

All the commissioners except Reverend Gibbs followed the direction. The Reverend continued to look at Matt for a few seconds before turning a stony face toward the camera.

"In a few moments, we'll proceed to the press room," Tyler explained. "The president will make a brief statement, then he'll introduce Chairman Bugatti. Dr. Bugatti will make a brief statement, and then we'll have a few minutes for questions. Are we ready?"

The commissioners filed onto the press room stage. Tyler pulled Matt from the line and held him back.

"Remember, stick to public information," Tyler whispered. "The charter, the schedule, the procedures. The press is *not* unbiased—either they're pushing an agenda, or they're trying to make headlines. Keep it factual, and keep it non-controversial."

Matt nodded. "I understand."

Tyler put a hand on Matt's shoulder. "You'll do great."

"Thanks," Matt said as he turned to follow the line. Tyler pulled him back.

"And don't tell them you're an atheist."

The commissioners lined up behind a podium bearing the presidential seal. The small room, its rear wall lined with television cameras, was filled with people, some seated, and as many standing. All of them rose as the president entered the room.

"Please be seated," the president said as he gripped the sides of the podium. "Justice Alonzo has just sworn in the seven members of the Presidential Commission on the Unexplained Deaths of Young Women. These distinguished individuals have accepted, at my request, the solemn and difficult task of ascertaining the causes, both immediate and contributing, of the tragic deaths of forty-nine young ladies." The president looked behind him to acknowledge the commissioners before introducing them.

"Dr. Cory Christensen, former head of research at Labbè Pharmaceutical, and Nobel laureate in medicine. Dr. Samuel Lipinski, Professor Emeritus of the Berkeley Institute for Health Policy Studies. Reverend Hunter Gibbs, author and pastor of the Stoneway Congregation. Virginia Van Hollen, retired CEO of Rohrbacher Pharmaceutical. Former Senator Loretta McDermott of Kentucky. Former Representative Victoria Woodall of Minnesota. All of them are highly accomplished and well-respected."

The president turned and motioned for Matt to come forward.

"I'm also honored to introduce a young man who is perhaps not as well-known, but who is no less impressive than his fellow commissioners, and whom I've come to respect: the chairman of the commission, Dr. Matt Bugatti."

Matt stood next to the president as cameras clicked. The president stepped aside as Matt took his place behind the presidential podium.

"Thank you, Mr. President," Matt said quietly. He looked at the faces before him, some with questioning looks, some scowling—none smiling.

"I know I speak for the entire commission when I pledge to you, Mr. President, and to the families of the young women who died, that we will pursue the truth wherever it leads. If it is in our power to do so, we will make it our mission to prevent such a horror from ever being repeated.

We will continue our preparations through the weekend. Hearings will begin next week."

The president shook Matt's hand before leaving the room.

"We have a minute for questions," Tyler said. The room erupted in shouting. Tyler pointed at a person in the front row. "Pete, you first," he said.

"Dr. Bugatti, what about the name of the commission, *on the Unexplained Deaths of Young Women*. We already know that the drug *Backup* killed these girls. Why do you say that their deaths are unexplained?"

Matt swallowed hard. "The charter of the commission is to determine direct *and indirect* causes. We have evidence, but evidence is not proof. We know some things but not everything. Whatever you may have heard, the cause of death is still not known."

The shouting resumed. Tyler pointed. "Jake."

"Mr. Chairman, since the abortion clinic bombing in Pittsburgh, the number of confrontations and arrests at clinics nationwide has escalated. Some say it's only a matter of time before another bomb explodes. How far will the commission look into these incidents?"

Matt gripped the podium as he pushed himself back. He looked at Tyler, who nodded slightly.

"The events at health clinics are outside the scope of this investigation," Matt said.

Tyler immediately pointed again. "Susan."

"Dr. Bugatti, what's your reaction to the public statements from CG Pharma that they support the work of the commission and will cooperate fully?"

"Since we have scheduled testimony from a number of CG Pharma's officers, naturally we welcome their cooperation."

Tyler scanned the clamoring and gesticulating crowd. His eyes settled on a short woman with graying hair, with one hand extended, silent, as if she were waiting to be called on in class. *Could that be...?*

"The woman in the back. You. I don't know your name."

The woman lowered her hand. "I'm Clara Kildee, on assignment from the Associated Press."

Tyler's eyes widened. *So that's Clara Kildee.*

"Your question?"

"Dr. Bugatti, do you know the names of the forty-nine victims?"

The room fell silent. Matt looked at the woman, whose face was guileless.

"Clara, I do not. But I will make it my first task to learn them."

‡ ‡ ‡

"That went beautifully," Tyler said to Matt as they exited the Rayburn Office Building. "You're a natural."

"I'm glad you think so. I was nervous as hell."

The two of them walked a few more steps before Tyler halted.

"Dr. Bugatti, I couldn't help but overhear you say to Reverend Gibbs that you don't believe in God."

"That's right," Matt said.

"But how can you not…" Tyler blurted, before stopping.

Matt smiled. "Not believe in God?" He kept walking as Tyler stepped quickly to catch up.

"The French mathematician Laplace wrote a lengthy book on the motion of planets, which he dedicated to the emperor Napoleon. The emperor asked Laplace why, in a book on the workings of the universe, God was not mentioned. Do you know how Laplace answered?"

Tyler shook his head.

"*I had no need of that hypothesis.*"

"Dr. Bugatti!"

Matt and Tyler looked toward an overweight, heavily perspiring man in a brown suit jogging in their direction. When he reached them, he gulped and paused to catch his breath.

"Dr. Bugatti," he huffed, "I'm Robert Hendrickson. I'm…"

"You're the vice president of business development for CG Pharma," Tyler said before Robert could finish.

"Yes, that's right. Can I have a word?"

"Mr. Hendrickson," Tyler said.

"*Dr.* Hendrickson," Robert corrected.

"Since you have agreed to testify before the commission, *Dr.* Hendrickson, it would be improper to speak with you outside the official proceedings."

"I just wanted to reaffirm the commitment of Compton-Genencraft to the success of the commission, and to impress upon you the potential impact of the commission's findings on the U.S. pharmaceutical industry, accounting for 350 billion…"

"Dr. Hendrickson, you're out of line," Tyler said. "This conversation is over."

Tyler took Matt's arm and hurried him forward, leaving Robert huffing and sweating.

"You'd better get used to that," Tyler said.

Matt stopped suddenly as he and Tyler approached the waiting limo. Next to the car stood a woman, strikingly beautiful, tall and dark-skinned, with black hair and blue eyes, so blue that they seemed out of place. The contrast caught Matt by surprise.

"Who's that? Another reporter?" Matt asked.

"No," Tyler groaned, "not a reporter."

The woman stepped forward as they approached. Tyler greeted her before she could speak. "Hello, Ronni. Out for a stroll? Dr. Bugatti, let me introduce Ronni Barraket from Stivers and Cartwright."

"Hello, Tyler," Ronni answered. "Hello, Dr. Bugatti. Congratulations on your appointment."

Matt was about to speak when Tyler cut him off. "Ronni here is a lobbyist for the American Life Defense League, an anti-abortion group. The ALDL has opposed nearly every social policy of this administration."

"The ALDL is an organization of concerned pro-life citizens," Ronni said, "but I'm not here in that capacity."

"Oh? Can you switch capacities just like that?" Tyler said. "Or do you mean you're not billing them for your time?"

"Dr. Bugatti, I'm an adviser to Senator Yolanda Herrera Peña of Ohio. The senator has asked me to convey to you her support for the commission, and her wish that you will come swiftly to a complete and honest account of this sad situation."

"Did you hear that, Dr. Bugatti? *Everyone* supports the commission. CG Pharma, ALDL, senators and who knows who else, they're all cheering for you and they all want the truth. What selfless, civic-minded patriots." Tyler opened the car door and motioned for Matt to enter. "Nice try, Ronni." Tyler climbed into the car and slammed the door.

Matt twisted in his seat to look out the rear window as the limo pulled away.

"Ronni *who?*"

"Barraket," Tyler said. "It's Lebanese, I think." Tyler looked at Matt, then he looked out the rear window at the distant figure on the curb.

"Forget it, Matt. You've got nothing in common."

‡ ‡ ‡

Matt hung his jacket in the hotel room closet and loosened his tie. He touched the screen of his cell phone and put it to his ear. The voice that answered was not his mother's.

"Marie?"

"Hello, Matt. How's Washington?"

"I'd rather be in Raleigh. Why are you at Mom's house?"

"She asked me to take her home. I take her home and spend the evening with her on bad days."

"How long have you been doing that?"

"Not long. A week, maybe. Just a couple nights."

Matt sat on the edge of the bed, elbow on his knee, head resting in his hand.

"I didn't know."

"You've been busy."

"Can I talk to Mom?"

"Sure. Here she is."

There was the sound of the telephone being handed off.

"*Ciao, Matteo caro.*"

"Hi, Mom. How are you feeling?"

"*Mi sento bene, caro. E tu?*"

The conversation continued, half English, half Italian, until Matt asked to speak to Marie.

"Is she always speaking Italian now?"

"With me, most of the time. My Italian has improved a lot."

"Marie, I really appreciate your help."

"It's nothing."

Matt paused. "I can take care of your time."

"I wouldn't take your money, Mr. Famous Rich Guy," Marie said indignantly. "This is what friends do for each other."

Matt squeezed his eyes shut. A tear fell from the tip of his nose.

"I'm sorry."

"You should be. Now do your duty. Your country needs you."

Matt ended the call and dropped the phone on the bed. He went to his laptop and logged on to a secure site specially created for the Bugatti commission, opening a folder labeled *Victims*, containing a list of files:

NOVOTNY_LYUDMYLA
MATZEK_KATARINA
BLASKOVICH_CYNTHIA

The list had forty-six more entries, ending with *MELNIK_DEBRA*. Matt opened the first file on the list and began to read.

19

Battle Lines

Yolanda checked her cell phone—again. She had no new messages, and she didn't expect any, but she continued scrolling through the list of old messages, and not talking with Steve Melson, the host of *Politics Weekly Forum*.

A voice in Yolanda's earpiece counted down, "Five seconds. Four. Three…"

"And we're back again with the *Politics Weekly Forum* round table," Steve Melson announced. "We all know the history: forty-nine girls dead, a drug company in denial, and a government slow to act. Senator Herrera, the Bugatti Commission begins its hearings tomorrow. What should we expect?"

"Steve," she addressed the host genially, "I *hope* that we will hear the truth, and I hope that the commission, and all who come before it, are committed to finding the truth. I *expect* that we will hear obfuscation and rationalization from the FDA and the drug maker, Compton-Genencraft. They had a chance to pull *Backup* from the market and prevent at least some of these tragic deaths, but this administration's extreme policies on abortion and birth control, and this drug maker's twisted priorities, placing profit ahead of the public's safety, have warped their judgment."

"Senator, you seem to have bypassed the entire investigative process," said a middle-aged man with glasses, a regular on *Politics Weekly Forum*. "We don't even know that this drug is connected with the deaths of these girls. In fact…"

"In *fact*," Yolanda interrupted, "since this drug was pulled from the market more than two weeks ago, no more deaths have been reported. The CDC announced a connection…"

"A *suspected* connection," the pundit interjected.

"…between *Backup* and these deaths," Yolanda continued, "and Kay Cardin…"

"Secretary of Health and Human Services," Steve explained.

"…contradicted the director of the CDC, who works for *her*, and kept this drug on the market. The president is the head of my party, and I support many of his policies, but these actions are the height of irresponsibility."

"Senator," Steve said, "I know that you have taken a strong stand on these issues, but my question was about the commission itself. Do you think that they are equipped to conduct this investigation fairly and completely?"

"The commission is evenly balanced in their views. My greatest fear is that they will separate into factions and that the investigation will end in a deadlock. I pray to God that won't happen, but I suspect that God will get very little help from the commission chairman."

"Why is that, Senator?"

"Because Dr. Bugatti is a known atheist."

‡ ‡ ‡

The video monitor in the office of Ronni Barraket displayed a title screen to the accompaniment of a Brahms cello concerto:

C-SPAN

10:00 a.m. EDT
Hearing
Presidential Commission on the Unexplained Deaths of Young Women

It was 9:45. Ronni perused the daily digest of articles on her computer, clicking most of them to skim their contents, reading a few of them in detail. Every few minutes, she dashed off an email—some to clients, some to colleagues, and some to the Stivers and Cartwright research department —oblivious to the C-SPAN background music.

"Good morning, Ronni."

Ronni looked up to see Jay Stivers standing in her doorway, dressed as if he'd just come from a round of golf.

"Did you have an early tee time, Jay?"

"Senator Sims. He's lined up on the embargo bill."

"Are we for it or against it?"

"As free-market conservatives, we're against it," Jay said, smiling. "As lobbyists for the National Association of Soybean Producers, we're for it. And now that the NASP is among the Honorable Alphonse Sims's major campaign donors, so is the senator."

Ronni nodded without a word. Jay looked at the video screen.

"The Bugatti Commission," he said.

"The first hearing is today. Senator Herrera is scheduled on three shows this weekend and I've got to prepare points."

Jay sat in a chair facing Ronni's desk. "I've been meaning to talk with you about your work for Senator Herrera."

Ronni looked up from her computer. She took her hands from the keyboard and laid them in her lap. "I'm listening."

"Your association with the senator is becoming quite well known. I hear you've even been representing yourself as a member of the Senator's staff."

"Jay, that's not true. I've never told anyone that I'm anything more than an adviser to Senator Herrera. I certainly have *never* said that I'm a paid staffer."

"Not everyone makes that distinction."

Ronni's mouth dropped open. "I don't understand the issue. Everyone at this firm has outside interests, and there's nothing in our contracts to prohibit them. You yourself are an adviser to a House committee chairman."

"That's different."

"How is it different? How?" Ronni stood up. "This can't be about my billings. I have one of the highest billing rates in the firm. I make a ton of money for you and Arnie Cartwright." She looked at the video screen. The hearing would begin in five minutes.

"It's not your billings," Jay answered. "I have to think about the firm's image."

Ronni nodded. "Oh, I get it. Senator Herrera is one of the staunchest pro-life voices in Congress, but because she also supports government programs to help the poor and disadvantaged, she's tainted. And so am I. And so are you."

"Ronni, you know our clientele. Ideological purity matters to them."

Ronni set her jaw. "I know. While you've been thinking about our image, I've been thinking about our clients. And I think they're not doing themselves any favors by being so dogmatic. Our clients might be better served if we advised them to compromise once in awhile."

"Ronni, I *do* advise compromise," Jay said with a strained voice. "But this is not a compromising world." He ran his hand over his bald head. "Not any more, anyway."

"Are you telling me to stop advising Senator Herrera?"

Jay sat motionless for a few seconds, then stood up and walked to the door. "Keep it low key."

As Jay left, Ronni noticed that the Brahms concerto had ceased. She looked at the screen just as the commissioners filed into the hearing room.

The commissioners' chairs were arranged on a two-level platform, three in front, four in back. Seven engraved plaques with the commissioners' names rested on the tables. Matt took his seat at the center of the front table, behind the name plate that read

DR. BUGATTI
CHAIRMAN

The commissioners faced another table reserved for witnesses. It was already occupied when the commission arrived. Beyond the witness's table were rows of seats, filled with spectators, and cameras lining the rear wall.

Though the room temperature was comfortable, Matt tugged at his collar, trying for a little more slack. He popped open a bottle of water and drank a third of it. The noise in the room slowly diminished as Matt shuffled a stack of papers, ceasing entirely when he adjusted the microphone closer.

"Good morning. Thank you for coming."

Matt announced the name of the commission and introduced its members. He gulped another third of the bottle before continuing.

"Our first witness is Dr. Lloyd Duncan, director, Centers for Disease Control and Prevention. Dr. Duncan, welcome. Before we begin, I'd like to read a brief statement."

Ronni, watching the proceedings from her office, leaned forward and turned an ear toward the screen.

"Last week, I was asked if I knew the names of the victims of this epidemic. At the time, I didn't. Now, three days later, I do know them. I've read the case files. They tell me everything we know about how these young women died —but not how they lived, or who they were." Matt drank from the water bottle. "I've called some of the parents, and I expect to call all of them in the coming week."

Ronni turned her other ear. *He called the parents?*

"I think it's important to get to know these girls. And they *are* girls, most of them. The youngest is fourteen; the oldest is twenty. They have girls' names—names like Kat, and Cindi, and Liddie. They have loving parents who are devastated by their loss."

Matt drained the last of his water. "When we get in the middle of this, when we're overwhelmed with facts and data and details, we can't forget these girls."

Matt read forty-nine names.

"Dr. Duncan, please begin."

Ronni leaned back in her seat and folded her arms as she studied the chairman of the commission. She pressed a knuckle to her lip, nodding slightly.

The CDC director gave a detailed account of the manner of death. The audience gasped when he displayed graphic autopsy photos. Though most turned away, Matt forced himself not to.

"Dr. Duncan," Matt asked at the end of the testimony, "were all the deaths from the same cause?"

"Understand, Mr. Chairman, that we did not perform most of these autopsies. Much of the information we have is second hand and incomplete. We can't say the cause of death was the same in every case, but the reported symptoms are consistent."

"Are they symptoms of a known disease?"

"They could be consistent with an auto-immune disorder."

"What exactly does that mean, Doctor?"

"These bodies self-destructed."

There were murmurs from the audience.

"What could have triggered this response?"

"We don't know."

"But that's not true, is it, Doctor?"

Matt looked behind him at the questioner, former Rohrbacher CEO Virginia Van Hollen.

"In fact, you announced your finding weeks ago that these deaths were linked to the use of the contraceptive *Backup*. Are you retracting that statement?"

"That statement was premature."

"But you did have evidence that many of these women used this drug shortly before their deaths. Is there a reason to think that there's *no* connection…"

"Virginia, really." The man interrupting was Dr. Cory Christensen, Nobel laureate. "You know better than that. You can't presume a cause to be disproved. That's not how it works."

"Don't lecture me, Cory. I *know* how *it* works. The CDC *knew* this drug was deadly, they *announced* that the drug was deadly, and the president forced a retraction to protect himself from criticism over the drug's fast track approval. *That's* how it works."

"Mr. Chairman, that's an outrageous charge!" shouted former Congresswoman Victoria Woodall. The room erupted in chaos, drowning out the shouting match between Virginia, Cory and Victoria.

Ronni kept her eyes on Matt.

Cameras clicked. Matt twisted in his chair to see who was shouting at whom. He looked at the turmoil in the audience. He stood.

"There will be order in this hearing!"

The noise continued. Matt signaled the security guards by the door to approach the table.

"Clear the room," Matt said.

The commissioners stopped their shouting, watching as the guards ushered spectators from the room.

"The press, too," Matt said.

Correspondents from a dozen news outlets protested as the guards escorted them to the door.

Matt remained standing in the room, empty except for the commissioners and the witness.

"These hearings will be conducted with decorum and with respect for the witnesses and for our fellow commissioners."

"Mr. Chairman," Virginia said, "if I may…"

Matt turned and looked directly at Virginia, his gray eyes blazing. Virginia inhaled sharply.

"I have to be allowed to question the witness, don't I?"

All the commissioners looked to Matt.

"Ms. Van Hollen, I'm aware of your views. You've been quite public about them."

Cory Christensen smiled.

"And I'm aware of your views as well, Dr. Christensen. And Ms. Woodall's." He looked at each face. "I know where all of you stand. I respect your right—I respect your *responsibility*—to hold your beliefs and to defend them. But this is a fact-finding commission. I will not tolerate bias, and I will not tolerate…"

"Mr. Chairman, really…" Virginia interrupted.

"…*and I will not tolerate* advocacy or incivility. If it continues, I will dissolve this body and report to the president that we were unable to complete our commission due to our inability to conduct ourselves professionally."

Virginia looked into Matt's eyes for another second before looking down.

"I would like to apologize to Dr. Duncan, and to my colleague, Dr. Christensen, and to you, Mr. Chairman."

"Very well." Matt turned back to the witness. "Dr. Duncan, the CDC has studied how often women use emergency contraceptives, correct?"

"Yes, Mr. Chairman."

"And based on the number of cases in which *Backup* use was confirmed, have you calculated the statistical likelihood that *Backup* usage among these forty-nine girls is simply representative of the population at large?"

The doctor smiled. "We have, Mr. Chairman. It's less than ten percent."

"Thank you, Dr. Duncan. One more question. You didn't dwell on the fact that all forty-nine girls were of Eastern European ancestry. Did you do a similar calculation of the chances that this, too, was a random occurrence?"

"No, sir, we haven't."

Matt pulled a sheet from his stack. "I have. The chances are remote—one out of a number so large, it takes seventy-five digits to write it. What does that tell you, Dr. Duncan?"

"It tells me that all these girls died from the same cause, and that only women of Eastern European descent are susceptible."

"Thank you Dr. Duncan. You're dismissed. This hearing is adjourned until tomorrow morning at ten a.m."

The witness left the room. The commissioners filed out. Matt remained at his seat, paging through a file, framed in a C-SPAN close-up.

Ronni watched Matt on the video screen in her office.

CHARLES O'DONNELL

He's in charge.

20

PROGNOSIS

It was as awkward a silence as any Matt had ever experienced.

Dr. Tobey had known Flora for more than thirty years; he'd known Matt from birth. It was Dr. Tobey who had called Flora almost fifteen years before to tell her that her husband, Giovanni, was in a coma from which he would never wake up. That was a hard call to make. The news he had just delivered was in some ways harder.

Flora looked at the floor. Matt put his hand on Flora's arm. "What's the prognosis?" he asked.

"There are treatments for the symptoms of Alzheimer's. They can help improve memory and cognitive functions. I'm sure your specialist will prescribe a regimen."

Matt felt his throat constrict. "The symptoms?"

"We can treat the symptoms. There's no cure."

"She's not even fifty-four. Isn't she too young?"

Dr. Tobey took a tissue from a box at the edge of his desk. He dabbed at his eyes and nose. "Early-onset Alzheimer's represents only about five percent of cases. Flora, your tests show that you have a genetic predisposition for Alzheimer's. The incidence of the disease among the population with your genetic makeup is much higher."

"How high?" Matt asked.

Dr. Tobey reached for another tissue. "Very high."

Matt waited for the rest of the answer.

"Almost one-hundred percent."

Matt squeezed Flora's arm. "If it's genetic, then…"

"Yes. It's inherited."

Flora looked up from the floor. She looked at Matt for a moment before pressing her hand to her mouth and sobbing.

Dr. Tobey handed Matt a sheet of paper. "You should be tested. This is a prescription for the test and the address of the laboratory."

Matt looked at the sheet without really seeing it. "What if it's positive? There's no treatment, right?"

"There is treatment. But no cure."

Matt folded the paper and slipped it into his pocket. "Thanks, Dr. Tobey."

"Flora," Dr. Tobey said, "you're a strong woman, with people around you who love you and will care for you."

Matt took Flora's arm to help her stand. Flora pulled her arm away and stood up.

"*Io posso alzarmi,*" she protested. "I can get up. I can walk."

As Matt and Flora neared the door, Dr. Tobey spoke.

"There is another option."

Matt stopped and turned.

"There are a number of clinical trials underway for new treatments. Some of them may still be accepting new subjects. I've heard rumors of one in particular that produced outstanding results in the earlier trials, almost complete remission in some subjects. There are no guarantees, but it's worth looking into."

"What drug is it?"

"The drug doesn't have a name yet. The company is Compton-Genencraft."

‡ ‡ ‡

Flora and Matt didn't speak on the drive home. Matt pulled into the driveway of Flora's house and turned off the car. Flora touched Matt's arm.

"*Mi vuoi bene, caro?*" Flora said. "Do you love me?"

"*Sì, Mamma.*"

Flora took Matt's hand, the look on her face a mixture of fear and longing. Matt's eyes filled with tears.

"*Vorrei andare in Italia,*" she said. "I want to go to Italy."

‡ ‡ ‡

Tyler Ross's office in the basement of the Eisenhower Building was small, more like a large, windowless closet than a useful workspace. Tyler's attempts to keep it organized were overwhelmed by his workload—the shelves were overflowing and his desk was piled high. Tyler and Matt sat at a table, the one useful work surface remaining. There were a few transcripts and exhibits on the table, with the rest stacked on the floor, within easy reach.

"How are Christensen and Van Hollen doing on their part?" Tyler asked.

"They can barely stand to be in the same room with each other," Matt mumbled.

"The draft, Matt, how are they coming with the draft report on the approvals?"

Matt looked up. He stared at Tyler for a few seconds. He shook his head.

"I haven't seen the draft. But they haven't told me they'd be late."

"I'll call Van Hollen." Tyler picked up the phone and entered a number.

"Matt, what's wrong with you?" Tyler asked as the phone rang. "You're someplace else."

"Nothing. I'm fine," Matt said. He continued to read the file for a moment before laying it on the table.

"Actually, it's my mother. She's…"

Tyler held up a hand. "Virginia? It's Tyler. Say, are you still on track to have a draft by tomorrow? Yeah. Yeah. Who do you want? Yeah. If you think that's necessary, of course. I'll discuss it with Dr. Bugatti. Okay. Can I have *something* by tomorrow? All right. I'll take it up with the chairman."

Tyler hung up the phone. "They'll give us what they have, but they want to call another witness—the CG Pharma research head. You know, Stroud. Cameron Stroud."

"We talked to him already."

"They have more questions. Christensen is convinced that this nasty reaction to *Backup* is related to specific genetic variations. He wants to know why it wasn't detected in the clinical trials. The trials are Stroud's department."

"Sure. Go ahead and schedule it."

"Consider it scheduled." Tyler turned to his computer and began typing. "Anyway, you were saying. Your mother."

Matt stared at the wall. "It's nothing. She's fine." Matt stood up. "I'm going for lunch. Do you want anything?"

"Where are you going?"

"The barbecue place."

"Nope. I'm good," Tyler said without missing a keystroke.

Matt had become a regular at Old Glory BBQ. It was the closest thing to North Carolina barbecue within miles—not quite the same, but good. The wait staff knew him by name. Matt had only to sit at a table and a pulled pork platter with coleslaw and cornbread would appear within minutes.

Matt nibbled the bread and sampled the pork. After thirty minutes he'd made hardly a dent and the food was cold. He rarely left food on the plate, especially barbecue. He loved it —in fact, he craved it.

Food was taken seriously in Matt's boyhood home. Flora's attention to detail and her pursuit of perfection, the foundation of her restaurant's reputation, was duplicated in her home. She never served barbecue. She had nothing *against* barbecue—on the rare occasions when the Bugatti family dined out, she enjoyed barbecue whenever Matt chose the restaurant. Barbecue was simply not in Flora's repertoire. It was a specialty, one she chose not to practice. The knowledge, the effort, the *time* that it took to master a cuisine was immense. She had to be selective. The alternative was to be second-rate. Flora could not abide the second-rate—it was not in her nature.

Matt handed his credit card to the waiter, who looked inquiringly at the uneaten pile of pork before heading for the cashier. While Matt waited for him to return, his phone buzzed in his pocket. He looked at the display: *Dr. Tobey.*

"Hello, Dr. Tobey."

"Hello, Matt. I have your test results."

Matt's mouth went dry. "Uh-huh."

"It's not good news."

21

SOLDIERS

Lucy Seidman appeared serene. She was prepared to do battle for Christ, having long since reconciled herself to her fate. She did not fear death. Life had become a burden, death a release. More than that, death was Lucy's reward, payment for the service that God had demanded of her, a divine settling of accounts. Her calm demeanor was the consequence of her surrender to a holy cause, and of the 30 milligrams of oxycodone she had taken that morning to deaden the pain of stage three ovarian cancer.

Lucy sat on a metal chair in Donald Lominger's front room. She followed Marlin Castor's directions as he opened a Velcro strap and adjusted the position and fit of the belt of explosives wrapped around her waist. It was shaped to follow the contours of her body; when properly worn, under a loose top, it would be nearly invisible.

"I checked out the clinic," Marlin said. "No metal detector. No search. No real security at all, in fact." He patted the belt. "You'll have no trouble getting in."

"That's surprising," Donald said.

"Yeah," Marlin snorted. "It's crazy. After the Pittsburgh bombing, every clinic in America clamped down. After a couple of weeks of quiet, they've all loosened up." Marlin stood up. "Don't expect that to last. If you're planning any more of these, you'd better come up with a different plan. After Thursday, security will be tighter than a virgin nun."

"Mr. Castor!" Donald whispered. He tipped his head in Lucy's direction. *"Please!"*

"Sorry, sweetheart. No disrespect."

The young woman with more than ten pounds of high explosives strapped to her body sat in front of Marlin with her hands folded in her lap. She looked up at him and smiled sweetly.

"Is it the same type as Pittsburgh?" Donald asked.

"Same mechanism, different design, bigger load. I used three kilograms in Pittsburgh. This one has five."

Lucy looked at Donald with half-closed eyes as he kneeled next to her chair.

"Sister, we've made all the arrangements. Your escort will pick you up in front of your building on Thursday at eleven a.m. Make sure you put on the belt exactly as Mr. Castor showed you."

"Don't arm the explosive until you get to the clinic," Marlin warned. "Enter the code and press *star*. When you're ready, press *pound*."

"Don't press *pound* until you're with the doctor, Sister Lucy," Donald said. He turned to Marlin. "What's the code?"

Marlin shrugged. "It's whatever you want it to be."

"Three sixteen," said Lucy.

Donald nodded. He held Lucy's hand and closed his eyes as he raised his face to the ceiling. "Yes, Sister," he said. "Glory to Jesus."

Marlin picked up the cell phone on the table and punched in a sequence of numbers, then closed the phone and handed it to Lucy.

"*Three one six star* to arm. *Pound* to detonate."

"Thank you, Mr. Castor," Lucy said. She closed her eyes and bowed her head. *"Thank you, Jesus,"* she whispered.

‡ ‡ ‡

"Where is it?" Marlin asked Donald.

Donald unlocked the trunk of his car and removed a bundle wrapped in a plastic grocery bag. Marlin opened the bag and inspected it.

"Fifteen thousand." Marlin twisted the bag shut and tossed it onto the front seat of his car. He lit a cigarette and climbed in.

"What's special about three one six?" Marlin asked as he started his car.

"John 3:16," Donald answered. *"For God so loved the world that he gave his one and only Son, that whoever believes in him shall not perish but have eternal life."*

‡ ‡ ‡

Lucy sat quietly in the waiting room of the Atlanta Family Plan clinic. Her escort sat next to her, gently stroking the back of Lucy's hand. They looked at each other, exchanging nervous smiles.

The nurse called a few names but had not yet called Lucy's. As they waited, Lucy took a cell phone from her pocket and flipped it open.

"Lucy?"

Lucy looked up. "Dr. Coleman!"

"How are you doing? Are you in much pain?"

Lucy's escort looked quizzically at the doctor. "Dr. Coleman, do you know Lucy?"

"Of course. I diagnosed Lucy's cancer. Lucy, do you need anything? You know, you could have come to the free clinic. I would have made sure you got everything you need."

"Cancer?" the escort questioned Lucy. "Is that why you're getting the abortion?"

Lucy fumbled with the cell phone. She tried entering *3-1-6* but instead entered *3-1-9*. *Oh, Lord,* she thought. She pressed *star* and the phone beeped.

"An abortion?" Dr. Coleman said. "That doesn't make sense. Lucy has ovarian cancer. I'm sorry to say that it's very advanced. She can't get pregnant."

Lucy tried a second time to enter *3-1-6* and again entered *3-1-9*. She pressed *star* and the phone beeped again.

"Lucy, what are you…" Dr. Coleman asked. As she watched Lucy's frantic keystrokes, she noticed the unnatural drape of her shirt, as if her middle were wrapped in a towel. A dreadful realization came to her.

"Lucy, no!"

Lucy punched *3-1-6* and pressed *star*. Dr. Coleman lunged for the phone. Lucy fell forward from her chair, sprawling on the floor, the cell phone sliding across the room.

"Bomb! Bomb! She's got a bomb!" Dr. Coleman screamed. The people in the waiting room froze for an instant before rushing the door.

Lucy pushed herself across the floor toward the phone. Dr. Coleman tried to grab Lucy but was unable to find a grip. Lucy's hand was within a foot of the phone when her forward progress stopped. Dr. Coleman was on the floor behind her with her arms around Lucy's legs.

"Oh Jesus, Jesus, Jesus!" Lucy sobbed. She kicked until one of her legs broke free. Dr. Coleman involuntarily loosened her grip as a heel caught her full in the face. Lucy covered the last twelve inches between her and the phone.

"I am heaven sent!" Lucy pressed the key.

The blast ripped through the clinic, killing seven and injuring twelve.

‡ ‡ ‡

"These only look like different issues, but they're the same issue."

"Explain that," Steve Melson demanded of the *Politics Weekly Forum* round table regular. Before he could answer, guest commentator Tony Marino of the American Life Defense League interrupted.

"They are *not* the same issue," Tony objected. "The concern that many Americans have over this administration's radical policy on birth control, which extends to the free availability of abortion-inducing drugs, must *not* be equated with the sickness that drives these terrorist acts. Pro-abortion factions would love for the public to associate the American Life Defense League with these clinic bombings. The ALDL loves life. We even love the misguided doctors, as the Lord commands us to do, who perform nearly a million abortions a year, but we hate the scourge they have brought upon this land."

"Too late," the regular said. "In the public's mind, you're already linked. And do you know why? It's because *your own* position is extreme. *Backup* does *not* induce abortions. As long as you insist that it does, the public will see the ALDL as a group of extremists."

"The science on how *Backup* works isn't settled," Tony responded.

"You *talk* like it's settled."

"If there's even a *chance*…"

"A chance is not a scientific conclusion."

"…that babies are dying, it's our duty…"

"Your duty to what?"

"…to stop it!"

"Stop it how?"

"Babies are dying!"

"How would you stop it? What would you do?"

"*Anything!*"

The round table was quiet for a beat. Steve Melson broke the silence. "We'll be back with *Politics Weekly Forum* after this break."

‡ ‡ ‡

Marlin Castor didn't usually watch *Politics Weekly Forum* on Sunday mornings, but he'd heard that abortion clinic bombings would be the topic of discussion. He'd watched the exchange, staring at the screen almost without blinking for the duration of the segment. It began with an account of the dead and injured in Atlanta, and ended with the incriminating admission from Tony Marino that no tactics were off limits in the crusade against abortion.

At the commercial break he clicked off the TV. He covered his face with his hands.

Sergeant Castor reporting, sir.

At ease, Sergeant. I have the report from your mission. Target destroyed, twelve enemy dead. Well done.

Yes, sir. Any other casualties, sir?

What?

Sir, I asked if there were any other casualties. Non-combatants. Civilian casualties, sir.

That's not your concern, Sergeant.

Sir, I don't pick the targets, I just blow them up. That's my job. You pick the targets. I want to know that you're doing your job.

Sergeant, you're out of line.

Sir, I don't think so. Lives are at stake.

That's enough, Sergeant.

Sir…

Listen to me, Sergeant. I give the orders, you carry out the orders. I am responsible for the consequences. I'm responsible, not you. You are a soldier. Do you know what that means? You're a tool, an instrument in my hands. You have no intention, no responsibility, and therefore no culpability. A tool, nothing more. Do you understand?

Yes, sir.

Dismissed, Sergeant.

But sir…

I said dismissed. Get out of my office.

Marlin's eyes snapped open when his cell phone buzzed. He took a deep breath before answering.

"Mr. Castor, we have won another battle."

Marlin closed his eyes. *Meeks.*

"Congratulations."

"It is a sign. God has tested me and I've proven worthy of his trust."

"Happy for you. Why are you calling?"

"I will raise an army. You must provide their weapons."

Darryl described his plans. Marlin's face went ashen.

"That will cost you," Marlin said.

"It's of no consequence," Darryl responded. "Whatever is required, God will provide."

22

TESTIMONY

DR. CAMERON STROUD took his seat at the witness table.

"Thank you for being here, Dr. Stroud," Matt addressed him, "and welcome back. I remind you that you are still under oath."

"I do know that, Mr. Chairman," Cameron said. "How may I serve this commission?"

Virginia Van Hollen began the questioning. "Dr. Stroud, although the mechanism is not precisely known, we have established with a high degree of certainty that the auto-immune syndrome resulting from the use of *Backup* is limited to young women of Eastern European ancestry. Do you agree?"

Cameron looked impassively at Virginia before turning to Matt.

"Mr. Chairman…"

"Excuse me, Dr. Stroud," Virginia said, "*I* asked the question. You will address your answer to me."

Cameron clenched his jaw as he continued looking at Matt. "That is an unforeseen and extremely unfortunate interaction, *Commissioner*. We are doing everything we can to understand the cause."

"I find it interesting that you describe the gruesome deaths of forty-nine women as an 'unfortunate interaction.'"

"I must ask the commissioners to please refrain from editorializing," said Matt.

"Actually, Mr. Chairman," said Cameron. " I said *extremely* unfortunate interaction, and it is precisely the type of response that the clinical trial is intended to uncover."

"Which brings us to the topic at hand," Cory Christensen said. "The clinical trials for this drug were somewhat unusual, weren't they?"

"I don't know what you're referring to, Dr. Christensen."

"There was no phase two trial. This drug went directly from phase one to phase three."

"Sir, the decision to bypass phase two was made with FDA approval, on the basis that the two primary components of *Backup*, the hormonal contraceptive and the oral retro-viral vaccine, have an established safety record. The FDA agreed that these drugs had been adequately characterized, and that large-scale testing of the *Backup* formulation could proceed."

"You say that the FDA agreed—with whom?" Virginia asked. "Who proposed bypassing phase two?"

Cameron leaned close to the microphone, speaking in a measured tone. "Commissioner. Compton-Genencraft made the recommendation for the reasons I have just outlined."

The audience began to murmur.

"Was the past history of these drugs the only consideration?" asked Virginia. "After all, shortening the approval process was to your company's financial advantage, by a lot, I would add. Weren't you eager to get this drug to market as fast as possible?"

Cameron's voice ticked up a notch. "That's a motivation with which you should be quite familiar, *Commissioner.*" He looked at Matt. "Yes, Mr. Chariman, the management of Compton-Genencraft wanted this drug on the market with minimum delay. But the FDA did not require a lot of convincing."

The murmurs in the audience rose to a loud buzz. "Quiet, please!" Matt shouted.

"Are you saying that the FDA was overly willing to bypass its normal approval process?" Cory asked.

"Dr. Christensen, I'm saying that the FDA wanted this drug on the market quickly, just as much as we did."

The noise from the audience rose to its highest level yet. It took Matt a full minute to quiet them.

"I have another question, Mr. Chairman," Dr. Christensen said. Matt nodded.

"Dr. Stroud, you know why these effects were not detected in the phase three trials, don't you?"

"If you're referring to the location of the trials, yes, that was another unfortunate and unforeseen circumstance."

"Indeed. I think we can say confidently that very few women of Eastern European ancestry go to free clinics in South Africa for emergency contraceptives. Whose decision was it to conduct the trials in South Africa?"

"Dr. Christensen, the clinical trial was designed by a consulting firm. Since a primary objective of the trial was to verify that combining an oral HIV vaccine with an emergency contraceptive was effective in reducing the incidence of HIV, it was necessary to conduct the trial where there was a high rate of HIV infection."

"So this was *not* Compton-Genencraft's decision?"

"No sir. We approved it, but it was part of the proposed design."

"I'm finished, Mr. Chairman."

"Mr. Chairman, if I may," said Hunter Gibbs. Matt nodded.

"Dr. Stroud, I am not a Nobel-winning scientist. I'm just a preacher. How exactly does this drug work? Doesn't it cause an abortion?"

"No, Reverend Gibbs. It works by delaying ovulation."

"But it could cause an abortion, couldn't it?"

"Commissioner Gibbs," Matt interrupted, "the question was asked and answered. And let's please stay in scope."

"But I believe this *is* relevant. The witness has just admitted that this drug was rushed to market without adequate precautions…"

"That's a conclusion that has not been established," Matt said.

"…by an agency of the government whose responsibility it is to serve the people…"

"Commissioner Gibbs, please, stay in scope."

"…and the *people* have grave misgivings about this drug. These actions by the government have moral consequences."

"Reverend Gibbs, I must ask you to stop this line of questioning."

"Is it surprising that some have taken extreme measures, even to the point of violence and death, to assert their will when their elected government will not?"

"You're out of order, Commissioner. Dr. Stroud, you don't have to respond to that outburst."

Cameron said nothing. The rest of the commissioners remained silent.

"Dr. Stroud," Matt said, "I have a question. In your experience, have there been other trials that Compton-Genencraft has conducted that compare with the trial for *Backup?*"

"Every trial is different, Mr. Chairman."

"I understand. Let's take an example. Your company is currently in trials for a drug to treat Alzheimer's disease. Is that correct?"

"That is correct."

"And you are now in which phase?"

"We've completed phases one and two, and are now in phase three."

"So, in this case, you chose *not* to bypass phase two trials."

"Yes, Dr. Bugatti, that's correct."

"And how has the drug performed?"

"Mr. Chairman," Hunter Gibbs interrupted, "how is *that* question relevant?"

Matt looked at Hunter, then he looked down. "It's not. Dr. Stroud, you don't have to respond."

"But I will respond, Mr. Chairman. In phase two we saw improvement in more than eighty percent of test subjects with mild to severe Alzheimer's symptoms, and nearly complete reversal of the disease's progress in more than twenty-five percent."

"And are you still accepting subjects for the phase three trials?"

"Mr. Chairman," Hunter said with a loud voice, "let's stay in scope."

Matt took a sip of water. "Dr. Stroud, no more questions. You're dismissed."

‡ ‡ ‡

Tyler sat at his desk, staring intently at Matt as he reviewed the draft of the report. Matt sat at the table, paging through the final section containing the recommendations of the commission, then closing the book, placing his hand on the cover.

"Nothing," Matt said. "Not a single substantive change. Nobody is at fault. Everything stays the same."

"They did recommend that the FDA not skip phase two trials. And they recommended broader authority for the FDA to order a recall."

Matt closed his eyes and shook his head. "That's nothing. The FDA already had the authority and they didn't use it." Matt stood and paced the floor. "I just can't accept that this was nothing more than an unlucky series of events."

"What *do* you think?"

Matt stopped pacing. "I don't know. I…I just *feel*…" Matt looked at Tyler. "I've talked with the parents of every one of these girls. Some of them I consider friends." He sat down at the table and picked up the report. "How can I tell them their daughters' deaths were just a terrible accident?"

"The report is based on the evidence. Were the facts misinterpreted?"

"No." Matt laid the report on the table. "Look, I know the president wants the report right away, and that the rest of the commission has already signed off. But it's *my* decision whether to release the report. What do you think I should do?"

"Follow your conscience. If you have misgivings about the conclusions, or if you don't agree with the recommendations, then don't sign."

Matt nodded. "I'll make my decision in a few weeks. When I get back."

"Back from where?"

"Italy. My mother wants to make one last trip."

23

DILIGENCE

"I'M DISAPPOINTED," THE president said. "Deeply disappointed."

Matt and Tyler stood by as the president paged through the commission's report.

"Mr. President," Matt said, "I need to be sure before I give my approval."

"It's not as if you're planning to convene more hearings, or gather more evidence," the president snapped. "You're vacationing in Italy, for God's sake."

"Mr. President," Matt said warily, "I assure you, I'll continue to review the testimony and exhibits during my trip. But I need to be certain that we haven't overlooked anything."

"Mr. President," Tyler said, "Dr. Bugatti has compelling personal reasons for making this trip at this time."

The president pursed his lips as he looked first at Tyler, then at Matt. "I've heard. How is your mother?"

"Her condition is deteriorating. Thank you for asking, Mr. President."

The president rubbed his chin. "Matt, I appreciate your diligence. We all want the report to be complete and correct.

But it's also important to give the public a sense of closure. The people need to be reassured. Besides, the rest of the commissioners have already approved the draft. What good can come from delaying its release?"

"Mr. President," Matt began in a steady voice, never diverting his gaze, "the commission was evenly split in their positions, and that was by design. The report represents the narrowest set of conclusions and the least controversial proposals that they could agree upon, and that was also by design." Matt pointed at the report. "That may be complete and correct, but it was also pre-ordained. Mr. President, I intend to provide closure for the public, but more importantly, I will answer to the parents. When I can face them and defend these findings with conviction, I will release the report."

"Very well. But I'm sending Tyler to Italy with you."

"That's really not necessary, Mr. President," Matt said.

"Indulge me, Dr. Bugatti. I'm the president of the United States."

24
Let the Day Begin

Yolanda had hoped for a clear, sunny day, symbolizing a new beginning and a bright future. Instead, it was a typical June day in central Ohio, mild and overcast. The dull weather did nothing to subdue the large and boisterous crowd.

The audience was diverse, numbering nearly five thousand—Latinos, of course, but also pro-life evangelicals and liberation theology Catholics; free-traders and union members; activists and isolationists. They were united in their concern for a country they were sure had lost its moral bearings, and in their enthusiasm for Senator Yolanda Herrera Peña.

The preliminary speakers—various county officials, a mayor, two congressmen—were effusive in their praise. *Committed,* they said, *tireless and inspirational.* They did their job well. When Yolanda stepped onto the platform, the applause continued for three solid minutes.

Yolanda hugged each speaker affectionately, including those whom she was meeting for the first time. She smiled and waved as she looked out on the throng gathered on the West Plaza of the Ohio Statehouse. The cheers continued as she acknowledged familiar faces from the platform, and a few unfamiliar ones. When she stepped behind the podium, it was a signal for the other speakers to sit in chairs arranged in an arc behind her. Yolanda, alone in the middle of the stage, surrounded by her retinue, with a backdrop of the stone columns of the statehouse, formed a striking image. It was no accident.

The crowd grew silent as she began to speak.

"Congressman Wayne, thank you for that warm introduction. Thanks also to all the speakers for their kind words, and for their commitment to public service."

Yolanda paused. "Public service," she repeated. "What shall I say about the calling to serve one's country and its people? Oh, it's like any other vocation in that it's best pursued with passion. Tradesmen are driven to master their craft. Parents raise their children with love. Clergymen seek to glorify God. If they have no passion, they toil without purpose.

"How many of our so-called leaders, whether in this building behind me or in Washington, toil without purpose? Too many—far too many—and they do so at a time when we can least afford it.

"This great nation rests on a foundation—as strong as its people, and sustained by their decency. But that foundation is cracked, and the America our founders built upon it is threatened. And yet, our leaders' passion is for other things, and they toil without purpose.

"The wealth of this nation is increasingly concentrated in the hands of a privileged few, while millions struggle. Young adults drift with no moral compass. Children go hungry and suffer from want of proper medical care. The lives of millions of unborn babies are snuffed out in the name of *choice*. Each of these injustices is a fault in the bedrock of America. And yet, we cannot call upon our leaders to shore up these flaws, for their passion is for other things, and they toil without purpose."

The crowd latched onto the tag line, erupting in cheers every time Yolanda said *"...and they toil without purpose."*

"When my beloved husband died," Yolanda continued, "I was sure I would never again find purpose in my life. He was everything to me. *He* was my purpose. But God did not take one purpose from me without offering another. It is *my* passion that this nation should realize a new beginning, from the foundation up, for *all* her people."

Yolanda gripped the sides of the podium. Her eyes shone and her jaw was set. The crowd gasped when, as if on cue, the clouds broke and a shaft of sunlight lit up the stage.

"My fellow Americans—my friends—I ask for your support, for your help, and for your prayers, as I seek the office of president of the United States."

The audience went berserk as loudspeakers blared the Call singing "Let The Day Begin," the lyrics of the song consonant with Yolanda's aspirational message, the rhythm resonant with the energy of the crowd: *Here's to the babies in a brand new world...here's to you, my little love, with blessings from above, let the day begin.*

Dignitaries, donors, and friends streamed onto the platform, each one pre-approved and admitted onstage by armed agents. Volunteers circulated through the crowd, collecting cards that had been distributed at the entrance, now filled out with names and phone numbers. Each volunteer carried a portable credit card reader to accept donations. The massive organization required to mount a national campaign, which Yolanda had been building quietly for the past four years, was abruptly thrown into gear.

✝ ✝ ✝

The pandemonium at the statehouse was nearly matched by the reception at the Hilton following the rally. Seats went for two thousand dollars each, but for an additional contribution of five thousand to the National Committee, the donor could sit at the same table as Senator Herrera. A photo with the candidate cost another five hundred.

Of the few seats reserved at no cost for select individuals, one went to Ronni Barraket. Near the end of the evening,

Ronni waited nearby as the line for photos with the candidate dwindled.

"It was a wonderful speech," Ronni said to Yolanda after the last photo was snapped.

"What did you think of the sunbeam?"

Ronni laughed. "Spectacular. How did you arrange that?"

"I didn't. God did."

Ronni stopped laughing. Yolanda waited a beat and then grinned widely, winking as she put her hand on Ronni's arm.

"It was pure luck. I had a half page to go, but when the sun hit me, I went straight to the punch line. You have to take advantage of the breaks."

"Always," Ronni said, laughing uncertainly.

"Well, then," Yolanda said, "the Bugatti commission. Where do we stand?"

"Our sources tell us that the report has been signed off by the commission, but Bugatti hasn't agreed to release it."

"What was the conclusion?"

"Nothing improper on the part of either the drug company or the FDA. A few minor recommendations."

"No improprieties? That figures." Yolanda looked at the floor. "It's hardly an outcome we can rally the troops around. We need a finding against CG Pharma and the FDA." She looked up. "But you said Bugatti hasn't signed off?"

"No. He has misgivings."

"That's a bright spot. At least we can keep the controversy alive. What happens next?"

"Bugatti is taking time to review the evidence before he makes a decision, in a month or less, I'm told."

Yolanda nodded. "Good. We can keep banging the drum in the meantime. And we have time to get to him."

"That might be a problem. He's leaving for Italy."

"Italy? Seriously?"

"It's a personal issue. Something to do with his mother."

Yolanda tapped her lower lip.

"Ronni, when's the last time you asked Jay Stivers for time off?"

25

ASSOCIATED PRESS

CLARA KILDEE'S PHONE was silent as she waited for an answer to her request.

"For how long?" the Associated Press bureau chief asked.

"A week," Clara answered, "two at most, but if I can't get the interview, I may need an extension."

"Do you even know where he's going to be?"

"Not exactly. His family is from Northern Italy, near Bologna. He'll probably be in the vicinity. But don't worry, I'll find him. And if I don't, the Italian press will. The Italians have been following this story fanatically."

"Then I'll have our Milan bureau cover it. Why should I send you?"

"Because it's *my story!*" Clara shouted. "I know the issues, I know the history, I know the people. Up to now, every article on this story has been under my byline. You can't give it to a foreign bureau. It's mine."

This time the silence lasted a full ten seconds.

"All right. You've got the duty. But try to keep expenses down."

"Expenses. Christ, I'm an old lady. I don't have expenses."

26

Obsession

Francis Compton took the call from his father.

"The report is perfect," Elliott told him. "We couldn't have hoped for a better outcome. No fault of ours, no fault of the FDA's."

"How do you know?"

"My Washington sources. I got the call ten minutes ago."

Francis sighed. "Dad, it would sure be helpful if you'd share your sources with me. "

Elliott snorted. "Not now, Son. When you're ready."

"Damn it, Dad, I'm forty-eight years old and the CEO of a major company."

"Son, don't waste my time telling me what I already know. These are highly placed sources. They have to be handled. They know me. They trust me. They *don't* know you."

Francis clenched his fist. "Fine," he said. "Then we've got nothing to worry about. As soon as the report comes out, we'll do a press release and get all this behind us."

"Not so fast, Son. We have a little problem."

"What problem? You said the report is perfect."

"The head of the commission, Bugatti, is the problem. He's balking. He needs more time, to 'think about it.'"

"I'll send Robert to put some pressure on Bugatti to release the report."

"Hendrickson? Forget it. You sent him once and he fucked it up."

Francis pressed his fingers to his closed eyes.

"I'll go myself."

"Way to take charge, Son. I'm proud of you. But you're not going either. I want you to send Stroud."

‡ ‡ ‡

Cameron smiled in a way that gave Francis shivers.

"Of course, Francis, I'll be happy to have a chat with Dr. Bugatti."

"Make sure your passport is valid. You'll need to go to Italy. We're still trying to pinpoint Bugatti's location."

"Dozza, most likely."

"What?"

"Dozza. It's a small town just outside of Bologna. It's where the Bugatti ancestral home is located. Bugatti is taking his mother for a family visit."

Francis stared blankly.

"Well don't look so dumbfounded, Francis. *Somebody* around here has to stay informed." Cameron stood up. "And once again, that burden falls on *my* shoulders."

Cameron headed out the door, but poked his head back in.

"Don't worry 'bout nothin', Francis. I'm in charge."

‡ ‡ ‡

At home, Cameron checked his passport—good for another year. He searched online for fares to Bologna and accommodations in Modena. Once he saved his options it would take just minutes to book his travel—as soon as he knew Bugatti's plans.

Cameron closed the browser and opened another file, labeled *Bugatti,* containing subfolders: *Biography, Ancestry, Family.* Each of them contained detailed data on Matt

Bugatti. Cameron had been collecting them for years. Cameron guessed that he'd spent hundreds of hours searching the Internet, making phone calls, and traveling. He'd been to North Carolina to talk to Matt's childhood friends and college classmates; to Wisconsin to meet Matt's co-workers; his upcoming trip to Italy would be his fifth, and his second to Dozza.

Cameron had dedicated many more hours to the study of mathematics, mastering obscure concepts of number theory. This knowledge was useful when attending conferences where Matt's colleagues, or Matt himself, were in attendance. These were Cameron's best opportunities to learn about Matt directly from Matt's peers, or, better yet, to observe Matt from a distance, to see the deference others paid to him, to memorize his mannerisms, which Cameron imitated in a mirror when he was alone. *Do you know who I am? Of course you do. I'm Dr. Matteo Bugatti.*

Cameron was always discreet, never arousing suspicion. His detailed knowledge of Matt's background convinced everyone he contacted that he was exactly who he said he was: an old friend of Matt's. They were only too happy to share their recollections for Cameron's growing database of Bugatti arcana.

He opened the file labeled *Achievements*. It contained the first article Cameron had ever collected—the first time he'd heard of Matt almost three years before.

AMERICAN MATHEMATICIAN WINS FIELDS MEDAL

Dr. Matteo Bugatti, 27, of the University of North Carolina has been awarded the Fields medal, the highest recognition bestowed on mathematicians under the age of 40.

Cameron re-read the article for the hundredth time. His hands were trembling.

Finally, Bugatti, we'll find out what kind of a genius you really are.

27

Dozza

"CUGINA!"

Twenty people shouted as Flora stepped out of the car at the home of Pierangelo and Stefania Bugatti. Matt followed, standing and looking around at the vineyards, gardens and pastures among the gently rolling hills of Emilia-Romagna. The weariness from the long journey dissipated instantly in the bright sunshine of a brilliant Sunday morning at the Bugatti villa.

The eighteenth-century estate had been in the Bugatti family for more than a hundred years. The main building, a massive, timber-framed structure of stone and earth, sat at the center of a hundred acres in the small *comune* of Dozza. Twenty years ago Pierangelo had converted twelve of its eighteen rooms to guest suites. Most guests came for the bucolic surroundings and the superb cuisine; some guests came for the experience of working in an Italian vineyard, or tending an Italian goat herd. Whether they worked the farm, toured the countryside, or strolled the streets of Dozza, the guests, without exception, raved about the accommodations and hospitality of the Bugattis. For the occasion of Flora's and Matt's visit, Pierangelo had blocked off all twelve suites, all occupied but one: two by Matt and Flora, one by Tyler Ross, and the rest by *i cugini Bugatti*.

A contingent of newspaper, radio and TV reporters had gathered across the road. Tyler stood in front of them, his arms extended, signaling them to stay put while the Bugatti family reunion took place. Some shouted questions, which Tyler tried to answer, but the process was ineffective—only a few reporters could speak any English and Tyler could speak no Italian.

Matt hung back as Flora kissed and hugged one relative after another, calling each by name. Matt hadn't seen any of them since he was sixteen and he remembered the names of only a few. Flora chatted with her relations as if she'd seen them all the day before.

One man broke away from the crowd and approached Matt. *"Il famoso Matteo Bugatti!"* declared the bald, portly middle-aged man. "The famous Matteo Bugatti! I'm your cousin Pierangelo." The man embraced Matt and kissed his cheeks. "Do you remember me?"

"Certo ti ricordo," Matt replied. "Of course I remember you. How have you been?"

Pierangelo held Matt's shoulders and beamed. "You still speak the language! And beautifully, too." Pierangelo put his arm around Matt's shoulder and led him toward the group. "We are all proud of you, Matteo. Such an important responsibility. And we're sure that you'll come to the right decision."

"I hope so. But I didn't expect you to have such an interest."

"Ma certo! All of Italy is talking about it, in part because a Bugatti is running the investigation, but also because we believe these drug companies and the American government must be held accountable for the deaths of those poor girls. The whole world looks to America to lead. But now, with the loose morals, the abortions, *mi Dio!* America is starting to look like Europe." He put his hand on Matt's shoulder and smiled. "You are doing God's work, *cugino.*"

Matt looked at the ground. "I'm only trying to find the truth."

Pierangelo smiled widely. "*Bene. Molto bene.*"

"*Matteo, caro,*" Flora said as Matt and Pierangelo approached. "Come meet your family."

The bedlam continued as the Bugattis got caught up and Tyler held the press at bay. Each relative welcomed Matt with an embrace, some holding babies or toddlers, insisting that Matt kiss them on the cheek. He was surrounded by Bugattis, touching, hugging, kissing and talking; one would not release him before another embraced him. His head turned this way and that as they pressed against him from all sides, everyone shouting at once. He stood straight and gasped for breath.

Matt saw Tyler across the road holding back the reporters. A taxi pulled up behind Matt and Flora's car. The sole passenger paid the driver and stepped out—Ronni Barraket stood alone as the taxi sped away.

"*Scusa! Scusa!*" Matt said as he worked his way to the edge of the group. As he walked toward Ronni the frenzy in the press pool resumed and reached a new high. Matt changed course in their direction.

"*Signor Bugatti! Signor Bugatti, per favore!*" they shouted, almost in unison. Matt raised his hands to silence them.

"*Mi dispiace,*" Matt said, "I'm sorry, but my mother and I are here on a personal visit. I ask you, please, to respect our privacy. But I know that you have questions. I will be able to answer some of them after lunch." Matt turned and walked away.

"*Quando? Quando?*" they shouted. "When?"

"*Quando abbiamo finito!*" Matt shouted. "When we have finished!"

"Ms. Barraket," Matt said as he approached, "*Che sorpresa!*"

Ronni knitted her brow. "Excuse me?"

Matt pressed his fingers to his eyes and chuckled. "That was Italian, wasn't it? I'm sorry. I meant to say, 'what a surprise.'"

Ronni smiled. "I took a chance that you might have some time to talk." She glanced in the direction of the reporters. "But it looks like I'll have to get in line."

"You're *out* of line, Ronni." Tyler Ross appeared next to Matt. "Any conversation with Dr. Bugatti outside the context of a commission hearing is improper."

Matt held up his palm. "Tyler, I'm sure Ms. Barraket knows the limits of propriety." He turned back to Ronni. "And I hope that you know that I won't be persuaded by anything other than facts."

"I know that, Dr. Bugatti. I've been following the commission proceedings from the start. I've gotten some insight into your character."

"Then you have me at a disadvantage," Matt said. "Tyler, you'd better get back to the press. They look restless."

"This isn't right," Tyler said as he walked back to the reporters.

"I'll send them some lunch," Matt said. "That'll quiet them down."

Ronni laughed. It was an endearing laugh, warm and genuine. Matt liked it.

"Is this your first time in Italy?"

"I've been to Rome once. I never made it outside of the city."

"Rome is impressive," Matt said. "But this…" He gestured toward the vineyards next to the house, each well-tended vine sending out canes covered with bright green, almost iridescent leaves. With his other hand he pointed at the hills in the distance, covered with olive groves and grazing flocks. "*This* is Italy."

"*Matteo, chi è questa bella ragazza?*" Pierangelo shouted as he walked toward Matt and Ronni. "Who is this beautiful girl?"

"That's my cousin," Matt explained to Ronni. "This is his estate." Matt waved. "*Pierangelo, quest'è la signorina Ronni Barraket.*"

"*Piacere.*" Pierangelo kissed Ronni's hand. He turned to Matt and whispered, "*Ronni! È un nome da uomo!*"

"You'll have to excuse my cousin," Matt said. "He's very direct."

"What did he say?" Ronni asked.

"He said that Ronni is a man's name."

"Oh." Ronni smiled at Pierangelo. "It's short for Rhiannon."

"*Ronni è un soprannome. Lei si chiama Rhiannon,*" Matt translated.

Pierangelo grinned. "*Ah, bella! Bellissima! Allora, Rhiannon, deve pranzare con noi. Venga, venga!*"

"My cousin is inviting you to lunch," Matt explained. "He'll be hurt if you decline, and you'll be missing out on one of the great dining experiences of Northern Italy."

"Then I accept."

The three of them walked toward the house, where most of the family had already entered for the midday meal.

"*Dirmi, Rhiannon,*" Pierangelo asked. "*Dove alloggia?*"

"Pierangelo would like to know where you're staying."

"There's a Sheraton at the Bologna airport," Ronni answered.

"*L'aeroporto? Non è possibile! Lei deve rimanere qui. Abbiamo una bellissima stanza proprio per Lei.*"

"If you want to experience Italy," Matt said, "the airport Sheraton is not the place. Pierangelo insists that you stay here."

"I couldn't."

"I understand," Matt said, "but Pierangelo doesn't. Perhaps you can explain it to him."

Pierangelo wore an eager expression that looked as if it could turn to dejection with a single word. Ronni looked at his round, pleasant face.

"All right. But I'll need a ride back to the Sheraton to get my things."

Matt smiled. "*Non c'è problema.*"

Most of the family were already seated at the long tables in the dining hall. Flora sat near the head of one table, in the seat of honor, to Pierangelo's right. Matt brought Ronni to meet her.

"Mom, this is Ronni Barraket, from Washington. Ronni, this is my mom, Flora."

Ronni held out her hand. "I'm happy to meet you, Flora."

Flora looked at Ronni with wide eyes, immobile at first, until a smile appeared as she took Ronni's hand.

"I'm happy to meet you, Ronni. It's so good of you to join us."

Ronni turned to see Matt staring at Flora.

"Matt?" Ronni asked.

Matt looked blankly at her, slowly blinking his eyes. "There are some seats at the end of the table," he said as he led Ronni away.

"Are you all right?" Ronni asked.

"Yes," Matt said. "It's just that…" He looked back at Flora. "Those are the first words of English my mom has spoken in almost a month."

The meal lasted nearly four hours and was splendid in every respect. Ronni answered Matt's questions about her work as a lobbyist, and as an adviser to Senator Herrera Peña. She never asked about the commission, and Matt never raised the topic.

"Your mother is lovely," Ronni said.

Matt looked across the table at Flora. She was chatting and laughing, as joyful as he had ever seen her, and the very opposite of the brooding, taciturn woman she'd been for weeks.

"Thanks. This trip has been wonderful for her."

"I heard that she's not well."

"No, she's not." Matt touched the corner of his eye and rubbed the moisture between his finger and thumb. "She has Alzheimer's Disease. But you wouldn't know it to look at her now."

28

SUPPLIER

MARLIN CASTOR SAT in a booth at the *Corner Café*, an establishment in a neighborhood past its prime, given over to feral pets and crack houses. Marlin did not know the name of the person in the booth with him—he'd only met him a few times before, and had always addressed him as *man*, as in *Hey, man, how you doin'?* But Marlin had a name for him. He called him the Supplier.

Marlin shook a cigarette out of the pack and put it between his lips. He lit up as he offered one to the Supplier, who declined.

"You can't smoke that in here," said the waiter, standing by the booth in a sweat-stained t-shirt and a dirty apron. Marlin looked around the café at the filthy walls, the decaying furniture, and the grease-coated hood over the stove.

"You're shitting me."

"It's a non-smoking establishment."

Marlin and the waiter stared each other down. The waiter blinked first. He looked down, wiped his hands on his apron, and walked off without a word. Marlin took a long drag, exhaling in the direction of the waiter before dousing the cigarette in a glass of water.

"You need to do better on the price, man," Marlin said.

The Supplier grinned and shook his head. "It's a premium product, my friend. Military grade, no pain-in-the-ass chemical tags—*un*-traceable."

"A thousand a kilo? That's ten times what the military pays."

"Look around you, General Patton," the Supplier laughed. "You ain't the army, and this ain't the PX. Besides, you never haggled over the price before."

"I never needed this much before."

The Supplier raised his eyebrows. "Yeah. That's right. Three kilos. Then five kilos. The first buy just before that clinic went up in Pittsburgh, the second right before Atlanta. This is some nasty business, Mr. Castor. You ain't blastin' stumps. And that's why I can't come down on the price. In fact, now that I know what you're into, I'll have to ask you for a premium."

Marlin sighed. "What premium?"

"An extra five hundred a kilo."

"Oh, fuck."

"That is a take-it-or-leave-it offer, Mr. Castor."

Marlin looked over the Supplier. He was a scrawny, gristly punk, a slow talker, but twitchy, like he'd smoked a pile of amp right after chugging a quart of gin. Marlin couldn't read him. In particular, Marlin couldn't tell if the Supplier could be messed with or not.

He recalled the last negotiation he'd had with Darryl Meeks.

That crazy religious fuck will pay anything I ask.

"All right. Fifteen hundred a kilo. I'll pass on the cost to the consumer."

"Deal. How much do you want?"

"Two hundred."

The Supplier twitched. "Two hundred *kilos?* That'll take some time. And you gotta front me half for raw materials."

"I need it all at once, man. As soon as I can get it."

The Supplier got twitchier. "You told me you never buy more than you need."

"That's right. I don't like to keep a lot of inventory."

"And you need two hundred kilos all at once. That's enough for what…forty bombs?"

Marlin shook a cigarette free, put it to his lips and flicked his lighter. Just before he lit up, he noticed the cigarette floating in the glass of water, a thread of brown stain winding its way to the bottom. He took the cigarette out of his mouth and put it back in the pack.

"Yeah. Forty. More or less."

29

RONZANO

MATT WOKE A half-hour before sunrise, just as the sky began to brighten. These were the hours he loved most, the time between waking and the rest of the world coming to life— the peaceful part of the day, still new and uncomplicated by events.

Matt found Pierangelo and Stefania in the kitchen preparing breakfast.

"*Ciao, Matteo,*" Stefania said in a low voice, hardly more than a whisper.

"*Ciao, Stefania,*" Matt said. "*Ciao, Pierangelo.* Why are we talking so quietly?"

Stefania looked surprised. Pierangelo started to laugh and Stefania joined him.

"I don't know! It's so early, and most of the guests won't be up for another hour, so we try to be quiet. But I don't think they can hear us!"

Matt smiled as Stefania and Pierangelo laughed, almost out loud, but not quite, until Pierangelo put his arm around Stefania's waist and Stefania kissed him, holding both of his cheeks.

"*Un espresso, Matteo?*" Pierangelo offered.

"*Doppio, per favore,*" Matt replied.

"I'll bring it to you. You go out and join your friend."

"My friend?"

"*Sì! La tua ragazza.*"

Matt peeked through the window in the kitchen door. Ronni Barraket sat alone at a table with a laptop and a cup of coffee.

"How long has she been there?"

"Oh, not long. Ten minutes. Go! She's all alone!"

"You know, she's not my girlfriend."

Pierangelo puckered his lips. "But why not? She's beautiful." He pointed two fingers at Matt, bumping his hands together. "And you two were together all evening." He turned back to the espresso machine. "The espresso will be ready soon. Your girlfriend is waiting. Go! Go!"

Ronni looked up and smiled as Matt approached her table.

"*Buongiorno,*" Ronni said.

"*Buongiorno a Lei,*" Matt answered. "May I sit down?"

"*Prego.*"

"I'm impressed," Matt said as he took a seat. "Your pronunciation is very good."

"I heard a lot of Italian last night."

"You must have felt out of place."

"Not at all. I felt completely at home."

"The Italian people are superb hosts. But an Italian family gathering can be a little overwhelming."

"It was nothing," Ronni laughed. "You should come to a Lebanese wedding if you want to be overwhelmed."

"I can't imagine," Matt said. "I'm glad you enjoyed yourself. I enjoyed talking with you. And I appreciate your keeping the commission out of the conversation."

"The time didn't seem right. But since you brought up the topic, I do have a question."

Matt nodded. "Okay."

"Why haven't you signed off on the report?"

Matt laid his hand flat on the table. "The commission has drafted a report and the draft is under review. We will issue a full and valid report with recommendations at the earliest possible moment."

Ronni frowned. "That's your stock answer."

"It's the answer."

"No, it's not. I asked why haven't *you* signed off."

Matt lowered his eyes, rubbing his chin. "There are missing variables."

"I don't understand."

"Why only Eastern Europeans? Why only young girls? The use of this drug was widespread, but only a small number were affected."

"Do you think this wasn't an accident?"

"No, that's not what I mean. I'm sure it *was* an accident. And maybe, with what we knew at the time, neither the drug company nor the FDA could have anticipated the outcome. But…"

"But what?"

"There's no chain of causality. We know that *Backup* caused the deaths, but that's all we know. We don't know how. Without knowing the actual cause, how can we keep it from happening again?"

"*Eccolo!*" Pierangelo appeared carrying a tray holding three double espressos and a carafe of hot water. He distributed the cups around the table, holding out the carafe to Ronni. "*Americano?*"

"*Sì,*" Ronni replied. Pierangelo diluted the thick espresso to the American consistency, then took a seat behind the third cup of espresso.

"*Allora, che fai di bello oggi?*"

"Any plans for the day?" Matt translated.

"I don't have any," Ronni answered. "What do you suggest?"

"*Ronni è libera,*" Matt told Pierangelo. "Ronni is free. I'll do whatever Mom wants to do."

"You will be very bored," Pierangelo said. "Flora will spend the whole day talking and eating with the cousins." He held out his hands. "You must take Rhiannon to Dozza and show her the murals. We will take care of Flora. You two can stay in Dozza until sunset." He winked. "It's very romantic."

"Pierangelo thinks you would enjoy a visit to Dozza. It's a beautiful town."

"I'd like that. Should I hire a guide?"

Matt asked Pierangelo the question.

"*Una guida? Certo! Matteo!*"

Ronni laughed. Matt sighed.

"I really do need to see what Mom has in mind, but if she's all right, I'll be happy to show you around Dozza."

"I have another idea." Tyler Ross stood behind Pierangelo. "How about we review the commission hearing transcripts, and you can tell me what gaps we need to fill, so you can sign off the report?"

"Tyler," Ronni said, "you have an odd way of popping up out of nowhere and derailing a pleasant conversation."

"And you have a way of pushing the limits. All last night you monopolized Dr. Bugatti and now I find you in this little *tête-à-tête*."

"We never once discussed the commission last night," Matt said.

"And this morning?"

Matt hesitated.

"I asked Matt why he hadn't approved the report," Ronni said.

"Oh, it's *Matt* now, is it? Dr. Bugatti, this can*not* happen. If you discuss the proceedings with this…*lobbyist*, you will compromise the entire commission."

"Tyler," Matt said, "I've answered that exact same question at press conferences."

"Did you give the exact same answer?"

Matt looked from Tyler to Ronni. "No. Not exactly the same."

Tyler closed his eyes. "This will not end well."

"Tyler, we'll go over the transcripts tomorrow," Matt said. "You know, you might enjoy seeing a little of the countryside. You'll be fresh for a working session in the morning."

"First thing," Tyler said. "I want to get through as much as possible before the press conference."

"What press conference?"

"The one I scheduled for you tomorrow at two o'clock. You and Ms. Barraket were having such a wonderful time yesterday that you never got back to the press." Tyler headed for the door. "I had to do something to get them off my back," he shouted as he left the hall.

Pierangelo looked at Matt like a befuddled child. *"Che cosa si trattava?"* he asked. "What was that about?"

"Non è niente," Matt answered. He translated his conversation with Tyler.

"There are gaps?" Pierangelo asked.

"Unanswered questions," Matt explained. "There seems to be a genetic factor in the deaths. No one can determine what it is."

Pierangelo patted Matt's hand. "You must go see your cousin Dario."

"Dario? Is he here?"

Pierangelo chuckled. "No. He is not here. He is in Ronzano, at the hermitage."

"What's he saying?" Ronni asked.

"I'm not sure. He wants me to talk to a cousin, Dario. But I don't know him. And he lives in…" He turned to Pierangelo. *"In un monastero?"*

"Sì! È un frate dell'Ordine dei Servi di Maria."

Matt turned back to Ronni. "He lives in a hermitage. It's like a monastery. He's a monk in the Order of the Servants of Mary."

Ronni and Matt were speechless as Pierangelo looked at them expectantly.

"You can go today," Pierangelo said. "He's there always. He can help."

"Pierangelo, I know what you're trying to do, and I appreciate your concern. But I don't think that spiritual counseling is what I need at the moment."

Pierangelo gave out a short, exasperated sigh. "You don't understand. Dario will introduce you to the director of the foundation."

"The foundation?"

"Yes, yes, the European Genetics Foundation. They are located at the Hermitage of Ronzano."

‡ ‡ ‡

Matt and Ronni drove through the Italian countryside, along a switchback road, past orchards and vineyards, to the top of the central hill of Ronzano.

"What do you expect to find at the foundation?" Ronni asked.

"Nothing, probably," Matt said. "We've been trying to find answers for weeks. I doubt there's anything this outfit could do that hasn't already been done." He turned to Ronni. "At the very least, I'll meet my cousin Dario. And it's a beautiful day."

Ronni scanned the panorama. The hill sloped away from the road, dotted with stone structures among green pastures, stretching to a distant mound topped by a domed church, the city of Bologna spread out below.

It's breathtaking, she thought.

The car continued down a tree-lined stretch, until a sign came into view, an arrow pointing down a narrow side road, above a second sign, reading:

EREMO DI RONZANO
EUROPEAN GENETICS FOUNDATION

"Here we are." Matt took a sharp left turn up the one-lane road, leading to a compound of simple buildings with stuccoed walls and tiled roofs. Matt and Ronni got out of the car and looked over the surroundings. The place was deserted.

"Let's go this way," Matt suggested. They headed down a path, past the corner of the largest building, to find an open door in the front of a simple structure, with a circular window above it, and a cross above that.

Matt and Ronni entered the chapel. It was plain, almost crude in appearance, with whitewashed walls, some decorated with frescos in varying states of decay. There was a vaulted ceiling over the altar, but over the pews there was no ceiling, only exposed beams and the underside of the tile roof.

"Posso aiutarvi?"

Matt and Ronni turned to face a man of medium height, with a round, fleshy face, a serene smile and bright eyes behind tiny gold spectacles. His hair was silver and needed cutting, curling around his ears and brushing the tops of his generous eyebrows. He wore the simple brown habit of a mendicant friar.

"Sì, grazie. Cerchiamo Frate Dario," Matt said.

"You are Dr. Bugatti, no?" the friar said in English.

"Yes, I am. How did you know?"

"We all have heard of you, Dr. Bugatti." The friar put his hand on Matt's arm. "I am Brother Alessandro."

Matt shook the friar's hand. "This is my friend, Ronni Barraket, from the United States."

"Hello, my child. Welcome to the Hermitage of Ronzano." Alessandro motioned toward the door. "Come. Brother Dario is in the vineyard. It's a short walk. I'll take you there."

The three of them left the church and walked toward the head of a narrow path.

"Brother Dario has told us about you. He remembers you as a child."

"I'm afraid I don't remember him. I haven't been to Italy in more than ten years."

Alessandro looked at Matt over his glasses. "He remembers you. And he prays for you, as we all pray for you."

The path led to the edge of a field. A few friars with broad hats were scattered among row upon row of meticulously tended vines.

"Fratello Dario! Vieni!" Alessandro cried. The friars poked their heads above the tops of the vines. One raised his arm

and made his way toward Alessandro. As he approached, a look of surprise and recognition brightened his face.

"*Cugino Matteo!*" He embraced Matt and kissed his cheeks. Dario was older than Matt, and a little heavier, with skin darkened and aged by the sun. But he had Matt's gray eyes and Matt's thick, dark hair. They shared the same features. If not for the difference in their ages, they might have been mistaken for one another.

✟ ✟ ✟

"I will take you to see Lamberto."

The words echoed in the hermitage wine cellar. Dario uncorked a bottle and poured three glasses. He held his up to the light. "Our *pignoletto. Prego.*"

"Lamberto is…who?" Matt asked, setting his glass on the table.

"Dr. Lamberto Magnani is the director of the foundation. When he discovered that you are my cousin he was very excited. He had many questions." Dario took another sip. "I'm sure he would rather ask his questions directly of you."

"How do you know him?" Ronni asked. "Do you spend time at the foundation?"

"Oh, no. Lamberto is a frequent visitor to the hermitage. He has many responsibilities, and life in Bologna can be chaotic." He poured another round. "He appreciates the quiet and solitude of the cloister." Dario drained his glass and set it down. "I have already sent word. Lamberto is expecting us. You have a car, yes?"

The drive might as well have been a trip in a time machine. The quaint fifteenth-century hermitage bore no resemblance to the gleaming glass and steel headquarters of the European Genetics Foundation. Lamberto Magnani was waiting in the reception area when Ronni, Matt and Dario arrived. He was a short, wiry man with sharp features and wavy salt-and-pepper hair.

"*Fratello Dario, come stai?*" Lamberto said, kissing the friar's cheeks. "And you are Dr. Bugatti, yes?" Lameberto shook Matt's hand vigorously. "It is a great pleasure to meet you."

"Thank you for seeing us, Dr. Magnani," Matt said. He introduced Ronni. "I understand you've been following the proceedings of the commission."

"Yes! We all have. It's a mystery. Perhaps the solution lies with the genetics. We have many theories, but sadly, no time to pursue them."

"That's a pity," Matt said. "It seems that no one has been able to solve the mystery, not in the United States, not here."

"But now *you* are here," Lamberto said. "Perhaps you would be willing to spend some time with our researchers. It could…what do you say, 'shake something loose?'"

"I'd be happy to."

"*Bene!* Come, there is a conference room we can use."

Lamberto led the way through a secure doorway, waving his badge to gain access.

"Dr. Magnani," Matt said, "does the foundation do research on the genetic causes of Alzheimer's disease?"

Lamberto stopped short. "What a coincidence that you should ask! This week there is a conference on that topic here at the foundation. We organized it when a world authority, an American, agreed to attend." Lamberto headed in a different direction, motioning for the others to follow. "He is here today. I will introduce you. You know, this is really an amazing coincidence, because he is also very familiar with your commission."

Lamberto opened the door to a conference room. Fifteen men sat at tables arranged in a *U* shape. The tall, young-looking man at the front of the room halted his presentation when Lamberto entered.

"*Mi scusi,*" Lamberto said. "I didn't mean to interrupt."

"No need to apologize, Dr. Magnani," the presenter said. "Dr. Bugatti, welcome to the foundation."

"Thank you. It's a pleasure to be here, Dr. Stroud."

30

GIDEON

MARLIN CASTOR LAID two bubble packs on the counter.

"Two pre-paid phones, on sale, fourteen-ninety-nine each," the cashier said as he rang them up. "With tax that comes to thirty-two dollars even."

Marlin handed over two twenty-dollar bills.

"Let me guess—teenagers?"

Marlin smiled weakly and silently took his change, picked up the bag and left the store.

Marlin opened the trunk of his car and tossed the bag in among ten other bags from ten other stores.

Thirty-six down, four to go.

The next discount store on Marlin's list was three miles away. He stopped en route at a mail drop, one of fifteen he'd arranged, each under a different alias, each holding a package from a different distributor of electronic components. There were eleven more shipments like it being held for him at eleven other locations. He crossed one more item off his mental list.

At four p.m. Marlin bought a ticket at a multiplex cinema, choosing a movie at random, avoiding the art film in theater 12. He passed by the snack bar and headed straight for 12, fourth from the last row, four seats in—right next to the Supplier. They were the only two in the theater.

"How's the movie?" Marlin asked.

"Excellent. It's a think piece, really well crafted. It'll get six Oscar nominations. It'll win one. Or none. Probably won't gross ten million." The Supplier sucked from the straw in his giant soda. "People's tastes are all fucked up."

"Yeah."

Marlin rapped his knuckles on the armrest as the two of them sat without speaking.

"So?" Marlin asked after five minutes.

The Supplier dug into his jacket pocket and handed Marlin a bundle in a brown paper bag. As Marlin peered inside, he recognized the markings of class B blasting caps.

"This looks short."

"There's twenty-five. I'll get you the other fifteen in a week."

Marlin rolled up the bag and put it in his pocket.

"Well?" the Supplier said.

"Well what?"

"You paid me for twenty caps. There are twenty-five caps in there."

"Half down, half on delivery."

"Right. That's a delivery."

"A *partial* delivery."

"Then I need partial payment."

"You're shitting me." Marlin looked at the Supplier, who was his usual twitchy self. The Supplier did not appear to be shitting him.

Marlin opened his wallet and handed over five twenties.

"What about the C4?"

"Three weeks. Maybe four. Could be longer."

"I need an exact date."

"Well, I can't give you an *exact date*. I have supply chain issues."

Marlin rapped the armrest.

"Any chance of a *partial delivery?*"

"Indeed. I prefer it that way. I don't like to mix up more than fifty pounds at a time, and I don't like to leave it lying around." He sucked from his soda. "It's not safe."

‡ ‡ ‡

Twelve lieutenants, twenty-two recruits, five prospects. Twelve in late stage, five not expected to survive the month. Five recruits dead.

Darryl Meeks scrawled the numbers on a tablet. He factored each one and arranged the numbers in ascending order. He circled numbers with biblical significance:

Five—God's grace.

Twelve—God's governance.

Twenty-two—two times eleven—Division, disorder and judgment.

Darryl folded his hands under his chin as he stared at the page.

Five, five and five. Twelve and twelve. Twenty-two.

Darryl listed the books of the bible:

The Law—Genesis to Deuteronomy—five books.

History—Joshua to Esther—twelve books.

Poetry—Job to Song of Songs—five books.

Major Prophets—Isaiah to Daniel—five books.

Minor Prophets—Hosea to Malachi—twelve books.

He listed two columns of numbers, drawing lines between them, joining the same numbers in each column. One number remained unconnected.

Twenty-two. The number of letters in the Hebrew alphabet.

Darryl wrote the names of the Old Testament books in Hebrew. Beneath each name he wrote three numbers, calculated from the name of the book in each of three methods of the *gematria*, the system of Hebrew numerology. He circled the numbers and drew lines between duplicates. They converged on one name.

Mishlei—Proverbs.

He looked up chapter 22 and read. He stopped at verse 3.

A prudent man foreseeth the evil, and hideth himself: but the simple pass on, and are punished.

Darryl stared at the verse for a long time. Then he placed a call to Marlin Castor.

☦ ☦ ☦

Marlin pulled into the parking area of the public playground, a half-dozen cars scattered throughout the lot. Mothers and fathers sat on benches as their children played noisily. Marlin got out of his car and looked around. Besides his own car, there was only one other that was not either a van, an SUV, or had a baby seat. He walked toward its passenger side. Through the window he recognized Darryl Meeks.

"You weren't specific on the phone," Marlin said, as he got into the car. "I suppose you'll want a status report."

"Among other things."

"My supplier is having problems. I don't have a date by which we'll have all the raw materials."

"Everything must be ready well in advance. We will have a very narrow window. Three weeks. That's how much time we have."

"I can't guarantee that timeframe. If you absolutely need it in three weeks, you might have to settle for less than forty."

"It must be forty."

Marlin pulled out a cigarette.

"I'll thank you not to smoke in my presence, Mr. Castor."

Marlin put the cigarette back in the pack. "Why *must* it be forty?"

"Did not the Lord cause the rain to fall forty days and forty nights? Did not the Israelites wander in the desert for forty years? Did not Moses stay on the mountain forty days and nights to receive God's commandments? Did not Jesus fast for forty days as Satan tempted him?" Darryl's voice rose. "*Did not Jonah warn the Ninevites of God's judgment for forty days?*"

Marlin sat silently.

"It must be forty," Darryl said.

"Right. Forty it is."

"There's another matter we must discuss. The Lord has sent me a warning."

Marlin closed his eyes. He badly craved a cigarette. "Yeah."

"We need a contingency plan. If any of the bombings should go wrong, it's absolutely necessary that our soldiers not be taken alive. You must procure enough ricin for forty doses, each big enough to kill in a time of two hours."

Marlin's throat went dry. "Ricin. That's bad shit."

"I'll thank you not to utter vulgarities in my presence."

"You don't want ricin."

"The Lord has revealed it."

"Whatever the *Lord* told you, you must have heard wrong. Ricin can take days to work."

Darryl gripped his steering wheel until his knuckles turned white. "You know what I need. Will you provide it?"

"I'll come up with something. But it'll cost you."

"The Lord will provide."

Marlin got out of the car and leaned into the window.

"Meeks, just what *is* your mission?"

Darryl looked at Marlin, the whites of his eyes showing all around his irises. Marlin took a step back from the car.

"God commanded Gideon to battle the Midianite host with only three hundred soldiers against an army too large to number. Gideon's soldiers surrounded the camp. They caused such a commotion that the Midianites turned on one another in confusion. The host of Midian destroyed itself, to the glory of God." Darryl opened the glove box, pulled out a bundle and tossed it on the seat.

"Here's another three thousand. For the poison."

31

POWERBALL

Twenty agents gathered in the briefing room at the FBI's Charlotte field office for an update on the investigation into the Pittsburgh and Atlanta bombings. Special Agent Dan Sessions studied his notes as the last of the agents filed in. At precisely nine a.m. he began.

"There are still no firm leads on the source of the explosives or the triggering mechanisms. This plastic explosive is homemade, fairly high quality, but untraceable. The triggering devices were built from parts available from any of hundreds of suppliers, and cheap cell phones available at discount stores everywhere." Agent Sessions tapped a key on his computer. An image of a young woman appeared on the screen.

"The Pittsburgh bomber, Robin Kline, is now known to have been diagnosed with pancreatic cancer. It's a nasty way to die. The poor girl probably figured she had nothing to lose." Agent Sessions tapped the keyboard. Another woman's picture appeared.

"Atlanta bomber Lucy Seidman had ovarian cancer. Untreatable, according to her medical records. Clearly, neither of these women had the skills to build these bombs.

Our theory is that they were recruited for these acts and provided with the devices. Who's responsible, we can't know for sure. But we have an idea. It was reported that Ms. Kline uttered the words *heaven sent* before pushing the button."

As Sessions pressed a key, a photo appeared of a man in cheap, ill-fitting clothes, of average build but with a conspicuous belly, and thinning brown hair plastered to his head. The man stood at the head of a crowd of protesters, arms raised and shouting.

No one in the audience noticed the details of his appearance, not at first. What they noticed were his eyes— wide, intense blue eyes that glowed in the shadow of a prominent brow—the eyes of a zealot.

"This is Darryl Meeks, our person of interest. Six years ago he founded the radical anti-abortion group known as *Heaven Sent*."

The next series of slides showed Meeks on stage at rallies, among protesters at abortion clinics, and screen shots of websites with pictures, addresses and phone numbers of abortion doctors.

"The group is known for their extreme tactics, including violence, either directly, or by inciting others."

Sessions advanced the slide to show Darryl Meeks surrounded by a crowd of people, all grinning hugely. Darryl was not smiling, despite the fact that he held a giant prop check which read:

Pay to the order of   <u>*Darryl Meeks*</u>   *$459,000,000*

<u>*Four Hundred Fifty-Nine Million and No/100*</u> Dollars

For<u> *Powerball Winner* </u> *South Carolina Education Lottery*

"Two years ago Meeks got lucky, as you can see. He took a lump sum payment of two hundred twenty-eight million dollars before taxes."

There were a few low whistles from the audience.

"Meeks is a self-proclaimed expert on biblical numerology," Agent Sessions continued. "He claimed that God had revealed the winning numbers to him in the bible. When asked what he would do with the money, he said 'I will do God's work.'"

"This guy's nuts," came a comment from the audience.

"Completely deranged," Agent Sessions agreed. "Since his windfall, Meeks has amped up his operation. The number and size of protests have increased exponentially. We suspect that Meeks is either directly planning these bombings or he's bankrolling them."

"Follow the money," one agent suggested.

"That's problematic. Meeks has moved all but three million to offshore accounts. We have no visibility to any of his transactions."

"Tail him."

"His house is under constant surveillance. Everything he needs is delivered. He never leaves."

"Wiretap."

"Also a problem. With no direct evidence, we're only able to obtain a warrant for a pen register or trap and trace under the Patriot Act on the grounds that these are terrorist bombings. We have a list of all the numbers to and from his home phone and cell phone."

"Any luck?"

"Not much. A lot of traffic with known *Heaven Sent* members, but that proves nothing. And Meeks likes to use pre-paid burner phones. We can't trap and trace those."

"I guess he's not that crazy after all."

"I said he was deranged," Sessions said. "I didn't say he was stupid."

Agent Sessions turned off the projector. "We did see a series of calls from multiple pre-paid phones to Meeks's home phone. The caller may have thought that he or she was safe by using burner phones."

"*The* caller? Do you think they were from the same person?"

"That's our working assumption. They were all placed from the same area in Washington, D.C."

152

32

PERSUASION

"*IL PAPA?*" MATT repeated.

"Whose papa?" Tyler asked.

"The pope," Matt said. "*Il Papa.* This reporter just told me that the pope has granted me an audience. He asked when I planned to go to the Vatican."

"No! Absolutely not! The pope is the supreme spiritual leader to billions of Christian believers. You're not qualified."

"Not qualified?"

Tyler bit his lip. "What I mean is, you're not a diplomat. The pope is a head of state. You can't represent the United States to a foreign power."

"Oh," Matt said softly. "Don't worry. I have no intention of meeting the pope."

Matt addressed the press in Italian. "I'm honored that the pope would take time to receive me. But I'm afraid that I will not be able to accept his gracious invitation."

There was a collective gasp. "*Signor Bugatti,*" a reporter spoke up, "one does not refuse an audience with His Holiness when one is offered."

"What'd he say?" Tyler asked.

"He says it would be an insult to refuse."

Tyler scratched his chin. "All right. Answer him, but don't commit to anything. I'll have to check with the White House."

"It is not my intention to go against custom," Matt said, "nor do I wish to offend the pope. But I am here on a personal visit, and not in an official capacity. I must confer with my government before I can commit to a time when I can visit the Vatican."

One reporter raised a hand. "*Signore*, if this is a personal trip, why were you at the European Genetics Foundation yesterday?"

"I was in Ronzano to visit my cousin, a friar at the hermitage. He introduced me to the director of the foundation, Dr. Magnani. My cousin is a close personal friend of the director."

"So your visit to the foundation was not connected to the work of the commission?"

"It was not."

"And your conversation with Dr. Stroud, the scientist from Compton-Genencraft—was that also 'unofficial?'"

"What's he saying?" Tyler asked. "Did he mention Stroud?"

Matt waved his hand at Tyler. "Dr. Stroud is at the foundation for a conference on the genetics of Alzheimer's disease. We greeted each other briefly."

The group of reporters murmured.

"Dr. Bugatti, did you visit the hermitage alone?" The question was in English, from a woman in the middle of the crowd.

"That woman looks familiar," Matt whispered to Tyler.

"Clara Kildee from the Associated Press," Tyler whispered back. "She's the one who broke the story in the first place." Matt was about to respond when Tyler grabbed Matt's arm. "What visit? What's a hermitage?"

"I'll explain later." Matt turned back to the reporters. "Ms. Kildee, is it?"

"Yes, Dr. Bugatti," Clara responded. "I'll repeat my question. Were you alone when you went to the hermitage, and later, to the foundation?"

"No."

"Weren't you in the company of a Washington lobbyist, Rhiannon Barraket?"

Tyler squeezed Matt's arm. "*What?!*"

"Ms. Barraket asked me to show her some of the countryside, and I agreed. At no time did we discuss the commission."

"Still, do you think it's proper for you to spend time alone with an adviser to one of the staunchest opponents of abortion rights in the United States Senate?"

"*Momento, momento!*" Tyler shouted. He pulled Matt away from the crowd. "What are you thinking?" he whispered. "Not only have you compromised your neutrality, but now the AP will be blasting the story to a thousand newspapers, radio and TV stations."

"I know my responsibilities as chair of the commission. There haven't been any improper discussions between Ronni and me."

"Listen to yourself—*Ronni and me.* You're not in high school and this isn't the prom. In case you haven't figured it out by now, let me tell you a couple of things. First, *appearances matter.* You and *Ronni* could be talking about opera for all I know. But it looks bad. And second, *the press is everywhere.*"

Matt looked at the ground. "I won't be seen again in public with Ms. Barraket."

"Not good enough. I don't want her near you. Send her back to the Sheraton. Better yet, back to America."

"Isn't that *her* choice?"

"You get her out of here, or I will."

Matt nodded. Tyler addressed the crowd.

"Dr. Bugatti allowed Ms. Barraket to accompany him on his personal visit as a courtesy. Ms. Barraket enjoyed her tour of Italy, but as of today she is no longer staying at the villa. Thank you, that's all the time we have today for questions."

Tyler pulled Matt away. The few correspondents who spoke English were immediately set upon for a translation of Tyler's remarks.

"Dr. Bugatti," Clara shouted, "what about the girls?"

Matt stopped and turned back to the crowd. He spoke Italian.

"The correspondent from the Associated Press has asked about the girls. I'm grateful for the question, because the girls are what matter. Throughout the course of this investigation, every question I've asked, every decision I've made, has been for one purpose: to do right by these girls. Whatever you want to assume about my actions, I ask you never to forget *them*. I certainly won't."

Matt walked away. The press shouted after him.

"What did you say?" Tyler asked.

"I reminded them of what's important." Matt stopped. "It's not appearances. It's the girls, and the truth. I'll do whatever it takes to find the truth and I don't give a damn about appearances."

"Is that what you want from Ronni Barraket? The truth?"

Matt glared at Tyler. He walked back to the villa without another word.

‡ ‡ ‡

Ronni opened her door to a soft rapping.

"Hi," Matt said. "I have a question."

"Would you like to come in?"

"I'd rather not."

"What did you want to ask me?"

"Why are you here?"

Ronni walked away from the door and sat in a chair next to a small table. "Please, come in."

Matt stayed by the door.

"You could have asked me that question two days ago," Ronni said.

"I know." Matt stepped into the room. "I'm not sure why I didn't…I'm asking now."

"But you already know why I'm here."

"I want to know what you thought you would accomplish."

"I'm a lobbyist. My job is to persuade."

"If you're trying to persuade me, you must have already taken a position. This is an investigation. There are no positions, only unanswered questions."

Ronni looked at Matt's face—not belligerent or accusatory, but questioning.

"Senator Herrera wants to make *Backup* an issue in the campaign. She wants a finding of fault on the part of the FDA and CG Pharma. When she heard that the report didn't blame either, she sent me to persuade you."

"How did she know about the report? It's confidential."

"There are no secrets in Washington."

Matt walked into the room and sat on the edge of the bed. "Persuade me? Persuade me of what? Did you think you could convince me to falsify the report?"

"Oh, no. No. I've been following the proceedings since they began. I admire the way you've handled the hearings. I can't imagine that you would accept a report that was anything but truthful."

"Then what?"

"I work in Washington, Matt. I know what the town is like. Some politicians lie. Some bend the truth. But most bury the truth."

Ronni reached for Matt's hand, then hesitated. "I know you're under tremendous pressure. It would be so easy for someone in your position just to sign off on a report that stops short of the whole story. I'm here to make sure you keep looking."

"So the senator can have her issue."

Ronni stood and walked to the window.

"Senator Herrera believes…" Ronni turned from the window. "*I* believe—that America is in a crisis. A *moral* crisis. Poverty, violence, inequality, intolerance…" Ronni clenched her fists. "The *waste!* The sickening, unconscionable, unforgivable *waste*. We waste everything—our resources, our relationships, our *children*. Born and unborn, Matt, we're *killing our own children*." She felt a tear roll down her cheek. She turned back to the window. "Imagine how great America could be—how great the *world* could be—if it weren't for this immoral waste."

"I can't disagree, Ronni. Waste offends me, too. I don't know if I'd consider it a *moral* issue."

Ronni wiped the tear from her face. "Isn't it? What is morality but acting on your values? How can someone want something valuable, work for it, sacrifice for it, and then throw it away? That's the opposite of acting on your values. It's the opposite of morality. And if you believe in God, you have to believe that what God made is precious. To waste what God has given us? That's a sin."

Matt nodded slowly. "A person could accept that premise whether he believes in God or not."

"I don't know if Senator Herrera can lead us out of this crisis," Ronni said, "but at least she understands it." She sat down. "Before she can lead, she has to get elected. To get elected, she needs issues. That's politics."

Matt took Ronni's hand. "Tyler thinks you're a bad influence. He says it's bad optics if we're seen together."

"Do you think I'm a bad influence?"

"No." Matt let go of Ronni's hand. He walked to the door. "Tyler wants you out of here."

"I don't want to go."

"I don't want you to go."

"What do we do about Tyler?"

"Don't worry about Tyler," Matt said, smiling. "When he finds out what I've got planned, he'll forget all about you."

"What do you mean?"

"Tomorrow I'm spending the day with Cameron Stroud."

33

Contest

It was a perfect day for shooting.

Cameron and Matt arrived at *I Cieli Aperti* shooting range at a few minutes before one.

"*Buongiorno,*" Cameron said to the man on duty. "*Sono il dottor Stroud. Ho una prenotazione questo pomeriggio.*"

Matt's head snapped in Cameron's direction. "*Bravo!* Where did you learn Italian?"

"I picked it up on a previous trip," Cameron said, continuing the conversation in Italian.

"It's very good."

"Indeed," said the man behind the counter. "For an American you speak well. And you, sir," he said, pointing at Matt, "you are not from Bologna. *Milano,* perhaps?"

"No," Matt said, "I'm also American."

"*Davvero?*" the man laughed. "Really? No American speaks Italian like you!"

"*Molto gentile,*" Matt said. "You're very kind."

Cameron smiled thinly. "My reservation, please?"

"Certainly. You are on range number four."

Matt and Cameron followed the signs to their shooting range, each carrying his weapon: Cameron, a Browning Twelvette shotgun, and Matt, a Bettinsoli X7.

"That's a fine gun, Dr. Bugatti," Cameron said. "How long have you had it?"

"Not long. Actually, it belongs to my cousin, Pierangelo. I brought it from America as a gift. It's really more of a hunting gun than a clay gun. But when I told him about your invitation he insisted that I use it."

"I feel outclassed. I've had this humble Browning since I was a boy. I never travel without it."

Matt inspected his shotgun. "I don't think you have much to worry about. This is the first time I've used this gun. And I'm not really a trap shooter. I prefer pistols or rifles."

"Free shot?"

"After you."

Cameron raised his gun. *"Pronto, lanciatore?"* he said. "Puller ready?"

"Sì!" came the response.

"Pull!"

The target streaked across the sky. Cameron fired; the target disappeared in a puff.

"Dead bird," said Matt. "Nice shooting." He pointed his weapon. "Pull!"

The target rose. Matt fired, but the target sailed downrange, untouched.

"Lost," Cameron said. "Don't worry, Dr. Bugatti. That one doesn't count."

"Out of practice," Matt explained. "I hope that's not a sign of how the rest of the day will go." Matt broke open the gun. "Your go."

Cameron fired at five targets in succession, destroying four. He stepped to the next station as Matt took his place.

"Impressive," Matt said. "I can see I'm in for a contest." He raised his gun. "Pull!"

Matt's shot shattered the target. The second shot missed. The next three were dead birds.

"Even up." Cameron bit his lip. "Not really a trap shooter, hey? I think you're sandbagging me, Dr. Bugatti." He loaded his gun. "Pull!"

Cameron broke five targets in a row. Matt nodded in appreciation.

"Well done." He stepped up to the second station. "Dr. Stroud, I'd really like to learn more about your work on the treatment of Alzheimer's."

"Why, sure. In fact, I'll be presenting a summary of my findings at the conference tomorrow. You're welcome to attend, and if there's anything you don't understand, I'll explain it to you."

Matt looked at Cameron, whose smile seemed unnaturally wide.

"I look forward to it," Matt said. "Pull!"

Matt missed the shot. Of the next four targets, Matt hit two.

"That happens to me all the time," Cameron said. "Great start, but then I fall apart at the next station."

"You know," Matt said, "I would think that genetically caused Alzheimer's would be more difficult to treat. Wouldn't a genetic predisposition make the disease more or less inevitable?"

Cameron loaded his gun. "Possibly," he said. "Or possibly not. Most cases of Alzheimer's have no clear cause. Pull!" The target shattered. "Suppose we can identify the specific gene, and suppose we can determine its mechanism. There's a chance we can intervene. And that success might provide insight into the treatment of other forms of the disease. Pull!"

Cameron hit three of the next four targets. Matt stepped up to the station and pulled a shell from his vest.

"Have you made a decision on the commission report?" Cameron asked.

Matt fumbled with the shell as he inserted it into the breech. "I'm sorry, but I really can't discuss it." He closed the gun. "Pull!"

Matt missed four targets before hitting one.

"I'm not asking for details," Cameron added, "just wondering when it'll come out. It's been hanging out there for a week."

"There are just a few loose ends to tie up," Matt said. "Nothing significant."

Cameron pulled two shells from his pocket as Matt continued.

"But, as long as we're talking about genetics, I do find it disturbing that the genetic link to the fatal reaction to *Backup* couldn't have been foreseen."

Cameron snapped the shells into his gun. "You're making a conceptual leap there, Doctor. We don't *know* that there is a genetic link."

"But that's highly likely, wouldn't you admit?"

Cameron held his gun level. "Not at all. Remember, the active drugs in this formulation have a long history of safety. If there'd been a genetic reaction, we'd have seen it years ago. Pull!"

The target sailed into sight. Cameron fired and missed.

"Lost bird," Matt said. "I'm not a medical doctor, of course. But the numbers are hard to explain without assuming a genetic cause."

"There is mathematics, and there is medicine. Pull!" Cameron missed. "There are other factors involved."

"That's what bothers me—the other factors." As Cameron aimed, Matt added, "What about the inactive drugs?"

Cameron lowered his gun. "The what?"

"You said that the active drugs have a history of safety. What about the inactive drugs?"

"'Inactive drug'—that's a contradiction in terms."

"You know what I mean. There are other ingredients besides the contraceptive and the oral vaccine, aren't there?"

"Well, yes, there is one," Cameron chuckled. "A compound with no function other than to regulate delivery. That was CG Pharma's innovation. No pharmacological effect. And no genetic link."

Cameron missed the next three shots.

"I'm gaining on you, Doctor," Matt said.

"All this 'doctor' business is a bit formal. You call me Cameron, and I'll call you Matteo."

"Matt's good enough."

"Your shot, Matt."

He hit four of his five targets. Cameron stepped up to the final station.

"Heck, Matt, you have me on the run."

"I'm still down by two birds."

"Pull!" Cameron blew the target apart.

"Nice shot," Matt said. "I was speaking with Dr. Magnani. He also suspects a genetic link."

"Of course he does. He's a geneticist. Everything is genetic to Dr. Magnani."

"I suppose. But in any case, I would think that with your particular expertise in genetics that you would have taken steps to test for any genetics-related sensitivity."

Cameron's wide smile had long since vanished. "I don't know where you got the idea that I'm an expert in genetics. I have some background, but it's not my specialty. And I told you, these drugs are safe." He raised his gun. "If we tested for every remote possibility we'd never get a product to market. Damn it, we're running a business. Pull!"

Cameron missed three shots before hitting one. Matt finished his turn with five straight hits. The round ended with Matt in the lead, sixteen kills to fifteen.

The second round continued with little conversation. By the time they had completed the third station, Matt's lead had increased by one.

"I'm sure you'll be happy to get back to mathematics when this is all over," Cameron said.

Matt closed his eyes and smiled. "I will. I understand math. It has rules. Politics?" Matt shook his head. "If there are rules in politics, I haven't discovered them. And the conflicts, the rivalries, the posturing…I won't be sad to put this behind me."

"Indeed." Cameron took his place at the station. "But all fields have their rivalries, don't they? Even yours?"

"And yours, too, no doubt. But we have tools to resolve differences in our fields."

"So does politics. They're called elections. Pull!" The target shattered.

"Not the same. We don't vote on the validity of a mathematical theory."

"Of course. We scientists have to make our cases with evidence and logic." Cameron pointed his gun. "For example, how do you plan to respond Dr. Petrescu's latest paper? Pull!"

Matt didn't notice the target, or the result of Cameron's shot.

"Dead bird," Cameron said.

"What paper?"

"In the *Journal of Discrete Mathematics*. He took issue with your proof that the Riemann Hypothesis cannot be demonstrated to an arbitrarily large limit. Pull!"

Again, Matt took no notice of the shot.

"Lost," Cameron said.

"What do you mean, 'he took issue?' Did he find a flaw in the proof?"

"He claims it isn't complete. I would have to agree."

"*You* would have to agree? What do *you* know about it?"

"Oh, well, discrete mathematics is a hobby of mine. And I did find Dr. Petrescu's arguments convincing. Pull!"

This time Matt's eyes followed the target to the point where it disintegrated.

"Dead. Pull!"

Cameron's shot was perfect. "Dead bird," he said. "You're up, Matt."

Matt missed five straight targets. By the end of the second round, Cameron led, thirty-four to thirty.

Cameron offered his hand. "It was a pleasure shooting with you, Matt."

Matt shook Cameron's hand silently.

‡ ‡ ‡

"Of course, Dr. Bugatti," said Lamberto Magnani. "You're welcome to use all of our facilities, for as long as you like. Can I help you find something in particular?"

Matt sat in Dr. Magnani's office at the European Genetics Foundation.

"I need to look up a paper in a mathematics journal. It's available online."

Lamberto nodded. "Certainly. But you could do that from anywhere, isn't that so?"

"Yes," Matt said. "I could. But I hope you'll be able to help me with another matter."

"Of course. How can I help?"

"I need to learn about genetics. Where should I start?"

34

CURSE

"YOU'RE STILL HERE."

Ronni sat at a table in the dining hall of the Bugatti villa. She looked up from her laptop to see Tyler hovering over her.

"I can see that Dr. Bugatti can't be counted on to put aside his personal feelings and remain professional," Tyler continued, "so it's up to me. I want you out of here by noon."

"This is becoming tiresome."

"I'm just getting started."

Ronni tapped the keyboard of her laptop. "I would have thought that by now you'd know that Matt won't be influenced by anything other than facts and logic. He certainly won't be influenced by me."

"Oh, that is so charming. Even if that were true, it wouldn't stop you from trying."

"I'm not trying to influence Matt in any way."

"Liar."

Ronni slammed her laptop shut. "Don't call me a liar."

"Ronni, you're smarter than that. You wouldn't be here if you didn't know—just as I do—that your presence alone is an influence."

Ronni locked eyes with Tyler for a few seconds before looking down.

"I'm not leaving. The fact is I like Matt. I like his intensity and his curiosity and his commitment."

Tyler leaned forward. "Ronni, what can come of this? Nothing, that's what. You and I are believing Christians. Bugatti is an atheist."

"We share the same values."

"Ronni, you *know* that's not true. Our whole reason for being is our God. The legitimacy of our lives is measured by our relationship with Jesus Christ. Bugatti can't share in what we have—what *you* have."

Ronni tapped her fingers on her laptop. "There's more to it than that."

"*No*, Ronni, there's *not*. There can't be more to it than Christ because *Christ is all there is*."

"Morning."

Tyler and Ronni turned to see Matt approaching, clothes rumpled and hair uncombed. His eyelids drooped.

"Good grief," Tyler said. "Where have you been? You look terrible."

Matt dropped into the chair opposite Ronni. "The foundation. I was doing some reading."

"All night?"

Matt looked at his watch. "Pretty much. I took a short nap around two."

Tyler looked at Ronni as if he expected an explanation. Ronni shrugged.

"So," Tyler said, "reading. Anything interesting?"

"Fascinating." Matt yawned. "Basic genetics. Dr. Magnani made some recommendations."

"What prompted this sudden urge to read up on genetics?"

"I asked Stroud about his research into Alzheimer's disease. He said…"

Tyler leaned against the table. "*Stroud?*"

"Yeah. He said that genetically caused diseases might be more treatable than idiopathic cases."

"Idiopathic?" Ronni asked.

"It just means no known cause."

"When did you talk to Stroud?" Tyler asked, his voice shaking.

"He's here for a conference at the foundation. We went shooting yesterday. After the match, I went to the foundation to talk to Dr. Magnani."

Tyler hung his head. "The press conference. That reporter *did* ask you about Stroud." Tyler looked up. "Dr. Bugatti, you are out of control." He gestured toward Ronni. "It's not enough that you schmooze with this lobbyist. You're palling around with a principal of a company that *you're investigating.*"

"We didn't talk about the commission."

"*It doesn't matter!*" Tyler shouted. The few others in the dining hall who had gathered for breakfast turned toward the commotion. "You've compromised the integrity of the commission. The Italian press has the story, and that persistent reporter, Kildee, is sure to feed it to the AP. I don't know if the damage can be contained."

"Don't overreact."

"Ha!" Tyler pointed to his reddened face. "Do you think *this* is overreacting? Trust me, I'm holding back." He pointed at Ronni. "*You*, go home. And *you*," he pointed at Matt, "stay away from Stroud!"

Tyler turned and stomped out of the room.

"He has a point, you know," Ronni said.

"I know, I know."

Ronni looked at Matt. He was on the verge of falling asleep. "You went shooting?"

"Trap. He's pretty good. He beat me."

"*Did* you talk about the commission?"

"Briefly. Obviously, he wants the report released as-is."

"But you know that's not the right thing to do."

"Actually, I don't know. I know that *you* want it changed."

"I just want the truth. The *whole* truth." Ronni's eyes seemed angry.

"Sorry. I'm tired."

"*Ciao, Rhiannon!*" Pierangelo approached the table. "Hi, Rhiannon! Hi, Matteo! How are you this morning?"

"*Ciao, Pierangelo,*" Matt greeted his cousin, "we're fine, and how are you?"

"Wonderful, thanks!" Pierangelo set down a tray. "A double espresso for you, and for Rhiannon, *caffé Americano.*" He pulled a chair to the table and sat down.

"Matteo," Pierangelo said, "you must spend the day with your mother. You are here for three days and you have seen Flora only for meals."

"Tomorrow, Pierangelo. There is a lecture I must attend this afternoon."

"A lecture today. Yesterday it was shooting. The day before that you worked."

"Pierangelo! You told me that Mom was catching up with the cousins."

"No more. Many of the cousins have gone home. Now Flora asks for you. We tell her you are busy and she gets angry." He patted Matt's hand. "Today you are with Flora."

"All right," Matt sighed. He pushed the espresso away. "But later. I need to sleep first."

"*Bene.*" Pierangelo stood and picked up the tray. "And Flora also would like Rhiannon to come."

Pierangelo disappeared before Matt could say a word.

"What was that about?" Ronni asked.

"Mom insists that I spend the day with her."

"Good. You should."

"I'm glad you think so. She wants you to join us."

"Me? Why?"

"I can think of several possible reasons, but there's only one that matters. She likes you."

"In that case, I'd love to come along."

There was a moment of silence.

"Whose idea was the shooting match?" Ronni asked.

"Stroud invited me. But if he hadn't, I'd have found an excuse to talk with him about his research."

"The Alzheimer's research."

Matt nodded. "I hear it's a breakthrough."

"Will it be in time to help Flora?"

"I don't know. I hope so. But, from what I've read, her form of Alzheimer's is relentless."

"What form?"

"It's genetic. It was inevitable that she would get the disease. It's in her DNA. Pierangelo told me that it goes back generations. It's the family curse."

Ronni felt a chill. "Does that mean...?"

Matt nodded. "I've been tested. I'm cursed."

"Oh, Matt."

"Don't worry," Matt said, smiling. "I've got a couple of good decades ahead of me. My dad died before he was fifty. I should make it that far at least, especially if Stroud is onto something. Damn, I really wanted to hear that lecture." He stood up. "You know, Stroud said something strange to me yesterday, that he had a background in genetics, but that he wasn't an expert."

"Why is that strange?"

"I checked his record. He's not just an MD. He's got a PhD in molecular biology."

‡ ‡ ‡

It was a two-minute report on *CNN Headline News*, an interview with the director of a San Francisco women's clinic.

"We are not intimidated," he said. "We will continue to provide a full range of reproductive health services, including abortions."

Darryl Meeks scowled as he watched.

"Are you taking *any* precautions against a possible bomb attack?" the interviewer asked.

"We are doing more in-depth background checks on our abortion patients."

"But no searches or metal detectors?"

The director pursed his lips and shook his head. "These are women in need. We will not treat our patients like terrorists."

Darryl's scowl deepened. *How anxious he is to kill babies.*

The cell phone on the table next to Darryl's chair chimed. He didn't recognize the number, a long string of digits, starting with *39.*

"Hello?"

"Hello, Darryl."

"Where are you calling from?"

"Italy. I was watching CNN."

"So was I. The abortionist in California."

"They are a determined bunch, aren't they?"

"The wicked shall fall by his own wickedness."

"Amen. But we can't be careless. They'll be checking out every soldier. Don't be hasty. We must be certain of our recruits *and* our recruiters."

"This is proving to be very difficult. We have already lost five soldiers to their diseases. We can't take forever."

"I know, Brother Meeks. Work diligently and pray, as I pray. God will provide."

Darryl set the phone on the table as the next CNN report aired.

"Senator and presidential candidate Yolanda Herrera Peña is nearing the end of her five-day European tour after stops in six countries. Her trip ends with the obligatory visit to Italy and the Vatican, where she was granted a private audience with the pope. She returns to the United States on Saturday."

35

BACKUP

"WHAT NOW, MR. Castor?" the Supplier asked from across the table in the most remote corner of a biker bar. The bar had no pain-in-the-ass smokeless policy, a fact that Marlin Castor appreciated as he lit up his second cigarette in five minutes.

"Poison."

"Let me guess—your backup plan."

"It's not *my* plan."

"Right. Whatever. Did you have a specific poison in mind?"

"Short-term, delayed reaction. No symptoms for an hour, dead in two. My client asked for ricin, but it doesn't meet the specs."

"Yeah. I know just what you need. Brodifacoum. It's rat poison. You can buy it by the ton."

"Where can I get it?"

The Supplier twitched as he laughed. "Home store, garden supply, Amazon—but it's no good to you as-is. You can eat handfuls of it and it'll just make you sick. If you want it to kill, it needs to be processed."

"Can you do it?"

"Poison's not my regular line. I'm just a dabbler. But I know someone."

Marlin crushed out his cigarette. "Forty doses, in three weeks. Can you handle that?"

"For two-fifty a dose you can consider it handled, my friend."

Marlin nodded as he lit up. "How does this stuff work, anyway."

"Nasty shit," the Supplier said with a shudder. "Nasty. It's like a super blood thinner. Once it gets in your system, you bleed out—death by internal hemorrhage."

36

DEAD BIRD

CLARA KILDEE FOUND Brother Dario to be a genial and accommodating man. Dario gave her the same tour that he gave to Ronni and Matt. She asked many questions, to which Brother Dario gave direct answers without evasion. Why shouldn't he? After all, hadn't she assured him that she and Matt were old friends?

"Matt told me about the foundation," Clara told Dario in the wine cellar as she accepted a glass of *pignoletto*. "Who would have expected to find such a facility on the grounds of the hermitage?"

"It's not so unusual," Dario said. "Did you know that the Vatican operates an observatory for research in astronomy? And that His Holiness has a council of advisers which includes some of the greatest scientists in the world? The Church is no enemy of science."

"No, that's not what I meant. It's the *contrast*—a fifteenth-century monastery and a twenty-first-century research facility."

"The laws of genetics were discovered in a monastery, by a Catholic friar." Dario refilled the glasses. "Nature has always been nature, since the creative act of God. Science can reveal its workings, but the discoveries of science do not offer salvation. For that, we must turn to the faith. God and nature—they have always been, and will always be. They must coexist, everywhere, not only at Ronzano."

"I'd love to see it."

"The foundation? Of course. It's not far. We can go now. I will introduce you to Lamberto."

‡ ‡ ‡

Lamberto, Clara and Dario shared coffee in the foundation cafeteria, before walls of glass affording a vista of the surrounding vineyards, and the hermitage at the top of the hill.

"Life," Lamberto said, gazing at the view. "It surrounds us. It inspires us." He looked at his guests and smiled. "Well, it inspires *me* at least."

"It's a beautiful setting," Clara said.

"I am quite sure I would die in the city," Lamberto laughed. "Out here, I can hear my thoughts. And Brother Dario and the hermitage are near when I need solitude."

"If I didn't know you better, Lamberto," Dario said, "I would say that you don't like people. You spend hours in the cloister. You live alone in the country with no one for miles. You should join the Order."

Lamberto laughed and patted Dario's hand. "Perhaps one day I will. I already live a friar's life!"

"Matt must have enjoyed his visit, if the amount of time he spent here is an indication," Clara said.

"I suppose," Lamberto answered, shrugging. "Dr. Bugatti spent the entire night in the library. He was there when I arrived in the morning. He did not look like he was having a good time. I had to send him home to get some sleep."

"He *did* look ragged when I saw him this morning," Clara lied. "But he also said that he was impressed with the library."

"Our little library?" Lamberto said with a bemused look. "We have some volumes, and some computers. Perhaps he meant our database. We call it *GenArchive*. We have nearly all the gene sequences ever determined for tens of thousands of species. And we collect automatically news items and research papers from all over the world. GenArchive may be the most complete database of genetics research in the world."

"Yes, that's right. GenArchive. May I see a demonstration?"

Lamberto beamed. "But of course!"

After a short tutorial, Lamberto left Clara alone at the library computer. Clara looked over the various data sources: genomes by species, journal articles by topic, research paper preprints, even references to genetics in the popular press, each broken down into a hierarchy of categories. Clara shook her head as she scanned the sheer volume of information. Then she began typing in search terms.

‡ ‡ ‡

"Have you made any revolutionary discoveries?"

Clara turned with a start to see Lamberto leaning forward, studying the screen. After four hours, she could barely see the screen herself, much less make sense of the text on the display.

"*Association of HCG4P11 Gene Polymorphism in Individuals of Eastern European Ancestry with Immune Thrombocytopenia,*" Lamberto read. "That's obscure. I don't think I've seen that one before."

"I was searching on immune disorders among Eastern Europeans," Clara said.

"Hmm. I have done that same search myself ten times. I think I would have remembered seeing this paper. Where did you search?"

"The preprint database."

"Ah, that could explain it." Lamberto scrolled through the paper. "Yes, I see now. This paper was never published. I can see why. The conclusions are rather speculative. The journals would certainly have refused to publish without changes. Did you search for the same topic in the publication database?"

"Yes, but I couldn't find it. There are other papers by the same researchers, but different topics. Are you familiar with this disease? Thrombo…"

"Thrombocytopenia. I have heard of it. It's an autoimmune disease that causes internal bleeding. Usually it's not serious." Lamberto rubbed his chin. "Still…"

"What are you thinking?"

"If there were a drug reaction linked to this same gene, it could aggravate this condition, or perhaps even induce it." Lamberto touched his head. "We know that the *Backup* drugs have a history of safety. But *something* is causing this fatal reaction. I must look at this further." Lamberto gently crowded Clara aside and tapped the keyboard. "I have sent the document to my computer. Now, I need to find Dr. Stroud."

‡ ‡ ‡

"Yes, I remember that research."

Clara had tracked down the primary author of the paper, David Tate, a professor of genetics at Vanderbilt University, and contacted him by phone.

"We never could get it past the referees," the professor explained. "I can't really blame them. The evidence was thin. Then our funding was dropped and we moved on to other things. We did that work more than five years ago. I put the preprint out on our website, but I took it down after a week or two. How ever did you come across it?"

Clara described GenArchive, the foundation database.

"Damn, that sounds like a hell of a setup. But why would a small-town newspaper reporter be looking for obscure research preprints on an Italian computer?"

"I've been covering the *Backup* deaths for the Associated Press."

"Yeah, damn shame, that. Big news last month, but I haven't heard nothin' lately. Do you think this genetic link might have something to do with it?"

"I'm a reporter. *You're* the scientist. I was hoping you could tell me."

"I kind of hadn't thought about it. Maybe…tell me, just how did those girls die?"

Clara described the manner of death in horrifying detail.

"Jesus, I had no idea. I just figured they got a bad batch of pills."

"But could it be related to your findings?"

"Could be. The way those girls bled out sounds like thrombocytopenia but a million times worse."

"So it's possible?"

"It's a long shot. A lot of stars would have to line up."

"Thousands of girls took the drug, but only forty-nine died."

"Then I guess it ain't out of the question."

Clara hung up the phone. Then she got a twinge of nausea.

"Only" forty-nine died.

‡ ‡ ‡

Lamberto found Cameron in the temporary office the foundation staff had prepared for his visit.

"The conference is going well, don't you think?" Lamberto asked.

"Y'all put on a fine meeting, Dr. Magnani."

"Thank you. We have all learned a lot."

Lamberto looked at Cameron's face: His smile was fixed and his eyes were unblinking. Lamberto took a step back as a word came to his mind: *marionetta*—marionette.

"Well, I just wanted to thank you for your contribution, Dr. Stroud." Lamberto turned and made it to the door before turning back. "Oh, where is my head? I forgot the reason I came to see you."

Lamberto described the paper that Clara had found.

"That's odd. Why is a reporter spending time in your database?"

"She is a colleague of Dr. Bugatti's. She seemed very interested in the database."

"A colleague of Dr. Bugatti's." Cameron's smile straightened. "Of course. Clara Kildee. Now I remember her. Dr. Bugatti introduced us." Cameron's smile returned. "The paper sounds promising. Have you inquired further?"

"No, not yet. I have no time today. Tomorrow."

"I have time now. I'll go to the library. Ms. Kildee can show me the article."

"You will not find her there. She left to make a phone call."

‡ ‡ ‡

The road to Lamberto's house wound among the hills south of Bologna. He lived on a hillside, in the center of a property of twenty acres, too steep and rocky for cultivation, but the purpose of the land was isolation, not agriculture. His neighbors shared his appreciation for solitude; the nearest house was three kilometers away.

Lamberto's house faced east; the hill behind him blocked the view of the western horizon. Sunsets were not a feature of his evenings at home. That was fine with Lamberto—he rarely got home before sunset anyway, and the rising sun streaming through his kitchen window invigorated him at the start of his day.

Lamberto parked his car under the carport. He gathered the stack of material he'd brought home with him, mostly administrative paperwork that he never found time to do during working hours. He exited the car and stepped up to the door. He was reaching for the handle when he heard a sound. Lamberto had no way of knowing it, but it was the sound of a shell being inserted into the receiver of a Browning Twelvette double automatic shotgun.

The blast tore away the side of Lamberto's face, nearly severing his neck. He was hurled backwards by the force, coming to rest sprawled on his side, three yards from the doorstep. The report echoed down the hill before silence returned.

Cameron stepped under the carport to inspect the body. Blood pooled around what was left of Lamberto's head, a red stream winding its way under Lamberto's car, the last of a blizzard of papers settling to the ground.

Cameron judged the shot to have been effective.

Dead bird.

37

FAMILY

DOZZA'S BRICK-PAVED streets were narrow and steep, taxing the legs, forcing a leisurely pace. Had the streets been broad, smooth and level, one's pace would have remained unhurried, by choice if not by necessity. One couldn't help but pause frequently to admire the brilliant murals covering the walls of the medieval buildings, the famous *muri dipinti* of Dozza.

Flora spoke fondly of her memories of the town. She'd once had family in Dozza and Giovanni had courted her here. She talked almost incessantly as she strolled the streets with Ronni and Matt.

The three of them enjoyed a relaxing lunch *all'aperto*, in the lengthening shadow of the imposing *Rocca Sforzesca*, the Sforza Castle.

"We visited Bologna only a few times a year," Flora recalled in labored English. "For a little country girl it was exciting. The big towers, the big churches, the piazzas, and the *people!* So many people, talking fast, moving fast. *Oof!* It turned my head around." She looked across at the castle, down at the brick pavement, and at the shops. A few tourists murmured as they snapped photos, but otherwise the surroundings were silent. "I prefer Dozza."

"It's lovely," Ronni said. "I think I prefer Dozza, too."

Flora sipped her coffee. "*Mio zio Renato non è lontano da qui*," she said. "My uncle Renato is not far. We will visit him after lunch."

Ronni looked at Matt with a *what did she say?* look on her face.

"Mom," Matt said, "Uncle Renato isn't here anymore. He's been gone a long time."

"*Ma ce stai dicendo*," Flora huffed. "What are you saying—that I don't know where my own family lives?"

"Mom, Renato died before I was born."

Flora scowled. "I know you never liked Renato, but that is no excuse to make fun of me. You shouldn't be so cruel."

"What's happening?" Ronni asked Matt.

"Mom's a little confused. She thinks her uncle Renato is still living here in Dozza."

"*Non sono confusa*," Flora protested.

The three of them said nothing for several minutes, until Ronni broke the silence.

"Flora, why did you come to America to live?"

"*Ha! Non potrei mai lasciare l'Italia!*"

"She said she could never leave Italy," Matt translated.

"But you came to America in the eighties, didn't you?"

Flora straightened herself in her chair. "*Chi sei?*" she snapped. "Who are you? Do you think you know my business better than I do? Giovanni, who is this? Is she one of your girlfriends?"

Matt turned pale. "*Mamma, non sono Giovanni. Sono Matteo.*"

Tears welled up in Flora's eyes. "You are not your father. Why would you even mention the name of that bitter old man to me?"

"You're thinking of my grandfather, *Nonno Matteo*. I'm Matteo, your son."

"I know who you are, Giovanni. You're my cheating husband."

‡ ‡ ‡

Matt and Ronni sat at a table outside the villa as the sun approached the horizon, the voices of Flora, Pierangelo, and Stefania coming from inside, engaged in an exuberant conversation. A bottle of wine and one of *grappa* stood on the table between Matt and Ronni. Matt had finished three small glasses of *grappa* and was pouring his fourth.

"Are you all right?" Ronni asked.

"That's the worst I've seen her. It just shook me up, that's all." He drained his glass and reached for the bottle.

"Is there something else?"

Matt lifted the glass, but paused and set it back down. "She said I was her cheating husband. It was a hell of a way to find out that my dad cheated on my mom."

"Are you sure it's true? Maybe she's imagining."

"I don't think so. They never let on, but it makes sense. He had plenty of chances. He traveled a lot. And I remember some tense times—tense for no reason."

"If it's true, then why did they stay together?"

"Family. If it had been just the two of them, they might have split up. That would have broken up a marriage. But the three of us—we were a family. There aren't many forces more powerful in the Italian culture than family." Matt drank the *grappa*. "But there's another reason: They loved each other, enough to forgive. They were two willful people who forgave each other a lot."

"Infidelity. That's a lot to forgive."

"Mom mentioned her Uncle Renato. Remember?"

"Yes."

"My dad told me the story of Renato. He fancied himself a revolutionary. He never missed a chance to preach against the multinational corporations and Italy's unholy alliance with the western powers. Mom's family didn't know how far gone he was until the late seventies, when he fell in with a group of terrorists, *Brigate Rosse*, the Red Brigades. He vanished just before the Brigades kidnapped and murdered Aldo Moro, a politician. No one in our families wanted to believe that Renato was involved, but they all suspected that he was. One was certain of it and said so."

"Who was that?"

"My grandfather, Matteo. He told everyone who would listen that Renato pulled the trigger. When they rounded up the Brigades in 1980, Renato was among them. Nonno Matteo took that as proof that Renato was a murderer."

"That's so sad."

"Yeah. It was hardest on my mom and dad. Nonno Matteo forbid Dad to see my mom. That's why they left Italy." Matt poured another *grappa*. "Here's the point of the story. You saw how the Bugatti family—Dad's family— welcomed Mom back to their home. The old grudges are no match for the family bond. The last time I was here, more than ten years ago, I could still feel the tension. But now..." Matt paused as a peal of laughter echoed in the dining hall, followed by a joyful stream of the Italian language. "All is forgiven. This isn't a homecoming—it's a reconciliation."

Ronni looked to the side, avoiding Matt's eyes. "Do you think that there are some things so terrible that they can't be forgiven?"

"I suppose," Matt shrugged. "It's a low bar for some families. I'm amazed that brothers and sisters, or parents and children, can turn enemies over the tiniest little things. It would never occur to me to sacrifice a blood bond for pride."

"Does that make them bad families?"

"They're different. I try to understand behavior in terms other than *good* and *bad*."

"But aren't there acts that even a good family—I mean a *loving* family—might not be able to forgive?"

"For my family, it would have to be something horrible."

"What if you killed someone?"

"You're talking about Uncle Renato."

"Not necessarily."

Matt could see a tear rolling down Ronni's cheek. "Ronni, what is it?"

Ronni pulled a tissue from her handbag. She dabbed her eyes. "I guess my family's not in the same league as yours."

"Ronni..."

"My father and I haven't spoken in years."

"Because of something you did?"

"Yes."

"What could be that bad? It's not as if *you* killed someone."

"But I did."

"Did what?"

Her voice caught. "I killed my baby."

"Oh, Ronni."

Ronni looked down, wiping a tear from her cheek. Then she looked directly into Matt's eyes. "I was a seventeen-year-old girl who made a bad choice. Then I made it worse with another bad choice. I wasn't some poor girl who got pregnant from rape or incest. It was my own stupid behavior that got me in trouble. And I ended my baby's life because I didn't want the…*inconvenience* of raising a child. Oh hell, I didn't…" She turned away. "I didn't even want the inconvenience of being pregnant." She pulled a tissue from her bag and dabbed her nose. "My mom is still polite to me. My dad will never forgive me. So, is that something your family could forgive?"

Matt placed his hand on Ronni's. "I don't know. But they should."

☦ ☦ ☦

Matt walked Ronni to her room. She kissed his cheek; he gave her a comforting hug before leaving her.

Matt sat on the bed in his room, staring at the floor. *I forgive you,* he thought. *You didn't wrong me, but I forgive you, because you need forgiveness.* Twice he went to the door, intending to go to her, to hold her again, to comfort her, to forgive her. Twice he stopped short and went back and sat on the bed. He imagined Ronni in his arms, holding her, whispering in her ear, *forgive yourself, Ronni, and be forgiven. I don't judge you. Don't judge yourself.*

Matt sighed and began unbuttoning his shirt. He'd undone two buttons when there was a knock at the door. Matt hastily re-buttoned his shirt and covered the distance to the door in two steps. He swung it open.

Pierangelo looked scared and uncertain. The man behind him, wearing the uniform of the *polizia giudiziaria*, did not.

"Matteo, the police wish to talk with you," Pierangelo said. "There has been a murder."

38

PRECAUTION

As ONE OF the last people to see Lamberto Magnani alive, Clara was of particular interest to the Italian police—not a suspect, of course—the police inspector who questioned her had assured her of that—but useful in reconstructing the timeline leading up to the crime. The inspector said that he considered the interview to be of little value, and Clara agreed—she left the station and returned to her hotel determined to scoop the police.

It took five minutes for Clara to convey the concept of a *bourbon and ginger ale* to the bartender in the lounge of the *Internazionale* Hotel in Bologna. Once she succeeded, he kept them coming as Clara hammered one search term after another into her laptop. After an hour and three bourbon and gingers, she was familiar with nearly every publicly known fact about Dr. Magnani.

Lamberto was universally admired. He engendered no controversy. The man was the unlikeliest of murder victims.

Brother Dario might know more.

Clara checked the time: just past ten in the evening—too late for a visit to the hermitage. As she drained the watery remains of her drink, she touched the power button of her computer, but she didn't press it. She had a familiar feeling—a hunch. She typed another search term.

Cameron Stroud.

Clara wasn't sure what she was looking for until she found it. She'd seen it before but had failed to make the connection—a line in Cameron's biography:

Dr. Cameron Stroud, MD, PhD, Vanderbilt University.

Clara checked her watch. *Ten-thirty p.m. in Italy, late afternoon in Nashville, Tennessee.* Clara placed a call.

"Professor Tate, it's Clara Kildee calling again."

"Yes, ma'am. Still searching for clues?"

"I think I may have found one. That paper we discussed—do you remember if a man named Cameron Stroud was involved in that research?"

Clara heard a sound like a disgusted groan.

"That asshole—pardon my language, ma'am. Yeah, Stroud was a PhD candidate at the time. He wasn't *officially* part of *that* research but he stuck his nose in everything. *Everything.* The boy couldn't stand being left out. He just had to be the smartest guy in every room. What a piece of work."

"Then he was familiar with this research? About the genetic link to thrombocytopenia?"

"More than familiar. He knew it better than I did. Like I said, smartest guy in the room. That's what was so hard to take—he was actually as smart as he thought he was."

"I can see how some might find that annoying."

"Annoying? Hell, this whole place is filled with smart guys with giant egos. They're all *annoying.* Stroud's different."

"Different how?"

"He's a fuckin' psycho—pardon my language, ma'am."

Clara didn't respond. She was distracted by the sight of Cameron Stroud conversing with the hotel clerk, visible through the lounge entrance. The clerk nodded and gestured in Clara's direction.

"I'll have to call you back, Professor."

Cameron thanked the clerk and walked into the lounge.

Except for the bartender and a man in the corner nursing a glass of wine, the lounge was deserted.

✝ ✝ ✝

Matt declined Inspector Costa's offer of another cup of coffee—he'd already had two cups in the hour and a half since arriving at the station. During that time he'd been questioned only briefly, giving an account of his whereabouts since the previous night, with particular attention given to the time that he was with Lamberto Magnani. No one had yet explained the reason for the interview, but Matt suspected.

"Has something happened to Dr. Magnani?"

Inspector Costa looked down briefly, then nodded.

"*Sì*," Costa answered, "Lamberto was killed at his home this evening. We received a call about a noise, like a gunshot. We sent an agent to investigate. His third stop was Lamberto's house." The inspector wiped his eye.

"You knew Dr. Magnani?"

"For more than ten years."

"Who would want to kill him?"

"No one. We know of no motive. There was nothing taken. So far as we know, nothing was even touched."

"How…" Matt began, unsure how to ask the question.

"Shot to death," Costa answered. "The officer described the scene. I am glad I was not there to see it. Shotgun." Costa swallowed hard. "To the face."

"Oh, no. I'm sorry, Inspector."

"*Grazie.*" He poured another cup of coffee. He held out the carafe to Matt. Matt held up his hand.

"Of course," Costa said, setting down the carafe. "There is no reason you should not sleep. Me?" He sipped his coffee. "I will be very late tonight."

"I only met Dr. Magnani a few days ago, but I liked him very much."

Costa nodded, stifling a yawn. "Your cousin, Pierangelo—he owns a shotgun, correct?"

"He does."

"It was a gift from you, wasn't it?"

"Yes, for his hospitality."

"And you have used the gun since you have been in Italy?"

"I borrowed it to shoot trap. That was yesterday. I returned the gun to Pierangelo this morning. He can tell you."

Costa waved a hand. "Don't worry, Dr. Bugatti. I know Pierangelo. I trust him. I know where he locks up his guns. I'm quite certain they were secure at the time of the killing. And he vouches for you, Doctor. No, you are not suspected. We only want to reconstruct events. Which brings me to your trap shooting partner."

"My partner?"

"You did shoot with someone else, isn't that right? But of course, if you were alone, then that is my mistake." Costa sipped again. "We will go to the range tomorrow in any case. *I Cieli Aperti*—that is where you were, correct?"

"Yes. Dr. Stroud made the arrangements."

"Dr. Cameron Stroud. Do you know him well?"

"No, in fact, yesterday was the first time we'd spent any time together. Surely you don't suspect Dr. Stroud."

"Oh, no. As I said, we merely want to reconstruct events. Dr. Stroud is visiting the foundation. He is working—he *worked*—closely with Lamberto. And he also brought his shotgun with him to Italy. But that's not why we want to interview him. I'm sure he can tell us much about the hours before Lamberto's murder. As soon as we are able to locate him."

‡ ‡ ‡

Matt was met outside the police station by Pierangelo, who'd waited in his car for the two hours that Matt was inside. Pierangelo took Matt's hand and squeezed it.

"You are not in any trouble?" Pierangelo asked.

"No. Why would I be? I'm not a suspect."

"Matteo, you are dealing with the *Italian police*. They suspect *everyone*."

Matt and Pierangelo were silent during the drive home, as Matt replayed the conversation with Costa in his mind.

Nothing taken, nothing touched. No motive.

Shotgun. No ballistics.

Matt recalled his shooting match with Cameron.

I was speaking with Dr. Magnani. He also suspects a genetic link.

Of course he does. He's a geneticist. Everything is genetic to Dr. Magnani.

Matt stared out the window. *It's nothing.*

Matt and Pierangelo arrived at the villa. They left the car and approached the door.

"Dr. Bugatti."

It was a woman's voice but the source was unseen.

"Who is it?"

A woman with short, gray hair appeared. "I'm Clara Kildee. I don't think we've spoken before."

"Not privately. You're a correspondent, aren't you? Associated Press?"

"Yes. We need to talk. Alone, please."

"Pierangelo doesn't speak English."

"That doesn't matter. It's not safe to be seen with us."

Matt told a bewildered Pierangelo to wait inside.

"What's this about?"

Clara motioned for Matt to step out of the light. "How well do you know Cameron Stroud?" she whispered.

"Not well at all. I've researched his background, and we've spent some time together."

"I've talked with someone who knows him very well, a former professor of his at Vanderbilt."

"Where he got his M.D."

"And his PhD. The man I talked to told me that Stroud is brilliant, but unstable. And he has a mean streak."

"He seemed okay to me. A little arrogant, maybe. Why is this important?"

"I think he may have killed Dr. Magnani."

"*What?* Why would you think that? Because a former teacher told you he has a bad disposition? And anyway, what would Stroud have against Dr. Magnani?"

Clara told Matt about the paper she'd discovered, her conversation with Lamberto, his intention to discuss it with Cameron, and Cameron's appearance at her hotel.

"He knows what killed those girls," Clara said, "and he's trying to keep it quiet. We've got to take this to the police."

"Come with me."

Clara followed Matt into the villa and to the kitchen, where they found Pierangelo and Stefania.

"*Pierangelo, lei é Clara,*" Matt told them. "This is Clara. She needs a place to spend the night."

Pierangelo nodded. Matt turned to Clara. "Pierangelo and Stefania will take care of you for now. We'll find something more permanent tomorrow. Somewhere you can't be found."

"The police—they have to be told."

"Not yet. I need to get to Stroud first."

"But *why?* The man is dangerous."

Matt sat at the table. "Even if your suspicions are true, it's not reason enough to kill a man."

"Then why are you hiding me?"

"It's just a precaution."

Clara dropped into the chair opposite Matt. "Why take chances? Tell the police and let them sort it out."

"No. Not yet."

Not until I know for sure. Not as long as there's a chance for Mom —a chance for me.

39

Tisha B'av

It was a familiar sight: a delivery truck with the words *Daily Bread* in colorful script on its sides, pulling up to the gated entrance of the home of Darryl Meeks. The driver pressed a button on the intercom and spoke a few words. The gate slid open and the truck entered.

The FBI agent had positioned himself such that the front door was visible through a small gap in the foliage, which otherwise blocked any view from outside the wrought-iron fence. With the use of a high-powered spotting scope, the agent was able to observe all activity at the main entrance. Though similar vantage points weren't available for the other doors to the sprawling home, the FBI agent was satisfied that anyone entering or leaving the premises would be detected by high-res cameras mounted in strategic locations.

Over a period of months, the only vehicles to enter or leave the grounds were delivery trucks: UPS deliveries were common, bottled water occasionally, and the twice-weekly deliveries of food and supplies from *Daily Bread*, always on Mondays and Thursdays, always at nine a.m.

The agent squinted into the eyepiece. *Delivery man, average build, green uniform, baseball cap. Met at door, subject not visible. Returned to truck. Retrieved first load of supplies, entered home.*

It was the same routine he'd observed every Monday and Thursday morning for the last fourteen weeks.

‡ ‡ ‡

Darryl opened his door to the delivery man. Darryl was wearing a green *Daily Bread* uniform and a baseball cap matching the delivery man's. From a distance, the two of them were indistinguishable. "How many loads today, Austen?"

"Four today, Brother Meeks."

"You know where to put them."

"Yes, sir. Where are you off to this week?"

"Austen, you know the rules. No questions."

"Apologies, Brother Meeks."

Darryl watched Austen cart three more loads into the house. After the fourth load Austen removed his cap and tossed it on a table in the entryway.

"I'll thank you not to leave your clothing laying around on the furniture," Darryl said. "Guest room, kitchen, bathroom and media room only."

"Yes, Brother Meeks. Sorry about the cap. Will you be back on Thursday?"

"Yes, Austen, just like always."

Darryl wheeled the cart back to the truck. The FBI agent observed him through the hole in the foliage.

Delivery man returned to truck after fourth trip. Left premises without further contact.

‡ ‡ ‡

"The Lord has revealed the day," Darryl said to Marlin Castor. "Tisha B'Av, the ninth day of the month of Av. Six weeks from this Thursday."

194

Whatever, Marlin thought. He sat in Darryl's rented car in a the parking lot of a strip mall.

"Our preparations must be complete at least four weeks in advance—two weeks from now."

"I have thirty-six done. It'll be tight, but two weeks should be just enough time to complete the last four."

"The last twelve."

"What's that mean, *the last twelve?* I have thirty-six. You need forty. That's four more."

"The arrangements have been difficult. Some of our soldiers have died. We need a reserve force."

"I'll have a hell of a time just getting *four* more. *Twelve* more? You'd better pray on that."

"I intend to. But I know you are not a praying man. I have *your* incentive here." Darryl pulled a bundle of bills from the glove box.

"It's not a matter of money," Marlin said. "It's lead time."

Darryl gave Marlin a look that Marlin had come to know well—*has not God provided? Will he not yet provide?*

"No promises," Marlin said as he picked up the bundle. "Anything else?"

"The backup plan."

Marlin reached into a backpack. He pulled out a package, wrapped in tape, containing forty capsules.

"Concentrated rat poison, conveniently packaged in individual doses. Take one and you'll feel the effects in less than an hour. In two hours you'll be dead."

"How many?"

"Forty."

"I need eight more."

"Impossible."

Darryl gave Marlin the Look.

"Here's what I suggest," Marlin said. "Disassemble the capsules and distribute the stuff among forty-eight doses. But wear gloves. And a dust mask."

Darryl put the package in the glove box. He pulled out another bundle. "Eight more."

Marlin picked up the bundle. "No promises."

"Six weeks from this Thursday. All preparations must be complete in *two* weeks—no later."

‡ ‡ ‡

The plane touched down at DeKalb-Peachtree airport, a small, general-aviation airport employing relatively few security measures—ideal for the private traveler who wished to avoid confrontation with the authorities. It was the only airport that Darryl Meeks flew into when traveling to Atlanta.

Darryl took the keys from the attendant and climbed into the car as the attendant loaded Darryl's bags into the trunk— bags that contained Darryl's wardrobe for the three-day trip, as well as twelve explosive belts and forty doses of concentrated brodifacoum.

‡ ‡ ‡

Donald Lominger admitted Darryl to his home as if he were welcoming a visiting dignitary.

"Brother Meeks! He is risen!"

"Truly he has, Brother Lominger."

"When is the day of battle?"

"The Lord has revealed it. Six weeks from Thursday. Are you prepared?"

"Three soldiers stand ready. But..."

"What is it, Brother Lominger?"

"One of our soldiers is nearing the end. In four weeks she'll be in too much pain to carry out her mission. In six weeks she may be with our Lord."

"I've made provisions. If we have a few casualties, we can still succeed. But keep recruiting. We're counting on you for three soldiers. I have their orders." Darryl handed Donald a handwritten sheet. "Savannah, Georgia. Columbia, South Carolina. Tuscaloosa, Alabama. You must make the arrangements. Memorize the list and destroy it."

Donald looked over the sheet. "This will be hard. Georgia's laws are lax. We can make an appointment with no waiting period. Alabama and South Carolina have waiting periods, I think. I may need hotel rooms for our soldiers."

"Make whatever arrangements necessary. But we must destroy these targets." Darryl handed Donald a small package. "Each soldier must swallow one of these capsules a half-hour before her appointment. They mustn't wait more than an hour after taking the capsule before detonating the belt. Do you understand?"

"I think so. Yes. I understand."

Darryl stood and put his hand on Donald's shoulder. "We'll talk again before the day of battle. Until then, we have much to do. Let us pray."

Donald knelt on the floor; Darryl stood over him, his face raised to heaven.

"Lord, bless this man, Your soldier, and those whom he leads into battle. Give them courage, Lord, in view of Your mercy, to offer their bodies as living sacrifices, holy and pleasing to You—this is their spiritual act of worship according to Your good and perfect will."

✞ ✞ ✞

Ronni's phone buzzed. She checked the display and answered immediately.

"Yes, Senator."

"Where do we stand?" Yolanda asked.

"Dr. Bugatti hasn't yet signed off on the report."

"What's his position?"

"Matt just wants to understand the causes and to keep it from ever happening again. He's not satisfied with the findings. They're incomplete. He won't sign off until he feels like he can explain the conclusions to the parents with a clear conscience."

There was a moment of silence. "Matt?"

"I meant Dr. Bugatti."

"Ronni, I realize that to achieve a positive outcome you'll need to establish a rapport with Dr. Bugatti. You're not in danger of developing a personal relationship, are you?"

"I know my responsibilities."

"Nothing good can come of it. You know that, Ronni. Bugatti doesn't share our moral values. He's not aligned with our cause. Personal involvement can only lead to conflict and disappointment."

"I'm a professional, Senator."

"Very well. I'm sure I can count on you to remain committed."

"You can."

"Good. When do you return?"

"My flight is in four days. I can reschedule if necessary."

"Do what you need to do. But don't stay too long. The date has been set—six weeks from Thursday."

40

IL PAPA

MATT AND TYLER sat in the *anticamera bassa,* the lower antechamber of the Papal Palace, Matt's mind wandering as Tyler repeated the protocol.

"The chambermaster will escort you to the small throne room where the pope will greet you."

Matt stared at the wall as Tyler spoke.

"You're not a Catholic anymore, are you?" Tyler asked.

"What?"

"You were raised Catholic, weren't you?"

"Yes. Sort of."

"Sort of?" Tyler repeated. "What's *that* mean?"

"We went to Mass on Christmas and Easter. When someone died we prayed a Rosary. They were more like social events than worship."

"Why did you renounce your faith?"

Matt turned to Tyler. "I didn't renounce anything. You can't renounce a faith you never had."

"Bugatti, don't you believe in *anything?*"

"Reason and decency."

Tyler's lips were pressed together in a straight line. "Right. As a non-Catholic, you won't kiss His Holiness's ring."

"Kiss his ring? Seriously?"

"I said you *won't* kiss the ring. You'll simply bow slightly at the waist and shake the pope's hand when he offers it. What's the matter with you? Are you listening?"

Matt's eyes remained briefly on Tyler before he turned back to the wall. "Yes, of course. Continue."

‡ ‡ ‡

Matt was at the funeral Mass for Lamberto Magnani when Tyler received word that the president had approved the papal audience. Tyler thought the matter important enough to tell Matt immediately. His driver took him from the villa to the hermitage and gave him directions to the church in gestures and halting English.

The tiny chapel of the hermitage was filled beyond capacity. Lamberto's family, numbering more than twenty siblings and cousins, occupied the front rows. The brothers of the Order of the Servants of Mary sat behind them, all of them present in the pews except for Alessandro, who said Mass, and his servers, Dario and another friar. The rest of the chapel was packed—the entire staff of the foundation and scores of friends and acquaintances attended. Matt stood in the rear of the church with dozens of mourners for whom there were no seats. Alessandro said the Mass in Latin, ending with the blessing of the body. The coffin was closed throughout the rite, as it had been during the vigil— Lamberto's disfigurement was beyond the skills of the funerary cosmetologist.

Tyler waited at the entrance as people exited the chapel. When Matt appeared, Tyler took him aside.

"Your audience with the pope is tomorrow at two p.m. You leave for Rome at nine."

"Is this really necessary?"

"It wasn't my idea, and it certainly wasn't the president's. Refusing a papal invitation would have been awkward. Senator Herrera and her gang would have played it up. We're in enough trouble with Catholic voters. The president had no choice."

"All right," Matt said with resignation. "Just tell me what I have to do."

"I'll brief you on protocol tonight, if you can tear yourself away from Ronni Barraket."

"I'll be ready."

Tyler turned away, and then stopped. "Was it a nice service?" he asked.

"It was comforting. Dr. Magnani was beloved by many."

‡ ‡ ‡

Matt stood back from the mourners surrounding the grave. As the casket was lowered, he felt a tap on his shoulder.

"Quite a gathering," said Cameron Stroud. "Almost more than the church could hold."

Matt eyed Cameron uncertainly for a moment. "Were you there? I didn't see you."

"I arrived late. I was off to one side."

Matt turned back toward the grave. Brother Alessandro spoke the final words as the mourners crossed themselves.

"Where have you been hiding?"

"Hiding?" Cameron said. "Hardly. Working, that's what I've been doing. When I'm not at my hotel, I'm at the foundation."

"Is that where you were when Dr. Magnani was killed?"

"Dr. Bugatti! You sound just like the Italian police!"

"They're looking for you, you know."

"They *were* looking for me, that's true. They found me. I spent a few hours in their gracious company last night. That was the first I'd heard about Dr. Magnani." Cameron shook his head. "What a shame."

"How did it end with the police?"

"Hard to say. My Italian is pretty good—not as good as yours, of course—but I may have missed some of the nuances of the interview. They did seem intensely interested in our little shooting match. We're their prime suspects."

"Apparently. I have an alibi at least."

"One more thing we have in common."

Matt turned toward Cameron.

"I was at the foundation all day," Cameron continued. "I didn't leave until after ten." Cameron looked at Matt's face. "You *are* just like the police. They were skeptical, too, until they verified the facts with the night attendant."

"They're satisfied?"

"Oh, of course. There's only one entrance to the foundation, with badge access. All the other exits are alarmed. The attendant saw me enter and he saw me leave, and the access records corroborate his testimony. Air tight. What's *your* alibi?"

"I was with my mother and Ronni Barraket."

"Very good. Barraket at least is credible."

Matt's head snapped in Cameron's direction. "My mom..."

"Dr. Bugatti, I simply meant that the police would *expect* your *mother* to be protective." Cameron turned toward the grave. "But in view of her dementia, she could hardly be considered a reliable witness."

The conversation in Dozza came to Matt's mind.

I know who you are, Giovanni. You're my cheating husband.

"How specific is your Alzheimer's treatment?" Matt asked.

"Specific? How do you mean?"

"There are a number of genetic mutations that are associated with Alzheimer's. I wonder which of them you're targeting. It's a gene therapy, isn't it?"

Cameron smiled slightly. "Indeed it is, Dr. Bugatti. We use a modified virus to deliver the corrective genes to the patient's cells."

"Which genes?"

"I know what you're asking—do we target the genes associated with the inherited form of the disease?"

"Yes."

"Well, familial Alzheimer's *is* relatively rare. It wouldn't be a high priority for a commercial drug."

"Is that a yes or a no?"

"Neither." Cameron smiled more broadly. "Actually, since the genetic link with familial Alzheimer's is well established, it made sense to verify the delivery mechanism on those genes. The effects would be the most easily detected, since the causal link is known. Those genes were the first ones we treated successfully."

Matt closed his eyes.

Chi sei? Do you think you know my business better than I do? Giovanni, who is this? Is she one of your girlfriends?

"How close are you to releasing the drug?"

Cameron shrugged. "We're still in trials We've observed some concerning side effects that require some more research. Five years, maybe—sooner, if I'm doing my job."

"Doing your job?"

"Researching the side effects. Oh, and getting through the approval process. It's my specialty. Without me, this drug might not make it to market for another fifteen years."

‡ ‡ ‡

Matt followed the directions that Brother Dario had given him after the funeral. They led him to the wine cellar of the hermitage, through a door in the rear, to a passageway beneath the cloister. Brother Dario, holding a kerosene lamp, met him in the darkened space, motioning for Matt to follow.

Dario led Matt through a maze of tunnels, barely high enough to clear their heads. Dario opened a door to a small room, containing a chair, a table and a bed. Hanging on the wall were a crucifix and a framed print depicting the assumption of the Blessed Mother. Sitting on the bed, looking cross, was Clara Kildee. She remained silent as Matt scanned the room.

"It doesn't look too uncomfortable," Matt said.

"Not if you're a nun," Clara said. "No offense, Brother Dario, but this is unacceptable. I don't expect a luxury suite, but you don't even have Wi-Fi down here."

"It's temporary," Matt said.

"Let's hope so, Dr. Bugatti. As long as I'm holed up here, you're on your own. God knows *I'm* not any help." Clara took a breath. "What have you found out? "

"Stroud has an alibi. He was at the foundation when Lamberto was killed."

"He told you that? And you believed him?"

"He said the police were satisfied, but I'll verify it. He's too smart to tell me something that can't be verified."

Clara's eyes stayed fixed on Matt's. "I have a bad feeling about that guy."

‡ ‡ ‡

Matt and Tyler followed the chambermaster through a series of rooms in the papal palace, to an impressively large hall, illuminated by the light from two gigantic windows. The decorations were simple, almost sparse. Opposite the windows, on a low platform, stood a large, plain chair, under a canopy decorated with the papal seal.

"Small throne room?" Matt whispered.

"Just throne room," Tyler whispered back. "The *small* throne room is up ahead. We wait here."

They were not alone. A few others waited quietly for their names to be called.

"*Dottor Bugatti, mi segua, per favore.*"

Matt and Tyler walked toward the guarded entrance where the chambermaster stood. He held up a hand.

"*Chiedo scusa, Sua Santità desidererebbe vedere solamente il Dottor Bugatti.*"

"He says it's just me from here on," Matt said.

Tyler stood aside. "Remember the protocol."

Matt followed the chambermaster through three more rooms before encountering the door to *la sala tronetto*, the small throne room. The chambermaster knocked and genuflected as the door opened.

"*Santità, il Dottor Bugatti dagli Stati Uniti.*"

The pope stood with his hands clasped, attended by two priests wearing the purple sash of a monsignor. He was taller than Matt expected, and surprisingly robust for a man in his seventies. His expression was kindly, another surprise, given the pontiff's reputation as a rigidly conservative defender of Catholic dogma.

The pope opened his hands as Matt stepped forward to greet him, with strict adherence to the protocol that Tyler had carefully explained.

The pope gestured again, dismissing his attendants. Matt was alone with the pope in the papal library.

"Dr. Bugatti, we're pleased to welcome you to the Vatican," the pope said, in a voice soft enough that Matt leaned forward to hear him.

"Thank you for allowing me to meet you, Your Holiness."

"We have followed with interest the proceedings of your commission. We are greatly concerned about the outcome."

"In what sense, Your Holiness?"

"Tell us, Dr. Bugatti, are you a respecter of life?"

"Yes, Your Holiness, I believe that I am."

"You are sincere, of that we are certain," the pope said, nodding. "And we have been told that your concern for the poor girls is also sincere, and that you are committed to finding the truth about their deaths."

"I am, Your Holiness."

"Yet you take no stand against the scourge of abortion."

"Your Holiness, respectfully, that issue is not before this commission."

"Oh, but it is. Sexual license, contraception, and abortion, what you grotesquely call *choice*, are three inseparable beliefs in a single creed, a creed which trivializes sexuality, which destroys the ideal of an exclusive relationship between husband and wife. The men and women who govern your country hold this false creed. They believe that life—God's most precious gift—is a commodity, with a price tag. They believe that so-called *freedom* can be purchased with the lives of the unborn. They cling to this false creed as firmly as we hold to the truth of scripture. That is why they so recklessly pushed this drug into the hands of these unfortunate girls. And now they are dead. Doctor, you must look beyond the facts. Motivation is also important in finding fault. If you don't hold these feckless bureaucrats accountable, you will send an unmistakable message to the world: In America, life is cheap." The pope clenched his fists. "The whole world looks to America to lead. You lead the world in culture and commerce and power. You cannot choose to lead in one arena and not in another. You must also be moral leaders. That is the burden which God has placed upon you for the many blessings He has bestowed."

"Your Holiness, you can be sure that if there is fault to be found, we will find it. But we are not a court. We can't hold anyone accountable. We find facts. And we do not concern ourselves with broader issues."

The pope shook his head as he stood. Matt walked beside the pope toward the door.

"Dr. Bugatti, you are a logical man. But logic and inquiry are devoid of morals. One must commit oneself to principle."

"The truth, Your Holiness. That is the principle to which I am committed."

"Ah. The truth. That's a fine sentiment. But I fear that for you, the truth is what you can prove. You are closed to the truth of God's word, and to the guidance of your own spirit. How limiting. How sterile."

"Your Holiness, I don't agree." Matt faced the pope, looking directly into the pontiff's eyes. "It's true, I reject the concept of a god. For this reason, you cannot call me a godly man. But if *spirit* is that which is unique in each of us, then I am a *spiritual* man. My values and my conscience are my guide. And it's also true that 'God's word' holds no authority for me. If there's truth in it, I'll discover it for myself. And if there's untruth in it, I'll discover that as well. To accept dogma..." Matt paused. He swallowed. "Your Holiness, respectfully, to accept dogma without thinking, *that* is sterile, *that* is limiting."

The pope opened the door to the chambermaster waiting outside.

"Dr. Bugatti, we pray for you. But since you do not believe in prayer, we have a more practical suggestion. We met with your Senator Herrera this week. You would do well to ask her advice. We found her to be a committed defender of life —a true soldier of Christ."

‡ ‡ ‡

Clara quickly consumed the few English-language books and newspapers that Dario had brought to her. She spent a few hours writing articles for which the deadlines had passed with no way to submit them. With all her entertainment options spent, she laid on the bed staring alternately at the ceiling, the crucifix, and the Blessed Mother.

If Stroud has an alibi, then I've got nothing to worry about. If he's lying, then I need to find that out.

Clara went to the door and opened it a crack, peeking out into the unlit corridor. She fetched the kerosene lamp and stepped out of the cell. The corridor curved out of sight in both directions, the pale orange light extending just a few yards.

To hell with this.

Clara headed to the right. The stone walls were interrupted occasionally by doors, all with the same heavy construction, all seemingly centuries old. She tried each one. Most were locked, or possibly frozen from disuse. She did manage to force one door open. Lamplight revealed a few sticks, the remains of furniture not unlike that in her own cell, but long abandoned. She came upon several flights of steps, each going down, leading her deeper into the earth. As she explored, one thought ran through her mind.

Where is *that god-damned wine cellar?*

The corridor took a sharp left turn. Clara could see another door directly in front of her. At first glance, it resembled all the others she'd seen and had tried to open. As she got closer, differences became apparent.

It seemed old, but not centuries old; heavy, but not quite as heavy. The door's surface was evenly worked, unlike the hand-hewn planks from which the others were built. It looked as if it had been made to resemble the other doors, but with modern tools and techniques.

Clara turned the iron handle and pushed. The door opened slightly before it encountered an obstacle. She pushed harder, opening the door slowly with a sound like a heavy object being pushed across the floor.

Clara stepped from the stone corridor into a medium-sized room containing a table and chairs, and a desk littered with papers and files. In the light of the lamp, Clara could make out a few other objects on the desk—a photo of two men whom she recognized as Lamberto and Brother Dario, and a nameplate, which read:

DR. LAMBERTO MAGNANI

"Hello, Clara."

Clara turned with a start as a man appeared from the shadows.

"Stroud," she whispered.

Cameron lifted his hand, holding a Chiappa compact nine-millimeter revolver.

"Old woman, you have made my life damned complicated."

41

MISSING

FOR THE DURATION of Matt's trip to Rome, Brother Dario was out of reach—the hermitage had one rarely attended telephone, and the brothers did not carry cell phones. Matt had no reason to think that Clara might be in danger—after all, only he and Dario knew her whereabouts—but the thought continued to nag his mind as he stared out the window of the airplane.

"I'll need a complete report of your conversation with the pope," Tyler said.

"I thought the conversation was confidential," Matt replied, still staring out the window.

"Yes, that's customary, but you are a representative of the United States government. You can be certain that the pope did not intend for you to be the final recipient of his message. The president must be briefed."

Matt repeated his conversation with the pope nearly verbatim.

"Unbelievable," Tyler said grimly. "It's bad enough that the pope is cocked to fire a salvo right at the president over the commission report, but you had to go and sass him. What were you thinking?"

"The pope spoke frankly. So did I."

Tyler gripped Matt's arm. "Dr. Bugatti, this is the *pope*. You do *not* accuse him of being narrow-minded, not to his face, not *ever*. He's the heir of Peter and God's representative on earth."

A flight attendant came down the aisle, stopping at Tyler's row. "Sir, I must ask you not to shout. You are disturbing the other passengers."

Tyler nodded as the flight attendant moved on.

"Settle down, Tyler. He's just a man."

"This man *speaks for God!*"

Matt studied Tyler's face. "Do you really believe that?"

Tyler looked straight ahead. "It doesn't matter if I believe it. A billion people believe it. Seventy-five million of them live in the United States, and some of them vote."

‡ ‡ ‡

The scene at the Bologna airport was bedlam. More than thirty correspondents shouted at Matt and Tyler as they exited the gate area, a line of police holding them at bay. Tyler walked to the front of the crowd and raised his arms.

"Dr. Bugatti met with His Holiness this afternoon for less than an hour. As you know, by tradition, their conversation is confidential. Not even the president of the United States will be told."

Tyler put his hand on Matt's shoulder, guiding him toward the exit as the shouting resumed. As they approached the door, two people moved toward them: Tyler's regular driver, and Pierangelo Bugatti.

"*Ciao cugino,*" Pierangelo said as he kissed Matt's cheeks. "*Siamo così orgogliosi di te.*"

"What's he saying?" Tyler asked.

"He says they're all very proud of me. Tyler, if you don't mind, I'd like to ride back with Pierangelo."

"Sure," Tyler sighed, "why not? But we've got to get closure on this report." He looked at his watch. "It's late.

We'll talk tomorrow. Eight o'clock in the dining hall, all right?"

"Eight o'clock."

Matt followed Pierangelo to his car in the parking garage. Matt reached for the handle on the front door.

"No," Pierangelo said, opening the rear door. Matt joined Ronni Barraket in the back seat.

"It's been awhile," Matt said. "Let me fill you in."

✝ ✝ ✝

Pierangelo pulled into the driveway of the villa and stopped at the front entrance. Ronni and Matt went directly to Ronni's room.

"Do *you* believe that Stroud could have done it?" Ronni asked.

"No," Matt said. "For one thing, he has an alibi. But Clara Kildee is convinced. Between the research that she discovered and what the Vanderbilt professor told her, she's certain that Stroud is a homicidal maniac."

"Incredible. But not so incredible that you didn't feel the need to keep Clara hidden."

"A precaution. The thing is, I'm not sure how to prove it one way or the other. Poor Clara is going to have to stay underground until I figure this out."

"Maybe I can help."

"How?"

"We have an excellent research department at Stivers and Cartwright. If anyone can get answers about Cameron Stroud, they can."

"Good. Make that happen. Meanwhile, I'd better look in on Clara."

Matt walked to the door, laying his hand on the doorknob, then turning back to Ronni. He thought of all that had happened since he'd last seen her: *interrogated by the Italian police, attended a funeral, sent Clara into hiding, faced down the pope.* Their last conversation, and Ronni's revelation, seemed a distant memory.

"Ronni, the other night…"

"Matt, I'm sorry to have burdened you with that. It wasn't fair."

"It's all right. I just wanted to say, you shouldn't be so hard on yourself."

Ronni shifted from one foot to the other. "I deal with it in my own way. In any case, what I think about it isn't important. Neither is what my family thinks. Only God can judge."

Matt looked at the floor for a moment. "Goodnight, Ronni."

As the door closed, Ronni took her cell phone from her bag and placed a call.

"Good afternoon, Senator."

"Hello Ronni. Where do we stand?"

"They've discovered the Vanderbilt paper."

There was a pause before Yolanda replied. "Who knows about it?"

"It was the AP reporter, Kildee, who found it. She told Magnani just before he was killed. And she told Matt—Dr. Bugatti."

"We thought that this might come out eventually. We just need to adjust our timetable. Kildee has been useful up to this point. She still can be. Where is she now?"

"Dr. Bugatti has her hidden. He wouldn't tell me where."

"Indeed. Why would he hide her?"

"Kildee thinks that Stroud murdered Magnani."

"Interesting. And Bugatti? What does he think?"

"He's not sure."

"Very well. Offer to help them with their investigation. You must appear to be cooperative. But be cautious with the information you share."

"Already in progress, Senator."

‡ ‡ ‡

It was early evening when Matt arrived at the hermitage. He reached Dario's cell, finding the door open, Dario and

Alessandro inside. Alessandro's expression was disapproving—Dario looked scared.

"*Perdonami, cugino*," Dario said. "Forgive me. I had no choice but to tell Brother Alessandro."

"Dario, why?"

"Clara is no longer in her room. We cannot find her."

42

REVELATION

AGENT SESSIONS PAGED through his notes as the Charlotte contingent of the Clinic Bombing Task Force filed into the conference room. There were twenty agents in the room; another forty attended via a secure web conference. A map of the United States was projected onto the screen, with tiny portraits scattered across every region of the country. Dotted lines showing the connections among them formed a dense web resembling a map of airline routes. The portraits were too small to be recognizable, with one exception: In South Carolina the face of Darryl Meeks stared out with piercing eyes. Dozens of lines converged on Darryl's picture—a major hub in a network of fanatics.

"Per our briefing yesterday, we have reason to believe that something big is in the works," Agent Sessions began. "We've made no more progress on identifying the locations of the planned bombings, but we suspect that there may be as many as thirty targets—and we think that number will continue to grow."

Agent Sessions clicked a small photo located in the middle of Georgia, expanding it to a portrait of a man with a pudgy face with pinched features and a crew cut. "Donald

Lominger works as a health benefits counselor. He also has ties to various religious groups, all legitimate, and, we believe, to *Heaven Sent*, although we haven't been able to establish that connection unequivocally. We suspect him of having recruited the Atlanta clinic bomber, Lucy Seidman. Our working assumption is that Lominger is the southeast coordinator in this conspiracy."

Sessions continued, clicking one portrait after another, providing the background of each one.

"But the most significant development since yesterday is this: we've identified, with a high degree of confidence, the source of the phone calls to Meeks from Washington, D.C." Sessions clicked the icon hovering over Washington. A photo appeared, an indistinct frame from a surveillance camera, but the person was recognizable.

"Who is that?" one agent asked.

Sessions clicked again. A complete dossier appeared, including photos of the suspect's associates.

"Holy shit," the agent said. "Is that who I think it is?"

"Yes," Sessions confirmed, "and the president has been briefed. Our D.C. agents are on it. The rest of you have your assignments. Questions?"

There were no questions.

"Dismissed," Agent Sessions said. "Oh, one more thing. Agent Hastings will conduct the briefings next week. I'll be in Italy."

✝ ✝ ✝

The two cars were in open country, miles from the nearest highway. It was just after daybreak and still cool, though the temperature in the Arizona desert would top a hundred before noon. Marlin Castor loaded the last bundle into the trunk of Darryl Meeks's car as Darryl stood by.

"Eight belts. That's the last of them." Marlin pulled a small package from his jacket pocket, tightly wrapped with several layers of packing tape, and handed it to Darryl. "The rest of your rat poison—your backup plan."

Darryl held the package in his hand, staring at it for a minute before laying it carefully in the trunk. He closed the lid and placed both hands on the car as he bowed his head.

"The army of Christ is whole. The day of His judgment is near. Blessed be His holy name."

"Do you have something for me, Mr. Meeks?"

Darryl opened the door of his car and motioned with his head toward the back. Marlin took a leather bag from the seat and pawed through the contents long enough to verify that it contained the agreed-upon one and a half million dollars.

"It's all here," Marlin said. "That concludes our business."

Marlin turned and walked away.

"Mr. Castor, I have a question."

Marlin stopped and looked back at Darryl with raised eyebrows.

"Do you know what these are for?" Darryl asked.

"None of my business."

"But do you know?"

"Yeah, I know."

"What do you think about it?"

"Meeks, you contracted with me to provide certain merchandise. I delivered and you paid. I'm not to blame for what happens next." Marlin turned away.

"Mr. Castor, we are in a holy war," Darryl shouted. "The armies of God and Satan will do battle for a great cause. Christ has anointed me as his general. Which side are you on?"

"It's your cause, not mine." Marlin hefted the bag. "*This* is *my* cause."

"*He who is not with me is against me*. You can't sit this out, Mr. Castor. You're a part of it. And I don't accept that you did it just for money, knowing what it was for."

Marlin walked back to Darryl. He set the bag on the ground and lit up a cigarette.

"I spent eight years in the Army. Four tours in fucking…"

"Mr. Castor, I'll thank you not…"

"...in *fucking* Afghanistan. That's where I learned demolition and munitions. I was the best. Whenever there was a critical mission, they called for Castor. Behind enemy lines, under fire—the more dangerous the better. I was the go-to guy. I never missed—*never*. Do you know why? Because I mastered my craft. *I* did. The Army didn't teach me, I taught *myself*. Army training is for shit." He took a drag on his cigarette. "For eight years I took orders from idiots with more education and less brains than me—cocksuckers who couldn't tell C4 from silly putty, Army brass who sat safe in their green zones, picking targets like they were picking out a tie. Then Castor blew 'em up. Bad targets, collateral damage, non-combatant casualties—those fuck-ups are on the officer pricks who pushed the button, not me. Got that? It's *not on me*." Marlin dropped his cigarette and crushed it. "Eight years of putting my ass on the line and what did I get for it? Army pay and a general discharge." He picked up the bag. "See? It *is* just for the money."

"You have no faith and no cause, Mr. Castor. I pity you."

"Spare me, you freak." Marlin took a step away but stopped and turned back. "I have a question for *you*. What makes you think you'll get away with this?" He held up the bag. "I'm set for life. I can disappear. Not you. You're too high-profile. And have you thought about your co-conspirators? Every one of them is a security risk."

"I am God's soldier and a servant to His will. I follow the path that He has revealed. My fellow soldiers share my bond."

"Someone will talk."

"We would suffer martyrdom rather than betray the Lord. They won't talk, and neither will I."

"Yes they will. You're crazy if you think otherwise."

Darryl clenched a fist. "What did you say?"

"I said you're crazy, you're nuts, you're fucking insane."

Darryl walked to the car, opening the door, reaching under the seat for a .38 caliber revolver. He leveled it at Marlin.

The first shot lodged in Marlin's chest, sending him to the ground. The dust cloud settled as Darryl approached Marlin and stood over him.

Marlin chuckled as he closed his eyes. Darryl fired two more shots, the last one into Marlin's head at close range. He picked up the bag and tossed it into the car, taking one last look at Marlin as his blood soaked into the parched ground.

He hath defied the armies of the living God.

43

EVIDENCE

MATT SCANNED THE tiny room from where he sat on the corner of the cot. All of Clara's belongings were still there with one important exception: Her laptop was missing from its spot on the desk.

"Where could she have gone?" Matt asked Dario and Alessandro. "We're miles from anywhere. Clara doesn't have a car. I suppose she could have walked to the foundation to find an Internet connection. But you said that no one at the foundation had seen her, isn't that right?"

"*Cugino*," Dario said, "we asked at the foundation and at the homes along the road. No one has seen her."

"She might have hitched a ride into town. She was determined to submit her articles. I'll go into Bologna and see if she's at her hotel." Matt stood up. "I'm sure she's fine. After all, the only way in or out is through the wine cellar."

"Dario," Alessandro said, frowning, "you must tell Dr. Bugatti."

"Tell me what?"

"*Cugino*," Dario said, "there is another way."

‡ ‡ ‡

Matt followed Dario through the labyrinth of tunnels, down flights of stairs, to the end of the passage. They stood in front of a massive wooden door.

"It was a secret known only to the brothers and to Lamberto," Dario explained. "It opens to Lamberto's office. Sometimes, during the day, Lamberto would leave his office to visit the cloister. Often I would meet him for a glass of *pignoletto* in the cellar."

"Why is it here?"

"The foundation building is set into the hillside. The plans were drawn to avoid the ancient passages, but they were very close. Lamberto decided to create this doorway. It was his secret escape."

Matt turned the handle and pushed the door open. There was no alarm. The hallway lights dimly illuminated the office through the open door.

"It looks normal," Dario said. "Everything in place."

"What about this?" Matt asked, bending down to pick up a scrap of paper. He walked to the door of the office and examined it in the light.

"What is it?"

"It's a bar receipt, from the *Internazionale* Hotel. Clara's hotel."

"She was here."

"Yes, she was. And I doubt she dropped this by accident."

‡ ‡ ‡

Tyler sat alone at a table stacked with folders in the villa dining hall, each folder containing a transcript of testimony from the commission hearings. Tyler checked his watch frequently. It was already past nine.

Tyler reached for the folders, intending to take them to his room before mounting a search for Matt Bugatti. He'd put half of them into a briefcase and was going for the rest when a man in a black suede jacket approached.

"You are Signor Ross, no?"

"I am."

The man showed an ID card. "I am Inspector Costa, Criminal Investigation. May I sit?"

"Of course. What is this about?"

"In truth, I am seeking Dr. Bugatti," Costa said as he sat. "We have more questions for him regarding the death of Lamberto Magnani. But he is not in his room. Pierangelo suggested that you might know where I can find him."

Tyler stuffed the remainder of the files into his briefcase. "No, I don't know where he is, and if *you* find him you can remind him that we were to meet at eight. Tell him that he's late."

"I will do so," Costa said. "And I hope also that you will tell him to find me if you see him before I do."

"It's a deal." Tyler stood. "Anything else?"

"I think not. Unless you might know where I can find Clara Kildee."

"Kildee? The reporter?"

"Yes. We wish also to question her further. But she has not returned to her hotel in two days."

"I have no idea where she is."

"Pity. No one knows. Not you, not Dr. Stroud."

"Stroud? Why would he know?"

"Well, he wouldn't, really. I suppose I am, what do you say, grabbing for the straws? But I sense that he is knowing something that he is not telling. He is a strange one, do you think?"

"I haven't formed an opinion." Tyler picked up the briefcase and set it on the table. "Oh, look. There's our man," he said as Matt approached the table.

"Hello, Tyler. *Buongiorno,* Inspector."

"*Buongiorno a Lei.* Do you have time to talk, Dr. Bugatti?"

"Of course. Can we talk here?"

"Dr. Bugatti," Tyler interrupted, "we have a report to publish, and you're late for our meeting."

Matt held up a hand. "I know, Tyler. I'm sorry. Inspector, will this take long?"

"Not long, I think. We just need for you to confirm some details. We are still trying to reconstruct events. If you like, you can come to my office later." Costa stood. "Oh, and we need also to talk to Clara Kildee. Have you seen her lately?"

"No."

"Very well. My office, then? Shall we say eleven?"

"Can we make it two this afternoon?"

"Until two. Then that will leave only Signora Kildee. We have already talked with Dr. Stroud."

"You talked to Stroud?"

"Yes, late yesterday afternoon. I must confess, I had misgivings about Dr. Stroud, but of course his alibi is very good. There is no way in or out of the foundation where he would not be detected."

Costa watched Matt's face as he turned aside.

"Is Dr. Stroud at his hotel? I need to talk to him."

"Yes, we talked at the hotel. But you had better to be quick if you wish to see him. He has finished his business in Italy. He plans to return to America soon. It would be better if he stayed, but we have no cause to keep him here. Dr. Bugatti, we will speak later."

As Costa left, Tyler opened his briefcase and pulled out a file.

"Dr. Bugatti, you can't put this off any longer. You need to finalize the report." Tyler handed Matt a sheet. "I think I know where your head is. I've drafted a new conclusion. If you agree, I'll circulate it to the commission for comment."

Matt read the page. "The president won't like this. At least half of the commissioners will reject it."

"You have the power to overrule the commissioners. I'll handle the president. We both know this is the right conclusion."

"This says that the FDA and CG Pharma were jointly negligent. It makes them directly responsible for one death and indirectly responsible for the other forty-eight."

"Correct."

"But we don't *know* that."

Tyler grabbed the sheet and jammed it into the briefcase. "Stop vacillating, Doctor. Is there *anything* in this world that meets your standard of mathematical certainty? Honestly, how do you function? How do you accomplish anything if everything has to be rigorously derived from first principles?"

"Don't exaggerate, Tyler. I don't need proof of everything, just the things that matter."

"The report, Doctor?"

Matt's shoulders fell. "Send it around. See what they say. But remember, I still have final approval."

Tyler closed the briefcase. "At last."

Matt watched Tyler leave. He checked his watch.

I've got to see how Mom's doing.

Then Stroud.

Then the police.

44

BRIGHT EYES

ENRICO STOPPED SWEEPING the steps as he greeted the American.

"*Buongiorno, Signor Nelson.*"

"*Buongiorno, Enrico, che bella giornata!*" the American answered. "What a beautiful day!"

"*Sì! Proprio una bella giornata!*" Enrico went back to sweeping.

The American climbed the stairs of the tenement, an old building in a poorer quarter of Bologna. It showed its age, despite Enrico's attentions. The American had been an intermittent tenant for years. He liked it there, not for its amenities, of which there were few, but for its sameness. It was indistinguishable from a dozen other buildings in the district, and from hundreds more in other poor quarters.

The American entered his third-floor apartment, locking the door behind him. It was a simple place, with a tiny bathroom, one small room that served as both the living area and the kitchen, and two small bedrooms. One bedroom was furnished with a chair, a metal gurney, and a nightstand littered with syringes and bottles containing assorted drugs.

On the gurney, unconscious and attached to an IV bag, lay Clara Kildee.

Cameron replaced the IV bag, then checked Clara's pulse and blood pressure. He lifted Clara's eyelids to examine her pupils. Satisfied that Clara could tolerate the dose, he filled a syringe from one of the bottles and injected the drug into the IV line.

Cameron sat on the chair as Clara came to.

"Rise and shine, bright eyes."

Clara's eyelids fluttered open. She tried instinctively to reach for the feeding tube in her nose, but her hands were restrained.

"Did you sleep well? Oh. Not feeling too talkative this morning, are we? Clara, really, that face! You'll hurt my feelings with a look like that. And after all I've done to make you comfortable. A little appreciation isn't too much to ask, is it?"

Clara's hand curled into a fist with one finger extended.

"Bitch." Cameron filled another syringe. "This ought to improve your pissy mood." He injected the IV.

The discomfort from the tube chafing Clara's nose and from the restraints digging into her wrists subsided. She felt a warmth between her eyes as the jumble of thoughts that crowded her mind ran together, slowed, and ceased. From an unbounded black expanse she became aware of a voice booming in her head. Had she been capable of thought, she might have wondered if it was the voice of God.

"Who did you tell, Clara?"

"Tell what?" Clara responded, machine-like.

"Who did you tell about the Vanderbilt research? You told Dr. Magnani. You also told Dr. Bugatti, didn't you?"

"Yes."

"Who else?"

"No one."

"Very good, Clara. I believe you. But Dr. Bugatti told others, didn't he? Who did he tell?"

"He might have told his cousin Dario."

"The good friar. I wonder, did Dario tell anyone?"

"I don't know. Dario knows about me, but Matt swore him to secrecy."

"That's reassuring. I'm sure Brother Dario is discreet. Who else?"

"No one."

"Now, Clara, that's not true. Dr. Bugatti told Miss Barraket."

"I don't know."

"Of course you don't know, but *I* know. Dr. Bugatti, the *famous* Dr. Bugatti, the brilliant, the wealthy, the handsome Dr. Bugatti, the celebrated genius, for all his gifts still suffers from the same weakness that afflicts all ordinary men, from the stone age, knuckle-dragging troglodyte to the twenty-first century, Fields-medal-winning mathematician: No matter how big their brains grow, they are still ruled by their cocks. Thank God I've been spared that curse.

"He told her. *Ronni.* Beautiful, big-eyed, big-titted Ronni, his confidant, his imagined lover. He told her without even thinking. He'd tell her anything, he'd do anything, just on the chance he'll get into her pussy. That's something *you* know about, Clara. The power of the pussy. You know how to use it, like a lure on a line, like a knife on a dark street. You all do, you and Ronni and all the other little whores sucking and fucking those slobbering, mindless slaves to their penises. Ronni and Clara. Young whore, old whore. You're all the same." Cameron filled a syringe. "The only difference between you and Ronni Barraket is forty years."

He injected the IV. Clara slipped into unconsciousness.

"Night-night, bright eyes."

45

SUSPECT

FIRST TRIP TO Italy—not how I imagined.

Agent Sessions looked down from thirty-six thousand feet on the snow-covered peaks of the Alps. He didn't mind flying economy class from Munich to Bologna, but the overnight trip in coach from Washington had soured his mood. He'd always wanted to visit Italy but the thought of living on a government *per diem* during the stay, not to mention spending the entire time hunting for a fanatical terrorist did nothing to cheer him up. He turned from the window, drained the last of his diet Coke, and sighed.

‡ ‡ ‡

Sessions left baggage claim and looked over the crowd, spotting two men standing together, one in a stylish black jacket, the other in a rumpled, over-sized suit, holding a sign that read SESSIONS.

The rumpled man lowered the sign to his side as Sessions approached. "Good morning, Mr. Sessions," he said. "I am Chief Inspector Gilberto Grassi, Italian State Police. Welcome to Bologna."

"Hello, Inspector. I'm Special Agent Dan Sessions, FBI." Sessions extended his hand to the stylish man. "And you are?"

"I am Inspector Costa, Criminal Investigation."

"You're not with the State Police?" Sessions asked.

"Inspector Costa is investigating a murder," Grassi said. "It is a local matter. But during the investigation he may have had contact with your suspect."

"We have someone in mind for the murder," Costa said. "An American. I wonder if perhaps we seek the same person."

"Seriously?" Sessions set down his bag, kneeling next to it, rummaging hastily through its contents. He pulled out a photo and showed it to Costa. "Is this your suspect?"

Costa blinked, arching his eyebrows. "No. It is a surprise."

‡ ‡ ‡

Ronni watched the taxi circle the villa courtyard before coming to a stop. A man emerged and scanned the surroundings, until his gaze settled on Ronni, sitting at an outdoor table in the shade of an olive tree. The taxi stayed put as he approached her.

"Are you Rhiannon Barraket?"

"Yes," Ronni said, removing her sunglasses. "And who are you?"

The man produced an ID card and a badge. "Special Agent Sessions, FBI."

Ronni closed her laptop and rested her sunglasses on the table. "You're a long way from home, Agent Sessions."

"May I sit?"

Ronni motioned toward the empty chair.

"I'm investigating a string of abortion clinic bombings," Sessions continued. "You might have heard about them."

Ronni tapped her sunglasses on the tabletop. "The ones in America, you mean. Yes, I remember. There were two bombings. That's not exactly a *string*. Have there been more?"

"Did I say 'string?' I guess that *is* overstated. You're right, it's just the two." Sessions pulled a file out of his bag and opened it. "Pittsburgh, two dead, one critically injured. Atlanta, seven dead, twelve injured, four critically." He closed the file and laid it on the table."

"Terrible," Ronni said.

"You're an adviser to Senator Herrera Peña, aren't you?"

"I advise the senator on matters of social policy."

"Including abortion rights?"

"Agent Sessions, are you interrogating me?"

"The senator is an anti-abortion crusader—a rather vehement one."

"You're investigating a domestic crime. Why are you in Italy?"

"Oh, that." Sessions opened the file. He handed a sheet to Ronni. "Some of the people on that list may have knowledge that could be helpful to the investigation. They're all in Italy. Do you know any of them?"

Ronni read the list. She knew them all.

Matt Bugatti
Clara Kildee
Tyler Ross
Cameron Stroud

Her own name, *Rhiannon Barraket*, was at the top of the list.

"Yes, I know who they are."

"Do you know their whereabouts?"

"Mr. Sessions, why are we having this conversation? Are these people suspects? Because I can tell you that that's ludicrous."

Sessions took back the sheet. "Bugatti and Ross are staying here in this villa, but they're not in residence at the moment. Kildee is checked into the *Internazionale* Hotel in Bologna, but her room doesn't appear to have been disturbed recently. Stroud is at the *Raffaello* in Modena, preparing to check out."

"If you knew, why did you ask me?"

Sessions put the files back into his bag as he stood. "Ms. Barraket, you're right, there have been only two bombings. But we have reason to believe that the perpetrators aren't done yet. In fact, we believe that more bombings, perhaps dozens, are being planned."

Ronni tapped her sunglasses on the table before putting them on. "You didn't answer my question. Do you think the people on that list are connected with the bombings?"

"That's what I'm here to find out."

Sessions walked back to the taxi. Ronni reached for her cell phone as soon as the taxi had left the villa.

✝ ✝ ✝

The chief pollster for the Herrera campaign clicked to the next slide, filling the screen with polling data from ten battleground states. Yolanda studied the figures for five minutes without saying a word.

"Senator?"

"We've stalled."

"You haven't lost any ground, Senator."

"*My* campaign does *not* stand still—not when I'm trailing in four out of ten key states and leading by single digits in the rest. Look at Ohio. I'm barely polling in the thirties."

Yolanda's campaign staff exchanged nervous looks until, finally, the pollster broke the silence.

"Senator, your stand on abortion is holding you back. It's the number one reason given for not supporting you. If you were to soften your position, we could expect a four-point increase across the board. That would put you ahead in eight of ten swing states."

"I won't back down. Even if this weren't a life-and-death matter, if I were to change my message at this point, I'd look like a craven opportunist."

Yolanda's media manager spoke up. "Senator, we're not suggesting that you *change* your position. But there are key markets where a very strong anti-abortion stance hurts your numbers. All we're saying is, emphasize different issues— child poverty, education, infrastructure investment—in *those* markets."

"What about my opponents? They won't stand down. They'll stay on the attack."

"That's exactly our point, Senator. The others are focused almost entirely on the abortion issue. It's the easiest way for them to create a contrast in the voters' minds. The more you talk about right to life, the easier you make it for them." He paused. "Senator…Yolanda, you're still the candidate to beat. If you pivot, they'll pivot too."

Yolanda pressed a finger to her lip. "I assume that you have something in mind?"

"Yes, Senator. We've worked up a campaign. With your approval, we can start the ad buys immediately."

"All right. Let's see the spots."

Before the media manager could cue the first video, Yolanda's cell phone buzzed. She checked the display.

Ronni.

"Excuse me. I've got to take this."

Yolanda stepped into the hallway. "Yes, Ronni. Where do we stand?"

"Did you know that the FBI is in Italy investigating a conspiracy to bomb abortion clinics?"

"I did not. Who is it?"

"His name is Sessions."

"What does he suspect? *Who* does he suspect?"

"He's not saying. But he has a list, and I'm at the top of it."

Yolanda closed the door to the conference room. "Ronni, stay calm. Keep me informed of anything you learn. I'll work it from this end."

"I'm calm."

"Good. Remember, we only have a few more weeks to go. And none too soon. My numbers have hit a plateau. We'll need something dramatic to break through."

Yolanda ended the call and immediately placed another, this one to FBI Headquarters in Washington.

"This is Senator Herrera Peña calling for Director Carmona."

Yolanda tapped her foot as the call was transferred.

"Mr. Director," she said, "I understand that you've expanded your abortion clinic bombing investigation to Italy. We should talk."

46

MALEDIZIONE

MATT HELD FLORA'S hand, stroking it gently. Flora smiled, her eyes closed, her breathing slow and regular, as if on the verge of falling asleep.

"*Si sente bene,*" she said. "It feels nice."

"How are you doing, *Mamma*?"

Flora laughed softly. "Why do you call me *mamma*, Giovanni?"

"She is like this all morning," Pierangelo whispered. "Today she calls me Renato."

"*Mamma, sono Matteo,*" Matt said.

Flora frowned and pulled her hand away. "Don't tease me, Giovanni."

Matt reached for Flora's hand, but hesitated. "I'm sorry, dear. Can you forgive your foolish husband?"

Flora smiled. "*Ti perdono.*" She held out her hand. "I forgive you."

‡ ‡ ‡

Matt and Pierangelo walked together in the vineyard.

"*La maledizione*," Pierangelo said. "The curse." He spat on the ground. "I've seen it too many times, since I was a boy. At first they are only confused, then they disappear, slowly, slowly, over the years, like the murals of Dozza, until only outlines remain, with no colors. If we didn't know them, if we didn't remember who they were, they would be unrecognizable. Poor Flora."

Matt stopped walking to rub a grape leaf between his fingers, a young leaf, shiny and smooth. He looked into the sky, clear and blue overhead, dotted with clouds toward the horizon. The sun was intense and the breeze was warm. "Poor Flora."

Pierangelo put his hand on Matt's arm. "We will take care of her, *cugino*."

Matt put his hand on Pierangelo's, smiling weakly and nodding.

La maledizione.
Mia maledizione.

47

SERVANT

DONALD LOMINGER OPENED his front door a crack to see who was knocking so insistently. Three large men stood on his porch; two more men stood at the curb next to two automobiles and a black van with *FBI BOMB TECHNICIANS* painted on the side.

The serious-looking FBI agent nearest the door held out his ID.

"Are you Donald Milton Lominger?"

"Do you have a warrant?"

"Are you Donald Lominger?" the man repeated.

"Yes, I am. Do you have a warrant?"

The agent handed Donald a folded sheet of paper.

"I need to read this."

"Sir, that warrant authorizes me and my associates to search your premises for illegal explosives and other related items. Please admit us or we will enter forcibly."

Donald squinted at the paper. "May I see your identification again, please? And the rest of you?"

The three men grudgingly showed their IDs. Donald opened the door.

"This is crazy," Donald said as the men entered. "I don't have anything like this. You're wasting your time."

The agents began their search with no hint of restraint.

"Hey, *hey*," Donald shouted at one agent who had just overturned a couch. "Take it easy."

The lead agent pointed toward a door, indicating that the search should be expanded to the rest of the house.

"Mr. Lominger, are you acquainted with one Darryl Meeks?"

"I'm not answering your questions. Don't I have rights?"

"You're not under arrest, Mr. Lominger."

"I'm calling my lawyer. Do you mind if I call my lawyer?"

"No, sir. You're free to call your attorney."

Donald opened the drawer to a metal desk on which sat an old tube-type TV, a computer and a bible. He pulled out a cell phone.

"Chief!"

The shout came from a back room. The agents converged on a closet, in which lay a belt consisting of five kilograms of high explosives and a detonator.

"Call in the bomb squad."

In the front room Donald opened the cover to his cheap cell phone. He keyed in the numbers *316**. The phone beeped. He pressed pound.

The two bomb technicians at the curb were hurled against the van by the force of the blast. It took a moment for them to recover. One of them rushed the house. The other noticed a bloody heap in the side yard.

"Kenny! Kenny! Over here!"

The agents bent over the body of Donald Lominger. One of them pressed a finger to Donald's neck. A gurgling noise came from Donald's throat as he opened his eyes.

"Shit, he's still breathing. Call an ambulance. We've got to keep this guy alive."

Donald closed his eyes. *Jesus, take me, your servant, into your presence.*

Kenny fetched a medical kit from the truck and began to administer first aid. The ambulance arrived shortly afterward.

The EMTs were able to keep Donald alive for another hour, until the brodifacoum took effect.

48

DECISION

"*TUTTO È STATO perfetto,*" Cameron said to the hotel clerk. "Everything was perfect. I'm looking forward to my next visit to Modena and to staying in your fine hotel."

"*Grazie, Signor Stroud,*" the clerk said, beaming. "*Buon viaggio.*"

Cameron extended the handle of his suitcase and hefted the strap of his bag over his shoulder. He turned away from the counter to find Matt Bugatti standing directly in his path.

"Dr. Bugatti. How unexpected. I could flatter myself by believing that you came all the way to Modena to see me off, but I doubt that's the case."

"It's not." Matt held out a sheet of paper, a photocopy of a receipt from the lounge of the *Internazionale* Hotel.

"We found this receipt in Lamberto Magnani's office."

Cameron examined it. "Dr. Magnani appears have enjoyed a drink now and again."

"Look at the date."

Cameron held the sheet closer. "I don't understand. Why is this important?"

"It's dated the day Lamberto died. And it's from the hotel where Clara Kildee is staying."

"That's hardly mysterious. I've heard that Ms. Kildee is quite the snoop, and a lush, too, from the looks of *this*. Magnani gave her the run of the foundation. She probably dropped it." Cameron handed the sheet back to Matt. "If you're so curious about it, why don't you ask Kildee?"

"We can't find her. She's disappeared."

"Ah. Well, I hope you find her and solve the baffling mystery of the bar receipt. I have a plane to catch."

Matt took hold of Cameron's arm as Cameron started for the door. Cameron jerked his arm away, twisting his body violently enough to send his suitcase and bag flying. He turned on Matt, eyes open wide, teeth bared, raising his hand as if he meant to strike. "*Don't...*"

Matt recoiled instinctively. Cameron took a step toward Matt before regaining his composure. He picked up his bag and suitcase.

"Dr. Bugatti, I do hope that we'll have a chance to collaborate—in the future. But not now. My car is waiting."

"We know about the secret door."

Cameron cocked his head. "Now, I must admit, that's more interesting than a scrap of paper. What secret door?"

"In Lamberto's office. It leads to an underground passage that exits through the hermitage."

"Secret doors! Underground passages! Medieval monasteries! *Damned* exciting stuff. I wish I could stay to hear how it ends. *Ciao*, Doctor."

"The door has no alarm. It's a way in and out of the foundation without being detected."

"That follows. Why are you telling me this?"

"It puts a hole in your alibi. You'd have had enough time to leave the foundation, kill Lamberto, and return without anyone knowing."

Cameron laughed, a deep guttural laugh that sounded like a recording. "What a sensational theory. It presupposes, of course, that I knew of the *secret door*, not to mention that I had a reason to kill Dr. Magnani."

Matt produced another sheet of paper, the cover sheet of a scientific article, titled *Association of HCG4P11 Gene*

Polymorphism in Individuals of Eastern European Ancestry with Immune Thrombocytopenia.

"This research was done at Vanderbilt."

"I see that."

"You went to school at Vanderbilt. In fact, you were there when this research was completed."

"Why, indeed I was. In fact, I even recognize some of the names on this paper. But I don't see *my* name on here anywhere."

"Clara talked with the primary researcher. He said that you were familiar with the research."

"The resourceful, misplaced Clara. What's *her* theory?"

"She thinks that you know the reason why those girls died after taking *Backup*, and that it has something to do with this research. She told Lamberto about it and she thinks that you killed Lamberto to keep it a secret."

"Dr. Bugatti, I have *no* prior knowledge of this research."

"According to this researcher, Tate, you did know about it, in depth."

"Is that what Kildee said? Well, she's wrong. But in any case, how would *I* know that she told Magnani anything? Kildee told *you* that she talked to Magnani. She didn't tell *me*."

"I'm going to the police with this information."

"That's your decision, Doctor. As for me, I have barely enough time to catch my flight. I'm sorry that I can't wish you luck with the Italian police."

Cameron left the hotel and entered the waiting taxi. Matt watched the car drive away.

He did it. He fucking did it. He killed Lamberto.

‡ ‡ ‡

There were two men in the interview room besides Inspector Costa that Matt didn't recognize. One introduced himself as Inspector Grassi of the Italian State Police; the other held out an ID and said, "Agent Sessions, FBI."

"FBI?" Matt said. "Why is the FBI involved?"

"Dr. Bugatti," Costa said, "Inspector Grassi and Agent Sessions are here about another matter. It is a plot to bomb clinics in America."

Matt looked at the two men. "Look, gentlemen, I have information for Inspector Costa. I don't think it's relevant to your bomb plot investigation."

"I'll be the judge of that," Sessions said. "Inspector Grassi has authorized me to be present at this interview."

"*Dottor Bugatti, prego,*" Costa gestured toward the chair. "Please, sit. What can you tell me?"

"I can tell you who killed Lamberto Magnani."

Matt told Costa, Grassi and Sessions about the secret door, the dropped receipt, and the Vanderbilt research. He confessed that he and Dario had hidden Clara and that he suspected that Cameron had either killed or abducted her. He laid a packet on the table containing the evidence.

"How long have you known these things?" Costa said.

"Since last night."

"Doctor," Costa said, "you could have told me this then, or this morning, when we spoke at the villa. I remember, I mentioned Stroud's alibi specifically, and you said nothing."

"I had to talk to Stroud before I came to you."

"You confronted the suspect on your own?" Sessions shouted. "What possessed you to do that?"

"The same question comes to my mind," Costa said. "Your story, it is fantastic. But before I did not have reason to detain Dr. Stroud. His alibi was too good. That has changed." Costa picked up the phone. "*Rosanna, l'aeroporto, per favore.*" He covered the mouthpiece. "Unfortunately, Dr. Stroud's plane is scheduled to leave in just a few minutes. You may have given him the time he needs to escape." Costa uncovered the mouthpiece. "*Sì, sono l'Ispettore Costa, della polizia giudiziaria.*"

Costa's conversation involved several airport personnel, growing increasingly frantic as the minutes passed. After a pause of a few seconds, Costa closed his eyes. "*Grazie,*" he said, hanging up the phone.

"Dr. Stroud is in the air. He will land in Munich in an hour. We will notify the German police to intercept him."

"This is a hell of a development, Bugatti," Sessions growled. "Withholding information and interfering with an investigation—it's up to the inspector, but if this were my case, I'd have you brought up on charges and thrown in prison."

"*Dottore, ho conosciuto la sua famiglia quando ero ragazzo,*" Costa said. "I've known your family since I was a boy. Your cousin Pierangelo and I grew up together, and I have shared many meals with him and Stefania. I was present when Dario was ordained. And I remember your father, Giovanni, and Flora, your mother. I feel that I know you as well. So this behavior surprises me. Had you told us what you know even a few minutes earlier, we would have him in custody."

"*Conosce mia madre?*" Matt asked. "Do you know my mother? Do you know about her illness?"

"*Sì. La maledizione.*"

"*Stroud ha la cura,*" Matt said. "Stroud has the cure."

"*Capisco,*" Costa said, nodding. "I understand."

‡ ‡ ‡

The Lufthansa plane came to a stop at the gate, the seat belt sign staying lit as an announcement played over the intercom in German, Italian and English.

"Ladies and gentlemen, please remain seated. There will be a short delay before you can depart."

A man in a suit entered the plane followed by two men wearing German police uniforms. The man spoke a few words to the flight attendant, who pointed at an aisle seat halfway to the back of the plane. The three men made their way down the aisle to the seat identified on the passenger manifest as that of Cameron Stroud. The man pulled a photo from his pocket and compared it with the face of the man in the seat. He frowned.

"Are you Cameron Stroud?" the man said in German-accented English.

"Mi dispiace. Non parlo inglese," said the short, heavy-set, dark-haired, mustached man in the seat.

‡ ‡ ‡

"In six weeks, multiple bombings will take place, targeting abortion clinics across the United States," Sessions told Matt. "We know when they will happen, but not how many or where, not precisely, anyway. Until recently, we believed that the man behind the plot was this man." Sessions laid a photo on the table. "His name is Darryl Meeks. He's the head of an outfit known as *Heaven Sent*, a violent anti-abortion group."

"You said 'until recently.'"

"We've had some new information. We've traced a telephone call from the Washington, D.C. area to Darryl Meeks, one of dozens of calls from the D.C. area that Meeks has received from burner phones, prepaid cell phones that are used once and discarded. We reviewed surveillance footage from the National Mall, from where these phone calls were placed." Sessions laid a second photo on the table. "This is the real mastermind behind the plot."

Matt stood up, almost knocking over his chair. The photo was of poor resolution, as if it had been greatly enlarged. The person in the picture, talking on a cell phone, wore sunglasses, but he recognized Ronni Barraket.

49

NIGHT PRAYERS

THE BROTHERS FINISHED Night Prayers and returned to their apartments, content from a day of labor and devotion. The hermitage was at its most peaceful in the evening hours, when the Friars of the Order of the Servants of Mary remained in silent contemplation, not speaking again until Matins at sunrise.

Dario entered his cell and removed his robe. He knelt by his cot as he folded his hands and fixed his gaze on the crucifix.

Signore, I pray that the innocent woman who was entrusted to my care will be returned safely. I pray that you watch over my cousin Matteo, and for Flora, that you may ease her affliction. I pray for your deliverance from this evil that has taken Lamberto from us and threatens us still. I pray these things in the name of the Father, and of the Son, and of the Holy Spirit.

Dario crossed himself as he stood. He turned slightly in reaction to the sting of a hypodermic needle penetrating the skin below his jaw, entering his carotid artery. In less than a second the drug took effect and he collapsed on the floor of his cell.

50
MOTIVE

THE BREEZE WAS still cool in the courtyard an hour past dawn. Matt had been there since before sunrise. Pierangelo brought coffee, but Matt refused his offer of a pastry; Pierangelo studied the pensive young man for a moment before retreating to the kitchen, leaving Matt alone with his thoughts, troubled and conflicted since seeing Sessions's photo, more so now as Ronni approached the table.

"I was looking for you yesterday." She sat down and smiled at Matt, holding up her hand to shield her eyes from the sun. "Not even Pierangelo could tell me where you were."

"I spent time with Mom. She's having a bit of a relapse. She was doing so well when we first got here, but now she seems more bewildered than ever."

"I'm sorry. It's good, though, that she's been able to reconnect with her family." Ronni put on her sunglasses. "You know, I saw your mother yesterday afternoon with Pierangelo. That's when I asked him where you were."

"I had to leave for a while. I had a few errands."

"Oh."

Matt looked at Ronni, wondering what her hidden eyes might have revealed.

"Dr. Bugatti!" Matt and Ronni turned to see Tyler approaching. "Oh, and, of course, Ms. Barraket. Why am I not surprised? It's just as well. You'll both want to hear this. The commission has voted on the revision. Four to two in favor."

"In *favor*," Matt said. "Who…"

"Who switched sides?" Tyler interrupted. "It was Lipinski, the ethicist, that swung the vote. Van Hollen, Gibbs and McDermott—the pro-life faction—all voted in favor, as expected. I tried to talk Woodall and Christensen into making it unanimous, but they wouldn't budge. At least they won't be issuing a minority report."

"What about the president?"

"He's accepted the conclusion and he's prepared for the repercussions."

"You changed the report?" Ronni asked.

"Yes," Tyler said. "The investigation concludes that CG Pharma's trials were inadequate, and that the FDA was negligent in allowing the drug to go to market. The report states that the FDA and CG Pharma are indirectly responsible for forty-eight deaths and directly responsible for another. If they hadn't colluded to avoid issuing a recall, Debbie Melnik would be alive today."

Ronni nodded. "It's the right thing to do."

"I was sure you'd find this news to your liking, Ronni. Dr. Bugatti, I'll inform the president that we'll issue the report at a time of his choosing."

"Not yet," Matt said.

Tyler blinked slowly. "Oh no. Now what?"

"It's Stroud. He's hiding something."

"What? What is he hiding?"

"He knows what killed those girls. And he's known for a long time."

"You *suspect* that he knows."

"He knows."

"This is *wonderful,* Dr. Bugatti. You've finally come to a conclusion without a geometrical proof. That's progress. But tell me, what makes you so certain?"

"He's willing to kill to keep it a secret."

"You think that he killed Magnani."

"Yes."

"That's insane."

"I wish it were."

"You know what?" Tyler said, "I don't care. Whatever you suspect, or know, or *whatever*, it's irrelevant. The commission's findings are based on the exhibits and the hearing testimony. Anything Stroud might or might not have done are facts *not in evidence.*"

"Tyler, seriously?" Matt said. "If I'm right, it changes everything. How can it *not* be relevant?"

"What about the report? Will you approve it?"

"Not now. See me tomorrow."

Tyler turned and walked back to the villa. "The president will hear about this and he won't be happy," he shouted.

Ronni waited until Tyler was out of earshot before speaking.

"Matt, what have you learned?"

"What have *you* learned? Your research department was going to look into Stroud's background."

Ronni took her laptop from her bag. She opened a file and turned the computer screen toward Matt.

Matt scanned the screen. "There isn't anything new here."

"I know. Apparently there's nothing we could find that Clara hadn't already discovered. By the way, how is she holding up?"

Matt saw his reflection in Ronni's sunglasses. "A little stir crazy, but she'll be all right."

"Poor woman."

Matt sipped his coffee. "I've been reading up on the senator."

Ronni removed her sunglasses. "You have?"

"She seems like a one-issue candidate."

"No, that's not true. Senator Herrera has a comprehensive plan for America."

"But she leads with abortion."

Ronni tightened her grip on her sunglasses as she tapped them on the table. "If a million children a year were dying of cancer, or from gun violence, and the senator were advocating for research or reform, no one would question her priorities. That's the paradox of abortion. But there's more at stake than the destruction of our posterity, as if that weren't reason enough to crusade against the slaughter of our unborn children. Our national policy says something about who we are as a people, and what it says affects how we think and act. The senator believes—and *I* believe—that abortion is a core issue. A change in the law would be the foundation for a culture of life. But today, in America, life is cheap."

"The pope said exactly the same thing."

Ronni replaced her sunglasses.

"How far are you willing to go?" Matt asked.

"To stop this scourge? Some things call for extreme measures."

Matt stood up. "I'd better go see how Clara is doing."

Matt walked back to the villa.

Crusade. Slaughter. Scourge. Extreme measures.

He paused at the entrance, pressing his fingers to his forehead.

Could she?

‡ ‡ ‡

Matt found Inspector Costa that morning in Brother Alessandro's office. Alessandro appeared to be on the verge of tears.

"Where is Brother Dario?" Matt asked.

"Dr. Bugatti," Costa said, "your cousin is also missing."

"*What?*"

"We last saw him at Night Prayers, after sunset," Alessandro said. "This morning Dario did not appear at Matins. His cell was empty."

Matt looked at Costa. "After sunset? Then it couldn't have been Stroud. He'd already left Italy by then."

"No, Doctor," Costa said. "We alerted the German police to intercept Dr. Stroud. He was not on the plane. He paid a man to board with his ticket. We believe that Stroud is still in Bologna."

Matt dropped into a chair and put his head in his hands. "I should have come to you sooner," he muttered.

"Yes, Doctor, you should have," Costa said, "but now is not the time for regrets. It is the time for honesty. If you know anything more, tell me now."

"I've told you everything I know, even things I'm not sure of."

"Stroud, you mean. You are not sure about him?"

"What's his motive?"

"It is your theory," Costa said. "It is the research. Stroud wishes to keep it secret."

"That's a reason to be evasive. It's not a motive for kidnapping—or murder." Matt raised his head. "He knows the cause and he's holding back. What is he so afraid of that he'd kill to cover it up? Is he protecting CG Pharma?"

"Perhaps he is protecting his reputation?"

"But *murder*? It's too far to go just to protect a reputation."

"But you think that he is guilty, no?"

"I do. But I can't prove it."

Costa put a hand on Matt's shoulder. "Matteo, I have been doing this for a long time. I can say, the facts will only tell you so much. You are a smart man, but intelligence alone will not solve these crimes. If your instinct talks to you, you must listen."

‡ ‡ ‡

Matt walked in the hermitage vineyard to collect his thoughts.

Lamberto and Clara knew about the research. Costa and Sessions know, but they're not in danger.

He stopped walking.

Ronni.

Matt headed toward the hermitage in a run, then stopped.

I never told Dario, but Stroud doesn't know that.

Matt's stomach turned.

Pierangelo.

Mom.

Matt sped back to the villa. He exhaled with relief when he saw Flora and Pierangelo sitting in the courtyard. He stepped out of the car and scanned the surroundings—no obvious threat—then he sprinted to the table.

"Mamma, Pierangelo, come inside."

"Giovanni? What are you talking about?" Flora protested. "I want to be outside. I want to enjoy the day."

Matt took Flora's arm and lifted her forcibly from her seat. "Pierangelo, help me. It's not safe out here."

Pierangelo jumped up and took Flora's other arm. Flora complained loudly as the pair hustled her into the villa. By the time they had seated her in the kitchen she was weeping.

"Giovanni, Giovanni, why do you torture me?"

"Mamma, I'm sorry." Matt reached for Flora's hand but she pulled away.

"Don't touch me. I can't stand you touching me. Unfaithful brute. You're a *brute*."

Matt grabbed Flora's arm. "Mamma, *listen to me*. I am *not* your husband. I'm your son, Matteo. We're not safe here. There's a man, a bad man, who may hurt you. Do you understand? Please, Mamma, *try* to understand."

Flora turned away from Matt and pressed her hand to her face. "The only one who hurt me is *you*. All the nights away that you didn't call, the money you spent, the neglect. *Why?* I asked myself but I didn't know why. I only knew that you were hurting me. And then—*then*—all the things that you did to hide your lies. You had answers for everything. You paid attention to me on a schedule, like an unpleasant chore. The pretend smiles, the awkward kisses, the way you touched me as if you were touching a piece of furniture. Did you think that I wouldn't know? *That's* when I knew, no, not when you ignored me, but when you worked so hard to deceive me. You could only be guilty of something terrible. That is when I finally believed what I could not believe, what I couldn't even *imagine.* You would have been more kind to kill me."

Flora covered her face and sobbed. Pierangelo put a hand on her shoulder. "*Cugino,* what is it?" he asked.

"It's better that you don't know. But you must be very careful. In fact, it would be better if Mom and you and Stefania left the villa. Do you have somewhere to go?"

Pierangelo shook his head. "We have guests. We cannot leave."

"Some of them are cousins. They could be in danger, too. You'll have to send them away. I'll make it right with them. Please, your lives are in danger."

"Very well. I will make arrangements immediately."

"I'll tell Ronni."

"There is no need for that, *cugino.* She has left already."

‡ ‡ ‡

Matt remained in the kitchen with Flora while Pierangelo and Stefania dealt with the guests. He tried unsuccessfully to raise Ronni on her cell phone—after five attempts he gave up.

Flora had calmed down enough to allow Matt to hold her hand. Flora's outburst had been a temporary distraction, but now his thoughts turned back to Cameron Stroud.

Why?

He looked at Flora's face. She looked back at him, her eyes lacking any sign of recognition. Then her mouth became grim and she shut her eyes as she turned away.

You could only be guilty of something terrible...what I could not believe...what I couldn't even imagine.

Matt sat up with a start.

If your instinct talks to you, you must listen.

He inhaled sharply.

Oh, Jesus. He's not just hiding the cause. He killed those girls deliberately.

252

51

BUSINESS

CAMERON INJECTED ENOUGH thiopental into Dario's IV line to send him from a twilight state into a coma. Dario's answers to his questions had convinced him that Dario possessed no incriminating information.

"God must be watching over you, *Fratello Dario*. The Servants of Mary will find you in your cell tomorrow in time for Matins, groggy and sick, but with no recollection of our time together. *Dominus vobiscum.*"

Cameron turned around to face the other bed in the room.

"You, Clara, are a different matter. I'm afraid that I simply cannot trust you to keep your mouth shut."

Cameron filled a syringe. He increased the dosage from that sufficient to induce coma to that necessary to stop breathing. He inserted the needle into Clara's IV line.

Cameron jerked his head toward the door at the sound of a sharp knock.

"*Signor Nelson! È lì?*"

Cameron went to the door, opening it a crack, holding the syringe, keeping his right hand behind his back.

"*Enrico, come va?* Is something wrong?"

Enrico's lips were pressed together and his eyes were narrowed. "I hope not, *signore*. But we do have a matter to discuss."

"Very well, but we must be quick. I'm about to go out."

"May I enter?"

"I'm afraid I can't invite you in. Really, I'm already late."

"As you prefer, *signore*, but it might be awkward for me to be standing here in the hall while we talk about the two unfortunate individuals in your bedroom."

Cameron manipulated the syringe between his fingers. He placed his thumb on the plunger.

"I'm listening."

"It was necessary last night to enter your apartment. Normally I would notify you first, of course, but my tenant upstairs reported the smell of gas. I had no choice."

Cameron imagined the sequence of motions—fling open the door, plunge the syringe into Enrico's neck, drag the body into the apartment and close the door. He looked past Enrico into the deserted hallway.

"You know my secret, Enrico. Where do we go from here?"

"We have known each other for years. You have been a good tenant. I see no reason to terminate our relationship. But under the circumstances I believe that I have the right to ask for certain considerations."

"Go on."

"Fifty thousand euros."

Cameron gripped the door. He shifted his feet.

"To be shared between me and my associate."

"Your associate?"

"*Sì.* Of course I told my information to another, as a precaution. He will have to remain anonymous, however. We speak almost every day. He would be very concerned if he didn't hear from me."

Cameron relaxed his grip on the door. He glanced behind him at the two unconscious forms in the bedroom.

"Enrico, I think we can do business. But I have something else in mind, for which I'm willing to pay more than fifty thousand euros—ten times more."

255

52

TRAITOR

DARRYL RECOGNIZED THE scene. He'd been there. The ill-maintained tract homes in an older, poorer Atlanta neighborhood looked the same as he remembered, with the exception of the still-smoking remnants of the home of Donald Lominger.

The reporters on site canvassed the crowd for witnesses. One neighbor described Donald as "a man with a big heart who loved the Lord." The news ticker at the bottom of the screen provided a running commentary: *Developing Story—Two FBI agents dead, one critically injured in Atlanta bomb blast. Location identified as home of social worker Donald Lominger. FBI declines comment.*

Darryl sat in the subdued lighting of his media room, switching from one news feed to the next. Details were sketchy, but one conclusion was inescapable—*Heaven Sent* had a security problem.

Darryl muted the sound, closed his eyes and bowed his head. *Lord, if I have failed you, let your judgment be upon me. If you doubt me, let this trial test my resolve.* He picked up his cell phone and entered a number.

"One of our lieutenants has fallen," he said.

"So I've heard," said the voice at the far end. "But that's not the end of it. There's an FBI agent in Italy. He's asking questions."

Darryl sat mute for a few seconds. The screen on the wall displayed a picture of Donald Lominger, the photo from his City of Atlanta Office of Social Services ID card, and a caption: *Lominger Suspected Of Ties With Anti-Abortion Extremists.*

"There is a traitor among us," Darryl said. "I have twelve lieutenants. Only I know them all. Brother Lominger's cell had two others. It must be one of them."

"Find him. Report back to me. And Meeks?"

"Yes?"

"Don't do anything crazy."

53

ARRANGEMENT

"MR. DIRECTOR, I have your call."

FBI Director Edward Carmona punched a button on his console. "Agent Sessions, what is your status?"

"The suspect has relocated from the villa to the airport hotel. She remains under surveillance by the Italian State Police."

"Continue."

"There has been some activity at the villa. Most of the guests have left, but as far as we know, Bugatti and Ross are still there. Stroud attempted to flee but the Italians believe he's still in Bologna. Kildee hasn't yet been located."

"This is about that murder, the genetics scientist, right? Jesus. How involved in *that* mess should we be?"

"It's an internal matter, but it does involve U.S. citizens. I'll follow your guidance."

"Stand clear for the present. It's a job for the State Department."

"Understood. Is that all, sir?"

"No. I've spoken with the senator. We've worked something out."

☩ ☩ ☩

Matt locked the last of the doors to the villa. Despite knowing that Pierangelo, Stefania and Flora were a hundred miles away, he couldn't shake the feeling that they were still in serious peril. Tyler had protested more over Matt's refusal to finalize the report for yet another day than he did over relocating to a hotel in Imola. Matt didn't think that Tyler was in danger, but he urged him to stay vigilant nonetheless. Satisfied that his family was safe and that the villa was secure, he drove to the hermitage.

Matt reached the end of the drive and stopped short of the parking area, spying a man in a black jacket near the entrance to the chapel. He turned toward Matt's car.

Inspector Costa wore a look of bewilderment.

Matt waved as he approached. "What is it, Inspector?"

Costa looked toward the chapel door. The call and response of the Latin Mass droned from within. "They are praying a Mass of thanksgiving."

"Thanksgiving?"

Costa put his hand on Matt's arm, moving his head in the direction of the entrance. "Go, *amico.*"

Sunlight spilled into the interior as Matt opened the door. One of the brothers looked back to see who was entering. He smiled at Matt, then he touched the shoulder of the friar next to him, who stood and turned.

It was Dario. Matt ran up the aisle, almost stumbling, to embrace his cousin.

☩ ☩ ☩

"I prayed for you, *cugino,* and for your mother," Dario said. "I prayed for the return of Signora Kildee. I prayed for God's protection. That is the last that I remember."

"It was a joyful beginning to our day to have Brother Dario back with us," Alessandro said. "God surely heard our prayers."

"It would seem that God is being selective in his prayer-listening," Costa said.

"*Ispettore*," Alessandro said, "we asked God for Dario's return, and he is here. Shall we not offer our joy to God in praise?"

"*Fratello Dario*, I have had a call from our lab," Costa said. "Your blood test indicates barbiturates in rather high concentration. You were drugged. This was not God's doing."

Dario rubbed his eyes, looking hung over. "It was a man who took me, and it was a man who returned me. God has the power to soften men's hearts."

Costa and Matt looked at each other. "Very well, *frate*," Costa said. "Perhaps God has not yet been distracted by other matters and we will soon have Signora Kildee with us again."

‡ ‡ ‡

Costa walked with Matt back to his car.

"The brothers' faith is charming," Costa said, "but I prefer not to rely on God to solve this mystery."

"You're not a believer, Inspector?"

"In God? No. I was, once, before I joined the police. Now, I have seen too many terrible crimes, too many good people hurt, and who do I blame for this? The criminals, of course, but is not God to blame as well? Dario is convinced that God has returned him to the hermitage, but Lamberto also believed in God, and he's dead. How do I solve this paradox —a loving and all-powerful God who lets these things happen?"

"There are not many atheists in Italy."

"Atheist? I don't think so. I still allow for, how would you say it, a 'margin of error?'"

"An agnostic, then?"

"That is fair—an agnostic who wishes he could know—or an atheist who hopes that he is wrong."

Costa stopped, resting his hand on the top of Matt's car. "Do you think it is Stroud?" Costa asked.

"Yes."

"But you are not convinced of the motive."

"That has changed. I know now why he killed Lamberto. If I'm right, then Dr. Stroud is a very dangerous man."

"What are you thinking?"

By the end of Matt's explanation, Costa was shaking his head.

"But you have only answered the question with another question. True, if Stroud killed the girls, he would have reason to cover his tracks, but why would he kill the girls?"

"I don't know," Matt said. "It's my instinct talking."

Costa tapped his head. "Matteo, I respect your intelligence." He tapped his chest. "And your instinct as well. But you are not a policeman. Leave the investigation to the professionals."

"I'll be careful." Matt shook Costa's hand as Costa eyed him skeptically. "I need to have a word with Alessandro. Goodbye."

Matt found Alessandro and Dario in the cloister.

"Brother Alessandro, I have a request, but it could put you in danger."

"What is it, my son?"

"I need discreet access to the foundation. And I need a place to hide."

‡ ‡ ‡

Ronni tried three doors before she was convinced that the Bugatti villa was deserted. She returned to the taxi.

"*All'hotel?*" the driver asked.

"Yes, please."

The taxi crept down the hillside to the main road back to the airport Sheraton. The driver was unaware of the car following at a distance.

Ronni paid the driver and got out of the taxi to find her path to the entrance of the Sheraton blocked by Agent

Sessions, Chief Inspector Grassi, and a uniformed policeman.

"It's Sessions, right?" Ronni said. She looked at Grassi. "I don't think that *we've* met, though."

"Ms. Barraket, will you please come with us?" Sessions said.

"What's this about?"

"I think you know what it's about."

Grassi motioned in the direction of a large black sedan. The policeman joined Ronni in the back seat.

From a spot a few yards away, the man who had followed the taxi from the villa watched with interest as the sedan drove off.

‡ ‡ ‡

"That's the deal," Sessions said. "Your full cooperation is required. The terms are non-negotiable."

"Tell me again," Ronni said, "this was the senator's idea?"

"It was agreed between the senator and the director."

Ronni studied Sessions's face, and that of Grassi, who sat in a chair by the door. "I know something that the senator doesn't," she said, smiling, "and I'm willing to share it with you. But first I'll need an arrangement."

Ronni made her proposal as Sessions listened, arms crossed and frowning.

"All right," he said. "If it checks out, I'll agree. But this stays between us."

‡ ‡ ‡

The sedan deposited Ronni at the Sheraton. She took the elevator to the eighth floor and walked to her room. As she unlocked the door she felt a hand at her back shoving her into the room. She stumbled forward as the door slammed behind her. She retreated to a corner.

It was dark, the only illumination coming from the outside light that entered through the gaps in the curtains. Ronni held her breath, fearful that she might betray her location. She guessed that the other occupant was still in the entryway, but it wasn't until her eyes had adjusted to the dark that she could see the outline of a man standing in the middle of the room.

"What do you want?" she whispered.

"You're not safe," Matt said, "and if you want to stay alive, you'd better be completely honest with me."

54

TRUST

DARIO ADJUSTED THE wick of the kerosene lamp, casting a yellow glow in the tiny windowless cell, resembling the room beneath the hermitage that Clara had occupied briefly, but smaller and dustier, with an even smaller cot. The only other furniture in the room was a tiny table on which rested a basin and a pitcher of water, and a chamber pot under the bed. This room and another, smaller one, located in a remote branch of the complex of passages, were to be Ronni's and Matt's homes for the foreseeable future.

Ronni sat on the cot, looking desperately at Dario, and at Matt, who stood beside him.

"Can you see, *signorina?*" Dario asked.

"Is this necessary?"

"Lamberto was shot to death at his house," Matt said. "Dario was abducted from the hermitage. Clara was taken in the foundation and removed through the main underground passage. She's probably dead. Given all that, these measures don't seem like an over-abundance of caution."

"How long will we have to stay?"

"Until we can figure this out."

"How will we do that? We're completely isolated. We don't even have Internet down here."

"I took care of that. Check your computer."

Ronni opened her laptop and tapped a few keys. Her email inbox filled with messages.

"We set up WiFi extenders from the foundation. The signal's not strong, but it's usable. We should be able to get what we need."

"What happens when my battery runs out?"

"Dario will send one of the brothers. He'll bring you a spare."

"You've thought of everything."

"Hardly. If I'd thought of everything, we wouldn't be here."

After Dario left with his shopping list, Matt stood at the door of Ronni's cell, not saying anything.

"What did the FBI tell you?" Ronni asked.

"That you're responsible for the abortion clinic bombings."

It was difficult to tell in the dim light, but Matt could see no reaction on Ronni's face.

"It's not true."

"They showed me a photo. You were talking on a cell phone to the leader of a militant anti-abortion group."

"Is that what they told you? I mean, is that *exactly* what they said?"

"No. They said that the surveillance photo was taken at the same time that the call was placed, and that it was placed from the same location."

"In other words, circumstantial evidence."

"Yes. Fairly convincing circumstantial evidence."

Ronni stood and walked to Matt, taking his hand. "Matt, I've watched you for weeks. I've come to know how you think. Not surprisingly, you think like a mathematician. For you, a valid conclusion follows from an unbroken chain of logic that starts with indisputable facts. In some ways, you were the perfect choice to lead the commission. You weren't persuaded by emotional arguments. You didn't accept the compromise conclusion because the facts didn't support it."

Matt looked down at his hand in Ronni's. "Why are you telling me this?"

"I want to know why, when the FBI shows you a blurry photo and tells you a story, you're so quick to jump to a conclusion."

"What *is* the truth?"

"It's not me."

"Who is it?"

"I can't tell you. I have a good reason why I can't tell you. You'll have to trust me. I know you, Matt. I thought that you knew me, well enough at least to know that I couldn't be part of this."

Matt squeezed his eyes shut. "I don't know what to believe."

Ronni put her hand on Matt's cheek. "If you didn't know me, if I were a stranger to you, would you give me the benefit of the doubt?"

Matt opened his eyes. In the light of the lamp, Ronni's face took on a golden hue, almost glowing. Her intense blue eyes softened, seemingly incapable of deception.

Ronni pressed harder against Matt's cheek. "Would you, Matt, if you weren't trying to prove to yourself that you can be objective in spite of your feelings for me?"

"Ronni…"

She leaned close and kissed Matt. He touched her face, lingering for a moment before pulling back.

"I trust you," he said. "But you can't keep me in the dark forever."

Ronni looked in the direction of the flickering lamp. "I was about to say the same thing."

"I wouldn't do this if it weren't necessary. Cameron Stroud has disappeared. No one knows where he is, not the Italian state police, not the FBI. I'm convinced that he's out to kill anyone who suspects the truth."

"That he killed those girls intentionally."

"You *know*?"

"Yes. I've known for weeks."

55

URBINO

THOUGH NATURALLY CHEERFUL, Pierangelo was nearing the limits of his patience after less than two days in the home of his cousin Ugo. The place was large enough to accommodate Pierangelo, Stefania, Ugo and his family in comfort, but Flora found no joy in the inner-city Urbino apartment. When she wasn't complaining, she was crying, or she was accusing Ugo of hounding her and Giovanni out of Italy.

"She needs air," Pierangelo told Ugo.

"At least one of us does," Ugo grumbled.

Pierangelo drove Flora to a park outside the city wall. By the time they arrived, Flora had calmed down; after ten minutes in the sunshine, she was chatting happily. Flora held Pierangelo's arm and called him *papà*. He smiled at her and patted her hand, stopping occasionally to wipe away a tear.

Flora and Pierangelo walked in and out of shadows along the footpath, winding among the trees, as the wind rustled the leaves.

"*Papà*, I want to go to Bologna. Can we go to Bologna today?"

"No, dear," Pierangelo answered. "We're far away from Bologna. We'll go back to Urbino after our walk, to Ugo's."

"Ugo." Flora stopped walking. She closed her eyes, a tear rolling down her cheek, her lip trembling. "Ugo. Ugo. *Papà*, I don't remember…" She turned and looked at Pierangelo as if she were seeing something completely unexpected. She nodded. "Yes," she said. "You're right, Pierangelo. We must stay with Ugo."

Pierangelo exhaled with relief. They turned around to walk back to the car. After a few steps, Pierangelo felt Flora's hand pulled forcibly from his arm. Before he could turn, a blow to his head threw him forward, sending him sprawling facedown on the path.

56

OPENING

MATT STARED AT the computer screen in disbelief.

The file included the complete text of the Vanderbilt paper, with analysis by a Stivers and Cartwright staffer, verifying Cameron Stroud's connection with the research. Matt read summaries of other studies on the genetics of Eastern European populations, auto-immune diseases, and clinical trials, cross-referenced and subjected to rigorous statistical analysis. There was a four-page psychological profile of Cameron, with a disturbing conclusion: *Stroud exhibits traits suggesting undiagnosed narcissistic personality disorder and obsessive fixation. His behavior is consistent with grandiose delusions of intellectual superiority, and feelings of invulnerability leading to impulsive, even reckless acts.*

The report concluded that Cameron had intentionally engineered Backup for deadly effect. He had, simply put, committed mass murder. Although Matt had reached the same conclusion, on the basis of far less evidence, there was one item that Matt couldn't accept, one that cast doubt on everything he believed or wanted to believe about Ronni Barraket: The report was dated four weeks ago.

"We started the background checks right after the announcement of the commission," Ronni explained. "We already had files on most of the commissioners and key witnesses. But there were two we had nothing on. We identified them as targets for our research department and gave them top priority. Stroud was one." Ronni took her laptop from Matt. She tapped a few keys and handed it back. "You were the other."

Matt scanned the thirty-page file titled *Bugatti, Dr. Matteo*. It described his upbringing from birth, including every significant life event up to the present—enrollment in college at age fourteen, the death of his father at sixteen, his PhD at nineteen. The report described in detail his brief career at Connectrix and the work that led to the Fields medal. The full text of the NSA investigation into the espionage case against Matt was appended, a case that Matt had been assured was classified. A late entry reported Flora's diagnosis with Alzheimer's disease.

"You have a damn fine research staff," Matt said.

"The best."

"Why?"

"Why do we do the research? We always do it, for every significant issue that concerns a client. We research the facts, and we research the people. We never know what will be important before we start, but it always pays off."

"How did it pay off in this case?"

"Read the end of your profile summary."

Although Dr. Bugatti will take a strictly fact-based, analytical approach to the investigation, his profile indicates a capacity for empathy with the victims. This suggests that Bugatti will be dissatisfied with any finding that is not both satisfactory to the victims' families and fully supported by facts. Since it is unlikely that the evidence before the commission will be conclusive, it's probable that Bugatti will intervene to prolong the investigation, perhaps excessively.

"This creeps me out," Matt said.

"I'm sorry. It's not personal. It's part of our process. This finding was key to our strategy."

Matt closed the laptop. "What strategy?"

"We needed the issue. Senator Herrera is challenging the pro-choice policies of her own party. She's running to the left on economic and most social issues, but far to the right on abortion. That's risky enough in a general election, but it's a non-starter in the primaries. When the *Backup* deaths became news, we saw an opening."

"An opening?"

"If the president's actions contributed to the deaths of these young girls, it would put his pro-choice policies at issue. We needed the commission to find that the FDA was at fault, but we also needed to prolong the controversy until the senator could establish her campaign and the field of candidates narrowed. Our focus groups showed that the approach was a winner."

"You make it sound like a game."

"We survey the landscape, size up opponents, form strategies, plan attacks, assess results, change tactics...if it's not a game, what is it?"

Matt paced the length of the tiny cell. "It's *not* a game. You exploited those girls' deaths. You knew weeks ago that the FDA wasn't to blame. It was Stroud all along. You should have brought it out. Lives were at stake."

Ronni stood. "Matt, yes, we thought it was Stroud but we didn't have *definite* proof. We needed the issue. Our targets were the pharmaceutical companies, the FDA, and the president, not a deranged maniac perpetrating mass murder. Anyway, by the time we started our research, the drug had already been pulled from the market. No more lives were at risk."

"What about Lamberto? And Clara?"

Ronni sat down on the cot. "That's not fair."

"Isn't it? You knew that Stroud was disturbed and dangerous. You could have stopped him. Don't you think that you bear *some* responsibility?"

Ronni's eyes glistened. "We *saved* lives!"

"How? How did you save lives?"

"I was the one who told Clara Kildee that *Backup* killed those girls."

Matt stopped pacing. "What?"

Ronni wiped a tear from her cheek. "Clara's stories about the deaths of young girls were showing up in my daily brief. I was also getting items about *Backup*, since our firm had lobbied unsuccessfully to halt fast track approval of *Backup* as an over-the-counter drug. When Clara went on *The Dr. Rob Show* the epidemic became national news and I made the connection. I sent her an anonymous email telling her that *Backup* was the cause."

"How did you know that?"

"I didn't know. It was pure guesswork. I had everything to gain and nothing to lose. If the girls were dying from some other cause, there was no harm done. But if *Backup* was the cause, the drug would be pulled from the market and the FDA would be blamed. We'd have our issue."

Matt resumed pacing. "You should have brought this information to the commission."

"Matt, *we needed the issue.*"

"I get that. It was still wrong to hold back."

"The senator is working for a cultural renewal of the nation. Getting her elected is the first step. That was *my* reason for holding back." Ronni leaned forward, gripping the edge of the cot with one hand, extending her other hand toward Matt. "What was yours? You suspected Stroud. But you waited until after Clara had been taken to go to the police. Why? Could it be that you didn't want to jeopardize Stroud's Alzheimer's research?"

Matt turned away from Ronni and leaned against the wall. Ronni walked to him and put a hand on his shoulder.

"We each have our needs, Matt. We each make our choices."

Matt turned to Ronni. "Do you have enough to prove that Stroud did it?"

"I think so." She opened her laptop and scrolled through a list of emails. "Look at this."

From: slemeux@stiverscartwright.com
Subject: This could be the bloody glove
To: rbarraket@stiverscartwright.com

Hey Ronni,

We got to someone at the clinical trial company. She insisted that conducting phase three in South Africa was CG Pharma's idea. Her company designed a plan for the U.S. and Latin America but CG pushed for South Africa. It quadrupled the cost of the trial. She didn't remember who it was at CG who made the call but we kept digging. We found a guy who'd left the firm but he was there when the trial was designed. He remembered. He said it was "that asshole Stroud."

Steve

"Stroud testified to the commission that it was the consulting firm that proposed the South African trial," Matt said.

"He lied."

"If he designed the drug to target a specific genetic trait, one that only Eastern Europeans have, then the lethal side effects would never be detected in an all-African trial."

"It all fits together."

"Hardly," Matt said. "It seems far-fetched at best. And why would he do it, anyway?"

"Our research staff thinks that Stroud has a pathological hatred of women."

"Of an extreme nature, it would seem," Matt said. "Or else he's just plain evil. I can't…"

The noise sounded like the slow opening of a door on a creaky hinge. Matt and Ronni held their breath. Matt slipped his hand into his computer bag, withdrawing a nine millimeter Beretta pistol. Ronni's eyes opened wide—*What?* she mouthed silently.

Matt motioned for Ronni to move to a corner next to the door, taking a position at the opposite end of the wall, leveling his weapon.

The door moved slightly. Matt applied pressure to the trigger. Ronni squeezed herself deeper into the corner.

"*Cugino?*"

Matt recognized the voice. "Dario?" he whispered, keeping the gun aimed at the door.

Dario emerged from the shadow as the door opened wide. He was not alone. Matt shifted his aim as the second man stepped into the light.

Even in the dim glow of the lamp, Pierangelo's injuries were startling—his face was purple and swollen, he kept one arm cradled in the other, favoring one leg as he walked.

Matt relaxed his grip, taking his finger from the trigger, engaging the safety and returning the gun to his bag. He helped Pierangelo to the cot.

"Pierangelo, you're hurt. What happened?"

"*Cugino,*" Pierangelo said. "There is a place in Bologna you must go to, you and Miss Rhiannon. You must tell no one. You must not tell the police."

"Pierangelo, why?"

"They have her. They will kill her unless you go. They have her. They have Flora."

57

HE IS RISEN

MITCH HOEVEN LEFT the Life in Christ Evangelical Church of Gibsonia, Florida, following mid-week services. The day was already uncomfortable, the humidity stifling, the late morning summer sun having driven the temperature into the high eighties. Mitch hurried to his aging Nissan, started the car and cranked the air conditioning to maximum. He sighed as the blast hit his face. He put the car in gear and drove twelve blocks to his one-bedroom house.

Mitch parked the car in the driveway and entered through the side door. The interior was dark, Mitch having closed the blinds on all the windows before leaving for church, hoping to keep the Florida heat outside. It would take several minutes for his eyes to adapt.

"Brother Hoeven."

Mitch squinted in the direction of the voice, trying to make out who had addressed him. He turned on the kitchen light.

A man stood in the doorway to the front room, flanked by two other men. Mitch recognized the one in the middle.

"Brother Meeks! He is risen!"

Darryl took a step forward. "God is calling you to answer for Brother Lominger."

Mitch's mouth went dry. "It's tragic. God is surely testing us. Who will take command of our mission in Georgia?"

"Did you hear me?" Darryl said. "You've betrayed the Lord and you've betrayed me. I am here to serve God's justice."

"Br-brother Meeks, I d-don't understand. Wh-wha," Mitch stammered, "...what is it that you think I did?"

Darryl nodded to the two men; they took Mitch's arms as Darryl put his face inches from Mitch's. "Brother Hoeven," he said softly, "be comforted in knowing that God's mercy is infinite. Confess your treason and pray for his forgiveness. You may yet this day be in his presence."

"You're m-making a mistake. I've done nothing but what you have t-told me to do. I am a soldier, loyal and true to G-god."

Darryl's eyes grew wide, his jaw clenched. "You are Judas Iscariot, and I condemn you," he growled. "I damn you, I *damn* you to hell. God has no mercy for traitors and neither have I." Darryl took two steps back, grabbed his shirt, and tore it open, buttons flying in all directions. "*Treason!* We are at war and you have conspired with the enemy. *Traitor!* You can deny it, but I know it's true, because *God has revealed it to me!*" Darryl jerked his head in one direction, then another. He found what he was looking for—a large kitchen knife, lying next to the sink. In less than two seconds he had it in his hand.

"Brother Mee—" Before Mitch could finish the sentence, Darryl plunged the knife into Mitch's abdomen, driving it upward with enough force to lift him from the floor. Darryl's men continued to hold Mitch as he slumped, blood pooling around his feet.

"Dispose of the body," Darryl said. "Clean the floor." He pointed toward a corner. "And find the buttons."

‡ ‡ ‡

Agent Hastings entered the briefing room at a hurried pace, dropping a stack of files on the front table. She looked toward the back of the room. "Put up the presentation," she snapped.

Hastings clicked through a series of photos: the ruins of Donald Lominger's house, remnants of the phone that had been used as a remote detonator, a graph showing the infrared spectra of chemicals retrieved from three different crime scenes.

"The forensics lab has confirmed that the explosive from the Lominger blast is the same as that used in the Atlanta and Pittsburgh clinic bombings. The mechanisms used to detonate the devices were also similar." She clicked the presentation forward, projecting a mug shot of a man with a gaunt, unshaven face and hollow eyes.

"This is Randall Joseph McConnell, a known trafficker in illegal weapons and explosives. He's known in certain circles as 'the Supplier.' Under a plea deal, McConnell admitted providing the explosives for the Atlanta and Pittsburgh bombs—and enough for forty-eight more."

The agents in the room gasped. "Forty-*eight?*"

"Yes. It's much bigger than we thought."

"Did McConnell give up the locations?" an agent in the front row asked.

"He doesn't know them. He *did* give up the name of his customer." Hastings advanced the slide. Some of the agents in the room grunted in disgust; a few averted their eyes from the photo—a body, partially decomposed and dismembered by scavengers. "This is the customer, Marlin Blaine Castor, former master sergeant and demolitions expert, U.S. Army Special Forces. He did four turns in Afghanistan. His record indicates that he was highly skilled, but that he had a chip on his shoulder. Insubordinate. He received a general discharge five years ago." Hastings clicked through the autopsy photos. "Sergeant Castor was shot three times. He'd been dead for a week by the time his body was found."

"He's not talking," said an agent in the back, causing a wave of laughter to spread through the room.

"Clearly," Hastings said. "And neither is anyone else."

Hastings clicked again. A map of the United States appeared on the screen, identical to the map that Agent Sessions had shown the week before, but with a large red *X* over Atlanta.

"Our informant gave us Donald Lominger's name; that and his connection to Lucy Seidman, the Atlanta clinic bomber, got us a search warrant. We haven't gotten warrants for any of the others in the *Heaven Sent* network—yet."

"You don't need a warrant to interview them," said an agent standing by the door.

"We've tried. We have one informant among them, but he dealt only with Lominger, and Lominger never mentioned Meeks. The informant gave us the date of the bombings and his local targets, but the rest have been stubbornly uncooperative. Word is, these fanatics would rather die than talk."

"Where do we go from here?" asked the agent by the door.

"If at first you don't succeed. We've targeted twelve persons of interest for more intensive questioning, starting with this one." Hastings used her laser pointer to indicate a spot near the west coast of Florida. "Mitch Hoeven is known to have had contact with Lominger. We're sending an agent down there today."

‡ ‡ ‡

As the plane rose from the runway at Tampa Executive Airport, its sole passenger, Darryl Meeks, punched a number into his phone.

"It is done," Darryl said.

"What is done?" asked the other party. The voice broke up.

"You're hard to understand," Darryl said.

"I've had to relocate. The reception here is terrible. You said it is done. What is done?"

"We have discovered the traitor. It was Mitch Hoeven, in Florida."

There was a scratchy pause. "Was?"

"God's vengeance is satisfied."

"*What did you do?*"

"Whoever will not submit to God's law, let judgment be executed speedily upon him, even unto death."

"Oh, no. Tell me you *didn't.*"

"Hoeven is dead."

"I told you to find him and *report back to me.* Was that not clear? What possessed you? Are you insane?"

Darryl gripped the cell phone hard. "What did you call me?"

"We could have managed him. There was no need for this impulsive act. You've greatly increased our exposure. Are you even sure that Hoeven was the right man?"

Darryl remained silent, staring straight ahead and with the cell phone pressed to his ear.

"Well?" the voice asked.

"I am God's anointed one. I am he whom God has chosen as his instrument of justice. As he revealed the lottery numbers to me through his holy scriptures, so he revealed to me the name of the traitor. I have calculated it. Do you doubt the Lord? Do you doubt his holy word?"

"We've worked too hard to jeopardize the mission needlessly. We can't afford to be careless. The FBI is here and they're onto us. They could move in at any time. You saw what happened in Atlanta."

"My mission is of God. No earthly power can stop me."

"Right. Nevertheless, I've decided to change the date."

"*You've* decided?"

"We can't give the FBI time to coordinate. Contact your operatives and give me a new date. The sooner the better."

"The date was chosen by God. You cannot change it. No man can change it. Do you doubt the Lord?"

"We don't have time for this. Get me a new date."

"*Do you doubt the Lord?*"

"*Get me a new date!*"

Darryl closed the phone.

The Lord has revealed it.

At the other end of the call an identical cell phone snapped shut. Its user was about to destroy it and dispose of the pieces when a knock came at the door. The occupant went to the door, opened it a crack, and then opened it wide. The two people faced each other for a moment before one of them spoke.

"Something's happened," said Ronni Barraket. "We need to move quickly."

58

VISION

MATT AND RONNI followed their instructions to the letter. Matt left his car on the side of a street more than two miles from the location of the meeting. They had no trouble finding a vacant space—the streets, as usual, were deserted at five a.m.

They encountered no one as they followed the circuitous route from the car to their final destination. Had anyone else been following them, either by car or on foot, they would easily have been detected.

The tenement was on a narrow street, midway between cross streets. It looked old, its brick walls cracked where mortar had failed as the foundation settled, the paint on the door and window frames largely peeled away, exposing the weathered wood underneath, livable, but not comfortably so, like every other building on the street, and on every street that Matt and Ronni had walked to get there.

Matt raised his hand as they climbed the short flight of steps, but the door opened before he could knock. A short, powerfully built man pulled Matt into the entrance, reaching out a split-second later to pull Ronni in after him. The man glanced up and down the street to verify it was deserted before closing the door behind him. The short man pushed Matt and Ronni forward, toward a second, taller man.

"*Bugatti, non è vero?*" the tall man said.

"*Sì,*" Matt said. "*Sono il Dottor Bugatti.*"

"*E Lei, è Barraket, vero?*"

"*Sì,*" Matt answered. "We're looking for Signor Nelson."

"*Lo so,*" the tall man said gruffly. "I know."

The short man pulled Matt's arms behind him and secured his wrists with zip ties. He frisked Matt hastily before turning his attention to Ronni, binding her wrists, then searching her, probing every part of her body.

"*Lei non ha niente,*" Matt said. "She doesn't have anything. Leave her alone." The short man looked at Matt and sneered. He undid Ronni's belt and unbuttoned her jeans. Ronni pulled away but the tall man grabbed her shoulders and pushed her forward.

"*Che cosa hai qui?*" the short man said. "What do you have here?" He slid his hand into Ronni's pants as she struggled in the second man's grip.

Matt hurled himself against the short man, driving him into the wall. Matt kicked him in the stomach twice as he fell, before the tall man brought the butt of a pistol crashing into the back of Matt's skull, sending him to the floor on the edge of unconsciousness. The short man lay doubled up, holding his stomach and moaning.

"*Basta,*" the tall man said. "Enough. Let's get them upstairs."

The two men led Matt and Ronni up two flights of stairs, to the door at the end of the hallway. Inside the room the air smelled unpleasantly of alcohol, sweat and urine. Matt's head throbbed; when the smell hit him he fought the urge to vomit.

The men forced Matt and Ronni into two wooden chairs and secured their legs and arms with zip ties. From where they were seated, the bedroom was visible through an open door, and in it, two gurneys, each with a person strapped to it. Their chests rose and fell slowly with each breath.

Cameron stepped out of the bathroom, wearing green scrubs, addressing the two men in Italian. "*Grazie*, Enrico," he said to the tall one. "You and Marco may leave us. Let's be especially vigilant for any signs of the police."

"We are prepared for the police," Enrico said.

Cameron held up a hand. "Enrico, please, let's not discuss our private affairs in front of our guests."

Enrico motioned with his head toward the door. Marco followed him out of the room.

"We're all together again," Cameron said, smiling. "Me, Matt and Ronni. And in the next room, Clara and Flora."

Matt lifted his head, forcing his eyes open, his vision blurred, trying to make out the two women. "Have you hurt them?" he asked.

"They're fine, just fine. They're a little subdued at the moment, but no permanent damage. None yet, that is."

"We're here, Stroud," Matt said. "We've done as you asked. Now let them go."

Cameron straightened himself. "Is that what you thought? That you would come here and I would release these two *females?* Is that what simple-minded Pierangelo told you? No, no, your poor cousin got it wrong. I have no intention of letting them go anywhere."

Matt pulled at his restraints. The sharp edges of the ties dug into his skin. "Then why are we here?"

"Dr. Bugatti, you are here, and *she* is here, because I wish you to be here. And here you are."

"You don't have anything to gain by harming us. We're not the only ones who know what you did." Matt said.

Cameron narrowed his eyes. "What I did? You know what I *did?*"

Matt shut his eyes tightly—his head felt as if it were being squeezed by a vise, compressing and relaxing with each heartbeat. "Yes, Stroud. We know everything."

"Do you? No, I don't think you do, because I haven't *explained* it to you. Of course, this *female* can't understand, no matter how patiently and simply I spell it out. But *you*, Doctor, you have the intellect to understand, to *appreciate* what I've accomplished. And *that's* why you're here." Cameron walked to a small table on which sat a towel and a china basin filled with water. He rinsed and dried his hands. "Dr. Matteo Bugatti, awarded the doctorate at the age of nineteen." He carefully folded the towel and laid it on the table. "Nineteen. I was almost twenty-five years old when I received my PhD, but, of course, I *also* received an MD. I think we can agree that there was a *little* more involved in obtaining *two* doctor's degrees. Your discoveries in mathematics I'll grant you were impressive, although I found the editorializing over your Fields medal to be somewhat fawning. 'A seminal work.' they wrote, 'of such depth and originality that Bugatti deserves a seat in the pantheon of mathematicians, in the company of Newton, Gauss and Euler.' Pantheon? *Really?* Don't get me wrong, Doctor, it was good work, *important* work, the product of a fine intellect. That's why, of all people, I believe that you are among the very few that can understand the difficulty of the problem and the ingenuity of my solution."

"The *problem?*" Matt asked, struggling to stay alert, the pain in his head intensifying.

"A very difficult problem." Cameron held out his hands, as if he were comparing the weight of two objects. "The starting point: an obscure genetic mutation, limited to a small population of Eastern Europeans, linked to an unpleasant but relatively benign disease. The end point: a painful death for deserving females."

"Why? Why would you do that?" Ronni said.

"Shut up, whore," Cameron spat. "Keep your fucking mouth shut. The doctor and I are having a conversation."

Matt looked at Ronni—her eyes were wide and her mouth was open. He looked at Cameron, who looked as if he'd just wished Ronni a good morning. "I'm not impressed, Stroud," Matt said.

"Doctor, let me continue. The difficulty of the problem was *not* in exploiting this genetic vulnerability. Any reasonably competent, properly motivated researcher could have done it, given enough time—given enough chances—enough *guesses.*

That's the sad state of medical research these days. Guesswork—they shoot drugs about which they know little into bodies about which they know less, just to see what happens."

"They're helping people, Stroud," Matt said. "You're killing them."

"Before you judge, Doctor, let me point out that those helpful people whom you admire so much have racked up hundreds of times more victims by accident than I have on purpose." Cameron looked at his hands, rubbing his palms together as if he were trying to remove some invisible substance. He went to the basin and rinsed his hands. "No vision."

"What did you say?" Matt asked.

"They have no vision. They know the formulae, they know the anatomy. They've memorized a million facts, they can regurgitate the clinical effects of a thousand drugs. But they can't *see*."

Matt's eyes opened. For a moment, he forgot about his aching head. "See what?"

"*Structure*. They're all stuck in a descriptive world. They think that reading is the same as knowing, and that knowing is the same as understanding. But you and I, Doctor, we know better. In your world, equations and theorems are just imperfect descriptions of the truth. In my world, DNA codes for amino acids, amino acids make proteins, and proteins function according to their *structure*. Do you know what makes me different? It's this: I know what a protein will do because I can visualize its *structure*."

Matt thought back to an earlier time, a seeming eternity ago, on the first day of a new semester, lecturing a classroom of prospective mathematicians.

Some of you will transcend that plateau, when you begin to see concepts as structures; when what was once abstract becomes real, even visceral.

"Now do you understand, Doctor? I didn't have the luxury of clinical trials to test my drug. In fact, I had to complete the trials knowing that the mechanism would *not* be triggered.

Conducting them in South Africa was the key. It was highly unlikely that women of Eastern European extraction would frequent free clinics in Johannesburg. But I didn't need to test it. I *knew* it would work because I could *see* it." Cameron rinsed his hands again. "I didn't anticipate the age selectivity, though. I expected the effect to be manifested in women of all ages, not only teen-aged girls." He folded the towel. "That was a bonus."

"Very clever," Matt said.

"Do you think so?" Cameron smiled thinly. "That is high praise indeed, coming from the great Dr. Bugatti. You know, I've followed your career with great interest. I make it a point to learn about men whose achievements are comparable to my own. They are rare, almost nonexistent. You are the only one who even comes close. That makes my disappointment all the greater."

"Disappointment?"

"I'm disappointed in you, Dr. Bugatti." Cameron opened the drawer of a credenza, removing a syringe and a vial of clear liquid. "When the Bugatti commission failed to discover my secret, I was satisfied that my role in the deaths would remain unknown." He inserted the syringe into the vial, pulled back the plunger and withdrew it. He walked to Clara's gurney and stood over her. "But then this disgusting old whore figured it out. How does that make you feel, Doctor? You were scooped by a *female*." He inspected Clara's IV bag. "Before she found me out, and before you so badly disappointed me, Doctor, I doubt that I could have brought myself to kill you, no matter how necessary it was to protect myself."

"Then take it out on me, Stroud. I'm the one that disappointed you. Leave these women alone."

Cameron spun around. "You don't just disappoint me, you *disgust* me. *Leave these women alone.* I thought you were better than that. When I read about you, when I talked to people who knew you, from all I'd learned about you, I was sure that you had the capacity to free yourself from the influence of these—these *fucking* females. At last I'd found someone else who could rise above his reptilian urges. How could it be otherwise? How could you have risen to our intellectual level and still be burdened with these animal desires and these pathetic sympathies? I should have known better." Cameron studied the syringe, running his fingers along its length. "And how could you have done this to me? *Me?* The one man in the whole world knows you, who…who *understands* you?" He turned toward Flora's gurney. "Do you see what you did to your baby? Do you understand what you made of him? Flora, the good mother. Flora, the nurturing mother. When you held his hand, you didn't make him touch your body, did you? Touch all your filthy parts, until his hands reeked of the smell of you. You stroked his hair, you petted him and cooed 'sweet boy, dear sweet boy' and held him close and then— you stopped. You stopped and you didn't push his face between your tits and down your belly and between your legs and hold him there until he choked while you moaned 'oh, oh yes, sweet boy, oh, dear *sweet* boy.' You didn't teach him to keep a seething silence, to hide himself in darkness, to make his secret plans, to see a different world, where you were dead and no female would ever have power over him." He inserted the needle into Flora's IV line. "No, you made him a slave."

"Stroud, don't!"

Cameron pressed the plunger. Matt pulled at his restraints, blood dripping to the floor as the plastic cut into his arms. He lunged forward, pulling the heavy chair on top of him.

Flora's chest rose and fell twice, then remained still. Matt passed out as he succumbed to the pain in his skull.

59

ATONEMENT

THE PACKAGE INCLUDED the details of clinics in four cities—Richmond, Norfolk, Raleigh, Charlotte—and four single-page dossiers, one for each terminally ill woman that Walter Tillis had recruited, each having received her instructions and her equipment, standard issue for the army of Darryl Meeks: one explosive belt and detonator, one fatal dose of concentrated brodifacoum. Darryl sat in Walter's neatly-kept but deteriorating mobile home, studying the package. Walter waited for Darryl's reaction, expecting Darryl's praise for his dedication and devotion.

"When did you last visit your soldier in Charlotte?" Darryl asked.

"A week ago," Walter answered. "She's strong. She'll be ready."

"A week. Just before we lost Brother Lominger."

Walter closed his eyes. "God bless his memory."

"He was betrayed."

Walter's eyes snapped open. "Betrayed! Who?"

"Brother Hoeven was a traitor."

Walter swallowed hard. "Was?"

"He is dead, by my hand and God's."

Walter bowed his head. "Dear Jesus, preserve us and our holy cause."

"There is an FBI field office in Charlotte."

"I don't know, Brother Meeks. Is there?"

"You know there is, Brother Tillis." Darryl slipped the package into his bag. "I discovered Hoeven's treachery in my calculations. It was Hoeven who gave the FBI cause to search Brother Lominger's house. I had thought that by eliminating Hoeven we'd be secure. But to be sure, I sought further guidance in the scriptures." He pulled a sheet from his bag and held it out to Walter. "This is the Lord's revelation."

Walter took the sheet, covered with lists of bible verses and rows of numbers, and a tangle of arrows running between numbers and verses, seemingly at random. Where arrows converged on words, letters were circled: T-I-L-L-I-S.

"There is another traitor."

The paper rustled in Walter's trembling hand. "Surely not I, Brother Meeks?"

"You have said it."

Walter gripped the paper with both hands, pressing it against his face. Walter wept.

"How have you betrayed me?" Darryl asked.

"I was weak, Brother," Walter said between sobs, "and frightened."

"Then you confess?"

"I didn't give them your name, Brother Meeks. I couldn't, though they asked me many times. Brother Lominger never mentioned you. And I didn't know that they had gotten to Brother Hoeven." Walter held out the paper, crumpled and tear-stained. "And now I'm accused by God."

Darryl reached into his bag. He pulled out a .38 caliber revolver and laid it on the table. Walter stared at the gun open-mouthed.

"Brother Lominger told me that you are a godly man," Darryl said. "I believed him. Brother Tillis, you may yet prove your devotion."

Darryl took the paper from Walter, returning it to his bag. He stood and placed his hand on Walter's head.

"Lord, by this blood sacrifice in atonement for his sins, may this man merit your mercy."

Darryl left the trailer to the sound of weeping, looking in every direction. The trailer was at least a mile from the nearest dwelling. He walked to his car and stood waiting until he heard the muffled sound of a pistol shot. He opened the trunk, removing a metal trash can, its interior scorched and soot-covered, setting it on the ground. He pulled the package with the details of Walter Tillis's targets from his bag, dropped it into the can, soaked it with lighter fluid, and set it ablaze. Once the package was consumed, Darryl pulled a cell phone from his bag and punched in a number.

"We are not safe," he said into the phone. "We must strike now."

"Good idea," said the other party. "But what about God's revelation? You said that no man could change the date. Has God chosen a new date?"

"I have chosen the date," Darryl said. "I can't wait for God."

‡ ‡ ‡

The phone on Agent Hastings's desk buzzed. The display read *Edward Carmona*. She grabbed the receiver and put it to her ear.

"Will you hold for the director?"

"Of course," Hastings replied.

She heard a click. "Agent Hastings, what is your status?"

"Hoeven, the person of interest in Tampa, has disappeared. After interviewing his acquaintances we concluded that Hoeven may have been in danger and we entered the residence on those grounds. The kitchen area appeared to have been cleaned recently, but forensics detected evidence of a large amount of blood."

"Anything else?"

"Yes. A button."

"What kind of button?"

"A shirt button, from a very expensive shirt. It's consistent with those used by a tailor in Columbia, South Carolina."

"Meeks's home town."

"Yes, sir. And we have records of Meeks having received deliveries from the same tailor."

"That's something. Not enough for a warrant."

"There's more. When we couldn't find Hoeven we went to our informant, Walter Tillis, Greensboro, North Carolina. Same situation: Tillis had disappeared and we entered the residence on the presumption of danger."

"And?"

"Tillis was dead of a self-inflicted gunshot wound."

"Jesus."

"There's more. The gun, a .38 caliber revolver, is the same gun that was used to kill Marlin Castor."

"*Jesus.* Hastings, get your team to connect the dots. I want a warrant to search Meeks's house."

60

COMMON INTEREST

CAMERON WALKED TO where Matt lay, put his foot on the chair and pushed it over. Matt rolled onto his side, still motionless. Cameron knelt beside him and inspected the location of the blow to Matt's head, then he lifted Matt's eyelid.

"A mild concussion. Better to let him sleep. I'll wake him for the main event." Cameron stood. "That would be you, Ronni. First Flora, then Clara, then Ronni. You needn't worry, though. It's entirely painless. You'll feel rather pleasantly sleepy, you'll drift off, and then, nothing. Bye-bye."

"There's a place in hell for you," Ronni said.

"Did I say you could talk? Did you not hear me tell you to keep your fucking thoughts to yourself?" Cameron filled another syringe. "I especially don't want to hear you prattling on about your primitive superstitions." He looked down at Matt. "Dr. Bugatti at least has freed himself from *those* chains. If you want to console yourself with fantasies of life after death and eternity with your god, go ahead. Just don't bore *me* with them."

"God will judge you."

Cameron spun on his heel. He thrust his hand in Ronni's face, holding the syringe inches from her nose.

"Is this what it will take to shut your filthy mouth?"

The door burst open. Enrico and Marco rushed in, carrying a man who looked as if he'd suffered at their hands, his feet dragging behind him as Enrico and Marco pulled him through the door. His head was bowed and his face was hidden.

"What? *What?*" Cameron shouted.

"*Quest'uomo ha chiesto di te,*" Enrico said. "This man has asked for you. He would not say why."

Cameron gripped the man's hair and lifted his head. The man blinked his eyes slowly.

Ronni recognized him immediately. Cameron noticed the look on her face.

"Do you know who this is?" Cameron asked.

"Yes. He's an aide to the president of the United States. His name is Tyler Ross."

"What's he doing here?"

Ronni shook her head.

"Perhaps Dr. Bugatti has an idea." Cameron pulled Matt's chair upright. He went to the table and picked up the basin, throwing the water into Matt's face. Matt sputtered awake, looking around the room, his gaze settling on Tyler.

"Dr. Bugatti, have you been telling tales? I gave explicit instructions that you were to come alone and tell no one."

"I didn't tell anyone."

Cameron shattered the bowl against Matt's head. Blood streamed down Matt's face and filled his eye. He slumped forward against his restraints.

Cameron grabbed Matt's shirt and slapped him. "Don't pass out. Don't." He gripped Matt's chin and turned his head toward Ronni. "When she's dead, that's when you can sleep. I'll even help you."

"It wasn't Bugatti."

Cameron turned to Tyler.

"It was her," Tyler said. "She came to me. She asked me to use my influence with the president to dispatch special forces to rescue these people."

Cameron looked at Enrico. "*Hai visto qualcosa?*" he asked. "Did you see anything?"

Enrico shook his head. "*Niente.*"

"I came by myself," Tyler said. "There's no one else."

Cameron bent down and got face to face with Tyler. "Why?"

"I'm not here to save them," Tyler said. "You and I have a common interest. Neither of us can allow Bugatti or Barraket to live."

61

DAILY BREAD

AGENT HASTINGS SPOKE softly into her radio microphone. "Perimeter secure?"

"Confirmed. Perimeter secure."

Hastings pressed the button to the intercom at the gate of the residence. There was a click from the speaker.

"Identify yourself."

"Federal Bureau of Investigation. We have a warrant to search the premises."

Hastings heard another click. After a few seconds her radio came to life.

"Suspect is leaving the house through the rear entrance. Will apprehend."

"Acknowledged." Hastings turned to a young agent holding an aluminum case. "Enter the code."

The agent tapped the keypad on the intercom. The gate remained closed.

"It seems Mr. Meeks doesn't trust the fire department with the keys to his kingdom." The agent took a small screwdriver from his case and removed the panel to the intercom, attaching a jumper between two contacts. The gate slid open.

Agent Hastings led the team of four agents through the gate. They encountered four more agents coming from the back of the house, two of them leading a man of average height, thinning brown hair, and a prominent belly. Agent Hastings looked closely at his face.

"Darryl Meeks?" she asked.

The man opened his eyes wide, looking terrified. "No, I am not Brother Meeks."

"Who are you?"

"I'm Austen. I work for *Daily Bread*. I'm the delivery driver."

‡ ‡ ‡

Months of deception had taught Darryl the skill of not noticing the car parked on the street near his house. He was so good at it that the FBI agent in the car almost believed that the driver of the *Daily Bread* delivery truck was someone other than the most wanted man in America.

Darryl turned into the driveway, pulling up to the gate. He leaned out the window and pressed the intercom button.

"Identify yourself," said Austen's familiar voice.

"Daily Bread, Mr. Meeks," Darryl said.

"Come up."

The gate slid open. Darryl continued up the drive, stopping the car in the exact spot that Austen had parked it less than a week before. He got out of the cab, hurried to the back of the truck, and filled his hand cart with the first load of groceries. He hauled the cart to the front door and rang the doorbell. It was an act he had rehearsed to perfection.

The door opened to a Glock 21 in the hands of Agent Hastings.

Darryl ran back toward the truck. Four more agents materialized, two on either side, brandishing weapons.

"FBI," Hastings shouted. "On your knees, hands behind your head. Do it!"

Darryl kneeled and bowed his head.

Eli, Eli, lama sabachthani—my God, my God, why have You forsaken me?

62

HEAVEN SENT

CAMERON INSPECTED THE syringe in his hand before looking up at Tyler. "What else did you and this whore talk about?"

"She told me that you're responsible for the *Backup* deaths," Tyler said. "She told me that you have Bugatti's mother, and probably the AP reporter, Kildee. She didn't trust the Italian police to handle the situation. She asked me to intervene."

"But you didn't. Why?"

"This discussion could be more productive if these two thugs would let me go."

Cameron motioned to Enrico. Tyler fell to his knees as Enrico and Marco released his arms.

"The commission report must be approved with a finding against the FDA and CG Pharma. The public must be made aware of the conspiracy, the twisted, wicked conspiracy between the highest levels of the government and industry to kill the unborn. If it becomes known that that this was all the work of one single perpetrator, that conspiracy will continue."

Cameron slowly rolled the syringe between his fingers. "Forgive me if I'm skeptical, Mr. Ross. I find it difficult to accept that you're willing to be a party to the killing of Dr. Bugatti and the rest of these…" He looked at Ronni, then in the direction of the bedroom where Clara and Flora lay. "The rest of *these*, just to ensure that the conclusion of a *report* isn't challenged? That's not much of a motive. I think you're lying. I think the authorities are on their way here now."

"He's not lying."

All eyes turned to Ronni. "He's telling the truth when he says he wants us dead," she said. "But he's not telling you everything."

Cameron looked at Ronni with contempt. He turned to Tyler with a look of equal scorn. He turned back to Ronni. "Keep talking."

"The FBI confronted me with a photo," Ronni said, "a picture of me in the Washington Mall, talking on a cheap, pre-paid phone. They accused me of conspiring with a man named Darryl Meeks to blow up abortion clinics. Their evidence seemed convincing—they'd identified the make of the phone used to contact Meeks, the same kind that I was using. And I was making the call at the same moment that Meeks received an incoming call from a burner phone located at that exact spot."

"You don't believe this. You can*not* believe this," Tyler interrupted.

"Shut up," Cameron said. He turned back to Ronni. "Talk."

"When I saw the photo, I remembered that day," she continued. "We sometimes use burner phones to talk with our more paranoid clients. It doesn't happen very often. That photo was of the last time I'd used one. The day stuck in my mind, because I recognized someone else in the Mall using the exact same kind of phone."

"Stroud, she's a lying bitch. Kill her."

"You know who I saw, Tyler. You know because you saw me, too."

"Stroud, listen to me," Tyler said. "She's lying, but what if she's not? So what? What if I were conspiring to bomb abortion clinics? Do you care? I need the report. If Bugatti dies, I'll sanction the findings and your role stays a secret. We both get what we want."

"Tyler Ross," Ronni said, "you've offended God and His son Jesus Christ. I pray that God will have mercy on your repentant soul."

Tyler struggled to his feet, lunging at Ronni. Enrico and Marco grabbed his arms and pulled him back.

"You say you're a Christian," Tyler shouted. "You say you care about the mass murder of innocents. But when a true soldier of Christ comes forward, you betray me. You betray me, you betray Christ and you betray His holy cause. Damn you! I have more respect for Bugatti, an *atheist*, than I do for you, a believer who won't stand with the army of the Lord." He spat on the floor. "Because you are lukewarm, and neither hot nor cold, I spew you from my mouth."

Cameron watched with amusement. He waved his hand. "Get rid of him," he said to Enrico.

"Stroud, wait!" Tyler said. "You need me."

"I don't need you."

"You're a hunted man. You can't run forever. What's your end game?"

"Do you think I'm worried about the *end game*? There is no *end game*. There is only what there has always been—me, and everyone else." Cameron glared at Enrico. "*Merda!* What are you waiting for?"

"Stroud, I have influence. I can protect you."

"I'm still skeptical. Does an aide to the president have that kind of pull?"

"I have friends, friends who believe as I do, brothers and sisters in Christ. They're at the highest levels, in every branch of government. They'll protect you if it means that our plan succeeds."

Cameron looked up at Tyler, spinning the syringe in his fingers. "If they can hide me, they can find me. If they can protect me, they can kill me." He shook his head. "Nice try, Mr. Ross, but I'll take my chances." He readied the syringe.

Enrico felt a vibration in his pocket. He pulled his cell phone out and put it to his ear. "*Pronto.*"

Tyler tore his arm from Enrico's grip and slapped the syringe out of Cameron's hand, sending it sliding across the floor. Marco put a choke hold on Tyler.

"*Ci sono le macchine della polizia fuori,*" Enrico said. "There are police cars outside. Three or four. The police are entering the building."

"*Come fai a saperlo?*" Cameron said. "How do you know?"

"We have eyes and ears in the streets," Enrico said.

Cameron turned back to Matt and Ronni. "One of you can't follow directions, and at this moment, I really don't care who." He retrieved the syringe and plunged it into Ronni's arm. "*Ciao,* Ronni. Say hello to Jesus for me. Enrico, Marco, *andiamo.*"

Marco rammed his knee into Tyler's stomach. Tyler collapsed as Marco followed Enrico and Cameron through a side door.

Four officers of the *polizia giudiziaria* broke through the door with guns drawn, followed immediately by Agent Sessions and Inspector Costa. Costa pointed at Tyler. "*Lui,*" he said. "Him." Two officers pulled Tyler to his feet.

Costa looked around the room. "*I medici.*" He pointed at Ronni and Matt. "*Qui e qui. Subito!*"

Two medical technicians with crash kits followed Costa's directions, one tending to Matt, while the other examined Ronni.

"*Non respira!*" he shouted. "She's not breathing!" He pressed a respirator to Ronni's face and began ventilating.

"*Dottor Bugatti, riesce a sentirmi?*" the second medic said as he examined the gash in Matt's scalp. "Can you hear me?"

"*Mia madre è di là, nell'altra stanza,*" Matt said. "My mother is in the other room. Help her, please, please help her."

The medic hurried to Clara, then to Flora. He pulled his respirator from his kit and began to resuscitate her.

Costa cut the ties around Matt's wrists and ankles. Matt got to his feet and staggered into the bedroom. He leaned over Flora's motionless body.

"*Sta respirando?*" Matt asked.

The medic lifted the respirator. He waited a few seconds before replacing it.

"*Non ancora,*" he answered. "Not yet."

Matt felt a hand on his shoulder. "*Lascialo lavorare,*" Costa said. "Let him work."

As Matt stood back, Costa opened his hand in view of the medic, revealing a nearly empty vial of sodium thiopental.

"*Merda,*" the medic said. "We haven't much time."

"Where's Stroud?" Sessions demanded, just inches from Tyler's face. Tyler tipped his head in the direction of the second bedroom. Two officers rushed through the door.

The walls were lined with shelves, stacked with linens and bedclothes; piles of trash bags sat in the corners. The officers winced at the smell of disinfectant with undertones of urine and feces.

They swept the room with their pistols. One pointed at a closed door on the far wall.

"*L'armadio,*" he whispered. "The closet." The officers took their positions next to the door, guns ready.

"*Polizia! Uscire!*" one shouted. "Come out!" They listened for movement and heard nothing. The first officer adjusted his grip on his weapon as the second officer gently grasped the knob, took a deep breath, and flung the door open.

"*Non c'è nessuno dentro,*" he said. "Nobody inside." He holstered his pistol and stepped into the closet. His footsteps on the floor of the closet made a hollow sound.

"*Vieni qui,*" he said. "Come here." The other officer joined him in the closet as he pulled up the floor board, revealing a space large enough for a man—or three men—to crawl through.

One of the officers went back to the main room. "*È vuota,*" he said. "Empty. They're gone."

Sessions cursed. He pulled a card from his pocket. "Tyler Ross, I am arresting you on a charge of conspiracy to commit an act or acts of terrorism." He read from the card and returned it to his pocket. "Do you understand these rights as I've explained them to you?"

Tyler hung his head as Sessions spoke. As he looked to one side he noticed the officer's pistol, unsecured in its holster. Tyler laughed.

"What's funny?" Sessions asked.

Tyler looked up. "Forgive me, Jesus. I am heaven sent." The officer holding him was unable to react in time to prevent Tyler from grabbing his gun, placing the muzzle under his chin and pulling the trigger.

63

PATTERN

MATT WOKE TO a persistent throbbing in his skull. His hand went to his face, then explored the extent of the bandages covering his head, pressing against his temple, still slightly numb, the site of a gash that had taken eight stitches to close. He touched the back of his head and winced at the sharp pain. He disconnected the pulse monitor from his finger, then tried unsuccessfully to sit up. Fighting waves of nausea, he pulled the IV needle from his arm and tried again.

"*Signore, la prego!*" The nurse rushed into the room and put her hand on Matt's chest. She tried to push him back down but Matt refused to be pushed.

"*Riesco ad alzarmi,*" he protested. "I can get up."

"You have to stay in bed, *signore.*"

"It'll be all right," Inspector Costa said from the doorway. "I'll take responsibility."

The nurse glared at Costa. "No. Look at him. He must rest."

Costa showed his identification. The nurse looked at it, then at Matt. "You rest!" she said as she left.

Costa put a finger on Matt's chin and turned his head to one side, examining Matt's face, purple and swollen, his left eye barely open. "You look terrible," he said. "How do you feel?"

"My mother."

"She is alive. They haven't told me anything else."

"Where is she?"

"She's upstairs."

"I want to see her."

"You know, the nurse is right. You need to rest."

Matt slid off the bed. He stood up in his hospital gown, looking around the room.

"Your clothes were ruined," Costa said, guessing what Matt was looking for. "We have disposed of them."

Matt walked toward the door, but Costa stood in his way.

"Matteo, wait." Costa went into the hallway and waved his hand. An officer came with a change of clothes. "You can't walk around with your ass showing."

☦ ☦ ☦

Flora's face was all but obscured by the ventilator, her chest rising and falling at precise intervals, as the heart monitor traced a jagged line, each spike accompanied by a beep.

"We are still testing," the doctor told Matt.

"But you know already, don't you?"

The doctor turned away. "*Signore*, please. We'll know more in a few hours."

Matt touched Flora's hand; it was warm but unresponsive. He walked to the corner of the room and dropped into a chair, his breath catching as he put a hand to his mouth to stifle a sob.

☦ ☦ ☦

"I hope you have that son-of-a-bitch in a dungeon." Clara Kildee sat up in her bed. "You have dungeons in Italy, don't you?"

"Unfortunately, Dr. Stroud has escaped," Costa said.

"Escaped. Oh, Jesus."

"We are searching for him."

"Well, *find him*. That twisted bastard is pure evil."

"You seem to be well enough to make a statement, *signora*."

Clara looked at Costa over her glasses. "You're damn right I am. I'll tell you everything. Your steno had better have a strong stomach."

Costa nodded and turned to leave.

"Did you find my laptop?" Clara asked.

"Your computer?"

"Yeah. I'm past deadline. I have a story to file."

‡ ‡ ‡

Ronni opened her eyes. She turned to see Matt sitting in a chair next to her bed. He was barely recognizable—what wasn't covered in bandages was discolored and disfigured.

"Oh, my god," she said.

"It's not that bad," Matt said. "I'll recover. So will you."

Ronni looked at the ceiling. "What happened?"

"Stroud got away. Tyler's in intensive care."

"What? Intensive care?"

"He shot himself with the policeman's gun. You're lucky you were out when he did it. I had no idea he was..."

"He was the one behind the clinic bombings. I know."

Matt sighed. "How much more do you know that you haven't told me?"

Ronni gave Matt a weak smile. "I've only known about Tyler for a few days, since the FBI questioned me."

"The photo. They thought it was you."

"They were certain of it. They hoped that I'd confess when they questioned me about it. When I saw the photo, that's when I knew it was Tyler. It was an unlucky coincidence that I happened to be in the Mall at the same time, using the same kind of phone."

"An unlikely coincidence, I'd say. I'm amazed that the FBI believed you."

"Oh, they didn't. But they promised the senator."

"Senator Herrera? What did they promise?"

"The senator is on the judiciary committee. The FBI had been feeding her information on the bombing investigation, but they didn't tell her about the photo. When the investigation expanded to Italy, I called the senator, and she called the director."

"It pays to have friends."

"Yes, it does. Yolanda defended me. She refused to believe any of it, but the FBI insisted. She made a deal—if I were involved, and I cooperated, I'd get lenient terms. It was a huge risk for her. If I *were* guilty, it would mean the end of her campaign. She put it all on the line for me."

"But it was Tyler."

"Yes, but they had no evidence. The only way to clear me was for Tyler to confess. So I made a deal of my own."

"You know, I'm not surprised."

"Matt, it was a bad situation," Ronni said, looking pained. "I didn't have many options."

"What kind of deal did you make?"

"When Pierangelo told us about the hostage situation, I went to Agent Sessions. He came up with the plan to set a trap, and I agreed to cooperate. I'd make an appeal to Tyler to resolve the hostage situation, but I'd also confide that I was suspected in the clinic bombings on the basis of the surveillance photo. I told him I was determined to use all my contacts to discover the truth. If we could get Tyler to incriminate himself, the senator would get credit for working with the FBI to break the clinic bombing case. It would be a major boost to her campaign."

"It sounds like a win-win, except for one thing. You used my mom as bait. You used me."

"We didn't create the situation. We only took advantage of it." She looked down. "We didn't think it would go the way it did. I'm sorry."

Matt stood and paced the floor. "You could have told me, Ronni."

"Sessions made me promise to keep it confidential. And you might not have agreed."

Matt turned his back to Ronni. He walked to the door. "I need to be away from you." He left the room.

"Oh, Matt," Ronni whispered.

‡ ‡ ‡

Matt kept vigil with Flora until Pierangelo and Stefania arrived, the three of them gathered by Flora's bedside to say their final goodbyes. Costa arrived with the magistrate; Matt signed the order and Pierangelo witnessed it. The doctor signed, then stood by the ventilator. Matt looked at Pierangelo, tears streaming down his cheeks as he nodded slightly. Matt nodded once to the doctor. The doctor threw a switch.

The rhythmic sound ceased. The heart monitor continued to beep for another minute, then faltered. Flora remained motionless as the trace flattened and the alarm sounded. The doctor stepped forward and silenced it.

"*Mi spiace, signore.*"

"*Grazie,*" Matt answered.

Matt left the room with Pierangelo under one arm and Stefania under the other. Ronni, her face wet with tears, waited outside the door.

"*Aspettate di sotto,*" Matt said to Pierangelo and Stefania. "Wait downstairs. I'll be a moment."

"Matt, I am so sorry," Ronni said.

"My dad died of a heart attack. He was on a respirator, too. This is the second time I've watched a parent slip away."

Ronni touched Matt's arm tentatively. "She's at peace now, Matt. She's with…" Ronni hesitated.

"With God?"

"It's what I believe." Ronni removed her hand from Matt's arm. "I'm sorry."

"For what?" Matt took Ronni's hand. "Ronni, I know we believe different things. When you offer me sympathy, I expect you to use religious terms. They're not the words I would use, but we come from the same place—we care about each other's feelings. Why does it matter how we say it?

Whether it's your religion, the other guy's religion, *no* religion —Ronni, that's not important. It's the same for everyone. We care because we're human, and we're decent." Matt looked back into Flora's room. The doctor had removed the ventilator. He was smoothing Flora's hair. She looked like she was sleeping. "For all the hurt and the pain that people are capable of inflicting on each other, there's a greater truth— that mostly, we're decent. That's what I believe."

Ronni wept as Matt embraced her. "I'm sorry, Matt, I'm so sorry. It shouldn't have been like this. Can you forgive me? Can you ever forgive me?"

Matt watched as the doctor drew a sheet over Flora's face.

Mi vuoi bene, caro?

Sì, Mamma.

Vorrei andare in Italia.

Matt bit his lip.

I want to go to Italy—Flora's last wish.

Matt put his hand on Ronni's cheek. "Yes, Ronni."

"Ms. Barraket."

Ronni turned to see Agent Sessions approaching. She wiped her cheeks on the back of her hand.

"We've got a problem," Sessions said. "The date of the bombings has changed."

"We have weeks," Ronni said. "Tisha B'Av. That's what your informant told you. That's what the senator told me, anyway."

"Not anymore. We finally got a warrant to search Meeks's house. It's Tuesday. Two days."

"But if you searched his house, you know the targets."

"I wish. This guy kept it all in his head. We turned the place inside-out. We were lucky to find the date."

"You don't have *anything?*"

Sessions held out a sheaf of papers. "Yeah, this." The papers were covered with bible verses and rows of numbers, digits circled at random, a tangle of lines superimposed on top. "The Charlotte office sent these. It's all nonsense. We've interrogated Meeks for the locations, but he's not talking."

Ronni glanced at the stack of papers as Matt took it from Sessions's hand.

"What about Tyler Ross?"

"He didn't make it. If he knew anything, it died with him."

Ronni closed her eyes and shook her head. "You'll need to do a blanket alert."

"I was hoping to avoid that. There are almost six hundred abortion clinics in the U.S. It'll be impossible to keep a lid on a nationwide alert. Some of those bombers will get tipped off. They'll retreat, or hit another target."

"You don't have a choice," Ronni said.

"Yes, you do."

Sessions and Ronni turned to Matt, who was paging through the stack.

"These look like nonsense, but they're not," Matt said. "There's a pattern here."

64

FORTUNA

IT WAS A bad day for the air conditioning to break down. Warm weather was the norm for mid-July in the Eastern Plains of Colorado, but the air ahead of the approaching front was stiflingly hot and unusually humid. The staff of the Family Plan Foundation of Denver considered suspending operations until the AC could be repaired, but decided that the needs of the disadvantaged were too great not to tend to them, even under adverse conditions. The waiting room had no windows; fans in the corners stirred the air but failed to provide relief. The women who sat reading old copies of *Women's Health, Shape* and *People* shifted in their vinyl chairs, suffering silently.

A thirty-ish redhead sat near the door, glancing up from her magazine at every woman who entered. She noted the appearance of every one, paying attention to their mannerisms and what they might tell her about their state of mind. They all wore tank tops and shorts in the sweltering heat, exhibiting varying degrees of anxiety. Redhead took two seconds per patient to make her judgment before looking down again and pretending to read the article.

Redhead heard the door click open for the tenth time. She looked up and prepared to look down again but paused. The woman who entered didn't wear a tank top, but instead wore an oversized short-sleeved top over capri pants. Her arms and legs were thin and her face was gaunt; the large clothes hung loosely on her thin frame. She gave her name to the nurse at the reception desk and took a seat, her eyes darting around the room for a moment before she took a breath and closed her eyes, smiling. She picked up a copy of *Redbook* and paged through it.

The nurse stood in the door to the examination area. "Ms. Schaeffer?"

The thin woman in the loose clothes stood up while Redhead scrutinized her. Redhead's attention was drawn to the drape of the woman's top, to an unnatural crease in the fabric, as if the woman had wrapped her waist with a wide, stiff belt.

The woman followed the nurse through the door. Redhead tilted her chin toward the miniature microphone on her shoulder and spoke softly.

"In the back."

‡ ‡ ‡

"Just have a seat on the exam table, Ms. Schaeffer," the nurse said as she paged through the file. "I need to ask a few questions about your medical history."

"When will I see the doctor?"

The nurse looked up and gave the woman a polite smile. "In a moment. First we have to get through these questions. Then I'll take your vital signs. Then I'll have you get undressed. Then the doctor. Okay? So, when was your last period?"

"I'd really feel more comfortable talking to the doctor."

"Dear, we have our procedures. Just a few questions."

"Please?" The woman had an imploring look and seemed near tears. The nurse closed the file.

"All right. I'll get the doctor."

The nurse left the room. The woman reached into her pocket and pulled out a cell phone. She pressed its keys, entering three numbers, and was about to press *star* when the door burst open and two men in heavy protective gear entered at a run.

"FBI! Drop the phone! Drop it!" one of them shouted. The woman slipped off the table and stumbled to a corner. One of the bomb technicians reached for the phone but she twisted away from him. She pressed *star.*

"I am heaven sent!" She pressed *pound.*

The technician ripped the phone from her hand and tossed it aside. He pinned her to the floor as the second technician lifted her top.

"Roll her over," he said. His partner did so, finding the Velcro closure of the broad elastic strip that encircled her waist. He opened it, revealing the detonator, connected to the leads of a class B blasting cap embedded in five kilograms of C4 explosive. The technician reached into his tool belt for his wire cutters. He snipped the wires, then carefully unwrapped the belt from the woman's body.

The first technician rolled the woman face down and pulled her arms behind her. Her body heaved with sobs that became softer until she sucked in a breath, crying out, *"Jesus! Oh, Jesus!"*

The technician keyed the microphone that was pinned to his shoulder. "Clear."

The nurse reentered the room in the company of Redhead. "Report," she said.

"I'm pretty sure she armed the bomb," said the technician holding the woman's arms. "She might even have pressed the key to detonate. That was too fucking close."

"No worries, man," the second tech said. "That's why we have the signal jammer."

Redhead turned to the tech with a fierce look. "The jammer is a *backup*. You were supposed to get to her *before* she started punching keys."

"Hey, hey, Red," the tech said, showing her his palms. "Back off. Bomb defused, perp in custody. No harm, no foul."

The look on Redhead's face went from scornful to disgusted. She tilted her chin to one side. "Phone it in. Denver is secure."

‡ ‡ ‡

Sessions took the call from Director Carmona in the hallway outside of Costa's office. He returned after five minutes. Matt tried to tell from the look on Sessions's face if the report was favorable, but Sessions didn't give anything away —at least he didn't look like he'd just heard bad news.

"Thirty-five bombers have been apprehended," Sessions said. "None of them were able to detonate their bombs."

"This is good," Costa said. "I'm sure the suspects can provide you with more information about the conspiracy."

"Unlikely," Sessions said grimly. "Fifteen of the suspects are dead and the rest are comatose. Some kind of poison, apparently."

"What about the other five locations?" Matt asked.

"If your analysis is correct, we should be hearing from them at any time." Sessions pulled a sheet of paper from his jacket pocket, a list of forty abortion clinics scattered across America. "I've checked off the thirty-five sites we've secured. So far, there've been no reports of attempts on any clinics that aren't on the list."

"*Ottimo lavoro, dottor Bugatti,*" Costa said. "Good work! How did you know?"

"Meeks needed targets," Matt said, "and he wanted God to provide them. His starting point was scripture, and his end point was a list of forty clinics selected from six hundred. The path from point A to point B was numerology. It's pseudoscientific rubbish but it follows rules. The problem is, the rules change depending on what you're trying to prove. Meeks could have applied any set of rules to get the name of a single target, and another, different set of rules for a

315

second target, and so on. If he had, there would have been no way that I could have reconstructed the list."

"But you did reconstruct it," Sessions said, "from the rules in Meeks's notes."

"Sort of," Matt said. "The notes gave me an idea of the *kind* of rules he *might* have used, not the *specific* rules that he used for this calculation. But they showed something much more significant."

"Such as?" said Costa.

"That whatever rules he used, they were consistent across all the targets."

"But how does that help?"

"I constructed a set of equations, based on a set of numerological rules. I wrote a program to solve the equations, but at the same time to *alter* the equations by changing the rules. It took a while, but the solution eventually converged on that set of forty locations."

"Why forty?"

"I made no assumptions about the number of sites. Forty is what the program came up with. It's very likely that Meeks had forty targets in mind from the start."

"That worries me," Sessions said.

"Why?"

"We apprehended the supplier of the explosives, a man named McConnell. He told us that he provided enough material for forty-eight bombs—these forty, plus eight more. One of those exploded at the Lominger house in Atlanta."

Matt blanched. "That means…"

"Right," said Sessions. "There are seven more potential disasters at large."

Sessions's phone buzzed. "The director," he said. "Excuse me." He went back into the hallway.

"I had hoped that the FBI could assist us in finding Stroud," Costa said to Matt. "Perhaps they will, when this day is over, but now they are focused entirely on the bombings."

"*Dimmi come posso aiutarti,*" Matt said. "Tell me how I can help."

"*Non puoi,*" Costa said. "You can't. You're injured. You must heal. And I will tell you again, my friend, leave the police work to the professionals!"

The sharp pain that Matt felt as he touched his bandaged head reinforced Costa's advice. "Very well. It's your case. What actions are you taking?"

"Matteo, we are doing the right things," Costa said with some irritation. "My men are interviewing the residents of the neighborhood. The national police have issued a country-wide alert, and we have notified Interpol."

"And what have you found?"

"Nothing. He's vanished. But a blond-haired Italian-speaking American cannot escape notice for long." Costa reached across his desk and rested his hand on Matt's. "Matteo, I promise, I will not rest until I find this killer. I owe it to the memory of Lamberto. But you must be patient. These things take time and hard work." Costa withdrew his hand. "And, if I'm being honest, it takes *la fortuna*—luck."

Matt nodded in seeming agreement and said nothing.

65

MONEY

THE TALL MAN with dark hair and sunglasses stepped up to the counter. The *barista* addressed him in English.

"Sir, and what are you having?"

The man looked at the menu, hand written on a whiteboard on the wall. "Just an espresso, *por favore*," he said in an American accent characteristic of the South—Alabama, to be specific—but the *barista* had no way of knowing this. To him, the man sounded like every other American tourist to step into the *Yeah Cafe* in the *Pigneto* neighborhood of Rome.

"*Certo, signore!*" the *barista* said as he set to work preparing the espresso.

The man paid for his coffee, tipping generously, and took a seat in the corner. He opened his laptop and logged onto the WiFi network, opening a browser window and typing his search terms.

matt bugatti commission

One result caught the man's eye.

CHARLES O'DONNELL

ABORTION CLINIC BOMB PLOT THWARTED

FBI Director Edward Carmona announced in a press conference today that a plot by the radical anti-abortion organization Heaven Sent to bomb women's health clinics in forty cities was prevented by FBI agents. The action by the FBI was the result of an ongoing investigation that began with clinic bombings in Pittsburgh and Atlanta. Director Carmona gave credit to senator and presidential candidate Yolanda Herrera Peña for providing information crucial to identifying the conspirators. Senator Herrera, also present at the press conference, in turn credited an adviser, Rhiannon Barraket, for her role in identifying a key conspirator in the plot. Ms. Barraket, an employee of the lobbying firm of Stivers and Cartwright, could not be reached for comment.

Director Carmona went on to cite the contribution of Dr. Matteo Bugatti for his analysis of evidence that led to the deployment of FBI resources to the targeted clinics. Dr. Bugatti, head of the Commission on the Unexplained Deaths of Young Women, known as the Bugatti Commission, remains in Italy to attend the funeral of his mother, who died unexpectedly during a personal visit. Dr. Bugatti, in residence at his family villa in Bologna, also could not be reached for comment.

The man drained his espresso as he read the article, then he closed his laptop and left the cafe. He boarded a bus and rode it to an older and less fashionable quarter, to a neighborhood of aging homes, some of which the owners made available to visiting foreigners traveling on a budget. The man walked from the bus stop to one such house, letting himself in as quietly as he could, trying to make it to the stairs unnoticed.

"Signor Nelson!" the owner called to him from the front room. "And is your day good in Roma?"

The man paused at the foot of the stairs, still wearing his sunglasses.

"*Bone jorno,* Mrs. Romitti," the man said. "Yes, good day in Roma."

"And where are you going? Are you going to the Colosseo? Are you going to the Vaticano?"

The man smiled widely. "Yes, Colosseo today. Very nice. Tomorrow Vaticano."

The woman gave the man a nicotine-stained grin. "*Bene, bene.* When you are in Roma, you must see the Colosseo, because the Colosseo is Roma. And you must see the Vaticano, because it is the Vaticano."

"How true, Mrs. Romitti, how true." He started up the stairs.

"And where are you eating?"

The man stopped on the stair, gripping the handrail. "Cafe. I am eating at cafe. Later I eat at *restauranto. Capeesh?*"

"Oh, yes, I know many good *ristoranti.* I tell you where you are eating, okay?"

The man clenched his jaw. "I don't need you to…" He paused. "*Grazzi*, Mrs. Romitti, but I already have a restaurant in mind."

"Oh, but I know *many* good *ristoranti.* You are not finding them yourself. I will write them for you."

The man didn't hear Mrs. Romitti's offer. He was already up the stairs.

The shades were drawn in the second-story room of Mrs. Romitti's boarding house. The man entered, set his laptop on a stand near the door, took off his sunglasses, and removed a wig, revealing his sandy-colored hair. He flipped on a light.

"*Aye!*"

Enrico and Marco covered their eyes. Enrico was stretched out on a couch; Marco was trying to make himself comfortable in a stuffed chair. "Why do you have to turn that on?" Enrico said.

"Why are you sleeping in the middle of the day?" Cameron countered.

Enrico sat up. "Because there is nothing else to do in this garbage dump. There is only sleeping, eating, and shitting. Four days we're here. You don't let us out, you don't even let us talk."

"It wouldn't do for Mrs. Romitti to know you're here," Cameron said. "She thinks I'm a confused American on his first visit to Rome. That's the part I'm playing. You need to play your parts."

"This is getting old. I'm thinking that I have better things to do. Marco, what do you think?"

"*Sì*, better things," Marco mumbled.

"You see? Marco agrees. I think that Marco and I, we will be leaving. And we will take the rest of our money."

"You'll get your money when I'm through with Bugatti."

"We gave you your chance with Bugatti. That was our deal. If you didn't make the most of it, that's not our fault." Enrico stood and stretched. "We don't care about Bugatti. We care about our money. And we want our money."

Cameron set his sunglasses and wig on his laptop. "I know where Bugatti is. We need to go back to Bologna."

Enrico snorted. "We are *sure* not going back to Bologna before we get our money. We are not going back to Bologna even if you give us what you owe."

"I need you in Bologna. How much more money do you want?"

Enrico spoke to Marco in dialect. The conversation lasted for more than three minutes, getting heated at times. Cameron had difficulty following, but he surmised that Enrico advocated cutting their losses, while Marco saw an opportunity for an even bigger payoff. At last Enrico turned back to Cameron.

"Two hundred thousand," he said. "And we don't leave Rome until we see half of it in our hands."

"*Questo non è accettabile!*" he growled. "Unacceptable! I've already paid you three hundred thousand. You'll get the other two hundred when we're finished, not before. Leave now and you get nothing."

Enrico and Marco exchanged a blank look before Enrico began to laugh. Marco joined him.

"*Arrivederci*, Signor Nelson," Enrico said.

"*Sì, arrivederci*," Marco repeated. They pushed past Cameron toward the door.

"Wait!"

Enrico and Marco stopped. Enrico had his hand on the doorknob.

"One hundred thousand."

"One-fifty," Enrico countered, "and fifty up front."

Cameron gritted his teeth. "Done."

‡ ‡ ‡

The three men drove quietly with their lights off down the path to the Bugatti villa. Enrico exited the car and approached the building. He tried the door. He signaled to Marco and Cameron that it was locked, then disappeared around a corner. It would be another thirty minutes before he reappeared.

"*Non c'è nessuno là,*" Enrico said as he approached the car. "There is no one in there."

"How do you know?"

"All the doors are locked. The windows are closed. I pried one open and went in. I listened room by room. They have all gone. Signor Nelson, I think your information is bad."

Cameron rubbed his lip. "Damn," he whispered.

"He's not here," Enrico said. "You don't know where he is. And the longer we stay in Bologna, the more danger we are in."

"*Lo so! Lo so!*" Cameron said. "I know!"

"Marco, go," Enrico said.

"Wait," Cameron said. "Let me think."

"No! We go now. Marco, *andiamo.*"

Two lights appeared from the rear of the villa, the headlights of a car heading straight for the three men. At the last moment the car veered to one side and sped up the path to the main road. Cameron was able to glimpse the driver just long enough to recognize him.

"*È Bugatti!*" Cameron shouted. "Enrico, you idiot, you let him get away. Marco, follow him!"

"*Cazzo!*" Enrico said, as Marco stepped on the accelerator.

‡ ‡ ‡

The chase led them to the Hermitage of Ronzano. Matt arrived thirty seconds ahead of his pursuers. He bolted from the car and ran for the wine cellar.

Cameron's car skidded to a halt next to Matt's. Cameron sprang out. He opened the rear door to retrieve a shotgun from the back seat. He grabbed the gun, but felt resistance. Enrico had a grip on the barrel.

"*Aspetta!*" Enrico said in a hoarse whisper. "Wait! This is a church. Are you going to commit murder in a church?"

"If I must," Cameron said. He jerked the gun out of Enrico's hand. "But he's not going into the church. He's going underground. If we let him get too far, we'll never find him." Cameron ran toward the wine cellar door.

"He's crazy," Enrico said. "Marco, let's go."

Marco got out of the car. He tucked a pistol into his belt. "We still don't have our money." He ran after Cameron.

"*Cazzo, cazzo, cazzo!*" Enrico cursed. He grabbed his pistol and followed Marco into the building.

‡ ‡ ‡

In a small, dusty cell, empty except for a few sticks of furniture, a crucifix, and an image of the assumption of the Blessed Virgin, Matt felt in his pocket for two clips, each clip loaded with fifteen rounds of nine-millimeter ammunition. He took one out as he unholstered his Beretta semi-automatic pistol, inserting the magazine into the grip and slapping it home. He pulled back the slide and released the safety. He waited, focusing on his breathing, in total darkness.

66

DEFERENCE

STEVE MELSON WAS almost fawning in the attention that he paid to Yolanda as they chatted amiably during the break. The combative tone that he used routinely with his guests, even when off-camera, was absent. Yolanda hardly noticed. It was the same deference she'd been given by everyone since the FBI's press conference the previous day—the respect one pays to the next president of the United States.

The floor director counted down the seconds to the end of the break.

"Welcome back to *Politics Weekly Forum*. We're here with senator and presidential candidate Yolanda Herrera Peña. Senator Herrera, in the wake of the dramatic announcement yesterday from FBI Director Carmona, your lead in the national polls has increased to more that twelve points over your nearest rival for the Democratic nomination. You lead all likely Republican nominees in the general election by eight points or more. Congratulations. But we're still weeks away from the first debate, and months from the Iowa caucus. Are you peaking too soon?"

Yolanda lifted her chin. "Steve, this has nothing to do with standings in the polls. The FBI, through their superb investigative work, avoided a catastrophe of historic proportions. I was honored to have been a part of it. Our office worked closely with Director Carmona throughout. It was one of my advisers, Ronni Barraket, who recognized that she had knowledge crucial to the solution of this conspiracy. She courageously consented to participate in an FBI operation that led to the apprehension of the leader of this plot. When Ronni asked my advice, I urged caution, but I recognized that the stakes were high enough to justify the risk, great as it was."

"Are you saying that you placed the life of one of your staff in jeopardy?"

"Steve, that was her choice. I didn't order her to get involved. I don't have that authority. But if I did, I'd have given the order. Hundreds of lives were at stake. It's the sort of decision a commander in chief faces daily."

"The public appears to think that you made the right call. Based on the numbers, the nomination is yours to lose."

‡ ‡ ‡

Yolanda returned to the green room after the segment. As she entered, Ronni stood up from her seat. Yolanda rushed to her and embraced her.

"Ronni, dear, thank God you're all right," she whispered. "Thank God, thank God!"

"Congratulations, Senator."

Yolanda took Ronni's face in her hands, looking at her sternly. "You had no right to agree to that insane scheme. Edward Carmona was ready to suspend Dan Sessions. He would have, if the press hadn't been so favorable. He chewed out Sessions in private, but he'll have to hail him as a hero in public." She looked into Ronni's eyes. "You had no right," Yolanda said. "Dr. Bugatti's mother dead, and you almost dead. What in God's name possessed you to take such a chance?

"I'm sorry," Ronni said. "For Matt. He had no say in any of it and he lost his mother. But I'm not sorry for the decision. You're going to be president."

"Not worth it. I don't want to be president at that price. When Edward told me about the photo, and that they suspected you were involved, I knew it couldn't be true. I would've dropped out of the race right then if it meant that you'd be safe."

"I know. That's why I did it."

Yolanda hugged her. "Never again, do you understand?"

"I understand," Ronni said. *No promises*, she thought.

The two of them left the studio, making their way through the noisy crowd of reporters to Yolanda's limousine. The shouting continued as the car pulled away.

"Tyler Ross is dead," Ronni said.

"I know."

"That will be a major embarrassment to the president."

Yolanda turned to Ronni. "No, it won't. We have Darryl Meeks in custody. The trail stops with him. Ross's role in the conspiracy will never be public. He entered an Italian hospital for an emergency appendectomy. He died of infection." Yolanda turned back to the window. "That's the official account, anyway."

"He shot himself!"

"The people will never know."

"Senator, that's not right."

"I know how you feel, Ronni, but we can't let this touch the president." Yolanda lowered her voice. "There's another reason to keep this quiet. The FBI suspects that Ross wasn't the only highly-placed official involved. If Ross were exposed publicly it could compromise their investigation. Of course, my office is cooperating fully."

They rode in silence for a few minutes.

"Where do we stand with the commission report?" Yolanda asked.

"It's been delayed, of course. Matt will write the truth— the girls were victims of a mass murderer."

"And neither the FDA nor CG Pharma could have foreseen that the drug would have been intentionally engineered to kill," Yolanda said. "That sort of blunts our message that they were in a tacit conspiracy to rush this drug to market, the FDA to advance a radical pro-choice agenda, and CG Pharma to pad their pockets. There goes my issue."

"Senator, you helped to thwart the bomb plot and save hundreds of lives. You don't need the issue any more."

"*You* thwarted the plot—you and Dr. Bugatti. I'm simply the willing beneficiary." She patted Ronni's knee. "That's all behind us now."

"Yes," Ronni said. "Behind us."

Stroud still at large—and Matt still in danger.

67

FULFILLMENT

Darryl sat alone in the interrogation room of the Charlotte FBI field office for more than an hour, motionless the entire time, eyes closed and head bowed, under the watchful eye of two agents behind a one-way mirror.

"What do you think, Greg?"

The other agent sat with his arms crossed, chewing the inside of his cheek. "He's too cool."

"Yeah. This waiting game isn't working." He stood. "Let's go shake him up."

The two agents entered the room. Greg took a seat across from Darryl while the other stood by the door.

"Your master plan is a failure, Mr. Meeks," said Greg.

Darryl raised his head and opened his eyes, his face still passive, saying nothing.

"Did you hear what I said? We picked up all your bombers before they got the chance to blow themselves up. *All* of them. A few of them talked before the poison killed them. They gave up some of your gang and now they're talking, too. It won't be long before we have your whole fucking army of God in custody."

"I don't believe you," Darryl said. His voice was quiet, but hard edged. "They would die before they would betray me."

Greg picked up a remote and pointed it at a screen on the wall. It flashed on, displaying a news channel broadcasting feeds from four locations, each showing a similar scene, agents of the FBI leading men in handcuffs from shabby houses. They were people that Darryl knew—his lieutenants, servants of Christ.

"Judging from appearances, I'd say that your crew isn't as anxious to meet the Lord as you thought they were."

The agent flipped the channel. Reporters were interviewing the staff of health clinics that had been targeted for destruction, but which were still intact.

"Take a look at this, Meeks." Greg laid a list of the targeted sites in front of Darryl. "Recognize that? It's two days old." He laid down three more sheets. They were lists of bible verses and the calculations that Matt had performed to identify the targets. "We're on to your numbers game. We knew the targets a day before the first chemo patient strapped on her suicide belt."

Darryl shook his head.

Domine, quo vadis? Whither goest thou, Lord?

Greg scooped up the papers. "All we need to do now is to recover the other seven belts."

Darryl's eyes opened wide. "What?"

"We know there were forty-eight belts in all. One blew up in Atlanta. Another forty we picked up today. That leaves seven."

Darryl stared past the agent.

Seven, the number of heavenly perfection, the number of wholeness.

He smiled. "The Lord's plan is not yet fulfilled."

Greg sighed. He looked at the agent by the door. "Kyle, bring him in."

Kyle left the room, returning a few seconds later with a man in an orange jumpsuit.

"Meeks, you know Austen, don't you? The *Daily Bread* truck driver? Your body double?"

Darryl looked at Austen with ferocity. "What did you tell them?"

Austen cringed at the outburst. "I didn't tell them anything, Brother Meeks."

"*Liar!*" he shouted. "First Hoeven, then Tillis, and now you. Has everyone betrayed me? Has the Lord completely abandoned me?"

"You're out there by yourself, Meeks," Greg said, "all by your lonesome. Ol' Austen here gave you up. Didn't even hesitate. One little threat and he folded like a napkin."

"Brother Meeks, I didn't!" Austen protested.

"*Liar!* You found the belts and you told *them*, the enemies of God, where they were."

"No, Brother Meeks!"

"*Stop lying to me!* You laid in wait for me, you were the bait in their trap. I'm here, and God's plan is ruined, because of *you.*"

Austen was near tears. "No, Brother, I couldn't have told them where the belts are. I don't know where they are."

"*Stop!*" he screamed. "You found them and you told them. You looked in the back of the truck and you found them. Don't deny it!"

Darryl lunged across the table at Austen. Greg intervened as two other agents entered from the area behind the mirror.

"Get him out of here," Greg commanded. The agents dragged Darryl off.

Kyle sat Austen in a chair. "Listen to me, son," he said. "We searched the truck. It's clean. There are no bombs in that truck. But if you know where they are, now is the time to tell me. You're in a lot of trouble, boy. You can still do the right thing."

Austen's lip started to tremble. His eyes teared up.

"Austen, tell us what you know."

"The store has two trucks," Austen choked.

‡ ‡ ‡

Agent Hastings and Director Carmona sat at the conference table in the director's office, both leaning slightly forward in the direction of a speaker phone.

"Agent Sessions, what is your status?"

"We had no opportunity to question Tyler Ross before he shot himself. We tried to keep him alive but treatment failed and he died less than a day later."

"Continue."

"We have no more leads. We've been asked to assist in the apprehension of Cameron Stroud. What is your direction?"

"Leave your agents there. I want you on the next plane to the U.S."

"Yes, sir." There was a static-filled pause. "Mr. Director, I want to apologize again for my rash decision. In my judgment…"

"Your judgment was flawed, Agent Sessions," Carmona barked. He took a deep breath. "Dan, we've had that discussion. Get yourself home. The American people want to greet their hero."

"Yes, sir."

The line went dead.

"Agent Hastings, next steps."

"Our staff in Charlotte is interrogating Darryl Meeks," Hastings said. "Our top priority is to recover the missing bombs. None of the other conspirators that we've taken into custody admits to knowing their whereabouts."

"Alternatives."

"None, sir."

"Unacceptable. Think of some."

"Yes, sir. We…" The phone in agent Hastings's bag chimed. She retrieved it. "It's the Charlotte office, sir." Hastings listened to the report. Her face turned ashen.

"Sir, we believe we know where the missing belts are. The grocery store, *Daily Bread*, has more than one delivery truck. We believe the belts are hidden in one of them."

"You *believe*?"

"We questioned the store employees. The owner has the truck. He took it this morning."

"That's a vehicle with—how much?—thirty-five kilograms of C4 in the back?"

"Yes, sir."

"And where is it headed?"

"Washington, D.C., sir, according to the employees."

‡ ‡ ‡

The Virginia highway patrolman got his coffee and bear claw to go. He left the lunch counter at the truck stop on highway 301 and headed back to his patrol car, passing a panel truck on the way, going a few steps past it when he stopped and looked back.

That's weird.

The truck appeared to have been crudely painted in white. The design under the paint was almost, but not quite entirely obscured. He could make out some writing, brightly colored script, not quite readable, but he recognized the initial letters of two words, capital D and B. He touched the paint—still tacky.

The patrolman knitted his brow, looking at the ground, not really thinking, but just wondering. Then he shrugged and walked to his car. As he approached, he heard his radio, unintelligible from a distance. He got in the car and checked his computer screen. *Nothing new.* He started the car and pulled out of the lot, heading south. As he did so, the text on his computer screen scrolled up, displaying the transcript of the radio bulletin just issued, for all patrols to be on the lookout for a panel truck with the words *Daily Bread* printed on the sides in colorful script. The patrolman continued south, unaware.

‡ ‡ ‡

Agent Hastings remained in the director's office for an uncomfortably long time before her phone chimed. She answered the call and put it on speaker.

332

"We have a report from a Virginia state patrolman of a suspicious vehicle at a truck stop on highway 301."

"Location?"

"Unknown. The patrolman saw the truck approximately ninety minutes ago."

"*Ninety minutes?*" Hastings shouted. "What took him so long?"

"The truck has been painted. The logo on the sides is no longer visible. He just recently noticed the bulletin and made the connection."

"God damn it. Where was the sighting?"

"Near Port Royal, just south of the Rappahannock.

"He'll be in Washington in ten minutes," the director said. "If he obeys the speed limit."

☦ ☦ ☦

The Washington Metropolitan policeman noticed the vehicle just before noon, a white panel truck that matched the description in the radio bulletin just issued. He keyed the mic on his radio.

"Car 503 northwest on Mass Ave Southeast past Independence. Have vehicle, white panel truck in sight. In pursuit. Request backup."

The car followed the truck through mid-day traffic, slowing as it approached a sign on the right.

FAMILY PLAN FOUNDATION OF AMERICA
NATIONAL OFFICE

The truck turned into the drive and pulled up to the security gate as the policeman parked across the street. He watched as the driver talked with the security guard. After a few words, the truck backed out and continued down the street.

The policeman radioed his position. He followed the truck through a series of right turns, putting him back onto

Massachusetts Avenue, heading toward the National Office of the Family Plan Foundation of America.

This time the gate was blocked by a Metropolitan police car, with two more police cars positioned on either side of the gate and an unmarked car parked to one side. Agent Hastings and three more special agents of the FBI stood behind it.

The driver of the truck accelerated, jumping the curb, breaking through the chain link fence and continuing across the lawn toward the building as six guns opened fire.

The truck slowed to a stop at the entrance. A few curious occupants came out of the door.

"Back in the building!" Hastings shouted. She approached the truck with her gun drawn. "If there's a rear exit, use it. Do it now!"

The onlookers scrambled to reenter the building. Hastings stepped closer to the truck, peeking into the driver's side window. The driver lay across the seat, bleeding from multiple wounds, including one in the head.

"Driver's down," she yelled. "Get the bomb techs in here." She holstered her gun. She had not yet let go of the grip when she noticed a movement: the driver's right hand, holding a cell phone, his thumb on the *pound* key.

It was the last thing that agent Hastings ever saw.

68

FOLLE

"*QUESTO È FOLLE,*" Enrico muttered. "This is crazy. You can't see nothing in here."

Marco flicked a cigarette lighter, illuminating the walls of the passages with a yellow glow. Cameron slapped the lighter from Marco's hand. It caromed off the wall and went out, immersing the three of them in darkness.

"That was not smart, Signor Nelson," Marco growled, putting his hand on the grip of his pistol. "How do you expect to find your man in this cave with no light?"

"Keep quiet," Cameron whispered. "I've been in this place before. I know it. I can see it in my mind." He felt his vest pockets. *Twenty shells.* He took two shells out and loaded his shotgun. "I can see in the dark."

"*Bravo,*" Enrico said. "Good for you. You find him. I'm getting out of here."

Cameron grabbed Enrico by the arm in a deliberate move, not feeling around for Enrico's arm, but simply grabbing it. Enrico wondered if perhaps Cameron really could see him.

"*Donna vecchia,*" Cameron said. "Old woman, what are you afraid of? That you can't see Bugatti? He can't see you, either." He let go of Enrico's arm. "Just do as I tell you."

‡ ‡ ‡

Enrico went first. He kept his right hand on the wall. *La prima stanza è sulla destra*, Cameron had told him—the first room is on the right. Enrico stepped carefully, edging forward, until his fingers encountered the door frame. He slipped his hand around the frame. The door was open. He drew a deep breath and held it. He smelled the cool, earthen smell of the rock walls, the slightly suffocating accumulation of dust, and nothing else. He listened.

Silence.

He moved slowly through the open door, trying to look around, but even with his eyes well adapted to the dark, he saw only blackness. He waited.

Marco went next, to the second room, on the left. Cameron waited a minute before following, stopping at the first room.

"Enrico."

"*Sì.*"

"Go to the next room on the right. Wait two minutes. Count it."

"*Sì, ho capito,*" came the whispered answer. "I understand."

Cameron went to the second room.

"Marco."

There was no answer. Cameron froze, his hand extended into the open doorway. He felt a slight change in air pressure. He swung through the doorway, bringing the butt of his shotgun up into the chin of the man in the room.

"*Coglione!*" Marco's voice cried out. "Fucker! It's me, Marco!"

"Why didn't you answer?" Cameron hissed.

"How can I know your voice when you are whispering? I don't know who you are! You could be Bugatti for all I can tell!" He moaned. "You broke my jaw, asshole."

Cameron knelt next to Marco in the dark and touched Marco's cheek.

"Aah!"

"It's not broken."

"I'm beginning to agree with Enrico. I think this is crazy. I think *you* are crazy."

"I'm going to the next room on the left. Enrico is in the next room on the right. Go to the room on the right after that one."

Marco got up and headed down the passage to the next room.

"Enrico?"

"*Sì.*"

"I've changed my mind. Let's get out of here."

"No. The money."

"I didn't think that you cared about the money."

"I care."

"Do you know what that fucker did? He almost killed me!"

"Marco. The money."

Marco grunted softly and moved on to the next room.

‡ ‡ ‡

It took more than an hour to check the main passage and all the branches. The three men faced a final door, just slightly open.

"The foundation," Cameron said. "He went into the foundation. Damn."

"Let's go," Marco said, no longer whispering. "We will find him later."

Cameron put his hand on the door. "No," he said. He pushed the door open.

Lamberto's office was softly illuminated by light from the hall, unchanged from the last time that Cameron had been there. It hadn't been that long since he'd searched the office for evidence of the Vanderbilt paper, and encountered Clara Kildee by accident. Cameron took immediate advantage of the opportunity, drugging her and dragging her through underground passages, through a cluttered wine cellar, to his waiting car, then to his flat in Bologna. He might have wondered at that moment if he'd made the right decision, had he not been Cameron Stroud, a man incapable of self-doubt.

The lights were blinding. Cameron reflexively shut his eyes.

"*Non ti muovere!*" Inspector Costa commanded. "Don't move!"

Costa's weapon was drawn, as were those of four uniformed officers of the *polizia giudiziaria* on either side.

Cameron knelt down, bringing his shotgun forward. He stopped when he felt the muzzle of a pistol pressed against the back of his skull.

"Marco, what are you doing?"

"I don't do nothing!" Marco said. "Enrico! Are you crazy?"

The man behind them had a pistol in each hand, one on Cameron, one on Marco.

"Enrico is gone," said Matt Bugatti. "He left an hour ago."

‡ ‡ ‡

Enrico left Cameron and Marco, keeping his right hand on the wall, stepping carefully, edging forward, to the first room on the right. He slipped his hand around the frame. The door was open. He listened.

Silence.

He moved slowly through the open door and waited.

Two seconds later a hand covered his mouth and the barrel of a gun dug into his temple.

"*Silenzio!*" Matt whispered in his ear. Enrico nodded. Matt pushed the gun harder against Enrico's head for emphasis, taking his hand from Enrico's mouth and removing the gun from Enrico's belt.

"*Signor Bugatti,*" Enrico whispered. "I don't even want to be here."

"Lay down on the floor. Stay quiet."

Enrico obeyed. Matt put his foot in the small of Enrico's back as a minute passed.

"Enrico," Cameron whispered.

"*Sì.*"

"Go to the next room on the right. Wait two minutes. Count it."

"*Sì, ho capito,*" Matt whispered.

Cameron moved on. Matt removed his foot from Enrico's back.

"*Vai,*" Matt said. "Go."

Enrico's breath rattled with a mixture of fear and relief as he made it past the door of the wine cellar into the open night. He hesitated only briefly before starting the car and tearing out of the parking lot of the hermitage. *They're on their own,* he thought.

‡ ‡ ‡

Marco's hands were in the air; Cameron's shotgun was still pointed at the floor. All three of the Italians kept their guns pointed at Cameron as Matt kept his pistols against the backs of the two men's heads.

"Dr. Bugatti, we have this now," Costa said.

Matt lowered his left hand. Marco sighed with relief. Matt kept his Beretta tight against Cameron's head.

"Dr. Bugatti," Costa said. "Matteo."

An image crept into Matt's mind, an image that he had tried for days without much success to suppress, but which had now returned. Matt closed his eyes to see it better.

Flora, strapped to a gurney with an IV bag hanging from a hook.

Cameron in green scrubs, inserting a needle into the IV line.

Flora's chest heaving, then falling still.

The doctor flipping the switch, the heart monitor faltering, Pierangelo's tears.

Matt pressed the gun a little more firmly against Cameron's head, conjuring up more images.

Flora, sternly disapproving when Matt disassembled the coffee maker to see how it worked.

Flora, glowing with pride when Matt received his doctorate.

Flora's tears when the doctors shut down Giovanni's life support.

Flora, chatting happily with her Italian family as her mind slowly left her.

Matt opened his eyes. Cameron still held his shotgun.

Make a move. Make it now. Make it.

Matt pressed the trigger, squeezing slowly, knowing the feel of it well, the precise amount of resistance before it gave way, the hammer fell, and the pistol fired.

"Matteo," Costa said softly. "Please. Don't."

Matt's lip trembled but his hand was steady.

"What's it going to be, Doctor?" Cameron said brightly in English.

Matt stared at the back of Cameron's head. The shotgun had not moved.

Matt removed his finger from the trigger, raised his pistol and stepped back. The two uniforms came forward and shackled Cameron and Marco.

‡ ‡ ‡

The police were waiting at the end of the drive to the hermitage to arrest Enrico. It had all gone according to plan.

The news item about Matt remaining in Italy for Flora's funeral had been Costa's idea. Ronni helped to arrange it through the Stivers and Cartwright media relations department. They had no way of knowing when—or if— Cameron would take the bait (though the psychologist on retainer from Stivers and Cartwright was highly confident that he would) so they staked out the foundation every night. Costa wanted to take Cameron at the villa, but Matt insisted on the confrontation in the underground passageways of the hermitage. Costa protested, but ultimately he agreed. He understood. In a face-to-face situation, anything can happen. No one would fault Matt for defending himself. It was risky, Costa knew, but it was the least he could do for his friend. He deserved his chance.

After all, Matt had been through hell.

Epilogue

Matt drove slowly through the neighborhood. The modest homes, the neatly kept lawns, the wide sidewalks on which residents strolled on pleasant evenings, stirred memories of his childhood, and the house, now vacant, where he spent it. *The house without Flora*—an alien concept, Matt thought, the same poverty of imagination he'd suffered after Giovanni died—the world without Giovanni, an idea that circumstances forced on Matt, not one that Matt could derive from experience or logic. *I can conceive of infinities within infinities, but not life without family.*

The Bugatti Commission issued its report, finding that the deaths of forty-nine young women were the act of a mass killer, a gifted but deranged researcher who now faced charges of capital murder. The commission further found that the FDA and Compton-Genencraft Pharmaceutical, while not directly responsible for the deaths of the girls, were unduly hasty in bringing *Backup* to market. Francis Compton, CEO of Compton-Genencraft, hired professionals to manage the situation. Through the brilliant work of the media relations arm of Stivers and Cartwright, their image was preserved. The public, generally speaking, held them blameless.

Nevertheless, there came a call for restrictions on fast-track drug approval, following a series of sensational articles by Clara Kildee exposing the cozy relationship between big pharma and certain government officials, who, denying impropriety, and to prove their sincerity, spoke out in favor of bi-partisan legislation, which passed both houses of Congress in a matter of days. Stivers and Cartwright lobbyists worked hard to defeat it, but public opinion in the law's favor was too strong for politicians to dismiss. The president signed *Liddie's Law*, as he called it, in honor of the first victim, Liddie Novotny—a sweeping reform that made no distinction among different types of drugs. Its immediate impact was to delay, perhaps by years, the introduction of a dozen or so promising treatments, including one for Alzheimer's disease from Compton-Genencraft. It was a consequence that Matt hadn't anticipated when he approved the commission report, and for which he compensated by making a donation to the Alzheimer's Foundation of America, in Flora's name, in the amount of five million dollars.

Matt last saw Ronni at an event for candidate Yolanda Herrera Peña. By then Ronni had left Stivers and Cartwright to work full-time for the senator's campaign.

"I'm still passionately pro-life, like the senator," she told Matt, "but I couldn't keep working for Jay Stivers. There are too many problems that the free market won't solve by itself. We all need to work together."

"Are you worried that you're working for a lost cause?" Matt asked.

Ronni bit her lip. "It's so unfair. The senator wasn't to blame for the Washington bombing."

"She took credit for stopping the clinic bombings. Her poll numbers soared. That was probably just as undeserved as her fall in the polls after the Family Plan bombing, don't you think?"

Ronni looked exasperated, then her expression softened. "I suppose. Still, I think it's a little early for the pundits to write her obituary."

"She's not out of the race as long as she has you, Ronni. I admire your dedication."

Ronni kissed Matt's cheek. "Thank you, Matt."

Matt patted Ronni's hand. Then he gave her a check, made

out to the senator's campaign, for the maximum amount permitted by law. Ronni thanked him and said goodbye for what both of them feared was for the last time.

‡ ‡ ‡

Matt continued down the street. *Three months,* he thought, since he'd stood in the Oval Office and accepted the commission to find the truth. It seemed like three lifetimes. *An investigation, a gathering of evidence, the drawing of conclusions based on facts and logic—no political posturing, no fanaticism, no psychoses.* How simple that perspective had seemed, and how bizarrely wrong it had turned out to be.

Matt was no child; he was not ignorant of people's failings. He knew that the path he had chosen, one of dispassionate analysis in matters of fact and theory, was not the path chosen by most—or even by many—but how could he have been prepared for the test to which his world view would be put?

Reason and decency—with no revealed dogma to which he could turn, they were his foundation: reason and decency. He would live by those principles until the rest of the world caught up with him. Nonsense, however durable, cannot persist forever.

Matt pulled into the driveway of a simple house, looking as if no sadness had ever touched it, like another house in that respect, not here, in Kenosha, Wisconsin, but in Raleigh, North Carolina, the home of Giovanni and Flora Bugatti, and their son, Matteo. The Raleigh house was empty now; this house, the one that Matt approached, was not.

Matt paused at the door before knocking. He hadn't looked forward to this moment, but he was determined. It was payment on a debt, one that he had assumed three months before, the first of forty-nine installments before the debt could be retired.

Matt knocked. A large man answered, with large hands and a thick neck, but a kind face.

"Mr. Novotny, I'm Matt Bugatti. May I come in?"

About the Author

CHARLES O'DONNELL WRITES thrillers with high-tech themes in international settings. His book *Moment of Conception* is a medical and political thriller set in Italy and Washington D.C. The book is the natural product of his fascination with all things political, and his realization that, perhaps, nonsense *can* persist indefinitely.

Charles lives with Helen, his wife, life partner and fellow political junkie in Westerville, Ohio.

ACKNOWLEDGEMENTS

I THOUGHT THAT writing my first book, *The Girlfriend Experience*, was the hardest thing I'd ever done, like birthing a porcupine at times. Writing *Moment of Conception* was harder, not because it's longer, or because the plot twists are less manageable, or the characters more complex, but because, after one novel, I have a better idea of when I'm doing something wrong. Working a problem is always easier if you don't know the answer—you only have to work it once.

The Girlfriend Experience is a good book, but *Moment of Conception* is better, because I'm a better writer than I was before, and for that I have many to thank.

My *Girlfriend Experience* readers have been awesome. Without their encouragement, praise, and criticism, I would not have had the energy or inspiration to write *Moment of Conception*. Some of them became my alpha readers, patiently combing through rough—I mean *really* rough—drafts to point out the obvious and not-so-obvious flaws. Thanks especially to Mike and Tim, alpha readers extraordinaire, and to the usual gang of O'Donnells.

I tried something new this time, posting each chapter as it was written on Wattpad and writeon by Kindle, and on my blog, Indie Omnibus. Thanks to the many readers who offered their comments, some good, some bad, but all helpful.

I still rely on the Kindle Community of indie authors for advice, and for answers to my many questions. They are always generous, courteous, and, unfortunately, too numerous to mention.

To Kristin, my editor: Thanks for your many corrections and suggestions, and for your encouragement—this is a better book because of you.

Special thanks to my friend Roberto, whose son, Matteo, is the namesake for my main character. I asked him, and he agreed, to edit the many Italian phrases in the book, but he gave me so much more, explaining nuances of Italian expression, and offering comments on Italian culture. *Grazie, Roberto. Ottimo lavoro.*

To Andreea, my cover designer: Thanks for conjuring up an image that so perfectly expresses the mood of the book. I love it.

And, of course, unbounded gratitude to Helen, life partner and fellow political junkie.

Charles O'Donnell
May 16, 2019

www.ingramcontent.com/pod-product-compliance
Lightning Source LLC
Chambersburg PA
CBHW060851210726
48293CB00006B/1755